SLEDGE HAMMER

hard to love series

P. DANGELICO

SLEDGEHAMMER (Hard To Love Series #2)
Copyright © 2017 P. Dangelico

ISBN 13: 978-0692935859 (Custom Universal)
ISBN-10: 0692935851

Published by P. Dangelico

Cover Design: Najla Qamber, Najla Qamber Designs
Proofreading: Judy's Proofreading
www.pdangelico.com

ALSO BY P. DANGELICO

Romantic Suspense
A Million Different Ways (The Horn Duet)
A Million Different Ways To Lose You (The Horn Duet)

Contemporary Romance/ Sports Romance
Wrecking Ball
Sledgehammer

Contemporary Romance
Baby Maker
Tiebreaker

CHAPTER ONE

YOU KNOW HOW THEY SAY never to go to the supermarket when you're hungry because you'll make some seriously ill-advised choices if you let your baser instincts rule your intellect? Yeah, the same logic applies to agreeing to see your ex-fiancé when you've had a soul-sucking week. I call it a perfect storm of awful circumstances. The state of New York called it arson.

"Deputy Dipshit!" I rake the bottom of a very nice Jimmy Choo high-heeled sandal, purchased on clearance at the Saks On Fifth Outlet, against the bars of the tiny holding cell. Which only serves to remind me that its sole mate was lost somewhere at the scene of the *alleged* crime. Go ahead and add that to the heap of reasons I wish a stray asteroid would destroy the planet tonight.

"Deputy Dipshit! I'll have you know I've been watching *Law and Order* since I was ten! I know my rights and I demand my phone call!"

"Ain't no one gonna come if you keep at it like that," a deep voice announces.

I look over my shoulder, at my one and only cellmate. Her long body is half hanging off of the metal bench, arm thrown over her eyes, wig askew.

"Sorry to interrupt your beauty sleep, princess, but it's

been ages since anyone's been back here."

"Name's Cassandra. And they always come at the top of the hour." Cassandra lifts her arm off her face and eyeballs the clock on the gray-green wall. "It's almost two. Someone will be around soon."

My inquisitive gaze glides over her expensive clothes and flawless makeup. Interesting riddle, this Cassandra. She sits up and crams her feet back into what looks like size fourteen, red patent heels. I'm momentarily shocked to discover that Louboutin makes pumps that size.

"Amber." My eyes cut from her feet to her face. "Nice shoes."

"Thanks." While she adjusts the long, straight hair of her wig, her dark doe eyes sweep up and down my person. "Girl, you look like a broken-down Cinderella. How'd you wind up in here anyways?"

"Bad company," I mutter while fiddling with the ripped edge of the vintage Badgely Mishka dress I found in a consignment shop.

Cassandra exhales tiredly. "Let me guess—you stalkin' yo ex, and show up at his house, and he married with five kids."

"Not even close," I reply dejectedly.

"Come on, Cinder. We probably here for another couple of hours. Might as well tell ol' Cassandra the story."

From what I can tell, ol' Cassandra doesn't seem much older than me. While I keep silent, she keeps watching me. Under her gaze, I feel naked, her sharp eyes performing a thorough examination of my mind and finding every dangerous turn and polluted crevice.

"You first."

"Stalkin' my ex. I showed up at his house, and he married

with five kids."

"Really?" I can't keep the doubt out of my voice.

"No, not really. He has two kids."

My eyes widen. "So...trespassing, or breaking and entering?"

Cassandra arches a well-groomed brow. "Nothing that exciting. Jaywalking. Also known as walking while fabulous," she replies with elocution that would've made linguistics expert *Henry Higgins* proud.

"You got arrested for walking?"

"If you must know, I was leaving my boyfriend's—" Her eyes narrow, lips press tight. "Ex-boyfriend's house." The dramatic pause is underscored with a sideways glance. "And on my way to the train station, the friendly neighborhood East Hamptons' officer came along. We got into it when he decided to write me a ticket for jaywalking. Which turned into public indecency. Which turned into resisting arrest."

"I burned down my ex's parents' house." That confession felt better than it should.

Cassandra sifts her perfectly manicured fingers through her long hair. "Good for you, Cinder."

"Not all of it. Just a small part—and it wasn't on purpose."

"Right. That's what I said when my boyfriend's wife found me on my knees."

I snort. "No, really. It was an accident."

Less than twenty minutes later, Cassandra has given me the CliffsNotes to her life story, how Christopher Hart was reborn Cassandra Hart, and I'm knee-deep in my latest tale of woe.

"Who puts drapes in the kitchen?! And how is it my fault

3

that someone spilled an entire bottle of booze on the floor?" Her serene eyes follow me as I wear out the concrete of the holding cell. "He watched them arrest me and said nothing!" Words are flying around as fast and loud as live ammunition.

"Jones? Amber Jones," a male voice yells. I rush to the edge of the cell and shove my face as close to the bars as I can without actually touching them.

"In here!"

Deputy Dipshit walks up with his eyes glued to the clipboard he's holding. "Time for your phone call."

"I can't wait to tell my lawyer how many different ways my civil rights have been violated this evening." At my fit of pique, Deputy D looks bored. "And hers," I say, pointing at Cassandra.

Reality: I don't have a lawyer, nor do I have the money to pay for one. And if I give myself time to consider this unfortunate fact I will unravel into hysterics.

I glance over my shoulder at Cassandra who gives me a thumbs-up. "Give 'em hell, Cinder."

"Let's go, Jones." He unlocks the door and guides me out. "Way to usher in 2017," Deputy D drawls in a thick New York accent.

Yeah, it's shaping up to a be real winner.

Five minutes later, I'm dialing Cam's number. Camilla Shaw: formally DeSantis, formally Blake, formally DeSantis. Camilla's the Laverne to my Shirley, the Robin to my Batman. My best friend since the fifth grade when an enamored Jimmy Murphy decided that slamming Cam in the face with a dodge ball was a good way to get her attention. He almost broke her nose, therefore, I almost broke his dick with a karate chop to the junk.

4

She spent the rest of the day following me around like a stray dog, thanking me over and over. When I figured she wasn't about to go away any time soon, I decided to adopt her. We've been best friends ever since. And thank God for that because I don't have many people in my life I can count on, and Cam's firmly entrenched at the top of that list...come to think of it, that's the entire list.

Someone picks up on the third ring and a loud grunt blows up the phone. "Is that beast mounting you again?" I say, holding the receiver away from my ear.

"Are you referring to my husband?" Camilla croaks, barely awake.

"Who else would be mounting you?" a super deep male voice grumbles in the background.

Camilla recently married Calvin Shaw, starting quarterback of the NY Titans. Long, boring story. They're expecting a baby sometime in the spring.

Her soft chuckle is muffled by a hand over the receiver. Then I hear a whispered, "Sorry, Boo. Go back to sleep."

More grunting follows. "That's the sounds of me trying to sit up. The spare tire around my waist keeps getting in the way."

"We'll have to discuss the joys of pregnancy some other time. I have a more pressing issue to deal with right now." For the first time all night a pang of shame hits me. I nervously flip the spiral cord of the desk phone in circles.

"Time's almost up, Jones," Deputy D shouts.

"Why are you calling? I thought you had a party to go to," Camilla slowly queries, only half awake.

"Funny you should say...umm..."

"Ambs—what is it?" I don't fail to note that humor is

conspicuously absent in her voice. The subtle hint of dread, however, isn't. She knows me too well.

"How do you feel about busting me out of jail?"

I get a solid two minutes of silence, followed by a deep sigh. "Where are you?" she snaps, the fog of sleep gone all at once. I pinch the bridge of my nose where a tenacious ache has taken up residence.

"Southampton county jail."

"Give me an hour."

* * *

"What now?" I say, stepping back inside the holding cell.

Twenty-nine, staring down the double barrel of thirty, and what have I learned? By the looks of my current circumstances, I'd have to say nothing.

"Now you wait for your lawyer, or if you can't afford one, a public defender will be appointed to you," Deputy D answers as he turns the lock.

Two and a half years ago, I hit a wall and made a vow to myself. It was time to start making better choices, choices that didn't remotely resemble the ones I'd made up until then. The kind of choices that look a lot like the one that just kicked in my front teeth and is making nonconsensual love to my mouth.

These choices almost exclusively revolve around one subject—Love. I've been chasing after it all my life. No shame in my game. The first step in recovery is admitting you have a problem. And what has Love done for me in return? Nothing. Other than leave me bruised and abused, and a little more hopeless each time. It was well past time for a change.

Swearing off relationships is the most adult thing I'd ever done. No more emotional ties that hold the power to

6

compromise the one thing that had been steadfast and true in my life since I was six, my desire for a career on the big screen—or little one. Either one will do.

Which brings me to what happened at Parker's parents' New Year's Eve party. Parker Ulysses Gregory (true story), was at one time my fiancé and the man I was going to spend my entire life loving.

We met in an acting class. I was the aspiring actress. He was the aspiring filmmaker slash director that wanted a better understanding of the acting process. He was also quiet, endearingly self-deprecating, and obsessed with his art—the very definition of right up my alley. It had all the makings of an epic romance. That is, when I still believed in fantasies like romance, affordable rent in Manhattan, and the Tooth Fairy.

Public service announcement, ladies. Those are the ones you have to watch out for. The cocky devils you see coming a mile away. You know why they say "the meek shall inherit the Earth"? 'Cause no one sees those fuckers coming. Now back to our regularly scheduled program.

Our love burned hot and fast, full of lust and butterflies and pawing each other in corner booths of dark and tragically hip downtown lounges. After years of bad first dates, Parker forced me to believe in Love again.

"See," my hopelessly romantic soul said, "fairy tales do come true." Clearly my romantic soul has the I.Q. of an earthworm. Actually, scratch that, an earthworm has some capacity for self-preservation.

When he proposed three months later, it didn't seem too fast. It seemed just right. Until it didn't. Until the small, subtle jabs started, picking away at not only the fabric of my love for him, but worse yet, my self-esteem.

Ex-douchebag: "Can you not wear the ripped jeans to lunch with my parents?"

Fine. I could accommodate the man I loved. Even if I thought his parents were wannabe, pseudointellectual pompous a–holes. Successful art dealers, you say? That specialize in contemporary artists such as Koons, Hirst, and Richter, you say? Wooptyfreakingdo, I say.

Ex-douchebag: "Why can't you wear a bra like every other woman?"

Umm, 'cause unlike other women I barely have any boobage. Forget that he was intimately acquainted with this fact. No bigs, I bought some bras.

Ex-douchebag: "Can you lower your voice when we're in public?"

I was using my quiet voice. Fine, I'll whisper.

Ex-douchebag: "Can you watch the swearing? It's unladylike."

What I wanted to say was *fuck you*. But I didn't. I tried. For him, I tried. I really did. It didn't work. It did *not* work. Profanity so often peppers my every day conversations that trying to stop it gave me a speech impediment. This went on until the jabs were no longer subtle and veiled, until they were downright mean.

Then came the proverbial straw that broke the camel's back. He asked me to turn down the part of the century, a regular spot on an acclaimed cable series because it required quite a bit of nudity. Somehow along the way *the genius* had forgotten I was an actress. Was I stoked about the nudity? Hell no. However, it is part of the job description nowadays. You'd have to be either grossly naïve or stupid to not expect it to happen at some point. Worst part—I did it. I turned it down for him. The depth of self-loathing I still experience whenever I think of it is unquantifiable.

By the time we broke up, I was a mere shell of myself. Someone I didn't recognize. Someone I didn't like. It took a full year for me to be able to look in the mirror and not feel shame, to not hate myself for being a willing participant in my own deconstruction. In hindsight, that's what it was. I was systematically taken apart one word at a time.

Before you go judging me, let me say that there was also a lot of good, too much good for me to simply kick him to the curb. He was great at taking care of me in his own way. He did all the cooking and food shopping and always made sure I had one healthy meal a day. He was very supportive when I was auditioning and did everything to help me prepare. And most importantly, he was great to my grandmother. My grandmother who during the time Parker and I were together had to be moved into assisted living because her Alzheimer's was progressing to the point that she could no longer be left alone, not even for a little while.

I am loyal to a fault. I'm talking organized crime, go-ahead-and-waterboard-me-it-won't-work style loyal when it comes to the people that stand by me. Which is why I put up with him for as long as I did.

In the two years since the demise of our relationship, I've slowly put myself back together. Cue the *Rocky* music. I worked on my craft. I booked two national commercials. I starred in two plays that got decent reviews. I read all the Law of Attraction books. The verdict is still out on whether those did any good. Though by the look of the cell I currently find myself in, I'm inclined to say no.

This was going to be my year. I felt like I was on the

precipice of something big. Something important. Something life-altering. Ever get that charge, that restless feeling and you know, just know you have to pay close attention to what happens next? I had that feeling all week.

"Jones, your lawyer is here," Deputy D bellows. This is not what I meant when I said life-altering.

I lift my chin off my knees, unfurl my tired body off the metal bench of the holding cell, and before stepping out, take a long last look at Cassandra. "Hey—are you going to be okay?"

Her eyes tell me she's seen worse and survived. One side of her full lips tilts up. "I'm always okay, Cinder."

Sure wish I could say the same.

"Come visit me at the store?" she adds.

"I will."

CHAPTER TWO

DEPUTY D LEADS ME DOWN a long corridor to a metal door with a tiny glass window. He said lawyer. Camilla couldn't pull off that act if her life depended on it—too honest and transparent. Which means she found someone on short notice. On New Year's Eve, no less. My best friend is a holy freaking rainmaker.

I'm bouncing on the balls of my bare feet, craning my neck to look through the small window. All I want to do is go home, crawl under the covers, and not come out for a week while I nurse my battered ego back to health and the promise of freedom is making me antsy. For the first time tonight, I feel marginally better. Until Dipshit unlocks the door.

I get a super clear view of whom is on the other side of it and then I don't feel better. No. As a matter of fact I feel worse. And just like that the shred of optimism I was fostering a minute ago circles the drain.

No, no. God, don't do this to me. I'll be good. I swear I will.

Camilla's husband's best friend. He's standing with one hand shoved in the pocket of his perfectly tailored tux. The top of his shirt is draped open, bow tie ends hanging down, eyes glued to the screen of his cell phone. I blink and blink, hoping and praying, but no, I'm not imagining it. This nightmare is real. I start to back out, and Deputy D slams the door shut behind me, the sound grating on my already raw nerves.

"What are you doing here?" My voice sounds strangely high and sharp.

He glances up. His thickly lashed brown eyes skim my face, take note of the black eye makeup which is undoubtedly halfway down my face, work their way lower to the ripped edge of my silver mini dress, then descend all the way to my bare feet. My toes curl in reflex, hiding from his scrutiny. I'm dying a million tiny painful deaths. A million. If there's a personal circle of hell for each and every one of us, this is mine.

I'm convinced that men like Ethan Vaughn are put on this planet to make the rest of us feel bad about ourselves. He's too...perfect. I hate that word, I really do, but there's no other way to describe this dude. A face and body that would make Adonis bristle in envy, successful, impeccably dressed. He's neat. He's very *neat*. It's past midnight and he's still pressed and clean. How the fuck is that possible? I bet he rinses his recycling before placing it in the blue bin. Probably farts perfume.

I don't buy it. I just don't buy it. My bullshit meter tells me something's off. Or maybe it's my black soul. Whatever, one of those two tells me that beneath the picture-perfect surface, he may secretly be a homophobe, or rude to waiters, or mean to animals. Who knows, maybe he likes to kick cats when no one is watching.

Mr. Perfect is still staring, and has yet to say a word. Nor does he have to. My skin is burning from his shrewd assessment.

Take a good look, you sick cat-kicking motherfu...

"I was under the impression you needed a lawyer." His deep voice is even and unaffected. Is he *under the impression* that I need him to get me out of a parking ticket? What's next, a yawn?

He slips his cell phone into his jacket pocket and crosses his arms. I meet his bullshit blasé attitude with one of my own. Except I go for bored, as if it's every day I hang out in jails looking like the newest member of the *Suicide Squad*.

"Aren't you a sports lawyer, or corporate lawyer, or something?"

"I'm licensed to practice."

Dandy. Just dandy. "Did you speak to Camilla? Is she coming?"

Camilla and Vaughn forged an unlikely friendship last year while she was working for Calvin, as a nanny slash teacher for his nephew, Sam. She has a soft spot for this guy, and for the life of me I cannot figure out why.

"Yes."

That's it? No other explanation? The silence continues. Apparently not. His cool gaze sweeps down my person once again and my spine snaps straight. I've got this. This is what I'm good at. On the inside I'm a blubbering, embarrassed mess, where as on the outside I'm stoic with a capital S, smooth as silk and just as cool. I'm an actress, playing pretend is my thing. I've got skillz in this department. Thus, digging down deep into my bag of skillz, I level him with my most devil-may-care stare.

"The prosecutor is asking for bail to be set at two hundred thousand."

"Wut?"

Forget the devil-may-care stare. Just forget it, because it falls right off my face, seamlessly replaced by shock and unmitigated fear. My heart begins thumping so hard inside my chest it feels like it's about to explode.

"Explain to me exactly what happened and don't leave out any of the truthful parts."

There's blood rushing in my ears. All I hear is *wah wah wah wah* truthful parts. I'm feeling woozy, my legs unsteady. Stumbling, I seek out the only chair in the room and slump down in it.

"I...I—" My chin jerks up to take a good measure of the man hovering over me. "Are you suggesting I would lie?"

"I'm not suggesting anything. I'm telling you to give me the truth and only the truth, or you'll be spending this night and every other night in the foreseeable future in a place worse than this."

Swallowing is an impossible feat, my throat dammed up by a hot chunk of terror. Under any other circumstance, I would rather shave with a rusty blade than expose my soft underbelly to this guy. However, as it stands, looking like a gullible jackass is a far cry better than serious jail time.

"Parker, my ex-fiancé, called two days ago and said he really needed to speak to me, that he was in town for his parents' New Year's Eve party. The Gregorys have it every year—"

"I know," Vaughn interrupts.

"How do you—"

"Never mind how."

His tone irks me in the worst possible way. It gets under my skin and makes me itch to hurl words that would make your ears bleed. Need I explain that I have poor impulse control?

He steps closer and I instantly tense. He half sits on the corner of the table, looming over me, and says...nothing. He simply waits me out as if he has he all the time in the world to torture me with his silence. Not for the first time I wonder who I raped and pillaged in a past life to deserve this crap. He's too close. His proximity is messing with my ability to form a single, cohesive thought. And I can smell him. *Christ, what is that?* It's seriously distracting—in a not entirely unpleasant way. Which only stokes my anger.

"Jones?"

"Right." I glance up and meet his intense gaze squarely. "He invited me. Left me three messages saying that he had something important to tell me. I have them if you need them."

"Personal?"

"At the time, I had no idea. It could've been work related." I sure as heck hoped it was personal, though. That, I do not say.

"Go on."

"There were over a hundred people there, most of whom were either drunk or high by midnight. The few times I saw Parker he kept saying he needed to talk to me, that he would find me the minute he got a chance. His parents had people there that were potential investors for one of his films and he was busy pitching to them. I thought nothing of it..." I fiddle with the ripped seam of my dress, every word coming out of my mouth making me more anxious as I relive the events. "I know a few of his friends so it's not like I was waiting around..." My voice loses volume. Who am I kidding? Of course I was waiting around. Even to my own ears the excuse sounds pretty thin.

"But he didn't."

"No," I murmur, shaking my head. "Then, right before midnight, Susan, his mother, made a toast congratulating Parker on his recent engagement." I glance up into a face as flawlessly static as a sheet of ice, nothing to indicate what he's thinking. "I was...surprised." Not exactly the right word but I'm keeping it PG. "He never even mentioned dating anyone."

My voice fades. Vaughn's expression hasn't changed one bit. Not a drop of sympathy or understanding to be found anywhere.

"I thought..." What the hell did I think was going to happen? That he'd fall to his knees and profess he'd made a mistake—beg me to take him back? Yeah, I did. I wanted him to grovel. I had no intention of taking him back—there was a greater chance of me curing cancer—however, the thought of Parker groveling made me maniacally giddy with delight.

"Let's get to the part where you started a fire."

My narrowed eyes cut back to him. If I ever again hear Camilla call this guy charming, she's getting tit punched without warning. "Why are you really here?"

"I owe Calvin a favor."

This night keeps getting better and better. I should've known. My relationship with Calvin can best be described as tenuous. I think he's a grouchy asshat. He thinks I'm...who the hell knows what he thinks, but I have reason to believe it isn't good. Thing is, he loves Camilla. He makes her happy. And as long as she's happy, we get along. God help him if he starts making her unhappy. I certainly don't want to owe the man, however, with an almost quarter million dollar noose hanging around my neck, I am not about to take my chances with a public defender.

"I bolted for the kitchen, Parker followed, we started arguing. You have to understand, between the catering staff and guests wandering in and out, it was chaos. So we're arguing, and I...I may have pushed two chaffing dishes onto the wood floor and, umm, you know those little thingies under—"

"May, or did?" he interrupts, eyebrow lifting into an arrogant arch.

"Did." His silence urges me to continue. "It was the party sludge! How was I supposed to know someone had spilled a bottle of booze on the floor?!"

The floor looked flambéed. It was kind of funny. Until it wasn't. Until the flames reached the drapes and the fire got out of hand.

"Nobody could find the fire extinguisher. Seconds later it reached the drapes. The rest you know."

Another full minute of silence ticks by. In the meantime I can feel his judgment all over me. Far worse than being considered dangerous, I'm being tried and convicted an idiot. In his eyes, I will forever be a screwup of the highest order, a bunny boiler, the crazy chick that almost burned down her ex's parents' house. And I couldn't even get that right. Put a bullet in me and call it a mercy killing.

"Who the hell hangs drapes in the kitchen?!!" I screech in my defense. All things considered, it's a miracle I haven't started bawling my eyes out yet.

A long, tortured sigh escapes my supposed lawyer. "Okay, this is the deal. You're being charged with arson in the fifth degree. Which is a Class A misdemeanor, the least serious. However, it still carries a possible jail sentence of a year if they can prove that the fire was intentionally set—"

Jail sentence? A year? This can't really be happening. Never once did I think there would come a day that I would pray for someone to have slipped the date rape drug into my champagne, but that day has come. Right now, I'm praying and praying hard. "What if I was rufied?"

His perfect brow wrinkles. "How much did you drink?"

"One glass of champagne." I look up and, for the first time, find concern in his big brown eyes. "I wanted to keep my wits about me."

"Did you pass out at any point?"

"Umm, no," I reluctantly admit.

"We'll proceed on the assumption that you weren't. Do I need to explain that the Gregorys are pillars of this community? It'll be your word against theirs—specifically Susan's."

"Susan never liked me. Parker was there. He knows it was an accident!"

"Regardless, it's her property. Susan is running the show and it will be her word against yours."

CHAPTER THREE

TEN MINUTES LATER WE'RE BEING escorted down the hall to a small courtroom. I'm shaking. With each step we take, my body vibrates at a rate that could very well spin me off the planet. Vaughn's steady presence beside me is the only thing preventing that from happening. Outside the courtroom, we sit on a bench and await our turn.

"Whatever happens in there, you are not to say a word." Vaughn's pointed gaze bores into mine. "Are we clear?"

I'm too tired to argue or defend myself. I'm too disillusioned with life. I nod and mean it as I briefly check him out. For the first time all night, I'm glad he's here—even though I'd rather pull my nails off with a pair of needle-nose pliers than admit that to him. No one paints a better picture of respectability and competence than this guy. It's got to lend some credibility to my cause...here's hoping.

"Jones."

My eyes snap up. "Hmm."

His gaze travels over my upturned face. "You can count on me."

Honesty and concern stare back at me. The concern is surprising. I've been around this guy a handful of times; we're virtual strangers. And yet the concern is real. And not in a detached, "sorry your life sucks" kind of way. No, it's real in a way that looks personal, like he has something at stake as well.

"Can I?" I intone, most of me riddled with skepticism while a small part desperately wants to believe him. He has no idea what he's asking. I don't *do* counting on people. I never have. Except now I have no choice.

"Yes," he unequivocally replies.

His quiet voice hits me in a soft spot I thought had grown callous. I can't handle him being nice right now. I can take anything except nice. Squeezing my eyes closed, I fight back the wave of emotion that pushes up my throat. "What about Cassandra?" My eyes blink open, and find him focused on me with a look of utter confusion.

"Who's Cassandra?"

* * *

Minutes later we stand in a small courtroom. A tired, disheveled young prosecutor to our right. Before us, a judge that looks straight out of central casting. He's about a century old, complete with bushy white eyebrows and a mustache. This is about right. This is my life in a nutshell.

"Really?" I mutter under my breath.

"Shhh," Vaughn whispers without glancing my way, his face a study in concentration.

"The man has an herb garden growing out of his ears. He can't hear a thing," I whisper-hiss back. On the edge of my vision, I notice Cal and Cam walk in and take a seat ten rows down. Relief crashes into me. The cavalry has arrived.

"Vaughn?" mutters the judge. Eyebrows that resemble two West Highland terriers climb up his forehead. "Any relation to Harrison Vaughn?"

"Yes, Your Honor, he's my father."

"Hmm, tell him Charlie Weebly says hello."

"Will do, Your Honor."

The judge drones on and on, reads the charges. Per my lawyer, I cringe and sweat as quietly as I possibly can.

"How do you plead?"

"Not guilty, Your Honor."

The judge addresses the prosecutor who has to look through some notes before he can answer back.

Vaughn quickly cuts him off. "Your Honor, the defendant has no record. And she was invited to the scene of the alleged crime. Her phone records will show as much. She hasn't made any attempt to contact the injured party in two years."

Two things. First, I'm slightly relieved. I know that Vaughn is not a criminal defense attorney so this could've gone either way. Second, I'm slightly in awe. Granted, I've never seen him in a work environment before, however, the confidence and command of the courtroom Vaughn is exhibiting is giving me goose bumps.

"Your Honor, there is significant damage to the victim's property," the annoyed and overly tired prosecutor retorts. "And there are a number of witnesses to the crime."

"Who were intoxicated, Your Honor," Vaughn counters. "There's evidence of drug use as well."

"What do you propose, Mr. Vaughn? This looks like a crime of passion. I'm disinclined to believe it won't escalate if I release her. Can't have her wreaking havoc in my town."

So now I'm *King Kong*. Great, just great.

"I'll be posting her bail, Your Honor."

My head whips around, my eyeballs urging Vaughn to look at me. To no avail, his unwavering attention remains on the judge.

Bushy eyebrows climb back up the judge's forehead. "I was afraid you were going to say that." He pauses, flips through some papers. "Fine. Let the record show that I will grant your request for a reduced bail in the amount of fifty thousand on one condition—house arrest until either a deal is reached, or a court date set."

"Your Honor, the defendant will lose her job and suffer serious financial hardship if she can't leave her home." Almost imperceptibly, Vaughn's eyes flicker to me and away. I catch it nonetheless. "I'm prepared to assume responsibility for Miss Jones. She can stay with me."

Say wut?

I'm getting whiplash. I keep staring at him, poking him with my eyeballs to get his attention, and yet nothing. I may as well not even exist.

"Fifty thousand dollars and she will be remanded in your custody, Mr. Vaughn. Good luck." The judge bangs his gavel. "Next case on the docket." His voice disappears as the high-pitch ringing in my ear drowns it out.

* * *

"You look like absolute dog shit," Camilla announces, walking over to me with open arms. We're outside the courtroom, waiting for Vaughn to file whatever paperwork is necessary to get me the heck out of Dodge.

"That good, huh?" Camilla throws her arms around my neck and squeezes me tight, which has me disappearing into the landscape of her body, my face squashed between two gargantuan-sized breasts. "You're thuffacating me," I feel the need to point out.

Holding me away from her, she inspects me closer.

"Where are your shoes, and what in the world happened to your dress?"

Looking down, I see what she's seeing. Not good. "I lost them in the kerfuffle. I need to find a ladies' room."

"Around the corner," responds the surly giant standing next to her. Arms crossed and legs slightly spread apart, his posture and raised black eyebrow are a dead giveaway that he's silently judging me. His expression says I'm the bad news he doesn't want his wife anywhere near. My expression says I wish I could flip you off but you will most likely be paying my bail thanks to your wife therefore I won't.

"I'm going to go sit on the bench, Boo. My feet hurt."

Boo leans down and places two quick kisses on his wife's lips. "Be there in a minute, honey."

I vomit a little in my mouth. "You guys are making me sick."

Camilla's thick lips spread into a huge, white grin.

Thankfully, the ladies' room is empty. I catch sight of the horror that is myself in the mirror and gasp. What was only hours ago a very neat bun is now a blonde nest for woodland creatures, my silver beaded dress is shredded in all the wrong places, and my smoky black eye makeup, the one I thought made my murky hazel eyes look green, has turned into skid marks running down my cheeks. It looks like a Chihuahua has wiped his little dirty doggy butt down my cheeks. I grab a bunch of paper towels and run them under the faucet.

As I stare at the image in the mirror, a surge of recalcitrance gets past the embarrassment, past the fear that I may have caused irreparable damage to my life. It lifts my chin, and squares my shoulders. I don't bother cleaning my face. Nope. I chuck the wet paper towels in the trash and wear that hideous mess as a badge of honor.

I stopped caring what anybody thinks of me a long time ago. The mess in the mirror, this is who I am in all my abundantly flawed glory. Heavy emphasis on the flawed part. No apologies made. No figs given. I do me, for better or worse—usually worse.

Outside the ladies' room, I locate a water fountain. In the middle of taking a huge gulp, voices from around the corner get my attention. Not like they're whispering, so you can't blame me for listening.

"Can't she stay with us?" That's Cal. His deep baritone is unmistakable.

"No. She's my responsibility now. It shouldn't take longer than three months anyway."

Three months? Groan.

"I don't like it."

"You don't like anything," replies my lawyer. Can't say I don't agree with him there.

"Do I have to warn you to keep your hands to yourself?"

Then, a raspy masculine chuckle. "You think I'd jeopardize my career over a hump? I could get disbarred if there's so much as a whisper of impropriety."

A hump? Okay, that stings. As much as I'd like to say otherwise, it kind of stings. Just a little. Which makes me hate myself. I should be immune to such nonsense. I have less than zero interest in this man, not even as a hump, not even as desperate as I am and I've got desperation written all over me.

I know I'm not his type. I'm sure he dates supermodels or supercelebrities or some such shit. And God knows he isn't my type. And yet, hearing that I'm not even good enough for a hump still stings...a teensy bit. And I have to live with him—for three months. If there's any justice in this world whomever he's *humping* will give him pube fleas.

"Under normal circumstances, I'd say no, but—"

"But what?"

Enough. I've had enough. I walk around the corner and all conversation ceases. "Ready?" I say, my game face on, the one devoid of any evidence that I've overheard them discussing me as if I'm nothing more than a hot burden to be tossed back and forth between them. There's nothing I loathe more than depending on other people. I've always been self-sufficient, having learned that useful skill decades ago when Eileen, also known as the slacker who gave birth to me, decided that she would simply pawn me off on my grandparents and start fresh with Dan.

Now I'm at the mercy of these two heroes. Bile rises up at the mere thought of it. Welcome to my life. Some people have cheerful, happy-go-lucky ones. Some have solemn, purposeful ones. Mine's got chronic bitch face interrupted by fleeting moments of mild amusement. This is not one of those moments.

* * *

It took another twenty minutes for me to be released, for Vaughn to make arrangements for my bail to be paid. They gave me back my purse, the only personal item the police confiscated when I was brought in, my coat and other shoe lost in the chaos of my arrest.

"I'll go get the car." Vaughn stalks away, his long legs eating up ground as he exits out the door and across the empty parking lot.

"Thanks for coming to my rescue," I mumble in a listless voice. I get a bunch of grumbled words from Cal, and an equal amount of, "You don't have to thank us," from Camilla.

Through the glass door, the three of us watch Vaughn's broad back disappear into the moonless night. As soon as he's out of sight, Cal faces me and exhales tiredly. He stuffs his hands in the pockets of his sweatpants and shrugs up his massive shoulders.

"I need to say somethin'—" Reaching up, he rubs his scruff-covered jaw. He seems unsure, as if he's searching for the right words.

"Spit it out, Calvin. I know you're dying to let me have it. Let's get it over with."

"Do me a favor, don't screw with him, okay. Just...go easy."

Huh? It takes me a minute to grasp what he means and about whom. He's worried about his friend? His wealthy, gorgeous friend whose major life issues probably include how to get on the waiting list for the next limited-edition Porsche, which he probably pronounces *Porscha* 'cause he's cool like that.

No. Just no. I've had the single worst night of my life. I've been conned, manhandled, falsely accused, arrested, and insulted. At the very least, it's making the top two. So is it any wonder that somewhere inside of me a fuse is lit that quickly grows into burning outrage. It really shouldn't be. And that's when Bad Amber takes over, punting reason and good sense to the curb.

"Yeah, sure. I'll be *suuuper* gentle when I breach his virgin anus for the first time. Can't make any promises about the second time, though."

Cal blinks twice, his mouth gapes open. Then he shuts it and his eyes narrow. "See, this is what I mean." He turns to

Cam, whose eyes are as large as dinner plates, and says, "This is exactly what I mean." Head shaking, he blasts me with that icy, gray gaze he's famous for on Sundays. "Not funny."

Shrugging, I glance at Cam. She's chewing on her bottom lip, desperately trying not to laugh while she attempts to pet her husband into a better mood. *Besties 4 eva.* Cal plants his hands on his hips and tips his head back.

"Relax, Calvin," I half-grunt, tired and generally pissed off. "Your sweet boy prince is safe from my evil sorcery. He's the only chance I have of staying out of jail. Besides, you can't go poking around there willy-nilly. You need to prep the area—"

"I can't listen to this," Cal mutters to his wife.

"She's kidding, Boo." The heavy petting continues. "Amber, tell him you're kidding."

Vaughn's pimped out Audi A8 pulls up to the curb. Black tinted windows, black hubcaps, black paint. Wild guess: he likes black. He gets out holding a man's winter puffer jacket. Wait for it, it's black. Ripping open the door, he walks up to us without a word and throws it around my bare shoulders. His moves are impersonal, brisk and efficient. He's a man on a mission, and the mission it seems is to swaddle me.

"What are you doing?" My question goes ignored. The jacket is as large as a sleeping bag, my head and bare feet the only parts of my anatomy sticking out. My eyes cut to Cal and Cam who are equally silent. This time I direct my question at the two stiffs standing next to me. "What is he doing?"

My best friend's puzzled frown matches mine. Before I have a chance to argue, Vaughn picks me up, kicks the door open, and carries me to the car. Being arrested in front of a hundred people because the owner of the house is screaming, "fire starter!" at the top of her lungs while pointing at me didn't do it. Losing a shoe as I was being manhandled into the back of a squad car didn't do it. Not even having my mug shot taken did it. However, being carried like I'm a small child by this man has managed to crush into dust what's left of my dignity.

Outside it's close to ten degrees, the concrete frozen over, and though I'm far from bummed that my bare feet do not have to touch the ground, I still can't hide my discomfort. My body is corpse-like in his secure hold while I stare straight ahead.

"Call me," Camilla shouts.

I turn to nod and notice Cassandra coming out of the door. Having been released, she heads for a waiting yellow cab. She's about to get in when she spots me. Punching her fists in the air, she shouts, "Cinder! Luv you, girl."

"Friend of yours?" the weirdo carrying me says. The note of amusement in his voice compels me to look at him. His lips quiver, on the verge of a smile that he eventually disciplines.

I tug my arm out of the jacket and wave at Cassandra. "She is now." As he gently places me in the passenger seat of the car, I force myself to look up at him.

"Thank you for helping her."

His eyes hold mine longer than I deem necessary. It feels like he's peering into my soul and judging me as damaged goods. It makes me excruciatingly uncomfortable, a state of being I'm accustomed to. My heart rate picks up speed. I'm dying to look away. However, I learned a long time ago not to back down from a challenge. That's why I stare back until he finally shuts the door.

* * *

The car ride back to the city is about as much fun as getting a Brazilian wax job, painful and seems to last an eternity. For a full hour Vaughn stares ahead with a blank expression. The few minutes of understanding we may have shared back at the courthouse have long been wiped away as if they never happened. He wants to do quiet. I can do quiet. This is a battle of wills I don't intend to lose.

"I trust you understand the importance of not contacting Gregory in any way, shape, or form. Not on social media. Not anywhere."

That tone. That tone is nails on a chalkboard to my ears. Lips thinning, I decide to nip this in the bud. "Look...umm..." *Mister?* Nope. That sounds weird. I start again. "Vaughn—"

My address prompts a slow turn of his head in my direction. His lids grow heavy and his mouth twists into a cynical smirk. I've never addressed him formally. It's usually Fancy McButterpants, or Fancy Pants—his chosen nickname by yours truly after I determined His Holy Fanciness needed to be taken down a notch, or two. But never Mr. Vaughn, and never ever by his first name. For some absurd reason calling him by his first name feels too intimate. It suggests ease, a friendliness that does not exist between us. Hence, I've never used it. Not once. Weird, I know. It is what it is.

"I don't intend to speak to that son of a filthy sow ever again, but someone needs to. He was there. He knows it was an accident." Parker may be an insecure, passive aggressive man/child, but he's not going to have me wrongfully imprisoned for an accident.

"David Pitt will be handling the case. He'll know how best to proceed."

"David who?"

"A colleague of mine. Practices criminal law—I refer all my clients to him."

"I can't afford him! As it is, it'll take me forever to pay you back."

"You don't have to pay anyone back. Calvin's taking care of it."

"I'm not a charity case. How much do you charge? Three hundred an hour?"

The dark humor on his face says one thing only—he might as well have called me a dumbass. There's that itchy feeling again. Breathing out a tired sigh, I try again. "Five hundred."

"You can't afford me."

"A thousand? Are you kidding me? What the hell have I been doing with my time? I should've gone to law school." This is the part of the program where I close my eyes and bang my head against the window. It will take me forever to dig myself out of this stink hole.

"I don't charge by the hour, Jones. I'm a business manager. I'm paid in percentages."

I glance at moneybags. Lost in thought, he's wearing a subtle smile. What does he have to smile about? Probably the karmic retribution I'm currently experiencing. "Finding this hilarious, are you?"

"Not at all," he answers without hesitation. Our eyes meet briefly and I can see that he means it.

"I want to know exactly what this is going to cost me because if it takes me holding up a bank, I'm paying back every cent."

"I think we've established that you're not cut out for a life of crime. Besides, Calvin's already paid up."

"Then I'll pay Calvin back. I want the exact amount."

I get a long-suffering sigh, coupled with a raised eyebrow. "The amount is zero."

The stretch of silence that follows leaves me drained, whatever energy I have left leeching out of me. What's the point of fighting it? Really? It doesn't make a lick of difference anyway. Way too often it seems my life is on a fixed track headed nowhere I want to go.

I steal another glance at my new roommate. He did nothing to deserve this. This is nobody's fault but my own. Time to embrace the fact that I will be at this man's mercy for the next three months. And God knows I could've done a heck of a lot worse than living with Fancy McButterpants in what is sure to be a fancy apartment. Best to start off on the right foot.

"Look, Vaughn, I get that I'm not your favorite person. I don't know what kind of favor you owe Cal that would require you to *volunteer as tribute*, but here we are, stuck with each other for the next...what is it that you said?" Arching a dramatic eyebrow, I add, "The next three months. I think we can manage to stay out of each other's hair for three months." I make a show of staring at his perfectly styled dark-brown hair. "Even though you use a ghastly amount of hair product."

Frowning, he squirms in his seat. "I do not use hair product."

"Agree to disagree. Anywho, this should be easy enough. You work days. I work nights. We'll hardly see each other. Absolutely no danger of anyone accidentally *humping*."

His reaction comes swiftly. His head whips around, guilt and surprise splashed across his supermodel-worthy features.

Finally—a genuine show of emotion. *Score one for team Jones.* Satisfaction turns the corners of my mouth up. No doubt about it, my life is a dumpster fire if this is the highlight of my evening.

His attention slides back to the road ahead. Three long minutes of heavy silence follow. "I didn't mean—"

"Easy there, counselor." The last thing I want is a long, awkward apology from him. "No harm, no foul. Hurting my feelings would require that I care what you, or any man thinks, and I assure you I don't. Quite frankly, after tonight, I am *this* close to moving to the Isle of Lesbos. All I need is your legal expertise and a bed to sleep in for the next three months."

He blows out a deep breath, his body relaxing while his hands tighten on the burl wood steering wheel. "You have it."

I turn in my seat to face him. I want him to see how sincere I am when I say this. "And I appreciate it. I know this sucks for you, too."

Holding my steady gaze, he gives me a curt nod.

CHAPTER FOUR

IT'S 4 A.M. BY THE time we reach my fifth floor walk-up in Greenwich Village. Vaughn insisted we grab some of my things before we head to his place. Every reason I had for him to wait in the car was rebutted with vigor. The futility of debating with a lawyer only hit me after I'd already wasted a pile of time. This is how that went—

Me: "You don't have to come up."

Him: "It'll go faster if I do."

Me: "I'd rather you didn't."

Him: "I'm coming with you."

Me: *What the f*—"Mmno, you're not."

Him: "Yeah, I am."

Me: "Let–me–hand–you–a–dictionary–so–you–can–understand–what–I–am–saying. You are *not* coming up."

Without warning, he yanked me out of the passenger seat and into his arms. After that, he proceeded to stalk into the narrow entrance of the building—which I didn't mind so much seeing as my shoe situation hadn't improved—and deposited me on my feet. Our eyeballs battled for supreme dominance of the galaxy. This ended in a draw. Then, without another word, he stepped past me and jogged up the stairs.

I mean, stubborn is putting it lightly. I don't want him in

my apartment. One, it's as big as a matchstick box. And two, it's a mess. I haven't had time to clean or do laundry in a week, couple that with the diminutive size of the space and you get a perfect disaster. I didn't want Mr. Perfect seeing it like this.

And now he's standing in my bedroom. Hands stuffed into his tuxedo pants pockets, he's looking around. What the hell is he doing in my bedroom? Damn, this is awkward. He's taking up way too much space, sucking up all the oxygen. I can't think with him in here.

"I'll help you pack."

Yeah, not happening, but I'm too tired to argue with him. Glancing around, his eyes fall on my unmade bed—and stay there.

"Are you here to do a health inspection or help?"

That snaps him out of whatever is going on in his head. I get down on all fours, my attention momentarily diverted as I grab my suitcase from under the bed. Bad move. Real bad. Because when I glance up, I find him in the process of opening the top drawer of my dresser.

"No! Not that one!" I screech.

Too late. Too freaking late. Vaughn is staring at the contents of the drawer, his expression frozen. Until I see his lips move. He's counting them. *Oh dear, he's counting them.* His eyes grow a little wider. He finally reaches seven and stops. Little does he know that eight is in the Amazon box near the front door.

"Don't touch," I say, with an exaggerated smirk.

A quick scowl darkens the perfection that is his face. "I wasn't planning to." His attention returns to the contents of the drawer. When he starts to close it, I decide to double down because it's that kind of night.

"Might as well leave it open. I have to pack those."

That perfectly styled head slowly turns in my direction. I get a blank, assessing stare. He thinks I'm messing with him, but I'm not. When I continue to stare back in silence, he blinks twice and rubs his face.

"You're bringing all of these?" he says more than asks, his tone reeking of disbelief. His doubt earns him a one shoulder shrug.

"I can't bring Jamie and leave Wes. Those two are an item. Sometimes I'm in the mood for Gabriel, sometimes Garrett. And Zeke has abandonment issues. He'll get upset if I leave him behind."

Guilty as charged. I name my vibrators after my book boyfriends. If you have a problem with it, get on your high horse and go file a complaint with the Bureau of I Don't Give A Stinking Shit.

He briefly squeezes his eyes shut and shakes his head, sighs deeply. "I'll be on the couch while you finish this up."

Fifteen minutes later, I've grabbed enough clothes for the week, packed each and every one of my book boyfriends, and swapped my busted Cinderella dress for a sweater and jeans. I walk into the living room to find Vaughn sitting upright on my couch with his head resting on the back pillow. He's sleeping so peacefully I almost feel bad waking him.

Watching him with unfettered access takes me back to the day we met. Not only is the godforsaken memory annoyingly preserved in high definition, it's also taken up way too much space in my brain—space that could otherwise be used for good. It was the start of football season. Minutes before I was to be picked up by *Calvin's manager* who, Camilla explained, also lived in the city and had offered to give me a ride to the stadium, my toilet backed up. True story. The dumb twats that live upstairs apparently like to play Russian roulette by flushing tampons. Which means everyone in the building suffered the consequences of their stupidity thanks to the ancient New York City plumbing. Hence, when the doorbell rang, I was expecting Eddie, my middle-aged building superintendent.

What I was not expecting when I opened the door to my apartment was the standard-bearer of masculine perfection in a custom-made suit. What I was not expecting was to get sucker punched in the cooter by a pair of big brown eyes framed with impossibly thick lashes. My brainwaves flatlined. You can't blame me—that face is a goddamn murderer of gray matter. It's flawless in a way that renders one incapable of doing anything other than staring, mouth agape. I catch myself doing it all the time, searching for a small bump, a tiny scar, an angle that's too steep or wide. And yet nothing, I can't seem to find a single one. Which aggravates me to no end. Which means I usually end up inadvertently glowering at him.

In my line of work, pretty boys are as common as flies on dog excrement. They've never been of any particular interest to me. I place them in the same category as exotic cars— typically useless and generally time consuming because someone's always trying to jack them. Therefore, you can imagine my surprise when somewhere in the background a harp began to play, butterflies took flight in my gut, and a rainbow came shooting out of my...well, you get the picture.

I gravitate toward shy, creative types. Types that don't reduce my attention span to that of a gnat because I suddenly develop the libido of a teenage boy. Who needs that kind of headache day in and day out? I've got shit to do. My laundry keeps piling up. My refrigerator hasn't been cleaned in a month. However, I will admit that if eyes had the ability to orgasm, mine would have that day.

So there I was, standing in my doorway drunk on lust. Until he smiled at me. That counterfeit smile rubbed me the wrong way. An ice bucket over my head, no challenge included. Still in the midst of healing from the third-degree burn of my latest bout with Love, I swiftly remembered that men were on par with Ebola, and all the reasons I vowed to stay away from humans with a penis for a brain returned with a vengeance. I glared, the smile fell off his pretty face, soon replaced by confusion, and the rest is history.

Since then, reshaping this reluctant attraction into indifference lightly garnished with a touch of resentment has been incredibly easy. And that's where I firmly stood on the matter—until now. Whether by choice or coercion, he's the only reason I am not a ward of the great state of New York. Now there's a heavy load of gratitude standing in the way of my resentment.

"Fancy." Nothing. Though I detect a very faint snore. Nice to know he's human; I was beginning to have my doubts. I get closer. "Vaughn," I say, a little louder this time. Still nothing. I hover over him, much closer than I'm comfortable with. The other choice is to touch him and I *reeaally* don't want to do that.

A whiff of his man aroma hits me and my eyelids get a little droopy. It's like stepping into an opium cloud, dangerously addictive. I stay there for a solid five minutes sniffing and sniffing, trying to ferret out what it is that's making me mental. His eyes slam open and meet mine.

Woops. Busted.

* * *

Fifteen minutes later, I'm standing in front of a turn-of-the-century limestone townhouse on the Upper East Side, one block from Central Park. Calling it impressive would be equivalent to me saying Ryan Reynolds has a pretty good body. In other words, woefully understated. There's money, and then there's Money. This is the latter.

"Did you neglect to tell me you're related to the House of Windsor?"

"Norma gave it to me," he absently answers while retrieving his keys from his jacket pocket. Loaded down with my suitcases, he trudges up the stairs to an elaborate wrought iron door.

"Didn't peg you as the kept man type."

His body goes rigid while his face adopts an expression of disgust. "Norma Ellington is my grandmother."

"Ellington? Ellington as in the real estate company?" The name plastered on every building that isn't named Trump in this city.

"Hmm."

He unlocks the iron door and we step into a vestibule. "What, no butler to greet us?" My quip goes ignored. Next, the carved mahogany door swings open. I cannot contain my surprise. Mouth gapping open, I am rendered speechless, which is close to impossible. I'm seldom surprised so this at least makes sense. What does not make sense is what I'm presently staring at.

"It's *The Money Pit*. You're living in *The Money Pit*." Stepping further inside, Vaughn right behind me, I look around, my eyes not quite sure what part of this wreck to settle on first. "Is the staircase safe to walk on?"

It looks like a demolition crew took out half of it while the rest is in a state of serious disrepair. The few pieces of furniture that are present don't seem to fit, the style ultra contemporary.

"I just hired a new contractor. I hadn't planned on a houseguest." While I stand there mesmerized, he walks past me. "Stay out of the living room, dining room, and…" He exhales tiredly, his broad shoulders dropping. "Better yet, don't go anywhere other than the kitchen and bedrooms." Without a backward glance, he begins to climb the stairs. "Stairs are fine—as you can see."

On the second floor, he leads me down a long hallway, until we reach two closed doors…next to each other. He's frowning again, staring blindly at the doors and frowning.

"You twist the knob to open the door."

That did not go over well. He levels me with a narrow-eyed glare and I'm immediately hit with regret. In my defense, I've been through a lot tonight. Sometimes my mouth does its own thing.

"Sorry, I'm tired."

"The master bedroom is under repair and these two are the only bedrooms with electricity."

"God's sake, Vaughn. I don't care if you have a cage hidden in a dirt pit behind that door. My brain is deep-fried and my soul is on life support. All I want to do is get horizontal and sleep for a thousand years."

I push open the door to bedroom number one. A king-size mattress with no sheets sits on the floor, the windows are bare, and a standing lamp offers the only light.

"You take my bedroom tonight. I'll fix this tomorrow."

"Absolutely not." I drag my limp body to the mattress and plop down. "Do you have an extra set of sheets and a pillow?" The look of sheer desperation on my face convinces him not to argue. He acquiesces with a short nod.

"These bedrooms share a bathroom in the middle," he states. You would think he's giving me the nuclear launch codes with the tone he's using. "Make sure you lock both doors when you're in there."

Minutes later he walks back into my bedroom, carrying towels, a stack of bed linens, a down comforter, and a pillow. After placing them on the mattress next to where I'm sitting, he stuffs his hands in the pockets of his tuxedo pants and pauses.

"Can I get you anything else?" He looks like he stepped out of the pages of GQ, none the worse for wear after what we've been through tonight. I'll admit I'm slightly annoyed by this. His eyes meet mine. There's something lurking in the dark depths of those eyes that I can't quite put my finger on. I shake my head and he turns to leave.

"Hey." Pausing, he looks over his shoulder. "Thank you for everything…really." Raising his hand, he stalls the rest of my speech. After which, he exits.

CHAPTER FIVE

BANG BANG BANG

I bolt upright in bed. I'm a light sleeper, always have been. So light that I need earplugs, a sleep mask, and blackout curtains to remain asleep. And to fall asleep? That's a whole other story. As in, it is unlikely to occur unless I get a little help from one of my mechanical boyfriends. This body runs on high RPMs. It takes a village (of electric man parts) to help me relax.

Momentarily confused and desperate to get my bearings, I push my black satin eye mask up my forehead. The sunlight coming through the bare window blinds me. Permanently, I'm almost certain. And then I realize where I am. *Groan.*

Bang Bang Bang

One glance at my cell phone tells me two things. One: it's way too early in the morning for construction workers to have arrived. And two: I only got two hours of sleep.

Said banging gets louder. Mumbling obscenities under my breath, I jump out of bed, jam on my slippers, and stomp out of my bedroom in search of the source of my misery. I step over tarps and painting supplies, walk under an open ladder—my luck's *shite* anyway so what difference does it make—and descend the stairs in a hurry.

AC/DC's Back in Black at seven in the morning? You have got to be kidding me.

Recognizing that the music's coming from the living room, I head in that direction. Angry stomping, I whip around the corner and my feet skid to a stop.

Whoa.

I blink repeatedly to make sure the hot piece standing twelve feet away with his back to me isn't a figment of my sex-starved imagination. Naked from the waist up, he's pounding away at the sheetrock. Tall, broad-shouldered, back muscles rippling every time he swings the sledgehammer against the far wall. His Levis are worn and I mean, really worn, not to mention in danger of falling off any minute now. Fingers crossed they do with the next swing. Fingers crossed. They're hanging so low over the pronounced muscles of his bubble butt that...

Wait...is he wearing underwear?

Nope. I can see crack. Butt cleavage. Yep, I am definitely staring at butt cleavage. My fascination with his butt cleavage produces a suspicious heat south of my waist. This is what happens when you've been without the feel of another human being for far, *far* too long. I knew I should've taken my friend, Justin, up on his offer to bone me into the next century. Once again, bad judgment on my part.

To say that my sex life is suffering a dry spell is akin to calling the Sahara a sandbox. It's been years. And by the looks of it, abstinence yawns before me for many more to come. But after the fiasco that was the last time—the sex so bad I actually got angry while in the midst of it, that's how utterly unsatisfying it was—abstinence seems the only reasonable way to go. Besides, I've got my boyz to get me through.

He's going at that wall like he's working out some serious aggression. On the next swing of the hammer, I'm reminded of the headache I awoke with. The delight wanes. Time to put an end to this nuisance.

"Hey." Nothing. He keeps killing the sheetrock, exposing a very nice red brick living beneath it. "Hey! Bob the Builder! Give it a rest, will you!"

Freezing mid swing, he brings the sledgehammer down gently. Then he drops it and turns around.

Da fuuu..."Fancy?" is all I can muster out, my voice strangely high. I know what the sheetrock feels like. I know because he may as well have slugged me in the gut with that sledgehammer.

Nostrils flaring, sweat dripping down a chest that belongs in a *Magic Mike* sequel, Vaughn stares back at me for what feels like a lifetime. So long I may need Botox. So long I'm starting to fidget under his pointed though slightly detached examination of me, myself, and I.

The song ends and the silence breaks the weird vibe traveling between us. And when I say weird, I mean not good, not good at all. *Huh.* What's his problem? I mean, besides having a total stranger live in his house and invade his privacy. Could be my vivid imagination is acting up. Could be. Yeah, that's it. Probably lack of sleep…probably.

He walks over to the sound system and shuts it off. When his attention returns to me, his lips twitch as his gaze zeros in on my t-shirt. Still reeling from the discovery of all the muscles standing before me, I have to check to see what it is that's amusing him.

"That's, umm, an interesting choice of nightwear," he finally says.

Cam and I have been exchanging prank Christmas gifts for the last ten years. This one is a personal favorite of mine. On the front of the oversized t-shirt, **The Duck U Lookin' At? ducking spellcheck** is written in bold black letters. On the back, there's a cartoon drawing of a duck flipping the bird.

I freaking love this t-shirt.

His chocolate brown eyes work their way down the length of my shirt, pause where it ends at the top of my thighs, linger for a while, then slide down to my feet. A baby v appears between his brows.

"Is that supposed to be chocolate ice cream?" He's referring to the top of my fluffy brown slippers. The ones I bought at the mall because they're a perfect metaphor for my life.

"It's the shit emoji."

"I was afraid of that," he mutters. Picking up a gray t-shirt off the floor, he starts wiping his chest.

I should've definitely taken Justin up on that offer.

* * *

"You're looking rather homespun this morning," I say as I pour a much-needed second cup of coffee and study the specimen seated across from me at the kitchen island. Elbows on the counter, I bring the mug to my lips while I openly examine his chest, the one he has yet to cover.

Who the heck would've imaged what was hiding beneath all that fine cotton and wool. When my eyes climb back up to his face, he arches a knowing brow. If he doesn't want me looking, he should put a shirt on it.

"Because I'm wearing jeans?"

"Because I've never seen you *uncoifed*."

I don't know what it is about him that brings out the

hobgoblin in me, but every time I'm anywhere near his divine self I'm gripped by an irrational urge to kick his shins and pull his hair, to get a rise out of him. Sadly, it's proving to be an impossible feat. The man has indifference running through his veins.

"I do not *coif* my hair," he replies, running a hand through it.

"Agree to disagree." The doorbell rings and we exchange a look of surprise. "Construction crew?"

He takes a sip of his coffee, watching me over the rim. "It's New Year's Day."

"Thanks, professor. I'll go." Hopping off the counter, I march to the tall window next to the front door.

"Maybe you shouldn't," I hear him shout. A tall brunette is on the front steps, attempting to peer through the wrought iron door.

"It's a woman," I whisper-shout over my shoulder.

I find him standing in the doorway of the kitchen, brushing the top of his hair back and forth in a gesture indicating what is clearly frustration.

I'm thinking an ex-something, maybe? Maybe. I'm not sure if he's dating anyone.

"What does she look like?" he growls, the little v back to decorating his brow.

"Pretty, tall and thin, long brown hair. She's in workout clothes." I look over my shoulder and catch him staring at my legs. His gaze casually slides away. Men, what simple creatures. And when I say simple, I mean stupid. "She looks like she just got her hair and makeup done."

"Alexa." More grumbling. I get the distinct impression he's unhappy about this uninvited visitor. Camilla had mentioned a while ago that Vaughn has a string of admirers. Although, having them show up at his house? Without an invitation? I wouldn't call it a string of admirers. I'd call it time to reevaluate your life choices, get a whole bunch of restraining orders, and most definitely an STD test.

It dawns on me, then. He's going to be entertaining these women in his bedroom, one door down from me...less than twelve feet from my ears. This is what I have to look forward to. Fun times ahead.

Jaw locked, he's staring at the ceiling. Discomfort is all over him, the muscles of his chest and arms taut.

"Want me to get rid of her for you?" I throw it out casually. I figure I'll help him out this one time. After what he's done for me, it seems only fair. However, if he's going to hit it and quit it on the regular, he's on his own. I will gladly feed him to the she-wolves, grab a bag of popcorn, and enjoy the show.

His gaze snaps back to me, his expression now bright with hope. "Could you?"

Could I? It takes some effort to tamp down the smug grin dying to spread across my face. "No sweat."

He looks genuinely relieved. This dude is full of surprises. As I head to the front door, a pronounced masculine cough gets my attention. Vaughn is pointing at my legs, a rosy glow under his tan, one I imagine he got sailing, or playing polo, or maybe counting stacks of cash outdoors.

"You might want to put some pants on."

Not that it matters, because I'm basically built like a thirteen-year-old boy, but I lift my t-shirt to reveal my pajama shorts. "Make yourself scarce," I say as I reach for the door.

The brunette, Alexa, has her finger poised to ring for the

fourth time. Seeing me, she tilts her head and frowns. Her gray eyes glide up and down my person, pausing meaningfully at the writing on my t-shirt.

"I'm looking for Ethan." When she attempts to look beyond me, I'm one step ahead, swaying to stay in her line of sight. "Ethan Vaughn."

"Bulgy eyes? Short?"

"No," she replies, voice dripping in condescension. "Tall and gorgeous."

"Oh, you mean, Fancy McButterpants. Yeah, he's...uh... indisposed at the moment."

"Is he okay?" Her concern is nowhere near genuine.

"I don't think so."

Surprise struggles to appear on her chemically frozen face. "I should check on him." When she sidesteps to enter, I once again slide in her way.

"He's got a raging case of diarrhea." That may have come out a little louder than necessary.

"Oh."

Her discomfort emboldens me to continue. "You know, the angry sort that makes you pray for a speedy death."

Her slender nose crinkles. "No, I don't know."

"Sure you do. We've all had it. He barely made it to the bathroom." She looks properly grossed out. "I'm sorry, what's your name?"

"Alexa."

"I'll be sure to tell Fancy you stopped by. That is, if he ever makes it out of the bathroom alive."

Her eyes turn into slits. "And you are—"

"Seriously overdue for a shower. Long night," I say with a side-eyed smirk. "Anysomethin', nice to meet you. Bye, Lexi."

"Alexa."

"Right."

With that, I shut the door and skip to the kitchen. Where I find Fancy leaning against the island with his arms crossed in front of that stripper-worthy chest, his face as neutral as the Swiss.

"A ragging case?"

"You're welcome."

"The angry sort?"

"You think she would've gone away if I suggested you had a tummy ache? That is a hardened stalker you've got there, Fancy Pants."

He shakes his head, his gaze falling to the floor. When he lifts his chin, he has his poker face back on.

"I got rid of her, didn't I?" Turning on my fluffy heels, I head upstairs.

* * *

After heading to the corner market, I spent the better part of the day in bed, worrying about my future and pretending to read. As late afternoon welcomes the dark, I crawl out of my bunker of despair and into the bathroom. I have no idea where Fancy is, nor do I care. The magnitude of my plight has finally sunk in and I can think of little else. After a terrible shower with practically no water pressure, I find a message from Camilla on my cell and call her back.

"Tell me everything."

"Well, outside it's Windsor Palace, and inside it's a dump." I run a finger along the lampshade and inspect the dust that it picked up. "I'm living with Miss Havisham."

"I mean, what happened at the party—with Parker?"

I was afraid of that. It's like someone stuck a pin in me. I instantly deflate, a thousand pounds landing on my shoulders. "I can't do serious right now," I mumble. "If I do serious, I'll get hysterical. I'll cry and I'm afraid I won't be able to stop."

"We won't do serious, then."

This is why I love her. No one understands me the way Cam does. "Okay, good." I breathe out a sigh of relief.

"Back to Ethan as Miss Havisham. Does that make you Estella?"

"Of course not, it makes me Pip. He's more Estella than I am."

"And the townhouse is a wreck?"

"It's *The Money Pit.* I don't understand how he can live here. And then, this morning, get this, I wake up to loud banging and find him looking like *Thunder From Down Under*, going crazy at the wall with a sledgehammer. I was about to go grab some singles until he turned around."

"Ethan? My Ethan? We're talking about the same person?"

"Yes. And slow your roll, you greedy grubster, he's not yours. You wanted *Shrek* and now you've got him. That one's yours. Good luck, by the way."

"I do love me some Shrek," she replies chuckling.

"Your husband hates me."

"He does not hate you."

"Is this going to turn into *Sophie's Choice* somewhere down the road? Don't send me to the killers."

"No one is going to the killers. Not even Parker unfortunately."

Dressed in the bath towel, I'm pacing, restlessly walking in circles, because even as I'm talking to Camilla, the scene at the party, with Parker so innocently, so nonchalantly telling me how in love he is keeps playing on a loop like the worst horror movie I can imagine.

In the shower, it came to me, the reason I flipped out at the party. It wasn't so much that it bothered me that Parker's in love and ready to live his happily ever after. No matter what, I would never begrudge anyone a chance at happiness. It was that he managed to make me lose trust in myself, in my own judgment. And all I keep thinking now is—what if I'm wrong about *everything*?

"She's a model," comes ripping out of me. "How original, right?"

"Was she there? Did you see her?"

"No. She was somewhere important doing some important stuff. That's not even the bad part. He finally got funded on the script we developed together and he's giving her the lead role. And he had the gall to tell me TO MY FACE that she's the best thing that ever happened to him."

Flopping down on my makeshift bed, I absently stare at the water stain on the ceiling. It takes the shape of my ex-douchebag's face and mocks me. "That's when I started flipping chafing dishes Jersey style. He basically called the two years we were together a mistake, that we were incompatible because of my *abrasive* personality, and it would be career suicide to work together." I scoff. "Oh—and he expects me to be happy for him. He actually said those words. He said *if I ever cared about him, I would be happy for him*. Fucker thinks he's the Dali Lama."

"I never liked him."

It's cold, a palpable draft swirling through the room. Shivering, I get up and drop the damp towel while I search in vain through my suitcase for my sweats. "I won't fare well as a prison bitch. You know I won't. My mouth will get me into trouble, and within a week someone will have me collared and calling me Sparkles."

My hands are shaking and it's not from the cold.

"That's not going to happen. Ethan, Cal, and I won't let it. You're not alone." Camilla's voice is fierce, her inner lioness coming through loud and clear. "Fucking Parker. I swear I'm going to get a voodoo doll and put a hex on his peanuts."

"Thanks, buddy."

"What are friends for?"

"To put hexes on exes?"

"Yup. I have to make dinner. Call you mañana."

"Sure."

Tossing my iPhone on the mattress, I turn and blanche. Across the open bathroom door, Vaughn stares back at me, his steady gaze unblinking. With a squeak, I grab the towel and cover my bare cooch.

Busted.

CHAPTER SIX

THE NEXT MORNING I ROLL out of bed, jam my slippers on, and shuffle down to the kitchen. Even though I'm barely conscious, I'm smirking. I haven't seen Fancy since I caught him staring at me naked.

So I forgot to close my side of the bathroom door, so what? Arrest me for being too preoccupied with the rest of my life to remember to shut a freaking door. How long he was standing there, I'll never know. Although judging by the fire on his cheekbones that I noticed when I walked to the door and slammed it in his face, I suspect it was longer than was absolutely necessary.

Do I give a hoot that he saw me naked? No. In my line of work my body is an instrument. If I was at all self-conscious, I wouldn't have a chance in hell of making it in this business. I'm just glad I remembered to shave, otherwise there would've been a lot to be embarrassed about. Single girl shaving habits, if you get my drift.

A distinct male voice drifts up the staircase. "Cedric, listen to me closely, you need to chill out. I promise you I'll get you everything you asked for…did I say everything? Yeah, I did…all you have to do is not fuck things up with any more negative press—"

Sounds like Fancy's hit the ground running. In the kitchen I find him seated at the island, cell phone to his ear, looking perfect as always. Before him is a plate loaded with scrabbled eggs and some kind of brown toast. I would expect nothing less.

"Did you hear what I said?"

I did and this Cedric sounds like a serious pain in the ass. He turns and takes me in—very obviously, I might add.

You saw it all last night, dude.

"I gotta go, Ced. No more nightclub brawls, ya feel me? Okay, later." Placing the phone down, he leans back in the stool and crosses his arms, his mouth pressed tight. I need about a gallon of caffeine before I can even begin to decipher that look.

"'Sup," I grumble. My sleep mask slips down and I push it higher up my forehead. No response from him. Maybe he's not a morning person, either. Maybe Cedric took everything he had to give.

In the massive refrigerator I find all sorts of healthy food. I push that crap aside and locate my Monster drink and frozen waffles. After dropping two of those suckers in the toaster oven, I pop open my drug of choice. Still no word from the man wearing the subtle frown behind me. I can, however, feel his relentless stare singeing the fine hairs on the back of my neck. Turning, I lean back against the counter and meet his examining gaze squarely.

"What?"

"Are we going to talk about it?"

"Talk about the fact that you're a filthy peeping Tom?" I shrug, indicating my total lack of interest in the topic. "I don't think there's much to say. Except that I better not find any videos of my bald eagle on some obscure Ukrainian porn site, or we're gonna have a problem."

"I wasn't..." His rebuttal fades into a tired sigh. "I specifically told you to close both doors."

I go with this just for fun. "Whatever, Tommy McPervertpants." He glowers and I hide my amusement by taking a big gulp of my Monster drink. The toaster signals that my waffles are ready.

"That's your breakfast?"

He's back to watching me intently. As soon as the caffeine hit my bloodstream, I figured out what that look on his face is. Equal parts displeasure and fascination. As if I'm some strange breed of extinct, scaly beast that's lumbered into his cave and left a trail of slime in its wake. I take a big bite of the waffle and wave the sucker around.

"These aren't even gluten free."

"You shouldn't eat that junk. I made scrambled eggs and millet bread toast. Help yourself."

Millet. Bread. Toast. Lovely.

"Thanks, but I'll stick with the junk."

He frowns at this. Apparently my diet does not meet his Holy Fanciness' standards. "Be at my office around noon and I'll introduce you to David Pitt."

"Is this really necessary? If you would just call Parker and get a statement from him—"

"David is one of the best criminal defense attorneys in the city," he says, interrupting. "Let's leave the lawyering to him. I won't risk anything going sideways with this case."

He won't risk it...mmmkay.

His cell phone rings and he glances at the screen. Lips thinning, he answers it. "Andi, I'll be there in twenty...I don't give a shit, tell Jerome I'll call him when I get an offer in writing…yeah, you can quote me." His gaze cuts to me, eyes running up and down my body, momentarily pausing on my oversized t-shirt. "I gotta go."

After hanging up, he makes his way around the island to where I'm leaning next to the sink. Mr. Perfect rinses his dishes before placing them in the dishwasher. He's standing awfully close. As a small woman, I place serious value on personal space and this man is all up in it. Like way up in it. He is definitely encroaching if I can feel the heat radiating from him on the side of my face, or the fine wool of his suit against the bare skin of my upper arm. And even though it's slowly making me mental, I don't budge.

"The new contractor should be here in an hour. I would appreciate it if you could let him in."

The opium cloud also known as his scent wraps around me and my eyelids get a little droopy. And yet—I don't budge.

"Sure," I say, staring blindly ahead. Whatever game he's playing isn't going to work. He's got another thing coming if he thinks I'm going to be cowed by a pretty piece of man meat with a cute bubble butt. Also, I've decided to go on the counter attack. If he gets any closer, I'm going to accidentally step on his anklebone. I'm wearing my poop slippers, probably won't do much damage, but it's not like I can shiv the guy. That wouldn't be right.

He looks down, his focus entirely on my nonexistent boobs. "Nice shirt."

I'm wearing my second favorite gift from Cam. It's another oversized t-shirt. This time, however, there's a cartoon drawing of a voluptuous naked female body on the front and back—complete with red sequin nipples.

"I always wanted big hooters."

He blinks. He blinks again. Cold and quiet, an iceberg stares back at me. This cohabitation thing is going to be really pleasant. He's going to make three months feel like a Siberian winter. Grabbing a paper towel, he dries his hands, chucks the paper in the waste bin, and turns to leave.

"You're fine the way you are," I hear him say as he walks out of the kitchen.

Huh?

The front door shuts, leaving behind a wake of confusion.

* * *

After fussing with my black jersey wrap dress for far too long because, really, who cares what I look like—never mind that I spent a little longer blow-drying my shoulder-length straight hair when I never, ever blow it dry—I grab my coat and purse, ready to head out when the doorbell rings. I open the door to the vestibule and find the new contractor along with a crew of men standing on the front steps.

"Hello there, blondie," he says in a gravelly voice while running his greasy eyes up and down my body. "You the assistant?"

"No. You the contractor?"

"The very one," the portly misogynist retorts. "Bill Morrison."

I quickly slip on my winter coat. And the answer is yes, I have a double standard when it comes to sexist name calling and leering. Women get a free pass. We have a long way to go to balance that scale, and God knows I'm going to do my best to contribute.

"You're an hour and a half late." His guys file past me and

into the townhouse, carrying heavy construction equipment, tools. All the stuff necessary to fix this money pit.

"I'm here now and we're wasting time talking about it."

This guy's attitude hits me in all the wrong places. He walks past me and into the living room. Against my better judgment, I follow.

"I have a meeting to get to, but we need to go over what the schedule is for the upstairs renovations."

If I have to live in this hazard pit for the foreseeable future, I can at least make sure it isn't detrimental to my health. I have a lot of energy, and I don't like to see stuff undone that should be done. And if it helps Fancy in any way, if I can give him something in return for getting me out of my "situation," why not.

I start ticking stuff off finger by finger. "The upstairs bathrooms should be the first item on your list. The water pressure sucks and the shower door is about to fall off the rusted hinges. Also can you please make sure Mr. Vaughn has a generator? They're saying we could get some nasty weather by the end of the week."

Looking around, he says, "We'll get to it when we get to it."

"No. No, that's not the answer I was looking for. The upstairs bathrooms get done first." Glancing at my cell, I realize I'm cutting it close. "The bathroom, Mr. Morrison. I've got to go."

* * *

Twenty minutes and a serious hustle later, I arrive on time at the address Fancy gave me on Lexington and 52nd. The building is art deco, nice although not exceptional in any way, just your run-of-the-mill city office building. The elevator doors open on the 30th floor, and I step into the reception area of Vaughn Sports Management.

Color me impressed. As I take in the shiny nickel letters spanning the maple-covered wall, I can't help but wonder if I'll ever get to see my last name somewhere that does not include a bill, a pink slip, or more recently, jailhouse discharge papers. If I remember correctly, Camilla mentioned that Vaughn is around Cal's age, which makes him either thirty-three or thirty-four, a mere three to four years older than me. And yet, look how much he's accomplished. I, on the other hand…no need to follow that sentence to its logical end.

The young receptionist sitting beneath said letters greets me and takes my coat and gloves, after which, she asks me to take a seat while she lets Fancy know I'm here. It's all very hush hush in the office. Beyond the reception area I can see people rushing back and forth, and wonder if he has a "no talking" policy for his employees. From down the hall, a very tall woman approaches. How to explain…

She's the embodiment of a 1950s bombshell. Jane Mansfield with natural red hair, fiery and bright and naturally curly even though she punishes it into a tight, low bun. Head to toe in black, all buttoned up, no hint of skin showing, big blue eyes hiding behind black-framed glasses. It doesn't take a genius to figure out she wears her clothes as armor. Also, she's wearing heels. Because five ten is insufficient. She feels the need to add a couple of inches to all that glory.

Reaching me, she holds out her hand and greets me with a perfunctory smile. "Miss Jones, nice to meet you. Andromeda Carrys, Mr. Vaughn's assistant."

Perfect. That's just perfect.

I'm staring. I know I am, but I can't make myself stop.

There's so much to take in. The hair. The skin. The Angelina Jolie lips. He must be in lust with his assistant. That's why he avoids the pussy parade. He must be. What man wouldn't be when he looks at this all day long. I'm practically in lust with her and I'm straight.

"Miss Jones?" Her voice is soft and feminine, and in direct contrast to how she dresses.

"Ah, yes," I say, shooting out of my seat. Restless, I smooth my dress for no reason whatsoever. The one that I now determine makes me look Amish. Then again, I could be in a crotchless latex jumpsuit and look Amish standing next to this woman.

Oozing sex appeal, Andromeda the bombshell sets off for Fancy's office while I obediently follow in her shadow. Apparently walking is a sensual act. I never got this memo. I guess we're doing this now—sexy walking. Must be the new thing.

She knocks twice and opens the door, motioning me inside, then closes it behind me.

"Sonavabitch is going down...romancing my client behind my back is an act of war," Vaughn says into the cell phone. He looks up and our eyes lock. His eyebrows gently pull together. For a moment he looks pleased which sets me at ease. "I went to see Sean's mother and made sure she understood that Kaplan doesn't have her son's best interest at hand...yeah, his mother loves me." Until his eyes scan me from head to foot and his mouth tightens. And my ease quickly turns to discomfort. Fidgeting, I stand there longer than I should. "Yeah, listen, I have a meeting. We'll discuss this later...I've already put in calls to two of Kaplan's clients offering them a better deal...I'd do it for free just to teach that fucker a lesson…okay…later, Barry."

Placing the cell on his desk, he rocks in his chair and fixes his shirt cuffs. "You can come in. I won't bite," he casually offers.

"I do."

The hell if I know where that came from. To cover up my extreme lack of control over the crap that comes out of my mouth, I do my best to look bored. He, on the other hand, looks like a guy caught surfing porn at work, wide-eyed and frozen.

"I'm kidding. Get real, Vaughn. Not if we were the last two people on a deserted island and I was in dire need of a meal."

That snaps him out of his frozen state, his lips gently turning up. "You wouldn't eat me if the alternative was starving to death?"

Clearly it's his turn to act like an ass. "I'd rather chew my arm off."

His phone rings. He glances at the screen, and grimaces. Smoothing his tie, he clicks it off. "I've seen the way you eat, Jones, and I say you last one day before you start eating me."

I can feel the heat blast up my neck. So I have an appetite, so what. This mouth needs fuel to operate. Meanwhile, his attempt to tamp down his amusement at my reaction is poor at best. His eyes betray him, turning into half-moons even though his mouth stays firmly in a straight line.

"You've been watching me? What a creeper. The peeping Tom thing makes sense now."

His reaction is swift. Gone is the amusement at my expense. Gone is the cocky half smile—sliding right off his face and onto mine. Pink blooms on his high cheekbones. He clears his throat and rocks his chair back.

"I...umm..." He scowls.

"Relax. I'm messing with you, counselor." I walk over and take a seat directly in front of his desk. My eyes are immediately on the move, perusing the room, anything to avoid eye contact. The intensity of his stares has tripled overnight and it's making me jumpy.

"So this is where you do your *Jerry McGuire* thing." The office is sparse, the colors muted, the furnishings simple. "Not what I expected."

I can tell from the periphery of my vision he has yet to take his eyes off of me. "Jerry McGuire is an agent," he says as he stretches his neck left and right. I'm also pretty sure he just puffed out his chest. What's gotten into him?

"I'm a licensed agent and a business manager. Not only is my job more comprehensive, it's also much more demanding."

Commercial break for an exaggerated eye roll.

The desk phone flashes. He answers. "June, hold all my calls...yes, all of them...I don't care who, all of them." He hangs up. "What did you expect?" he asks, his voice softer this time.

"I don't know...something a little fancier maybe."

"I'm rarely here." He leans back in his chair and laces his hands behind his head. His tailored white shirt clings to his chest. The one I know is all cut muscle under fine cotton. It demands attention and I hand mine over willingly. Until he coughs.

My eyes crawl back up to his face. "Too busy partying on yachts with superstars and strippers?" The glare I receive in response is positively nasty. "What? I watch *Ballers*."

"That's Hollywood, Jones. I live in the real world, where an important part of my job is teaching my young guys how to be responsible with their money." He has yet to take his eyes off of me. "Can't do that effectively if I blow mine on things like exorbitant rent."

"Solid point," I answer, even though I stopped listening at "blow".

What is he doing with his eyes? This is not a figment of my overactive imagination. He is definitely acting strange today. "Are you feeling okay?"

He looks momentarily confused. "Yeah. Why do you ask?"

Cuz you're acting like a nut job. "No reason. Where's your buddy? Let's get this party started."

"Down the hall." He dials the phone and says, "Ready whenever you are."

A few minutes later a guy around Fancy's age walks in holding a file. Equally fit, he's a bit shorter than Fancy and a hundred times more jovial. The devilish smirk he wears seems to be permanent. We get up and he walks over, an extended hand leading.

"David Pitt, nice to meet you." His grip is firm and dry. I like him instantly.

"Any relation?"

Pitt's smirk widens into a mischievous grin. "Only if it'll get me a date."

"Cheeky. I like him."

"Dave." The warning comes sharp and fast. I look over and find Fancy Pants scowling, hands on his hips and the set of his shoulders rigid.

Turning back to Pitt, I say, "He's no fun."

Pitt looks over at his friend. "I like her."

"You don't have to like her, you have to get her out of these bullshit charges," he grounds out. We all pause at the noticeable anger unpinning his voice. Realizing his error, Vaughn brushes his face with his palm. "You know what I mean."

Pitt's focus returns to me, his face tight in an effort to hamper his amusement. "I looked at the case file. It shouldn't be too difficult. First and foremost time is our friend. We want cooler heads to prevail. And if we put enough time and distance between us and the event, we may have a shot at getting the charges dropped altogether."

Hallefreakinlujah.

"I'm sure Ethan has instructed you not to contact Gregory in any way. That's my job. Let me be the liaison."

I nod in agreement. That will not be a struggle. Quite frankly, I don't entirely trust myself. If I were to lay eyes on the *p.o.s.* ever again, I could very well find myself indicted of first-degree murder. With cause, this time. "Should I block him?"

"No. Leave it alone. We don't want to inflame the situation. Don't answer if he contacts you. The first hearing is scheduled for the beginning of February but I'm going to ask for a postponement. I don't need to remind you not to leave the state, do I? Ethan would forfeit his bail money and you would be sent back to prison."

My gaze immediately snaps to Vaughn, and finds him shaking his head. "Calvin's money."

"My grandmother is in assisted living in New Jersey. I need to see her."

"Tri-state is fine," Pitt tells me. "I'll get a note to the judge if you provide an address."

Fifteen minutes later, after we've hammered out schedules and agreed on dates for our next meetings, the three of us walk out of Vaughn's office and into the hallway— smack dab into drama.

Female voices arguing in the reception area cause the three of us to turn. A busty blonde holding two bags from BLT Steak is head-wagging at Andromeda who's bearing down at her with an expression that can only be described as sexy boredom.

A quick glance at Fancy's face tells me this is another dedicated member of the pussy parade. Really? Does this guy's dick have a vibrate button?

The expression he's wearing is so tragic I almost feel bad for him...almost...maybe a little bit.

"Isn't that—" Pitt says absently.

"The paralegal we fired."

"The one that you—"

I don't miss the slight widening of the eyes and the stiff shake of Vaughn's head, all of it directed furtively at his business partner over my head. Maybe not. And by the looks of it, he already has pube fleas.

CHAPTER SEVEN

THE NEXT DAY I HEAD to midtown, to the offices of Glaser Talent Agency to meet with the man that has been not only a steadfast supporter of my career the last eight arduous years, but also a good friend. The building is sandwiched between a florist and a deli on a busy street off Broadway. Marty is old school. He's still in the small space he started in forty years ago, refusing to move to a better location when his business took off because he feared it would be "bad luck."

"What's up, kid," the man in question says from behind his cramped desk in his equally cramped office.

The familiar smell of pastrami and the sound of the lunch rush drift up from the deli below. I walk in and throw myself down on the old leather chair in front of his metal desk as I always do—seems to be a ritual with us, slip off my beanie and mittens, and place my motorcycle boots on the corner of his desk. He pushes them off. Also part of the ritual.

"What's up, my dear Martin, is that you left a particularly depressing bit of news on my voicemail the day before New Year's."

"I was in Florida. I thought you'd want to know."

"I was so sure I had it," I admit, exhaling my frustration. Shafted once again after my third callback. I lost out on a supporting role on a time travel series that was written by a best selling-romance author. Long story short, Camilla had managed to get me an audition. It turns out the author happens to be Mercedes' daughter's best friend—Mercedes being Calvin's estate manager of sorts. I say of sorts because Cal and Cam considered her family. At any rate, I got an audition. I even flew out to L.A. to meet with the producers on the third callback. To get so close and come away a loser was a blow of epic proportions.

"Sorry, kid. The network wanted a known commodity. They went with a household name." He fiddles with his glasses, pushing them up the bridge of his nose. Unfortunately, not being famous is often the biggest obstacle to becoming famous. "Look, it's time for you to make a change. I could have five auditions lined up for you in L.A. this week alone."

As I start to argue, he cuts me off. "You can't keep putting your life on hold for your grandmother. I hate to say it, but she could be in a bad way for a very long time and you're not getting any younger. It's the nature of the business."

He's right. Except my grandmother is no longer the only thing keeping me from moving to Los Angeles. Lips curling around my teeth, I cringe as I give him the bad news. "I can't leave the state of New York for at least the next three months and it has nothing to do with my grandmother."

"You're not making any sense, kid."

"Let's just say that after I got your message, the shit hit the fan."

* * *

One Maple is *the* hot spot in Manhattan, an upscale lounge that's a perfect blend of uptown sophistication and downtown trendiness. Our regulars mainly consist of music industry moguls and professional athletes, your occasional film and television star. And then there's the common folk. And when I say common, I mean the Wall Street millionaires that are about as common in this city as the jumbo-sized rats.

It's my third night back to work since *that unfortunate event* as I like to call it, and the week already feels twice as long. It's not even midnight yet and my feet are already aching. Lately I find myself wondering if it's time to hang up the bartending towel. By the look of my feet, which at present resemble pink sausages stuffed into casing that's too small, I can't help but think that maybe I'm getting too old for this. I've worked for this restaurant group for years, and although there was a time when this job was a boatload of fun, lately the good times have waned and the jokes a little harder to muster up. Not to mention, the customers ruder.

"Hey, baby doll. I'm back."

Case in point: rude customer *numero uno*. I can only assume this douchebag's inability to understand that I will in fact never ever see his "crib" nor ride in his "whip" is due to either oxygen deprivation when he was being birthed, or one too many testosterone shots. Ignoring him, I go about business as usual. This bar is packed three rows deep with bodies and although I'm one of four bartenders on duty tonight we still have to hustle.

"Hey—Abby, hello."

I've corrected him twice to no avail. Without a glance in his direction, I continue mixing two cosmos for a group of models sitting at the end of the bar with yet another Wall Streeter.

"Unfuckingbelievable," I hear him mutter to his equally

rude friend. "How long you gonna continue ignoring me. Hey, I'm standing right here!"

"No shit," I bark in exasperation. "Too bad you didn't drip down your momma's leg with the rest of your brothers and sisters."

Nothing. It went right over his head. Explain to me how this guy is allowed to trade millions of dollars for his company. Turning away, I start on a large order for one of the VIP tables crowded with NY Gladiators. Their season came to an embarrassing end a couple of weeks ago thanks to the Seattle Seahawks. At least, that's what Kevin, one of the other bartenders, whispered when they all filed in earlier.

Kevin's eyes meet mine. The universal signal for "get this jackass off my back" is exchanged and we switch places.

"That odious man is back. It's like he gets off on upsetting me."

I glance up into Sarah's wide doe eyes, her full lips puckered. She's been complaining about one of the players all night. "Any news on the grant yet?"

I don't envy Sarah. If the life of an actress is tough, that of a documentary filmmaker is exponentially worse, the struggle real as she waits to hear if her funding is approved.

"No. Can somebody else take that table?" I glance around her, at the VIP table the Gladiators are occupying, the table that will without a doubt earn a hefty tip.

Sarah who graduated top of her class at NYU film school, brilliant documentary filmmaker Sarah, Sarah who looks like a Lilliputian-sized Whitney Houston, barely five feet, happens to be as dumb as a bag of d...rocks when it comes to men. It's usually an endless source of entertainment for me. Except for tonight. Tonight I do not possess the required patience to be amused. I raise an eyebrow. It's either that, or stab myself in the eardrum so I don't have to listen to another minute of this.

"He can't be that bad."

"He asked me if he could borrow my magic wand for his trip to Vegas. The time before he asked if I could take him to *Middle Earth*. It's been shit like this all night," she snaps.

"And you have no idea why?"

Her expression morphs from confusion to suspicion. She knows me too well. "What's your point?"

"Have you looked in a mirror in the last decade? Put a freaking paper bag over your head if you don't want the attention. Now go deliver these drinks to the table where that *decidedly terrible* man is sitting."

"I miss having Camilla around to rein you in."

"Shoo." I wave. "Off with you. And don't forget to shake that moneymaker. Mama needs the cash." She gives me the stink eye over her shoulder and I laugh for the first time tonight.

The crowd parts and I'm greeted by a pair of friendly dimples. Longish, disheveled chestnut hair. Light brown eyes capable of casting a spell from across a room. Not on me, of course. I'm immune to such nonsense. I'm talking on the general female population. What started as the worst, most awkward date in the history of dates last summer on the Fourth of July has turned into a fantastic friendship.

Justin Harper, also known as Dimples, ranked fourth best wide receiver in the league last year. He caught 111 passes for 1,521 yards and 11 touchdowns.

Or so I've been repeatedly told.

Yawn. I am not a football fan. But seeing as my best friend is married to a player and my other dear friend is one, I make a real effort to pretend to be interested whenever the topic comes up.

Justin's ready smile and easy swagger part the crowd at the bar without effort. "Hey there, *sugar*." He pronounces the pet name with all the sarcasm in the world.

"What are you doing here, man candy?" Seems only right to return an equally offensive pet name. "Don't you have curfew with a play-off game only a few days away?" He pushes past a few suits, takes a seat, and hands me a shopping bag. Peering in cautiously, I pull out an official Titans jersey with his name on the back in big block letters.

"I don't know what to say." My lips pull up into a creaky smile. Does he want me to wear this hideous thing? Awkward.

"You can say that you'll wear it when you come to the game on Sunday."

"Umm..."

"My sister's still overseas. I won't have any family there."

Jeez Louize, why didn't he just punch me in the tits? I rub the achy spot over my heart. His much older sister, a sergeant major in the army, is the only family Justin ever talks about. I suspect that the parts he hasn't told me include a lot he'd rather forget. "What about that accountant you were seeing?"

"Uhh, yeeeaaah, that's over."

The surprise is all over my face. And disappointment on his behalf. I thought Justin had met a good one, someone that was genuinely interested in him as a person and not all the jazz that goes hand in hand with dating a celebrity athlete.

"Since when?"

"Since I forgot to call her back and woke up in the middle of the night to find her standing at the foot of the bed, staring at me."

"There's no good explanation for that."

"Not one."

"Did you change the locks?"

"That same night—so you'll do it. You'll be cheering for Team Harper on Sunday."

The big goofball tilts his head and bats his lashes a few hundred times. "Watch this—" he says, "BAM." Then he smiles, showing off his dimples.

I reluctantly smile back. Such a goofball. "If somebody's gotta cheer your lazy ass on, it might as well be me."

"I knew I could count on you, Jo." He thumps the bar with a loose fist and slides off his stool. A pretty redhead backs up, bumping into Justin's side—not at all by accident—then gazes over her shoulder with a huge smile that Dimples, ever the Southern gentleman, returns with not one but two, "pardon ma'ams."

Leaning over the bar, he places a quick kiss on my cheek and whispers, "Gotta go and get my beauty rest. This gorgeous face needs to be camera ready for national television on Sunday," probably more for the sake of the redhead that's still gobbling him up with her eyes than anything else. The redhead pouts and huffs and turns back to her friends.

"Yeah, yeah. Beat it. Some of us have to work for a living."

Justin beams a bright smile at me. "Oh, hey—you never called me back on New Year's?"

* * *

I splurge on a cab ride home even though I'm wearing a heavy down jacket, a hat, and gloves. It's in the teens again, so cold my breath has mass. Los Angeles weather beckons me every time my body spasms from the frigid temperature.

Around 2 a.m. I trudge into the house and ascend the stairs as quietly as possible, tiptoeing down the hall. A slice of light bleeds out from under the closed door of Fancy's bedroom. As soon as I walk past it, the light turns off. That's the third time that's happened this week. Does he have Spidey sense? I know I'm being quiet.

I flip on the light in my bedroom and freeze. Except for my jaw, my jaw hits the ground with a thud. My fairy godmother must have broken into my room while I was at work. She must have. There's no other possible explanation. Eyes wide and unblinking, I slowly step inside and turn in slow circles. I don't know what to gape at first, the sixty-three-inch television hung on the wall, the dark wood furniture, or the tufted bed. The entire room looks like it stepped out of the pages of *Elle Décor*. There's even a nice rug covering the ancient, scuffed-up wood floor. And drapes. Thank God for drapes.

I'm dumbstruck. Mindlessly, I grab the remote, turn on the television, and lose my ever loving shit. Quietly, though, *veeery* quietly. All the channels. All of them. And...Apple TV and Netflix. I'm dead. I must be. I must've died and gone to heaven.

Forget that it's way past midnight. Forget that he may or may not be doing something naughty to himself. The urge to spew gratitude propels my body to Vaughn's bedroom door. Once there, though, I blank. The light comes back on. Definitely Spidey sense.

"I can hear you," he calls out, his voice rougher than usual.

I can't figure out how to make my vocal chords work. He's made me stupid. The man murders gray matter. Without asking, I open his door and...umm...stare. In my defense there is a lot of skin on display.

He's sitting up in bed, leaning against a tufted leather headboard that matches my brand new white one. His chest is bare, the sheet pulled up to his lean hipbones. I suspect he's naked under that sheet, but manage to maintain some semblance of civility and control the impulse to do a full-fledged investigation. With discipline worthy of a ninja, I force my eyes up to his face. Where I find him putting on glasses—horn-rimmed glasses to be precise.

Guys with glasses have never done a thing for me. Never. Until now. Now they're doing something. Something that makes me uncomfortably warm in this notoriously drafty house.

He rubs his eyes, eyebrows rising and falling. I know he got an early start; I heard the shower running at five this morning. He must be exhausted. What's he still doing up at this hour anyway? Behind those glasses, his soft, sleepy eyes conduct a brief examination of my face while he patiently waits for me to say something. I have yet to produce a single sound. It's starting to get a little weird so I point to the room next door.

"You don't like it?" His shoulders fall a little in what looks strangely like disappointment. "I did the best I could on short notice. You can change it if you want."

Don't like it? Is he drunk? Better yet, am I drunk? Why would he be disappointed?

"Don't like it? I...I don't know what to say. Love isn't a strong enough word. I can't believe you...Netflix...Apple TV."

His mouth kicks up on one side. "You seem more excited

about Netflix than you did about me getting you out of jail."

"It's Netflix. You have no idea how many hours of uninterrupted, mind-blowing pleasure you've given me." That sounded different in my head. Two spots of heat appear on my cheeks while his mouth quivers in amusement. At my expense, of course.

"You're definitely more excited about this than getting out of jail."

"I owe you a big one." Okay, why does that sound filthy too? I'm tired. That's it. I'm just tired. In the meantime, heat spreads all the way down my neck.

"You don't owe me anything." He yawns, seemingly oblivious to my clumsy innuendo. Thank God his mind is not the cesspool mine is. I watch him rake his long fingers through his hair, which musses it up even more, which makes him look even sexier than he did a minute ago, which makes me glower. This is becoming a vicious cycle.

"Anyway, thanks. I'll let you get back to it. Sleep that is— or not. Whatever it was that you were doing."

He frowns, confused at my change of pace and tight voice. I can't fault him. I'm confused, too. Confused as to why I would have this kind of reaction to this particular guy. In my line of work I see one pretty face after another and none have ever affected me like this. Or is it infected? Whatever. They're one and the same as far as I'm concerned. I'm about to close his door but his voice stops me.

"How'd you get home?"

"Cab. But I usually take the subway."

He suddenly perks up, the sleepy look in his eye clearing. His lips thin. "That's dangerous."

"I've been doing it for six years. Hasn't gotten more

dangerous as of today."

He stares. No blinking. I'm not even sure he's breathing. "Use my car service. I'll have them wait outside for you."

What? Wait, what? "Mmmthank you, but that's not necessary."

"It is if I want to get any sleep." He runs a harried hand through his hair and presses his thumb and index finger over his closed eyes. "You work Tuesday to Saturday. It'll be outside waiting."

Not a chance in hell am I doing that. However, I'm all too familiar with the fact that arguing with him is pointless.

"It's late. I'll let you get back to sleep. Thanks again," I say quickly, hooking a thumb toward my room. Before he can respond, I duck out.

CHAPTER EIGHT

"HI, MARCO. HOW IS SHE?" I say to the young man walking toward me, the physician's assistant assigned to help care for my grandmother. Sleeves of tattoos, piercing through his eyebrow and God knows where else. In other words, hot as bawls. I wouldn't mind moving in here and having Marco assist me. He shakes his head, his demeanor serious. And the small amount of joy I was feeling drains out of me in an instant.

"Not a good day. She threw her oatmeal at Ethel this morning." Ethel, the woman my grandmother shares a suite with.

My spirits sink to the bottom of the crapper. "I'm sorry—I don't know what else to say."

"No need to apologize. It's the disease. Can't do nothing about it other than be patient." Seeing the demoralized look on my face, he continues. "She'll be happy to see you."

All I can do is nod and hope he's right. Because I don't know what I'll do if she starts throwing things at me. Nine years ago my grandmother was diagnosed with early onset Alzheimer's. It seemed to be progressing at a slow pace until six months ago when slow unfortunately turned into rapid.

I knock on my grandmother's door and enter. The room is

bright and tidy, the care at this facility exceptional. Which is why we all agreed that she would live the rest of her life here. My grandmother picked this place herself. Turning away from the window, she stares back with a soft smile and a vacant look in her eyes. And I know—I immediately know she doesn't have a clue who I am.

"May I help you?"

"It's Amber, Grandma." In her pale blue eyes, I can see her working through it and not coming up with anything. "Do you remember me?"

I don't want to stress her out, which could possibly lead to one of her meltdowns, so I pretend. I'm good at playing pretend, brilliant at it actually.

"Margaret?"

Her face lights up. "Yes."

"Would you mind if I visit with you for a while?"

She gets a bit flustered, smoothing the velvet pants of the track suit I got her last Christmas while she thinks it over. "I'm not really dressed for a visit."

"That's alright—"

"And I don't have anything to offer you."

"I already ate."

Timidly, she motions to the empty armchair near hers. I sit quietly and stare out the window with her.

Forty minutes later with a heavy heart I'm headed out the door. The head of administration for the assisted living facility, a lovely woman in her late fifties, catches me before I can walk out the front entrance.

"Miss Jones. May we have a word?" Her uncomfortable expression sets me on edge. I'm really not in the mood for small talk, but I definitely need to stay in her good graces.

"Sure. Is everything alright?"

Her mouth purses before she speaks. "Unfortunately, no. We never received last month's payment and this month's bill is due today. You're aware of our policy. If you're more than three months behind we'll be forced to evict your grandmother."

Every hair on my body stands on end. Fucking Eileen.

* * *

Things that go bump in the night never scared me. I learned a long time ago that the things I should be scared of seldom hide under the bed or the closet. They rarely look like the boogeyman. Only in bad fiction are villains so heavily drawn. The villains in most of our lives are family and friends, lovers. People making choices. It's as simple as that. Some we agree with, some we don't, and some that leave deep and lasting scars.

We had an agreement. All three Jones women. My grandmother, Eileen, and I. It was the first and certainly the last time we would all agree on something. My grandmother was going to sell her lucrative funeral business, property and all, and put most of it in a trust to pay for her care. Two small portions were set aside. One for my inheritance and the other for Eileen. Because my grandmother insisted that she didn't want her condition to hold me back from pursuing my career, she made Eileen the trustee. In other words, in charge of my grandmother's money. The money that was to pay for the assisted living facility she had picked out herself when she was still able to do so.

My grandmother was notoriously punctilious, neat and orderly, everything was always done by the book and on time. She would clutch her pearls in horror if she knew her bills aren't being paid.

An hour later I finally reach Long Island, my mood as dark as pitch. After a solid ten minutes of pounding on the front door and pressing the doorbell, it finally rips open. My thirteen-year-old half sister stands with a spindly arm on her hip and her head tilted. It's like looking in the rearview mirror, at myself sixteen years ago. Stringy blonde hair, freckles, that sullen, narrow-eyed sneer on her face. The purple braces and expensive clothing are the only things that distinguish the past from the present.

"Audrey."

"Amber," the cheeky little shit retorts.

Over her head, I scan inside the house and find nothing. It seems empty other than the sound of the television blasting. "Where's Eileen?"

"At the mall."

"Busy laying waste to the family coffers?"

"The what?"

"Never mind," I grunt, blowing on my fingers to make sure frostbite doesn't set in. "Tell your mother I came by and that I need to speak to her. And tell her it's urgent."

"She's your mother, too!"

"Don't remind me."

With that, I trot down the front steps and march out of there as if my pants are on fire.

"When did you get your period?"

Huh?

The motorcycle boots I bought in a thrift store for the cost of a sandwich come to a hard stop. My heel hits a patch of ice. Somehow I manage to right myself before my face gets intimately acquainted with the sidewalk. Turning, I find

Audrey with her arms crossed in front, putting on her best tough girl act. She may be able to fool other people with that scowl but not me. I invented that look. To me, that look says scared shitless and lost.

I barely know my half sister and it's pretty much my fault. All the animosity between our mother and me has spilled onto her. And frankly, up until now, her personality resembled more flora than human being. Before today she's only ever spoken two words to me—yes and no—and this abundance of verbiage is usually accompanied by a dirty look.

Am I a little resentful that Eileen works hard to look like mom of the year with Audrey when all she worked hard to do was to get rid of me? Yes, I'm a little resentful. I say only a little because if Eileen is anything, she's consistent. Over the years, I've watched her pretend to be a better mother, but in the end her selfish nature always prevails. Like everything else she's done in her life, it starts out with a bang and quickly turns into a whimper.

I swallow a heavy dose of guilt as I watch Audrey play with her braces and nervously shift from one purple Ugg boot to the other. Why did I ever think that Eileen was going to be any different with her? The truth punches me in the gut. Because I was thinking of myself, of my own pain, of my own anger—of my own issues. And if there's one thing that scares me, it's not things that go bump in the night or hide under the bed. It's being anything like my mother.

* * *

"Okay. Start again."

After I ascertained that Eileen had left Audrey home alone, I went inside and got comfortable. Dan, her father, is due in twenty minutes from his dental office. I figured it was best to have the conversation over the bills with the slacker, also known as my mother, in person, with witnesses present, and Dan is honest as the day is long.

"Brielle said that everyone else already got their periods and the later you get your period the smaller your boobs are and boys like big boobs."

I grab my Diet Coke off the coffee table and take a long, slow sip in an effort to temper the words that want to come screaming out of my mouth. Audrey doesn't blink, waiting patiently for my answer as if I'm about to come down from Mount Sinai with the word of God.

Was I this clueless at her age? No, I don't think I was. I was also too busy raining hell down on Eileen any way I could. From putting dog shit in her mailbox, to setting it on fire on their front steps, to constructing a makeshift slingshot and hurling it at their white garage doors.

"Brielle is a freaking genius."

"Really?"

"No, Audrey. I can't believe that you would listen to that twat."

Oops, by the wide seafoam-colored eyes I'm looking at I'm not supposed to use that word.

"I mean chick. Whatever, you know what I mean. Why didn't you Google it? Why would you take the word of that brainiac?"

"Brielle knows stuff. Her sister's a senior and she's dating the captain of the baseball team and he's super cute."

"Well, bully for Brielle. Too bad her older sister is dumber than she is." I rub my temples to soothe the tension headache this conversation is causing and consider what Camilla would say to a scared thirteen-year-old girl. "It doesn't matter when you get your period, Audrey. It's genes. Mom is really tall and I'm not. I probably got that from my father, but who knows for sure. I got my period just after my thirteenth birthday. And trust me once you get yours you'll wish you could've waited longer."

"Mom has implants," she blurts out. Like I didn't notice the double Ds Eileen was sporting after her trip to the "Bahamas" last year.

"I think it's a little early for you to be thinking about stuff like that."

"I sing," she blurts out, again. I guess this indicates a change of topic. I'm both surprised and pleased—at both the change of topic and the discovery that Audrey has something she's passionate about. "And play the piano."

"Are you any good?"

Her eyes meet mine for a fleeting moment before they move to the stain on her leggings. Picking at it, she shrugs.

"That's great, Audrey. Maybe you can play for me sometime? I'd love to hear you sing."

As she nods, we hear the door leading to the garage open and the click-clack of heels on the tiled floor. A minute later Eileen walks into the living room carrying several large bags from various clothing stores. Typical.

My mother's problem is that she's beautiful. I came to this conclusion at the ripe old age of fifteen. She's a doppelgänger for Christie Brinkley in every way except where it counts. Where as Ms. Brinkley parlayed those looks into a magnificent career, my mother parlayed it into a kid out of wedlock. A career would entail getting out of bed at a reasonable hour and putting in some effort also known as work. Eileen couldn't be bothered. She's self-centered and naturally lazy as fuck, couple that with beauty and you get a perfect disaster.

Eileen the beauty queen. Her nickname in high school. I've heard the story a billion times. So of course every time she would mention it, I would respond with something like this, "You made it through high school? I thought you only went as far as junior high." Or "Your Special Ed school went all the way to high school?"

I was a kid. I was angry. Don't judge.

Her turquoise eyes land on me sitting next to Audrey on the couch, and she stills.

"Amber? What are you doing here?"

"Took you a minute to remember my name, did it?"

She gives me one of her surly looks. One that makes her look like the wicked stepsister in *Cinderella*.

"Mom, can Amber stay for dinner?" Audrey says, her tone holding the typical angsty desperation of a teenager. Meanwhile, I am horrified.

"If she wants to."

"Nope. Nope, can't. I can't," I answer over Eileen. Leaping up from the couch, I remember why I came in the first place.

"I'm here because we need to talk." Tilting my head in Audrey's direction, I add, "In private."

"In the kitchen. Audrey, stay here."

"But Mom! I want Amber to stay, and if you guys fight she'll leave."

Audrey is seconds from tears, the expression familiar. I can't count how many times Eileen's had me in tears over the years. Not that I've ever let her see it. The organ under my sternum throbs and I know it's time to leave. I can't get caught up in this. I have too many battles of my own to fight.

Eileen follows me into the kitchen without answering Audrey.

"I went to see Grandma." I cross my arms and lift my chin, readying for battle. Unfortunately my mother is three inches taller, six with her heels on, so I'm still forced to look up. She sighs tiredly and lifts an eyebrow. As if I'm an annoying mosquito buzzing in her ear she'd like to swat away.

"They'll evict her if you don't pay the damn bills. You know that, don't you?"

"I'm a little late sometimes. Big deal. I'm busy, you know."

Busy? My blood pressure skyrockets, irritation transforming into full-blown anger.

"It's not a little late! You haven't paid for two months! I'm warning you, pay the bill or I'll take you to court."

"Take me to court? With what? You can't afford it." She scoffs. She loves scoffing, does it any chance she gets.

"I'll borrow against my inheritance if I have to. Or I'll get a loan. But I promise that if we have to move her, I will make your life a living hell."

"You've done plenty of that already! I'm used to it by now!"

"Hey, hey, hey. What's going on here?" Dan says as he walks into the kitchen. His green eyes, the same color as his daughter's, meet mine. I can't help comparing that while my mother's are filled with righteous indignation, as if she's the victim, Dan's are filled with empathy.

"Your wife stopped paying Grandma's bill. The Sunnyvale manager told me that they'll evict her if it's not paid ASAP."

"I'm a little behind! That's all," Eileen shouts. Dan shoves his hands into the pockets of his khakis.

"Everybody calm down. Your grandmother is not going to be evicted. We'll send the payment out first thing tomorrow morning. I promise you." I don't doubt Dan. Not for a minute. In the twenty-two years I've known him he's never disappointed me. Not once. Dan Peterson is a stud in every way that should matter—he's smart, kind, and dependable. "You have my word, Amber."

Hearing his vow makes every muscle in my body go slack. I give him a brief hug and plant a kiss on his cheek. "Thanks, Dan."

He gives me a sympathetic, lopsided smile partially hidden under his blond goatee and pats my upper arm. With that, I march out of the kitchen and out the front door without a backward glance at my mother. I'm almost at the end of their street, on my way to the bus stop, when I hear Audrey calling my name. I look over my shoulder and find her running toward me, skinny arms flailing, purple Uggs flying. When she reaches me, her cheeks are pink from running in the biting cold, her expression unsure.

"You forgot your purse." She hands me my messenger bag. "I programmed my number in your phone." Her expression stills, waiting for me to comment. When I don't, she continues, "Maybe—I don't know, maybe we can hang out...sometime?" Her gaze moves around nervously. She fidgets with the sleeves of her jacket, pulling them over her hands.

"I'd like that."

Her eyes slam into mine. "You would?"

"Yeah."

"Okay, cool," she says grinning from ear to ear. "I'll text you."

"I'll stay here until you get back inside, so run your butt off."

"Okay," she says cheerfully and takes off in a sprint back home. Maybe something good can come out of this mess. Maybe, in the process, I've gained a sister.

CHAPTER NINE

IT'S SUNDAY—THE BIG DAY—and we're all at the stadium in The Coach's Club across from the locker rooms where the players' families sit, waiting for the AFC Wild Card game to begin between the Titans and the Cincinnati Bengals.

Most of clan Shaw is in the house, the box loud from all the enthused members of our party. Which includes Amanda, Calvin's sister, and her son, Sam, who have been here since Christmas. Three other Shaw brothers, who I hadn't met before, and Camilla's parents.

"I'm starting to understand why you love this game so much. Hot, ripped men running around in tight, shiny pants—" Mrs. Football Hoe, otherwise known as my best friend, arches an admonishing brow. "No need to be embarrassed. I approve."

I called the nursing home this morning and confirmed that Eileen had sent the check. No doubt with Dan standing over her, making sure it got done. Which is the only reason why I can relax and enjoy myself now.

"Tackling each other to the ground? What she-devil thought this up? I'd like to shake her hand. The only thing that could possibly be improved upon is if they took off their jerseys."

"You're missing the point." Camilla's expression is tight. She's on the edge of her seat and the game hasn't even started yet.

"Am I? These dudes are brave. And not because of the hits they're about to take." I watch a couple of the players warming up while I suck down my diet soda. "Those pants are white. Number fifty-four looks like he's packing some serious heat. Can you introduce me?"

"No. He's married."

"Lucky bitch."

Feminine laughter gets my attention. I glance over my shoulder, to find Fancy is talking to an elegant Asian woman dressed in designer clothes. She pushes a dark drape of hair over her shoulder and bats her lashes, her face in jeopardy of cracking in two from the force of her smile.

"Who's that?"

Camilla looks over at the two of them.

"Dr. Lucy Davis. That's Davis as in her parents own the team. She's a pediatric surgeon and just got back from Syria where she was working with Doctors Without Borders."

Whatever. I organize a canned food drive for the homeless shelter in the Bowery every Thanksgiving. Do I go around bragging about it? No.

We watch them for a while. Fancy says something. She laughs again. They exchange smiles. Hands stuffed in his pants pocket, he rocks back and forth on his expensive Italian loafers. That's when I catch it—a glimpse that tells me it's all an act. I can't name it. I can't describe what it is, but I know it when I see it. The smile he's giving her is a fraud. What a little actor. Takes one to know one I guess.

"Well, she laughs like a hyena, so there."

Camilla tears her eyes away from the tall figure on the field warming up and smirks at me. "She does not laugh like a hyena."

The fabulous Dr. Davis throws her head back and laughs at something Fancy said for the umpteenth time. Brows up my forehead, I'm ready to gloat.

Camilla takes one look at my expression and says, "She's a very nice person."

Irritation crawls over my skin as I watch the two of them for a beat longer. "Christ, does he ever take a day off?" I mutter under my breath.

"Who?"

"Your friend—the pied piper of pussy. They show up at the house, at his office. They probably stalk him on his morning run. I'd really like to know what he does to these women. Does he shoot thunderbolts out of his dick?"

Camilla's brow furrows as she continues to stare at the man in question. Fancy's attention steers in our direction. He looks at Cam and smiles. Then his gaze jumps to me and the same smile dies a sudden death.

The hell is his damage? He's been hostile all day, acting as if I've offended him somehow. Which is impossible because we barely said two words on the ride over. I mirror back a frown of my own.

Four hours later the jubilation that was permeating the room is nowhere to be found, the mood that of a funeral. Fitting since it was a massacre. The Titans offense ran into a buzz saw called the Bengals defense. Camilla spent the better part of the game facing the wall because she couldn't stand to see Calvin being pile driven into the ground one more time while muttering, "I fucking hate this game," over and over.

It's a miracle he wasn't split in two. Even I had a hard time watching.

Walking gingerly, Calvin is one of the first players to hobble into the room. We all say our goodbyes and clan Shaw departs for home. Fancy pulls himself away from Dr. Davis' side, where he's been all afternoon, and makes his way to me.

"Ready to leave?"

"In a little while. Harper's going to need me to hug it out and kiss his boo-boos."

Hands on hips, he exhales loudly. "Is something going on between you two?"

"What do you mean?" I look up and find yet again, a frown. "Ever hear the expression *turn that frown upside down.*"

This does not amuse him. On the contrary he's starting to look a touch annoyed. What's he got to be annoyed about? Is his designer underwear riding up?

"You're wearing his jersey."

"So?"

"And you want to wait for him?"

"Breaking news: Harper and I are friends."

A very tall and very fit guy with dirty-blond hair and a tan that looks like it was earned the hard way, by working outdoors, walks up to us. He's appallingly handsome in a way that does not appeal to me whatsoever. He's a life-size version of a Ken doll—the XXL version. He's also wearing jeans and a flannel shirt, and for a moment I wonder who let this guy into the Coach's box.

He slaps Vaughn on the shoulder like they're bros. "'Sup, brotha," he says. As suspected.

"Hey, man. I thought you were on the farm," Fancy retorts. Also as suspected; those muscles did not grow themselves.

"Just got back. I got a favor to ask, can you take a look at the ESPN contract for me? I need a set of eyes I can trust before I sign."

"Sure. Email it to Andi, and I'll look it over tomorrow."

Tall, blond, and tan sets his butterscotch eyes on me, flagrantly moving from my face to my feet. By the time his attention makes the round trip back up to my face, he's wearing a gleaming white grin. For obvious reasons, I do not smile back. His eyes skip from me to Fancy, trouble brewing in that golden gaze.

"Is this the little lady?" he asks Fancy.

"Dane, don't."

"Did your friend wander off the Ponderosa? I think there's a 1950s TV show missing its main character." I turn to address the beefcake directly. "This is New York, bubba, we don't use that kind of language 'round here."

He snorts and smiles wider. Men, God's test-run before she created woman.

"She dudn't know who I am?" he asks Vaughn, his accent especially thick for my benefit, a big smile still draped across his chiseled face.

I turn my amusement to Vaughn. "Really? This is the company you keep?"

"Amber, this is—"

Tall and tan cranes his neck to scan my jersey. "This one's a stinger. Harper's got his work cut out for him."

My eyeballs are going to pull a muscle if he keeps this up.

"Quit it, Dane," Vaughn finally adds.

In between Vaughn and Tall and Tan, I spot a few of the players walking into the room. Among them is Harper, freshly showered and ultra-handsome in a well-fitting navy suit. Except he looks really bummed, which sparks warmth in my cold, cynical heart. His big puppy dog eyes search and find me in the crowd. I wave and he answers with a tired smile.

"'*Scuse* me, I have a friend to console." I push past Vaughn and his goofy friend and hold out open arms for Justin who lumbers into them without hesitation.

"You played a great game," I say, patting and rubbing his back.

"We sucked," he mumbles.

"How do you feel? You took some nasty hits."

"Achy. I'll sit in ice when I get home."

"You need some company?"

"Nah. I'm gonna take a couple of Tylenol PMs and sleep it off."

A masculine cough gets my attention. Or maybe it was the weird vibe branding the side of my face. Justin, who happens to be seven inches taller and had to hunch down for me to hold him, stands upright.

"Good game. Great stats," Vaughn says to him.

"Don't matter. We lost," Justin answers, much more subdued than he typically sounds.

Vaughn's pointed gaze turns on me. "Ready to go?"

Dry amusement tips up Justin's lips on one side. "Forgot you two live together."

"Hopefully not for long." The minute the words are out of my mouth I regret them. The weird thing is, I don't know why. It's not like I could hurt Vaughn's feelings. And he probably feels the same way about me, but for some reason there's a pit in my stomach. My gaze skitters away, to some very interesting lint on the floor.

"I know you're disappointed, Harper, but you'll get plenty more chances." Vaughn's voice is unaffected. If my jab bothered him, his voice doesn't betray him.

"Ready to go?" Once more, that low, soft voice addresses me. I nod and Vaughn turns to leave. After I kiss Justin's cheek, I follow my roommate out the door.

The car ride home is conducted in painful silence. A storm is brewing next to me. I can feel it gaining momentum with every silent minute that ticks by. I've never seen Fancy mad. Not that I have a lot to reference, but I've never even seen him mildly upset. He's always the one guy in the room with a crooked grin and laid back attitude, even if it rings phony half the time. At least, it does to me. To everyone else he's the second coming of Prince Charming.

In the underground garage, he pulls into his parking space and shuts off the engine. "Is something going on with you and Harper? You never answered my question."

Any guilt I was feeling over the bitchy comment is immediately replaced with irritation. "I don't see how that's any of your business."

I hop out of the car and attempt to take my aggression out on the door, by slamming it shut, but I'm thwarted by one of those pesky "soft close" features. German engineering and all that jazz. Not bothering to wait for him, I head to the elevator.

"It's my business if you're dating my client," he says, right on my heels.

"I didn't know," I say with a shrug. I'm a bit surprised, though Justin and I don't often discuss work and never once have we discussed Vaughn so there's that. As soon as we step into the elevator, I direct my gaze to the panel, avoiding all eye contact with the man standing way too close to me.

The elevator opens onto the sidewalk and I head toward the townhouse without a backward glance, the wind chill making my eyes water.

"Who do you think negotiated that monster contract for him? Brought him to New York."

I stop and turn, almost crashing into him. He takes a small step back. Barely a step. I'm forced to step back myself. It's either that, or shout at the chest six inches from my nose. "Are you looking for a round of applause? Is that it?"

"What I want is to be kept abreast of who my clients date."

"Why? Does he have to get permission?" I march around the corner and jog up the stairs of the townhouse, burning with a need to get as far away from him as possible. Vaughn gets the keys out and opens the door while I blow on my frozen fingertips and daydream a million different ways to torture him. As soon as the front door swings open, I hustle inside, and proceed to hang up my puffy jacket in the hall closet with Vaughn dogging my every step.

"I need to know these things in case I have to deal with a baby mama situation."

My steps screech to a sudden halt in the middle of the staircase. He did not just say that to me. I turn and take in the man standing three steps below me.

Fuuureaking men. You have sex on a first date, you're easy. You don't, you're frigid. Tell them you love them, do nice things for them, you're clingy. You don't, you're selfish and cold. I could go down the list of contradictions for hours. And now I can include being friends with a professional athlete makes me a gold digger.

"You're one to talk, Typhoid Mary! When it's pretty damn clear you've slept with half the women of Manhattan!"

"What did you call me?" The look of shock on his face would be funny if I wasn't so pissed right now.

"I called you a purveyor of disease. But here's a term you'll understand—slut!" I'm on a roll now, no end in sight. "When was the last time you had an STD test? You should've warned me that I needed to bleach the toilet seat every time I need to use it."

The shock on his face transforms into a fresh fit of anger. All puffed up, he suddenly looks two inches taller, his color high. "Are you, or are you not *dating* Harper?"

Turning up the stairs, I stomp to my bedroom door and step inside. "Ask your client," I shout, after which I slam the bedroom door in his face. "I'll go to jail before I let you manage me!"

* * *

Bang bang bang. I reluctantly crack open an eye. *Bang bang bang.* If that's the construction crew, it's gonna get murdery up in here. *Bang bang bang.* Actually, it sounds more like knocking. Ignoring it, I snuggle deeper under the covers but the knocking only grows louder.

I barely slept three hours. Reason number one, because I was so worked up by the altercation. And number two, because I could not assuage the tension I was feeling by said altercation with one of my electric book boyfriends. Just as I was settling in for a good workout with my dear, dear Gabriel, doubt started to creep in. One of those suckers sounds like a chainsaw and I couldn't remember which one.

What if he heard me? What if he walked in while I was using it? The bedroom door is so old it has a keyhole, no other lock.

"Jones?" Needless to say, I'm in no mood for him now. "You awake? Jones?"

Motherfu…

I shove my sleeping mask up and grab my iPhone off the nightstand. 5:30 a.m. He can't be serious. I have a private party to work tonight that will run way past midnight.

"Jones."

"Go awayyyyy!"

The door to our mutual bathroom swings open and I pop up in bed. "Hey! I didn't say you could cooo…"

My eyes focus. Standing in the bathroom doorway dressed only in sweatpants, he's leaning against the doorframe with his arms and ankles crossed like he has a right to be there. If he's trying to get a rise out of me, then he just knocked it out of the ballpark.

"You're sweating," I grind out through clenched teeth. For the love of modesty, his chest is glistening.

"Tends to happen when I run."

This dude must have a death wish. "Well—go do it elsewhere."

"I have something I need to say first."

He looks determined. I volley back a look that says I'm ready to crack nuts if need be, the slow-to-develop irritation I'm feeling inching closer to critical mass.

"Did you hear enter? No. No, you did not. Get out." I flop back down and cover my face with the down comforter.

"I'm sorry for what I said last night."

So he thought waking me at this hour was a good idea? "I don't give a fresh load!" I shout extra loud, the sound muffled by all the goose down. Nothing but the best for Mr. Fancy

96

McButterpants. "Beat it, Vaughn."

"Regardless, I still apologize. I know you're not with Harper."

That does it. That pushes me right over the edge. I pop back up and throw the black satin mask at him. It lands squarely in the middle of his sweaty chest and slides down.

"You don't know a damn thing. I could be doing the entire team for all you know."

Straightening, he stands with his legs spread apart, his body infused with a fresh need to argue. "So, you're admitting you're with him."

"Vaughn," I say über calmly. "If you don't get out, I will bludgeon you with this." Reaching under the bed, I grab Gabriel and hold him up, all fourteen inches and two pounds of solid plastic and metal. The end of the cord almost whacks me in the eye.

Vaughn's face drops. Determination turns to doubt, turns to resignation. "I'm taking a shower," he mutters and stalks back into the bathroom.

"Good choice!" I yell, waving Gabriel around for good measure. Except it's not good. It's soooo not good. Because I'm instantly picturing him naked. Flopping back down, I cover my face with my pillow. My pale skin feels blowtorched. Abstinence is a dangerous thing.

* * *

By the time the private party wraps up at 2 a.m. and I punch out, I'm a character out of the *Walking Dead*. Stepping out the back door, into the alleyway, every muscle I possess braces at the gust of below zero wind that hits my face. It's so cold my brain hurts.

The headlights of a shiny black town car parked a few

yards away turn on and my suspicion perks up. I keep a close eye on it as I pass, my hand already on the can of mace I carry in my purse.

The tinted window slides down and a man eyeballs me. Around fifties, judging from the silver threaded into his black hair. His dark eyes look eager. Why the hell would they look eager? My suspicion grows.

The driver's side door bursts open and he pops out. The noise makes me jump and wheel around.

"Miss Jones?" He holds up his hands as if to apologize. "I'm Fredo Alvarez. Mr. Vaughn sent me to pick you up."

He's wearing a long black wool coat and what looks like a suit underneath. *Groan.* It all makes sense. My face must say everything I'm thinking because the guy takes a tentative step closer.

"Look, Mr. Alvarez, I already told Mr. Vaughn I was not in need of a car. Sorry he wasted your time." With that, I turn and keep walking. Not surprisingly, I hear hurried steps behind me.

"I really need this job," he shouts, desperation kicking his voice up a notch. I stop and turn. He looks anxious. He definitely looks anxious. "This is the first job offer I got in two years." He's talking fast, the anxiety spreading to his voice. "My cousin works for Mr. Vaughn. That's how I got this gig."

Are you kidding me? How is this my life?

"I've been out of work so long I don't mind begging."

Wow. No messing around—he went for the knockout punch. My shoulders slump in defeat, my heart bloodied and bruised. Without a word, I start walking back to the town car. Mr. Alvarez doesn't know it but my Achilles heel is someone laying their weakness at my feet. Show me your boo-boo and my resolve folds quicker than a bad hand of cards. He couldn't have played it any better.

"Come on, Mr. Alvarez. You're driving me home," I mumble, so grumpy I could chew glass.

"Fredo. Please call me Fredo."

While he holds the door open, I slip into the back seat and glance up at him. The anxiety that was all over Fredo's face a moment ago is gone, replaced by a small smile threatening to grow larger. "Call me Amber, Fredo."

I should've known he'd get the last word. Freaking lawyers. *Score one for team McButterpants.*

CHAPTER TEN

TEN DAYS. TEN DAYS WITHOUT seeing hide nor hair of him. Unintentionally, we both did our best to avoid each other, falling into a routine of sorts. Well—maybe not so unintentional. Like clockwork, I hear the shower run at the ungodly hour of five thirty every single morning. From that point on, I wait an hour and a half before going down to an empty kitchen because I know he leaves for work by seven.

If I were a better person, a more mature person, a wiser person, I would simply forgive him and brush it aside as no bigs. Spoiler alert: I am none of those things. I knew he didn't have the highest regard for me—especially not after the scene at the jailhouse—however, being labeled a baby mama? Which in his thesaurus has only one synonym, gold digger. Mmmmno. No. You can call me many terrible things, but you cannot call me a gold digger. That, I will not take kindly to. And frankly, it stings. I was laboring under the false impression we were friends...of sorts. Whatever, friendly–er. But I guess we aren't. We're not even back to square one. We're pre-square one. We're not even talking.

I can hear the water running. It started five minutes ago at exactly five twenty-five. I hear it so clearly I may as well be lying on the bathroom floor. No way am I getting back to sleep.

To say that my nerves feel scraped raw is putting it lightly. Not only because I will be a wreck tonight when I sling booze until 2 a.m., but worse, all I can do as I lie here growing angrier by the second is picture water cascading down his stripper-worthy body in slow-mo.

My ovaries are staging a near riot. My lady parts are meeting with their union leader, estrogen, ready to go on strike. For whatever reason, this turkey gets my juices running, something not a single other person has managed to accomplish in the last two and a half years. Go figure.

A loud crash intrudes into my filthy thoughts. Really loud. Curiosity and a touch of worry kick me into action. I jump out of bed and head for the bathroom door. With my ear smashed against solid wood, all I get is the sound of the shower running.

"Fancy? You okay?"

"No."

I rip open the door and halt. *Holy shite.* The glass shower door is shattered, broken pieces everywhere, some of them on top of Vaughn who is standing in the middle of it clutching his bleeding hand.

"Don't move," I very calmly order.

In a flurry of activity, I run back to my room and shove on sweat pants and sneakers, then I run to Vaughn's room and locate his. Once I'm back in the bathroom, I gingerly step over the broken glass scattered on the floor and reach into the shower to turn off the water still coming down on him. He's shivering and the water is hot. I wrap Vaughn's bleeding hand in a towel.

"I'm going to help you step into your sneakers and then

we'll get you dressed and go to the hospital." He remains quiet, nodding in understanding. This is not good. God help me if he swoons.

"Lean on me while I help get these on you." I bend and help him step into his running sneakers, lace them tightly. Then I escort him out of the shower, where I locate a towel and wrap it around his waist.

Vaughn follows me into his room. "My sweats are on the top shelf in the walk-in closet."

I grab them and return to find Vaughn calmly sitting on the end of the bed, holding his now blood soaked towel close to his bare chest.

"Keep pressure on it," I tell him as I help him get his sweatpants on. Next comes his zip-up hoody. I hand him a clean towel to replace the blood-soaked one and we head downstairs. All the while I keep a close eye on him, looking out for signs of potential swooning. I am screwed if that happens. No way can I handle two hundred pounds of dead weight.

After I help him with his down jacket, I grab mine and bolt outside to hail a cab with my wounded roommate in tow. The extreme quiet is starting to worry me.

"Lenox Hill emergency room. Take Park," I bark at the cab driver, the adrenaline finally catching up with my mouth. The silent man next to me is unusually pale, his brow furrowed by pain. "Don't faint on me. Okay? We're almost there."

His big brown eyes meet mine, his full lips edge up weakly. He gives me a small nod as we pull up to the emergency room entrance. I throw the driver a twenty and tell him to keep the change.

If it's one thing I know, it's my way around a hospital. I have my grandmother's condition to thank for that. The waiting room is mostly full. I lead Vaughn to an empty seat. "I'll take care of it. Let me." His stares back for an amount of time I deem less than comfortable. Then he hands me his wallet.

Silent and serious, he holds my gaze until I walk away, headed for the check-in desk, taking the uncomfortable moment with me.

* * *

"I had to give you two layers of stitches. The laceration was deep," the young surgeon states in a perfunctory manner.

"At least, it's his left hand," I cheerfully throw out for consideration. Why does that sound dirtier than I intended? God knows this guy does not need to use his hand; he's got women lining up for that honor.

"Make an appointment to see me in fourteen days to remove them," adds the doctor.

"I'm supposed to leave for Florida tomorrow," grumbles the patient. Vaughn's color has returned. And with it, it brought a hella bad attitude. Sitting on the emergency room gurney, he takes the sweatshirt I hand him and shrugs off the hospital gown.

I am a sicko. A sick human being. Because what do I do? I stare. I stare so openly that I'm surprised I don't have a cartoon bubble above my head of two people doing it doggy style. For the love of chests, the man is injured. He still has blood smeared on his abdomen and I'm ogling him like we're at an all male burlesque. Classy.

"Bring your hot-as-fudge assistant."

Vaughn's attention snaps up to me. "Hot as fudge?" He

scowls. Somebody's grumpy. He usually handles my teasing without so much as a bat of a long, thick lash. "I travel solo when I'm working."

"Think, Vaughn. She can help you dress." I toss this one up with a wink.

Judging by the look on his face, you'd think I offered him a steaming slice of dog shit pie. "Andi's like a sister to me."

Wow. He sure seems bent out of shape over my suggestion about his assistant. This man is full of surprises.

"You have a sister?"

"No—but if I did I would feel the same way about her as I do Andi."

"Okay. I get it. You're not in lust with your assistant. I just assumed…"

"You assumed wrong," he barks.

My eyebrows shoot up my forehead. For the first time since I've met this man, he's not perfect. No, siree. He's angry and impatient, and generally in a bad mood. And it makes me smile. I'm smiling like the village idiot because although it took twenty some odd stitches in his left hand to do it, the shiny veneer is gone.

After the doctor finishes bandaging the turkey's broken wing and hands him a prescription for painkillers, we grab a cab back home, during which he is dead quiet and in deep contemplation for the entire ride.

"I'm going to clean up some of the broken glass," I announce as soon as we get back to the townhouse.

Vaughn walks past me, into the living room, the only room in the house that's almost done being renovated, and throws his big body down on the couch.

"Hell no," he snaps, looking up at me with an incensed

glare. "Let that fucker do it tomorrow. Then, I'm gonna fire his ass. He's lucky I don't sue him."

"Whoa there, counselor. You can't fire him now that I have something to hold over him. He's going to be working double time by the time I'm through. Besides, it will take forever to find someone else. You know it will. And I have to do something about the glass—it's the only working bathroom we've got if you get my drift." He grumbles something I can't make out, his attention directed over my shoulder. "Use your words."

His attention swings back to me. Although he's wearing a determined frown, nothing in his eyes suggests he's heard me teasing him.

"I keep thinking it could've been you. You could've been seriously injured." His eyes flicker away.

It's a constant source of surprise and amusement that my best efforts to poke the bear simply bounce off of him. At the moment, however, I'm feeling neither amused nor surprised. What I am feeling is a strange burn in my chest.

"I don't see how it's any better that you were injured. So we agree. You're giving me the green light to blast him."

His lips twitch, then slowly begin to lift up. "Fine. But don't touch anything," he orders, his tone brooking no argument. "I'll take some of those old pieces of sheetrock and lay it over the glass on the bathroom floor. At least we can use the toilet tonight."

It's Sunday, which means I usually have the night off. Unfortunately I'd volunteered to work a private party so I call One Maple and switch with a bartender who owes me. It's clear that logistically I have to help *the patient* prepare for the trip the stubborn ass insists on taking tomorrow.

"Party tonight. Where can I get the prescription filled?" When my query is met with silence, I turn away from the fridge to get a look-see and find him steeped in deep thought. Seated at the island in the kitchen, he's staring at the glass of water before him.

His phone rings again, for the umpteenth time. It's been ringing nonstop since we left the hospital. I'm actually surprised he's letting most of the calls go to voicemail.

"I'm not taking that junk." He sounds strangely forlorn, or sad, or something like it. Which bothers me. An urgent need to make him feel better gets a hold of me. Ten days ago I was ready to make a eunuch out of him and now I want to see him smile. The man is turning me into *Sybil*.

"You look like you're in serious pain, Vaughn. I don't want you to suffer. And since I can feel your pain as acutely as if it were mine, I'll take a couple of those babies with you—only out of solidarity of course—and then, just for giggles, we can do a marathon of *The Leftovers*."

"Negative on the pill party."

"All kidding aside, let me fill the prescription, in case you need one tonight to help you sleep. Your lobster claw is going to be throbbing later." With the way the doc bandaged his left hand, it basically resembles a lobster claw, as I've affectionately been referring to it. It's also totally useless.

He holds up said claw and stares at it with a pout, which turns into a grimace. The pain etched onto his refined features bothers me. I turn back to the stove and grab the pan.

"Word of caution, I haven't cooked in a really long time so...you know..." I say, shrugging. I push the scrabbled eggs off the pan and onto a plate with two slices of that millet bread he likes that tastes like dirt. "Just sayin'." I place the plate in front of him. "Also, you should know that my cooking repertoire is extremely limited. We'll have to get takeout when you get back. And I know what a health food freak you are so tell me where to pick up the grub you like."

His eyes meet mine. There's something fathomless in them. Whatever it is, it pulls me in and won't let go. The *Monday Night Football* song comes on and he blinks out of the moment. Saved by the proverbial bell. Even though I'm going to break out in hives if I hear that ringtone one more time.

He takes a tentative bite of his eggs. "Not bad. Needs a bit more seasoning, but otherwise really good." Smiling, he digs in.

That earns him an obvious eye roll. "I was on tenterhooks. So glad you approve, Fancy Pants."

"What else can you make?"

"What else? Mmmm, let's see—" Truth: I can't cook to save my life. My food is always one of these horrible things: too salty, too bland, or too overcooked. "I make a mean margarita."

He smiles and I get happy, happy that I've done something to pull him out of this strange funk he's been in since the hospital.

"I wouldn't call that nutrition."

"You'd be surprised at how many people would disagree with you." While he finishes his eggs, I turn to wash the pan.

"I had a lot of allergies when I was a kid."

The inflection in his voice gets my attention, the admission tentative, as if he threw it out as bait to see if I would bite. In all honesty, I want to bite. As much as I try to stop myself, I do find him interesting, drawn to him in ways I don't want to contemplate. So turning, I wait for him to continue.

"I was kind of sick for a while." He glances up to measure my reaction. Whatever he finds persuades him to continue. "Ever hear of Celiac disease?"

"I've heard of it, but I'm not familiar with what it is."

"It's an intolerance to wheat proteins, and if left untreated can trigger a host of other problems—including cancer. I have to eat well to feel good and I've been doing it for so long it's second nature to me."

"That's why you don't drink beer."

"Yeah. No barley or rye, either."

The doorbell rings.

"If this is one of your stalkers, I will—"

"It's Andi," he says, interrupting the beginnings of my mini tirade. His lips press together in a stiff line. "She's coming with me."

* * *

"I don't understand. You tell people you're gay?"

Plush mouth pursed, Andi wiggles it side to side while considering her answer. In the meantime, I hand her a glass of soda and she takes a sip.

"I don't *tell* people I'm gay. I told a new client that was getting excessively pushy about hitting on me that I'm not a fan of men and somehow he translated it as me admitting I was gay. News spread faster than athlete's foot in a locker room."

As soon as she walked in the front door, Andi began gushing personal information from the spigot that is her mouth as if the valve were broken. Which has now turned into one of the most entertaining and simultaneously bizarre conversations I've had in a long time.

"Doesn't it bother you—having to lie?"

"Ethan works exclusively with football players. I'm not saying they don't know how to behave themselves, but it shuts that conversation down before it even begins, and frankly, makes my job a lot easier."

"Does Fancy know? I mean Ethan."

"Fancy?" She chuckles. "Cute—it suits him. And yes, he's fine with it. Anyway, if I play my cards right, with Ethan's help, I can become a full manager and bring in my own clients. Maybe even some female athletes. So when he sells the business, I'll have some leverage with whomever buys it."

My ears perk up, the topic suddenly interesting. "Ethan is selling his business?"

"If he gets the job as head counsel for the Titans, he has to."

"Did Ethan say he would help you?"

She nods and sips her soda. "Yeah. He's so generous. I've learned more from him in one year than I did working with Titans Player Personnel in three."

"Speaking of the patient," I say. Treading lightly, we both head out of the kitchen and into the living room. Sprawled out on the very uncomfortable modern couch, Fancy is snoring. We watch him for a minute, then look at each other and smile. She motions to the door and I follow.

"You can throw the contracts I brought over in his suitcase," Andi states, one foot out the door. "I'll be here by eight tomorrow and the car by eight thirty."

"Got it. I'll have him ready."

"Amber, I know we just met but I feel like I can say anything to you."

Obviously—she's been talking nonstop. But why does this

suddenly make me uncomfortable? *Groan*. The answer hits me in the gut. Because if she divulges her life-long crush on her boss, I'll get queasy. Looking into her eager and open expression, I brace for the worst.

"I'm really glad he met you. I couldn't figure out how such a great guy didn't have a girlfriend."

Umm. Okay. Not what I expected. More importantly though, I can't have her running around thinking or spreading rumors that Ethan and I are an item. Not with the possibility of Ethan getting disbarred. *When did I start thinking of him as Ethan? Huh, weird.*

"We're not anything. It's a long story that you don't have time for, but in a few months I'll be gone."

Her delight wanes. "Bummer."

"Nope. Besides, I'm not looking for anything, and neither is he."

Her expression, wavering from suspicion to doubt, clears a moment later. I can see she doesn't believe me. Regardless, she keeps her opinion to herself. "See you tomorrow." In kitten heels, she gracefully glides down the limestone steps.

"Andi." She turns toward me with a smile. "You and Ethan?"

Her pert nose scrunches up while the rest of her face twists into a disgusted scowl. "Gross. He's like a brother to me. Incest isn't my thing."

After her colorful remark, she holds up an arm and in seconds a cab comes to a breakneck stop before her. That's never once happened to me. Not freaking once. And I've lived in this city for nine years. Apparently hailing a cab is a sensual act. I never got this memo.

* * *

"Gee wiz, what's this?"

With feigned innocence, I hold up a jar of hair product. Ethan steps out of his walk-in closet, two suits hanging from his good hand. As soon as his eyes zero in on what's in mine, his expression turns sulky. I, instead, revel in my victory. "I'll just put this in your fancy beauty case."

"It's a shaving kit."

"Whatever, it's Louis Vuitton."

His brow bunches and he looks away. "I like the good stuff," I'm pretty sure I catch him muttering under his breath. A stretch of silence follows. It prods me to glance up. I find his gaze heavy on me again. This time, however, his expression is contrite.

"What?"

"I need to apologize." He drops the suits on the bed.

Abandoning the shaving kit among the rest of his things in the suitcase on the floor, I stand. "I overreacted," I say, offering an olive branch of my own.

"No, you didn't." Walking closer, he sits at the end of his bed. "I shouldn't have said that." His eyes, filled with remorse, meet mine. "I shouldn't have insinuated it about you."

"You see a lot of that in your line of work. I get it."

"Doesn't matter." In frustration, he rakes his fingers through his hair. "I don't want you to think that I make snap judgments about people like that. That's not who I am." He watches me expectantly. This expectant look is developing into a habit with him.

For what, though, I don't know. Judgment? Absolution? I don't hold it against him. I don't know much, but I do know there's a heavy penalty to pay for carrying grudges around. I learned that lesson the hard way.

"I know you're one of the good guys." After everything he's done for me, this fact is indisputable. God knows if someone asked me to take in a virtual stranger, I'd immediately direct them to the Bellevue Hospital psych ward.

His eyes hold mine for a beat too long. Whatever crosses between us makes me uncomfortable. This entire conversation is making me uncomfortable. I shove my hands in the back pockets of my jeans to stop them from fidgeting.

"Is that what you think?" he murmurs.

"Yeah. I do."

The mood grows more serious with every second that ticks by. He plucks at the loose end of his bandage. "I don't know what I would've done if you hadn't been here."

"See, I'm good for something," I throw out, hoping to tease him into a better mood. He doesn't take the bait, though. Silence falls again. I'm about to leave when he clears his throat.

"No, Jones. You're just plain good."

My stomach drops. What in the ever-loving hell am I supposed to do with that?

"Friends, then?" I suggest in yet another attempt to steer us into a less awkward conversation.

He looks up then. "You want to be friends?"

I shrug, trying to act cool when I'm anything but. "This has the makings of an epic friendship. You've seen me naked. I've seen you naked—"

Even though his face doesn't change, I detect a smile in his eyes. "I knew I caught you looking at my junk. You couldn't help yourself, could you?"

"You almost knocked me unconscious with that thing

when I was helping you with your sneakers."

"It did not get anywhere near you."

"The tip was *this* close to my eyeball."

"Not true," he says flatly, though he's biting on his bottom lip in a poor attempt to curb his amusement. "Not even close."

"How did you expect me to explain the black eye? Don't answer that. Point is, we've both seen each other's privates and have come away unimpressed." His smile flattens. "I see a frown. Are you saying you don't want to be my friend? Because I'm ready to give you a matching lobster claw on your right hand if you answer in anything other than an emphatic yes."

"I already think of you as my friend." His steady gaze is all over me again and I'm instantly back to fidgety. I don't know what to say to that. I stare back blankly, blink a couple of time, scratch my neck. This conversation has lasted maybe fifteen minutes, and I'm as exhausted from the roller coaster of emotions as if I'd worked a double shift.

"You do?" Might as well go with the truth. And the truth is I'm both surprised and confused.

"Hmm."

"Then it's settled. Friends. Let's hug it out."

Leaning in, I wrap my arms around his neck, doing my best to keep a respectable distance between my breasts and his chest, because I am a respectable girl of course. Except the moment we touch I realize it's a mistake. Too late. Too bloody late. One minute I'm standing, and the next he pulls me in and I'm sitting in his lap. His arms slide around my waist, squeezing tightly, while he plants his nose on the side of my neck and inhales.

Sweet Jesus Christ Superstar.

Every muscle I possess braces, my breath held hostage by the tightening of my throat. To say I'm shocked is a bit of an understatement. I sit there like a lump, overwhelmed by the warmth of him, the scent of laundry detergent mixed with something subtle and uniquely him, the heavy beating of his heart, the pressure of his touch. It bleeds into me and unlocks some of the discomfort.

In small increments, I begin to thaw, and feeling me relax, he relaxes, too. It feels so good to be held I simultaneously want to run out of the room screaming, and tie him up and abuse him like I do my sex toys. Neither of which will happen. Not only is it forbidden in all caps, but I don't even qualify as a hump. Let's not forget that beauty.

He's having a vulnerable moment. That's all this is. Everybody needs a hug once in a while. Even man-hoes. He's obviously not getting any from his parade of women. Which is why, I pat his back twice, the gesture wooden and clumsy, and pry myself off his lap.

"Good," I say, all business. "Great. Glad we had this talk."

I swear he's looking at me like I kicked his three-legged puppy. Now I definitely want to run out of the room screaming. "You're all packed." I'm pretty sure my smile looks creepy. Positive actually. It's being held up by sheer force of will.

"You have your Tylenol PM ready?" He nods in response. "I'll put your suits in the bag tomorrow morning. Good night." I wave, which ends up looking like a quasi-Nazi salute. *The heck is wrong with me?* Everything, that's what.

He watches me intently as I back out of his bedroom. As

soon as the door closes, I exhale the breath I was holding, my shoulders sagging along with it. This trip of his couldn't have come at a better time. Nothing like a little distance to smother the weird vibe that's taken up residence between us.

CHAPTER ELEVEN

IT'S BEEN FOUR DAYS SINCE he left and not only does time seem to be standing still, but also, the house has grown twice as large and lonely. The moment Morrison and his men walked through the door the day after he left I knew he'd gotten to him first. The contrite look on Morrison's face was a dead giveaway.

"He called you didn't he?"

"He did."

"And."

"And I'm to…uh…do as you say."

Squinting at the clear lie, I say, "I call bullshit."

"Fine," he barks. "He said I should consider myself your bitch until the end of the job or he'll make sure my license is pulled."

Sounds about right. "The bathrooms, Mr. Morrison."

Lawyers…I should've known.

Fancy: Burn down my house yet?

The text comes in as my hand is dive-bombing into a bag of cheese puffs. You can imagine my predicament. Fingers covered in orange, I try and fail to use my elbow to pause the

Animal Kingdom episode I'm thick in the midst of. A text from my roommate? My roommate who is, at present, in Jacksonville. My roommate who has never texted me before. Why is my roommate texting me at 1 a.m.?

I use my knuckles to answer, fumbling to not leave a florescent orange trail all over my bedspread.

> **Me: Im in the midle of sphitzing the coch with lighter fuid as be speck.**

Oopsy. Leave it to spellcheck to fail me the one time I need it.

> **Fancy: Are you drunk?**

> **Me: Cheez puf hands.**

> **Me: Cal me.**

As soon as the phone rings, I get a strange sensation in my belly that feels like some distant relation to excitement...best not to examine that too closely.

"What are you wearing?" His voice is low and husky and full of mischief. If that doesn't deserve an eye roll, I don't know what does. This is what you call male humor. It requires a penis to find this funny.

"What if I said I'm wearing the Hello Kitty underwear I picked up at Target on sale." Phone cradled between my shoulder and ear, I finish washing my hands in the bathroom.

"I'd say that's surprisingly hot."

So predictable. "What if I said a strap-on?"

"I'd say let's change the subject."

Sooo predictable. "How's the lobster claw faring?"

"Having to watch my assistant cut my meat isn't exactly on my list of favorite things."

"I bet."

"You were right. I couldn't have done this without Andi," the man on the other end of the line mumbles.

"No shame in your game, counselor. I was going to suggest getting a temporary handicap sign next." I'm expecting a chuckle. At the very least, a snort. Instead I get a good three minutes of silence. I don't do well with silence. I immediately feel the need to fill it.

"What are you still doing up? Didn't you get your usual, obnoxious 5 a.m. start?"

"Yeah, I did...I couldn't sleep." I hear a long-suffering sigh and my ears perk up. The silence grows tense. I'm about to break the stalemate, but he beats me to it. "I'm not a slut."

Oh boy. I was hoping and praying we were going to gloss over that part of our little tiff...guess not.

"Soooo, we're not going to pretend I never said that? Because I thought we were."

"I'm not a slut."

Sigh. What does he call it? Being generous with his dick?

"I'm not."

I want to say *agree to disagree*, I really do, but I can't do it. Something in his voice tells me he's dead serious about this, and by the mere fact that he's bringing it up almost two weeks later says he's obviously been thinking about it.

"Why does it matter what I think?"

"I'm not a slut," he repeats more forcefully.

"Okay, well, then I guess you date a lot? Is that closer to the truth?"

"No. I haven't dated anyone in a while."

"Fancy—every time I turn around there's a woman stalking you."

"That doesn't mean shit. Do you believe me when I tell you I'm not a slut?"

The silence crackles with tension, anticipation screaming through the phone. Thing is, I do believe him. Ethan is many things, but not a liar. Not to mention there's absolutely no reason for him to lie to me. I'm nobody he needs to impress.

"I believe you," I grumble. Even though a nagging voice in the back of my mind tells me it's easier to believe he's a slut, easier to curb this budding *friendship* between us which feels dangerous.

"Good. I'm going to sleep. Call you tomorrow."

With that, the line drops. For the next few minutes, I stare at the screen of my cell phone wondering what the heck just happened. Then again it's becoming a trend where he's concerned.

* * *

I started receiving texts. Lots of them. At the most random times. And most of them look like this:

Fancy: What are you wearing?

Me: A frown.

Fancy: A wise woman once turn that frown upside down.

Me: A wise woman is now saying stop texting while she's trying to vacuum.

Fancy: Why are you vacuuming when the cleaning service is coming in two days?

Me: The house is covered in dust. I'm not waiting.

Fancy: How did court go?

Me: David got the postponement. Still don't know why. I'd like this to be over as soon as possible.

Fancy: David knows what he's doing.

I didn't doubt that for a minute, but I won't deny that I'm antsy for this to be resolved as quickly as possible.

Fancy: Flight boarding. Txt ltr.

Later that day…

Fancy: What are you wearing?

Me: Dust. Lots of it, Miss Havisham.

Fancy: ????

Me: Never mind. Getting in the shower. Ltr.

The phrase "fell into a friendship" comes to mind. Whether it was by proximity or circumstance doesn't matter, it happened seamlessly. I've never had this level of comfort with anyone, not this quickly, not even with Justin. As much as I love

Justin, he is five years younger, which once in a while becomes glaringly apparent—i.e. there are only so many times I can spend the day playing Madden and drinking beers.

By the end of Ethan's ten day trip I'm feeling a lot better about the state of our unorthodox friendship, the sizzle between us turned down to a respectable level. Whatever that means.

It's eleven by the time I see him standing in my bedroom doorway holding his luggage. Hair mussed, tie hanging loose. He looks tired. And he's wearing his glasses...and scruff. God help me, the torture. He gives me a lopsided smile and I give him one in return, cheeks stuffed with popcorn and all.

"What are you wearing?"

"A thmile." I cover my mouth to stop the popcorn from spilling out. "Wecome hoe. Welcome home," I reiterate after swallowing.

Dumping his luggage at the door, he walks in and starts pulling off his tie.

"What are you watching?"

You. You're by far the most fascinating thing I've ever seen. "The Leftovers."

He discards his suit jacket and I get a tweak of something called unease. Taking another handful of popcorn, I nervously cram it in my mouth. I'm a nervous eater. This is normal behavior for me. What is not normal behavior is my roommate pulling a *Magic Mike* routine in my bedroom.

"You look tired." In a daze I watch him unbutton his dress shirt. I have absolutely zero control over what my eyes are doing and at present they choose to be glued to those wicked fingers. The things they are doing to those buttons.

"Hmm," he answers, or rather grunts.

I begrudgingly look up and say, "Is this a bad time for me to ask what it is you're doing?"

"I don't have a TV in my bedroom and I can't read. My eyes are shot." Abandoning the half unbuttoned shirt, he starts unbuckling his belt and unzipping his slacks. My discomfort grows exponentially larger. The slacks fall to the floor with a thud, his shirttails falling over his black boxer briefs. At this point I may as well be standing in an oven. So much for the sizzle being dialed down. I'm freaking roasting.

"It's cold in here," he grumbles.

"You think?" Meanwhile, I'm sweating golf balls.

"Hmm."

"You're aware that this is inappropriate, right?" Sadly, not for the reason he thinks. The way he's back to unbuttoning his shirt, slowly and deliberately with heavy-lidded eyes on me, is starting to rev my engine and that's the last thing I need right now. I need my engine to shut down, to go night night, otherwise I'm going to have to rub one out the minute he leaves. It's either that or I can sign myself up for another sleepless night.

"You've seen me naked, Jones. I've seen you naked." He imparts this wisdom with a raised eyebrow. The understatement of the year. I don't think I'll ever get the image of him naked out my mind—ever. "I recall you being unimpressed," he adds, his lips quirking.

He's left his undershirt on. Thank God for small favors.

Lust. That's all this is. A normal bodily reaction to being deprived of what a body needs. No mystery here. Would I be surprised if my mouth watered at the sight of a burger had I not eaten a meal in years? No. Thus, I absolve myself of any guilt over this reaction.

Standing next to the bed, his expression sleepy, he waits for me to...what? Give him permission? Damn, this is awkward.

"Scootch over."

"Scootch? Say that again and I'll be forced to revoke your mancard."

If the look on his face is any indication, he finds something funny. I'm just not sure if he's silently laughing *at* me, or *with* me. "You've seen my mancard. Does it look like it can be revoked?"

"Indirectly. I looked at it indirectly. And only because it was in my face, making threatening gestures." My rebuttal is met by another raised eyebrow. "Fine," I mutter sourly and move over for him. The minute he crawls into my bed I get a hit of his scent. One hit and I'm high as a kite.

"How's your hand?" I mumble, my lips numb because I'm quasi tripping. He shoves his left hand inches from my face.

"Jeez, I'm not interested in smelling it, Vaughn." Grabbing his wrist, I hold it farther away, and turning it left and right, perform a thorough examination. Where the stitches were removed, the skin is still bright pink.

"Does it hurt?" I gently brush my index finger over part of it and he flinches. My attention cuts back to his face. "Does it?"

"No." His gaze falls to my lips. "So, what are we watching?" he murmurs. I can't tear my attention away from his heavy-lidded eyes, those impossibly thick, dark lashes. *The end of me*, I want to say but don't.

"*The Leftovers*. Only the strangest show ever." And just to illustrate that God has a sense of humor and routinely likes to get his kicks by messing with my life, we both turn to look at the television screen and find the lead male character, the very sexy Kevin Garvey, balls deep in some random chick, the scene complete with the requisite vigorous pumping and grunting.

It's official, I'm not getting any sleep tonight.

"What do you like about this show?" The question sounds tentative, as if he doesn't quite know how to approach the subject. Heat races up my neck for the umpteenth time in the last twenty minutes.

"Don't let the graphic sex fool you. The writing is excellent and the acting superb."

Grunting, grunting, and more grunting. In the meantime, my sweat glands are getting a serious workout.

"Is that your type?" he asks, his tone cautious, his gaze still fixed on the sex scene I could be enjoying if he wasn't sitting next to me.

"What do you mean by type?"

For fuck's sake, is this scene ever going to end?

"Muscles, ink." He doesn't look at me and I don't dare look at him. This line of questioning is rife with danger.

"I don't have a type."

"No type?" he turns to look at me and I do the same. No matter how hard he tries to look indifferent, his expression teeters on the brink of curiosity.

"Not physical. I think attraction is in the mind of the beholder. Everything else is lust and that wears off faster than an orgasm."

He gets quiet, thoughtful, which compels me to explain. "I'm attracted to people with passion, that have figured out what theirs is and go after it. I'm attracted to kindness and intelligence…I guess I'm attracted to some kind of awesome."

"Was Gregory awesome?" he says in a flat voice, not giving anything away.

And the groovy mood we were sharing a second ago takes a nosedive. The last thing I need is to be reminded of just how bad my judgment is, how astray I let it lead me. There's nothing worse than not being able to trust yourself. It has a paralyzing effect on your entire life.

I turn to watch the television again, the scene mercifully over. "No, he most definitely wasn't." Time for a change of topic. "Andi said you're selling your business."

When he doesn't answer right away, I steal a brief glance. It's his turn to be under the microscope and I can tell he doesn't like it.

"Only if I get the job as lead counsel for the Titans."

"Why would you give up the business you've built to work for someone else? You're obviously one of the best in your field."

"Because I've always dreamed of being a general manager. Getting the job as lead counsel gets me one step closer."

There's animation in his face when he speaks, a spark in his eyes. He's suddenly full of energy where minutes ago he looked sleepy. Passion—he's full of it.

"What about you? Have you always known you wanted to be an actress?"

"Since I was six. Whenever my mother was dating somebody new, she would drop me off at the theater and give the kid working twenty bucks to make sure I didn't leave."

"Jesus."

I force a smile. Not because I harbor any pain about it,

because I don't want *him* to feel bad. His eyes fill with sympathy, his features softened by it.

"Put the Kleenex away, Fancy Pants. I'm fine with it." He continues watching me with rapt attention. "I saw *Little Orphan Annie* one day and fell in love. I wanted to do what the kids in that movie were doing. My grandmother used to call me *The Purple Rose of Cairo* because I looked like I wanted to step into the screen."

"Have you ever wanted to do anything else?"

"No. I love everything about it." My thoughts drift to Marty and the weekly harassment I've been receiving from him to move. "My agent wants me to move to L.A. He says I have a much better chance of finding work there. He says I'm wasting time here."

"Is he right?"

I give it a minute of honest thought before I answer. "Yeah," I say, exhaling my frustration.

"How come you haven't moved already, then?"

"My grandmother."

He nods in understanding. "How bad is she?"

"Bad. It's Alzheimer's. She rarely recognizes me anymore." Although he's still nodding, something tells me he's holding back. "What does that look mean?"

"I know you want to do right by your grandmother, but it sounds like you're driving with your foot on the brake."

"It's too late for metaphors. Spit it out."

"I think your grandmother would want you to move to L.A... to give it a real shot."

It seems so simple from the outside. Logic tells me he's right. That's the reason my grandmother made Eileen trustee after all. But my conscience tells me she needs me, that Eileen can't be trusted. And I would die a thousand deaths if something happened to her while I'm in Lala land living my dream. Either way, I lose.

"I can't leave her. She was always there for me."

The quiet is heavy, the moment transforming into something I could never have anticipated, something meaningful.

"Success requires sacrifice." His voice is steel wrapped in velvet and packs a punch I can feel in my solar plexus. His eyes, filled to the brim with understanding, hold mine. Something tells me he knows something about sacrifice.

It's still dark out when I awaken to a foghorn in my ear. Cracking my eyes open, I turn in the direction of the offending noise and freeze. The owner of the foghorn is inches from my face, sleeping soundly.

The television is still on, the cable box reading 5:30. We must've fallen asleep watching it last night. He murmurs something before belting out another horrid sound. And I mean horrid, like braying mule, something's dying horrid. If I wasn't still half asleep, I'd be laughing my ass off right about now.

I give myself only a minute to admire him. I'm already on the verge of serious like and it would be downright stupid to encourage that feeling. We're a million miles apart in every way that counts, not to mention neither of us is looking for anything that even remotely resembles a relationship.

Despite the strange sounds emanating from him, he's the most handsome man I've ever seen. But what's even better is that he's generous and kind. A good egg, as Camilla would say. He sucks in a breath and cuts another one loose. I quietly crawl out of bed and into the shower. I shouldn't be enjoying this. I really shouldn't be. But I am.

CHAPTER TWELVE

My relationship with my grandmother is complicated, our history not a pretty one. I was angry and upset when my mother moved out to marry Dan. I felt like a refugee, neither belonging with Dan and Eileen nor with my grandparents. So naturally I acted out a lot. Which exasperated my grandmother who was trying to run the funeral home by herself because of my grandfather's failing health.

It was a recipe for an unhappy home.

Don't run.

Don't shout.

Stop screaming.

How in the world did you break that lamp?

How did you get so dirty?

Try to be quiet for ten minutes.

Don't do that inside, go outside and do that.

Stop talking.

Stop talking!

Stop talking!!

You're impossible, you know that.

And the worst by far…

I'm calling your mother to come get you.

It wasn't until I met Camilla and started spending time at

her house, with her parents, that I realized I wasn't the worst kid on the planet.

It took a long time for us to find common ground and it pretty much started after my grandfather died. I spoke less. I played less. I laughed less. Essentially, I became less. I was terrified my grandmother was going to send me away to God knows what unknown relative—in my mind there was always one out there—that I would've done anything to please her.

Regardless, once we started to get along, we got along. I helped her with the business, and in returned she never discouraged me from my interest in acting. Also, my grandmother was wise to my mother's bullshit. We had that in common. Our mutual disapproval of Eileen went a long way to bridging the gap between us. The problem was that my grandmother seemed to try to right all the wrongs she felt she committed with my mother through me. Ergo, she was unbearably strict.

"Margaret?" I say as I walk up to her in the activities room of the assisted living facility. She looks up from her needlepoint with a soft smile.

"Yes," she says, her eyes lighting up at the sight of me. For a minute the happy look on her face almost brings tears to my eyes. I miss her looking at me like she knows who I am. I never thought that losing the person you love most a little at a time would be worse than all at once but I was wrong. So wrong. Because who are we without our memories? Without our history. An empty vessel moving through life? *Where did your memories go, Grandma?* I imagine them floating over her head, in the ether, always out of reach.

Her eyes cloud when she realizes she can't place me, like a vacancy sign went up—nobody's home. A look I've come to know well. I take a seat next to her and for the next twenty minutes we make small talk. She answers with one word answers mostly, treating me like the stranger I am to her.

"Okay. I'm headed home, but I'll be back in a few days to see you." She gives me another polite smile that says she doesn't give a shit either way. "Margaret?"

"Yes?"

"What would you say to a friend that wanted to move to a different city to pursue her career?"

Her eyes move away, out the window overlooking the bare maple trees. "Is it something that makes her happy?"

I can't speak, biting the inside of my cheek to stop my bottom lip from trembling. Instead, I nod.

"Then she should go."

"But...what if it means she has to leave something important behind?" I manage to get out even though my voice cracks.

Looking me squarely in the eyes, gaze steadfast, she says, "She should go after whatever makes her happy."

* * *

By the time I get home from visiting my grandmother I am drained, parboiled, *finito*. All I want to do is get into my crappiest sweats—the ones that are threadbare, full of holes and feather soft—and eat. Eat everything I can get my grabby hands on.

To that end, I'm happily stuffing my face with pizza when a man walks into the living room. And when I say man, I mean part deity because holy cow patties he looks like he could walk on water. I stop chewing as my eyes do a slow, appreciative perusal of him.

"Hot date?" I casually throw out for consumption. Not

that I expect him to answer in the affirmative since I have yet to see him show any interest in any female since I've moved in.

He stuffs his hands in the front pockets of his suit pants and...says nothing. *Hmm.* His gaze moves away from me and my stomach slowly starts to sink.

"It is a date," I blurt out. A nasty prickling sensation burns my gut and travels all the way to my throat. His face is tight, his eyes shifty. He takes his cell phone out and glances at the time.

"I should get going."

Someone's stabbing my chest. Why is someone stabbing my chest? "Really? Wearing that?" I deadpan, my mouth running away with me while my brain struggles to comprehend what the fuck is happening. *A date? He's going on a date? No, no, I won't allow it,* it keeps saying.

He looks down. "What's wrong with what I'm wearing?"

"Nothing—if you like looking desperate."

A frown doctors his face. He seems conflicted about something. Although, what do I know? I couldn't have predicted this if I had a goddamn crystal ball.

"I don't have time for this." He turns to leave but pauses mid step, like he's about to say something else. The earth stops spinning in that moment. I hold my breath and hope for...I don't know what I hope for. In the end, he keeps his silence and continues walking.

My mood plummets another thousand feet as I stare at his back. I haven't been this demoralized since I was five and discovered Santa didn't exist because I caught a very loud and drunk Eileen, having returned from a date, wrapping presents at 1 a.m. There was more tape than actual paper on my gifts that year.

"Have fun," I say weakly. He waves as he disappears around the corner.

Have fun? No. Do NOT have fun. Have a goddamn miserable time as a matter of fact. I hope she falls and skins her knees. I hope she chips her perfectly polished nails.

Snatching up my cell, I dial the number of the one person I know I can hoist one long, uninterrupted rant on. "Harp, you busy? Good. Meet me at that crappy sports bar on Second and Seventy-First. Yep, see you in twenty."

The bar is small and dark, more likely frequented by bus drivers and construction workers than Upper East Side professionals, therefore it's easy for Harp and me to share a drink and catch up without him being harassed every two minutes for autographs or disgruntled assholes that lost money on fantasy football because Justin "didn't do them a solid."

I get there before Harper does and waste no time filling the hole in my gut that feels a lot like jealousy and disappointment with vodka tonics. The Knicks game is playing on the small television in the corner, the low buzz of conversation is all around me, and yet I don't hear or see a thing.

"You started without me?" a familiar voice calls out. "This must be bad."

I look over my shoulder and find Justin smiling down at me, dimples on full display, the flat brim of his Mets baseball cap pulled low and his disheveled brown hair spilling out the sides. He pulls his hands out of the front pockets of his dark designer jeans and shrugs off his down jacket, places his phone and keys on the bar, and takes the stool next to mine.

Three hours and who the hell knows how many drinks later—I certainly wasn't counting—I'm still listening to him drone on about his ex-girlfriend. Insert gun in mouth, pull trigger.

"She's the one that got away."

It takes a minute for it to sink in (alcohol and such). For me to give him my most disdainful glare. "Why do people say that? Why is that a thing? She's not a lost child. It's not like she casually wandered away when you weren't looking. You didn't lose her. She sprinted away." The hurt look on his face that I'm not drunk enough to ignore makes me pause. "Sorry. I'm sorry. I'm drunk and angry and…don't listen to me. What do I know? I don't know jack."

"What is it with you tonight? Why so pissy?"

I immediately get a clear picture of Ethan at a fancy-shmancy dinner with some long legged model. Then the whole picture turns red, my ears glowing with the evidence of my irrational fury. I say irrational because, let's face it, he's not mine. I have zero business feeling possessive, or jealous, or slightly heartbroken about this. Fine, more than slightly. What did I expect? It's not like he's a monk. He didn't take a vow of celibacy. Even though I wish he had.

"Because he's not a monk!"

"'Scuse me?"

"Never mind. We haven't finished with you yet. Every girl needs a grand gesture."

"She's in med school. She doesn't want to see me."

"So that's it? You're just—giving up?"

"She said to let her be." Then he sighs…sighs like a little bitch.

Utter disgust takes over my face. "Justin—"

"Yeah."

"I want you to pull down your pants." Justin draws the beer bottle away from his lips and looks over at me, confusion marring his movie star good looks. "Stick your hand between your legs and check to see if you're still in possession of your GODFORSAKEN chestnuts. I've listened to you cry about this girl for six months. Six months of whining! If she's so special, you go down there and fight for her."

"You're right," he says, slow nodding. "You're right."

"Are you a man, or mouse?!"

"I'm a man! I'm a man, dang it!" he shouts, slamming a large fist on the bar.

"Hey, man," interrupts the crusty bartender. "Time to pay the bill. We closin' in ten."

Instantly subdued, Justin flips open his wallet and fishes out his credit card. "Yes, sir."

Time to head home and face the piper. Or is it pay the piper? Fuck, I'm drunk. Time to go home.

* * *

With Justin's arm hooked around my neck, we amble down the street until we reach the townhouse. Standing at the bottom of the stairs, he leans closer and I catch a strange twinkle in his eyes. "Wanna mess around?" After this beauty, he waggles his eyebrows.

"No." I chuckle. I know it's cold because I can see my breath. I can't, however, feel much thanks to a large consumption of a controlled substance. Head shaking, I swat him away. "That ship sailed."

"Am I ever going to live that down?"

"Yes. But that doesn't mean I'm going to sleep with you."

The front door rips open and Ethan walks out, onto the

front steps. His shirtsleeves are rolled up and his jacket and tie are gone. The stormy look on his face both confuses and amuses me.

"Woopsey. I think I broke curfew," I whisper a little too loudly. Okay, maybe it's closer to a shout.

"Harper, do I have to get you a cab?" Ethan snaps.

"Nah, dude. I've got a car waiting." Justin motions to the Uber Black idling at the curb.

Ethan crosses his arms. He has yet to take his eyes off of me. "Good. Get in it."

My eyebrows scramble up to my hairline. "Big Papa izzz mad." Now I'm definitely shouting. Justin takes one look at me and we both break out in drunken giggles.

"Get in the car, Justin."

After giving Ethan a slow two-finger salute, Justin takes my hand and plants a kiss on the back of it. Then he turns and lopes to the car.

"Thanks for the drinks and the company, Dimples." I blow my buddy an exaggerated kiss and he catches it in the air.

"My pleasure, darlin'."

Once alone, Ethan and I spend a good two minutes—that feel surprisingly like an eternity—playing the staring game. He wins. I trudge up the front steps and past Big Papa as his intense, reproachful gaze tracks every move I make.

"You're drunk."

"Brilliant observation, counselor. What tipped you off?" I walk a semi straight line to the kitchen with Ethan right on my unsteady heels.

"How much did you have to drink?"

I open the fridge and grab a bottle of water. "Enough to

get me good and druuunk." I sound churlish. I know I do, but I'm just too shitfaced and hurt to care. "Did you have a nice date?"

The silence weighs as heavy as a metric ton of snow. In simpler terms, it's heavy. And goes on, and on, and on. Doubt pierces the fog of alcohol. Ugh, I may have given myself away. Turning to assess the damage, I find him wearing a decidedly uncomfortable expression.

Oh boy, he knows. He knows that I may be carrying a teeny tiny torch for him, and he's trying to find a way to let me down gently.

"What?" I snap, the alcohol wreaking havoc with my impulse control—the little I actually possess, that is.

"Nothing, it's that—" His jaw pulses with tension.

This is going to be bad. I can tell. Placing the water down on the island, I grip the edge of the granite counter and hang my head in defeat.

"Just say it. The suspense is killing me." I can't look at him when he cuts my heart out.

"It was with a guy."

Huh?

My head snaps up so fast I may have pulled a muscle in my neck. My chin's hanging loose and I'm pretty sure a little spittle ran out the corner of my mouth. His eyes flicker to mine and away.

"Did you say…a guy, as in male?" I must be drunker than I thought I was.

"Yeah, there was a guy waiting for me at the restaurant."

For once in my life, I'm having a real hard time finding the right words. "I…I'm sorry. I'm just…in shock." Never in a million years did I think…why *didn't* I consider it? Because

I'm a bloody idiot, that's why. I'm a self-absorbed fuckwit. He's never with a woman. For the love of penis, he even has me chase them off. If that's not a clear indication, I don't know what is. "Are you bisexual, or full-on gay?"

Don't be full-on gay. Please do not be full-on gay. I beg you, God. I will never ask for anything else…and I mean it this time.

I didn't think anything could make me feel worse than watching him walk out the door to go on a date, but this just did it. If he says full on gay, there's a ninety-nine-point-nine percent chance I'll start to cry.

"I'm not gay."

The breath I'm holding hisses out slowly. "Okay," I say, nodding. "Okay, so you're bisexual. That's good news."

His head tilts and his brows lower. "I'm not gay, or bisexual—and why would it be good news?"

Why would that be good news? Good question. I blink. I blink some more. Thinking on my feet is nearly impossible. "Never mind. Never mind. Do not mind me."

"Not that there's anything wrong with that," he quickly adds. Exhaling loudly, he does a thorough inspection of the kitchen ceiling while he repeatedly runs a hand through his hair, turning it into a disheveled mess.

Not for other men. I enjoy man-on-man action as much as the next girl, except when it involves the man I'm currently lusting after.

"It's Norma. She thinks I'm gay. She set me up with her Pilates instructor."

Again—speechless. Now is not a good time for me to be drunk. I need all my faculties intact to find my way around this labyrinth of a story.

"Your grandmother thinks you're gay?"

"Apparently," he mutters, rubbing the back of his neck. "Otherwise she wouldn't have insisted I go on a date with *Daryl*."

"Why would you agree to a date with *Daryl*?"

He blasts me with a squinty-eyed glare that has me taking a step back. "I wasn't informed whom I was meeting."

"Whom? Seriously? You're using good grammar at this hour?" I get a subtle hitch of an eyebrow and I'm immediately chastened. "Right. Sorry. Your nana thinks you're gay."

"Which means that you're coming with me to my grandmother's birthday party."

"Nooooo," I say, head shaking. "Sorry. No-can-do."

"Yeah, you can and you will." From the look on his face, I don't stand a chance of talking my way out of this. "Don't make me call in my favor."

"You wouldn't."

"You owe me, Jones. And this is how you're going to repay me."

CHAPTER THIRTEEN

IT'S DAYS AWAY FROM MARCH, and the weather continues to be as hideous as ever, no end to the cold in sight. One loathsome word has been bandied about all week—the dreaded N word, nor'easter. Also known as mayhem accompanied by blizzard like conditions that tend to dump a ridiculous amount of snow in a very short amount of time. Possibly the only thing capable of bringing this city to its knees. Not even a couple of psychos and some planes could accomplish it.

My phone chimes with an incoming text.

Fancy: *Alien* the director's cut or *The Matrix*?

He's been on the road for the last two and a half weeks—Dallas, El Paso, Charlotte, Miami—and seems to be racking up enough frequent flyer miles for a free trip to the moon. I've been getting a lot of calls and texts, usually at night and typically under the guise of checking in on the status of the construction. Which has been progressing at an accelerated pace since the day Morrison got his ass chewed out. Although that portion of the conversation usually lasts about a minute and then we're on to the next topic.

Me: Tough choice. Where are you and why are you

still awake?

Every time I get a text or the phone rings and the picture of his sweet bubble butt appears on screen with McButterpants stamped across it, my heart beats a little quicker. It is downright horrible how eager I am for even a scrap of his attention. I'd love to say something poetic and liken it to a flower being drawn to the sun, but in reality I'm a crackhead looking for her next fix.

Margin note: I took that picture surreptitiously. He has no idea.

Fancy: Indy. had a bad day. can't sleep.

The last leg of his trip ends in Indianapolis for the NFL scouting combine, a week long event for his young guys that have declared for the draft to showcase their mental and physical abilities.

The smart choice would be to pretend I never got that text. It's midnight. I can always say I fell asleep.

Me: Wanna talk about it?

Repeat after me, my pride whispers. *I am a weak, pathetic excuse for my gender.* A moment later my phone rings. There's no guessing who it is because I've assigned the song from the movie *Arthur* called *Arthur's Theme (The Best That You Can Do)* by Christopher Cross, to Ethan. Seems only fitting since he's so worried about disappointing his nana that he agreed to be set up on a blind date.

The chorus plays...*When you get caught between the moon and New York City...*

"Hey." His voice is low, the edges rough from overuse.

"You sound like shit."

He chuckles and I instantly feel my spirits lift. After a deep sigh, he grumbles, "One of my guys tested positive for PEDs today."

One of the things I respect most about him is how much he genuinely cares about his clients. "It's going to effect how he's drafted?"

"Yeah."

I can feel the weight he carries around in his voice, in the tired way he exhales. "I know how hard you work to help them be successful but you can't save them all, Fancy Pants. They're grown men."

"He's a twenty-one-year-old kid with too much responsibility."

"I'm sure you warned him."

"I did." He's back to grumbling his responses. A stretch of silence follows. I can almost hear him thinking on the other end of the line.

An irrational urge to take all his worries away, to soothe every hurt comes over me—and that's just plain stupid. This man does not need me to kiss his boo-boos. He's beautiful and successful and has friends and family. He doesn't need anything from me.

"Alien," I say. "Night, Vaughn." I hang up before he can say another word, before this craving becomes a full-blown addiction. I'm out of the boo-boo kissing business.

* * *

I warned Morrison to hook up a generator. I warned him repeatedly. Ethan agreed it was only wise considering the state of the ancient electric wiring in this behemoth of a house and Morrison said he would take care of it. But did he? No. Of course not. Hence, here I am alone, since Fancy has yet to return from his trip to Indianapolis, stuck in a house with too much open space, no electricity, and no heat.

Wrapped in my down blanket, I glance outside the living room window and see nothing other than a sheet of continuously falling snow. It's whiteout conditions. Traffic hasn't come to a complete halt yet but I give it another half hour until the streets look like a scene out of *The Day After Tomorrow*. Thank God I had the foresight to buy a couple of candles at the market when I went food shopping. Though a couple of candles aren't going to do jack to keep the frostbite away.

A noise at the front door gets my wary attention. The lock clicks open and a large hooded figure blows in with the cold wind and snow. Under the cover of the inky darkness, I stand there paralyzed, my heart hammering away.

Who the hell else has the keys to this place? One of the construction guys?

In nanoseconds I'm calculating how quickly I can reach a solid object and what my chances are of surviving outside in only my pajamas, and I suck at math. Amazing what the human mind can do when pumped up on adrenaline and life is at stake.

The intruder pulls his snow-covered hood down and my knees almost buckle.

"What are you doing here?!" I screech.

"I live here," the intruder answers flatly. Angry stomping, I stalk up to the jackass and hit him squarely in the chest, and in the process drop the blanket. I may as well be standing in an icebox. No problem, my anger's keeping me toasty. Catching my wrists as I flail against him, the jackass chuckles.

"This is how you thank me for walking twenty city blocks in a blizzard for you?" I rip my hands out of his hold and plant them on my hips. He drops his snow-covered down puffer jacket by his feet and looks down with a heart-stopping grin.

"Don't smile at me like that!" I snap. "And let's get one thing clear, I am immune to that bullshit." On a roll now, my arm slashes through the air. "You're not supposed to be back 'til tomorrow! I thought you were one of the construction guys trying to break in. I was about to go *Crouching Tiger* on your ass—"

"Wait, what?" His smile falters. He blinks, blinks again in comprehension, which turns into a bark of laughter, which turns into deep belly laughing. *Jerk.*

"I'd rather you go *Hidden Dragon*," he barely manages to get out.

"You're laughing? I amuse you? You're not gonna be laughing when I sock you in the coin purse."

He quickly covers his privates. Smart man because I am flat-out furious right now. I get a little testy after an adrenaline rush. I don't like to be scared, and it happens almost never, but when it does I get mad-dog angry. With that, I grab my blanket and stomp upstairs.

Fifteen minutes later my temper has cooled considerably, along with my body temperature. It's freezing in my bedroom. Even buried under a mountain of my clothes and a down duvet.

"Joooooones. I have a nice fire going downstairs. I have a pallet all set up for us in the den. Come downstairs."

I push the duvet off my face and find him leaning against the doorframe in his Harvard sweats, a wool beanie, and gloves.

"You scared the shit out of me."

"I meant to text you that I was on my way, but Cedric called and drained my battery."

"Freaking Cedric."

"Freaking Cedric. Come on, let's get you warmed up."

Downstairs, the fireplace in the den is blazing, the room glowing from the warmth and light radiating from it. There's a pallet made up of blankets and pillows and sheets I recognize as his set up right in front.

The snow is still steadily falling. I can see it out the floor to ceiling window. As I take in the scene, it's not just the snow that's falling, something inside of me feels like it's falling as well. Probably my stomach because it's one of the most romantic settings I've ever witnessed.

After I hung up on him two nights ago, I promised myself I'd put some breathing room between us. This unlikely friendship is on the verge of...affection? Yeah, affection—or something in the same emotional family. At least, for me it is. Point is, it's running away with me, and I need to herd it back into a space where I can manage it and not let it manage me. You don't hang out at your favorite bar if you're a recovering alcoholic for shit's sake! That's not a sign of good judgment.

Minutes pass silently as I stand there frozen, feeling awkward—something I haven't felt around him since that night in jail.

"Look at the bright side," he finally says, breaching the heavy silence. "At least Morrison finished renovating this room. No more drafty windows." He walks past me. Grabbing the fireplace poker, he fiddles with the logs.

My heartbeat quickens as I walk over to the pallet.

Slipping under the covers, I pull the blankets up to my chin, and stare at the ceiling while he gets in next to me.

"I'm starving. Do we have any food in the house?"

"If by food you mean that nasty almond milk you like, and that cereal that tastes like wood shavings, then yeah. I went to the store earlier."

Ethan gets up on an elbow, staring down at me with one of his killer smiles.

I glare back. "I was already there, getting my fix on. It's not like I went out of my way for you."

"You kind of did."

"No, I didn't," I insist, narrowed eyes directed at the man cheerfully smirking down at me.

"You did, admit it. You thought about me and little cartoon hearts appeared in your eyes like one of those emojis you love and you thought, what can I do for Ethan?"

"Are you stroking out?"

"And then you said to yourself, I know. I'll make sure he has all his favorite foods."

"You've lost your ever loving mind," I continue, talking over him.

"Whole Foods is a hike. You really, really went out of your way."

"That's not how it went at all."

"Agree to disagree," he taunts.

My smile cuts loose against my will. Somebody revoke my badass card. I've turned into a trained seal with this guy.

"Save my spot while I get the food you bought me out of your deep, *deep* desire to please me."

"If you value your future children, Vaughn, you will never utter that sentence to me again."

146

On his way to the kitchen, he steps over me and I try to smack his hip but he nimbly moves out of the way in time.

"You want some?" he shouts from the kitchen.

"No, thanks. I'm not a termite."

Fifteen minutes later the six-foot-two termite is back. "Mmmm, those wood shavings sure hit the spot," he singsongs while rubbing his flat abdomen in circles. He peels off his hat and gloves, pulls the sweatshirt over his head and off, revealing an undershirt. It rides up and I swiftly avert my eyes. Once done with his striptease, heavy emphasis on the tease part, he gets under the covers...and scoots closer and closer. A little too close for comfort. I can feel his body from my shoulder to my ankle.

"Jeez, Vaughn. Stay on your side, will you. I'm not a pregnancy pillow. Hug yourself if you're lonely."

His chuckle is deep and dark and gives me dirty thoughts. For a moment I wonder what it would feel like if he—

"We need to be close to transfer body heat," he snickers.

Before he got back into our makeshift bed, he threw another log on the fire, turning the room into a sauna. Not to mention what his proximity is doing to me. Time for an exaggerated eye roll. "Did that bullshit line work for you in high school?"

"Umm, no."

The strange inflection in his voice piques my interest. I look over and find him watching me. "I'm getting a rapey, *One Hour Photo* vibe from you right now."

"Why is everything a movie reference?" He's propped up on an elbow again with genuine interest on his face.

"It's my jam," I reply, tucking my hands under my head.

"Why movies? Why not books, or music?"

The sound of his low, intimate voice does funny things to my nether region. I'm trying to fight this thing growing between us tooth and nail, but it's getting harder and harder each day. Translation: I am screwed with a capital S. He can't be sweet and smart, thoughtful and funny all wrapped up in a package that looks like that and not give a girl ideas. It's like dangling chum in front of a shark. In case you missed it, he's chum and I'm the shark in this scenario.

"I like those things too, but I love that you can tell an entire story with just one glance, and that it can mean something different to each person."

"Hmm, good point."

"And then there's always the grand gesture, the moment of redemption. The boy gets the girl—or the boy. The crooked cop does the right thing and turns himself in. The hero gives his life for the drowning kid...the grand gesture hardly ever happens in real life."

"You like it when the boy gets the girl?" he murmurs, his eyes taking in every salient point on my face one piece at a time.

My face registers one thing only—suspicion. He's in a strange mood tonight. And try as I may, I can't figure out where he's going with this.

"He doesn't always get the girl, Fancy. But I do love the grand gesture. Every epic love story has a grand gesture."

The silence impels me to look over again. Brown eyes twinkling in the firelight, all the hard planes of his face outlined in gold. Ugh, somebody save me from myself.

"Still getting that *One Hour Photo* vibe from you." So what do I get after comparing him to the creepy stalker Robin

Williams played in that movie? I get an even bigger smile out of him. Men, explain them to me. "Are my insults ever going to score a hit?"

"No."

"I didn't think so."

"But keep 'em coming. I'm excited to hear what comes out of your mouth next."

"Fancy?"

"Yeah?"

"Why do you live in this dump?"

Sighing, he parrots my pose and lies back with his hands tucked under his head. The sigh indicates this is a much more serious conversation than I'd intended.

"This was the house my grandparents lived in when my mom was a kid. She grew up here."

"And?"

"And they were going to turn it into a commercial property so I asked Norma to give it to me instead. I'm fixing it up for my someday family."

"Are you close to your mother?"

"She passed away when I was fifteen." He turns and meets my eyes. "Ovarian cancer."

Stop. Somebody make him stop. That hurts. Damn that hurts. It feels like I just got double barrel kicked in the sternum. My gaze shifts to the ceiling in fear I'll lose it. I'd assumed he'd led a charmed life. What a dumbass. I, better than anyone, should've known not to draw such conclusions, to not judge him based on appearance. Things are rarely what they seem.

The ache fades into the background and a large dose of shame takes its place. "I'm sorry. That must've been really hard for you."

"It wasn't easy.

"I'm not close to mine," I blurt out. Again, my mouth doing it's own thing. "I don't even think of her as my mother. More like a distant relative I'm forced to tolerate every once in a while."

"How come you're not close?"

"It started when I was born. We had a falling out over a small discrepancy." My voice is toneless, dispassionate. The benefit of a bad experience is that once it's wrung out of you every drop of emotion, it's done for good. "She was under the impression that babies care for themselves. Eileen was your quintessential party girl. Not much time for maternal bonding when she was juggling multiple boyfriends. When I was eight she met Dan and decided that raising his son and a daughter was way too much work so she left me with my grandparents."

"And your dad?"

"Don't know who he is. Neither does Eileen. But honestly, that's never bothered me."

One minute of silence drags on, two.

"You better not be looking at me with sad eyes, Vaughn, or you're going to get bitch slapped and I'm just the bitch to do it." I look over and find him with his head propped up, a crooked smile and half moon eyes twinkling. "What about your father?"

His face lights up. "He's great. The best. We're very close. He's one of the reasons I went to law school. He's a federal judge."

That makes me smile. God knows why, but it makes me feel better knowing that his dad was there for him when his mom was sick.

"Did he remarry?"

"No...he was only forty-five when she passed." His gaze cuts to the fire. "I guess some people only get one chance at love."

"Love?"

At the query his gaze returns to me, the emptiness that filled it a moment ago replaced with curiosity. "Yeah, love. You know, romantic love, soul mate kind of love."

I can't. I can't even. The snort cannot be contained. "Soul mate love?"

"What? You don't believe in soul mates?"

"Are you serious?" His nonreply prods me to continue. "If you believe in that, then I've got some horrible news for you. Brace yourself, the Easter bunny isn't real, either."

Surprise, shock, doubt. Each one takes a turn on his face.

"You don't believe two people can fall in love and stay in love? What about all that grand gesture stuff?" He's searching for clues that I'm messing with him, which he is not going to find because I am as serious as a tax audit.

"Yeah. That's why we need movies and books and music. Because real life is as bleak as shit. And as far as falling in love, you can thank some powerful chemicals for that. The rest of it is a made up thing—like Christmas—to get us to spend money on holidays. It's purely a commercial construct."

"But you've been in love?"

"Of course, I have. I was in love with Damien Gatti in the fourth grade. He told everyone he caught me picking my nose, which was pure fiction by the way. In the seventh grade it was Billy Hansen. He never looked my way once—actively avoided me on a number of occasions. Turns out, he was looking in Jon Renavitch's direction. In the tenth grade it was Steve Boran. He was in love with me. He was also in love with the entire cheerleading squad. Need I go on? You're personally experiencing the repercussions of my last altercation with love."

I've baffled him. He's baffled.

"What about Cal and Cam?"

Tucking my hands under my face, I give his query good thought. "Random act of God. Black Swan event. Even a broken clock gets it right once in a while. Call it what you want."

His brow furrows. In his eyes, I can see that now familiar streak of stubbornness asserting itself. "My parents were crazy about each other."

"And your father never remarried. What's love done for him?"

"But they had it. When it was good it was great."

"This from the man who avoids relationships like the plague." I fluff my pillow and get comfortable.

"Maybe it's about finding the right person," he says staring into the fire, gold tracing the sharp line of his jaw, of his straight nose. He almost looks sad as he says it.

"And maybe unicorns run wild in Yellowstone National Park. Careful, counselor. Someone might mistake you for a romantic."

"And if I am?" His attention returns to me. He's smiling, but there's no humor in his eyes. Or his voice for that matter. I'm only half awake and I can still see he's hiding something.

"Whatever helps you sleep at night." Adjusting my pillow, I get comfortable. The dry heat is making me drowsy, my eyelids fluttering shut. "Fancy…"

"Yeah?"

"Thanks for coming home early," I mumble somewhat coherently, sleep seconds from claiming me.

"Sweet dreams, Jones."

Turns out, my dreams were all about him. And there was nothing sweet about them.

CHAPTER FOURTEEN

IF MY LIFE WAS MY anything like my favorite romantic comedy of all time, *When Harry Met Sally*, this would be the part where the super cute montage would play. Cue the running in Central Park together. Cue us sharing an ice cream Sunday at Serendipity and him wiping whip cream off the side of my mouth with his finger, then sucking on it. Cue us going to see *The Book of Mormon* and chuckling as we exit. And I would be wearing hats. Because naturally all cute montages require hats, even though I never wear hats in real life. Breaking news: none of that nice shit happens. You know what does however? Bickering—lots of it.

"Try it," he says—or rather, taunts.

"I don't wanna try it. Just looking at it makes me want to hurl."

"I never took you for a coward."

"I'm a coward because I don't want to put that in my mouth? Look at it! Why would anybody in their right mind put that in their mouth?"

The silence that follows makes me nervous. I glance up from my cell phone—I routinely like to torture myself by checking Facebook to see how fabulous everybody else's life is in comparison to mine—and find him coming around to my side of the kitchen island armed with a dish of the kale he's been cooking.

"Get away from me with that!"

"A small taste isn't going to kill you." I jump off my stool and run to the other side of the island, keeping a safe distance between the stuff he's holding and my mouth. "It might actually add a couple of minutes to your life."

"Or, I might gag on it and choke to death."

"You wouldn't die. I'd perform the Heimlich and if necessary mouth-to-mouth resuscitation," he informs me with a smug smile.

For obvious reason, I glower back. "You're creeping me out."

"Then you'll owe me for saving your life."

"Another reason not to touch that sludge."

The doorbell starts ringing. And rings. And rings. My eyebrows shoot up my forehead. "If this is one of your pussies, I will lose it."

"One of my what?"

I don't wait to see what his face makes of that, I take off for the front door. "Hold your goddamn horses!"

The incessant ringing is making me mental. I rip open the front door because I need to make my irritation clear, and find the perpetrator of this crime against my ears looking up at me with a sullen pout.

"Audrey?" I mumble in bewilderment.

"Amber."

Still a cheeky little shit. "What are you doing here?"

She struts right past me wearing a backpack large enough to trek across Antarctica with, banging it against my hip in the process.

"Ouuuch. Jeez, what do you have in there, a dead body?"

"No," she answers, as if it were an actual possibility.

"What are you doing here?"

"You said we could hang."

"Uh, yeah, but generally you call first and make plans." Ignoring me, she drops her backpack and kicks off her Uggs, shrugs off her down jacket.

"Is that your boyfriend?"

I turn and find Fancy standing in the hallway, sleeves rolled up, jeans hanging on his hips, feet bare. I'm so used to his masculine bling, I hardly notice it anymore. And yet I can imagine what any other straight female would be thinking— even a thirteen year old one.

Drying his hands on a dishtowel, a wide grin breaks across his face as his gaze jumps from me to Audrey. Meanwhile, Audrey stares up at him with stars twinkling in her green eyes.

Another one bites the dust.

"She's a fun size version of you."

"Hel...uh...I mean heck no. He's not my boyfriend." Ethan scowls at me. Looks like I may have wounded his delicate male ego. "Can you please take your animal magnetism elsewhere? I need to have a chat with my sister and you're scrabbling her brain."

"Sister?" He looks mildly shocked at first. A second later his amusement returns with a vengeance.

"Half-sister," I amend.

"There is absolutely no chance of me missing a minute of this," he replies with way too much interest in his voice.

Awestruck, Audrey continues to walk around like she was invited to do so.

156

"How did you know where to find me? Does Eileen know you're here? And how did you get here anyway?"

"Google. You mentioned his name. No. A bus."

"That's…disturbing. Phone please," I order, holding out my hand.

"Please don't call them yet. Please!" In seconds, she's on the verge of tears, her face contorting. *Teenagers, smh.* "Please, Amber. You know how she is. She's the worst mother! She leaves me home alone all the time and she never picks me up from school on time. I'm always the loser sitting on the front steps at school waiting for the crappy parent."

Dramatic streak a mile wide in this family. Family…*huh.* Yeah, I guess we are some kind of family.

"First of all, watch your language." Trust me, the irony is not lost on me. I get a super sulky look for that. "Second, Dan is a good man. He's a good father. Some people don't even have one parent, let alone two."

As soon as the words are out of my mouth, I realize that there's another person in the room who can attest to that. His eyes hold mine for a minute longer than I deem necessary while something big passes between us. I can't explain what it is, but I can feel its significance.

"How about some hot chocolate?" Ethan drapes the dishtowel over his shoulder and raises his winged eyebrows in question.

"Okay." Audrey beams sunshine and rainbows up at him, her smile so broad she's in serious danger of popping off her purple braces.

Minutes later in the kitchen, Audrey and I take a seat at the island while Martha Stewart, also known as Ethan, is making fancy hot chocolate. I eyeball the purple container with French writing as he turns and slides two mugs across the granite counter.

"You get your hot chocolate powder at *Vosges*? Really?" Across from me, he takes a sip, heavy-lidded eyes watching me over the rim of his mug.

"You know I like the good stuff," he murmurs in a voice that can only be described as seductive. It makes me uneasy, this subtle, but not so subtle change in him. "Why are you squinting?"

"I'm not *squinting*," I answer. I'm suspicious by nature, therefore I shrug his strange behavior off as me being suspicious by nature.

"You are."

"Agree to—"

"And what's with the A names?" he says, talking over me.

I shrug. Because really, the truth is simply that pathetic. "Most likely Eileen was too lazy to get beyond the first letter of the alphabet."

He snorts. "That can't be true."

"I wish I was kidding."

"I want to be just like you when I grow up."

I glance at Audrey and find her staring at Ethan with a goofy grin decorating her face. "No, you don't," I argue, horrified at the thought of Audrey aiming so low. I want so much more for her.

She turns to face me, her expression suddenly serious. "Yes, I do. You're my hero."

"Did you sniff glue before you came over? I'm not even a grown up. In fact, you'll probably beat me to it. You're probably a better grown up at thirteen than I am at almost-thirty."

"I'm nothing like you. You're super cool and I'm a loser. You're not scared of anything. And you have a super hot boyfriend."

I'm speechless. Also, I stopped listening after she called herself a loser.

"I will address the ridiculous things you've just said in order of importance. First of all, don't ever, *ever* call yourself a loser again. I hate that word. *Hate* it. What does that even mean? What are you losing at? From where I stand you're smart, funny, and you have your whole life ahead of you to get it right. I don't even have medical insurance. I eat all the wrong foods at the wrong time of day. I didn't finish college." I can tell by the look on her face I have yet to sway her opinion. "I don't even know how to drive a car! Second, let's use the word *super* a little more judiciously. You're throwing it around willy-nilly."

"You don't know how to drive?" says the eye candy across from me, the baby v between his brows only making him more appealing. This attraction thing is getting really inconvenient.

"No. And him—" I say, pointing to said eye candy. "He doesn't even like me."

"I like you," someone murmurs in a disgustingly low, sexy voice.

The hell?

I do a double take, my focus returning to the hot piece who just spoke. Casually leaning against the counter with his arms crossed, highlighting his spectacular biceps, his smug expression is directed straight at me. I don't like it. I don't like it one bit. My eyes narrow and my lips curl around my teeth in displeasure. At my *are you freaking serious face*, his smile gets even brighter.

"He had to bail me out of jail for starting a fire at my ex-boyfriend's house!"

"That is sooo cool," says the junior criminal in training that I share blood with. All I see is purple metal for days.

"Stop smiling. That is *not* cool. Not even in the least bit, Audrey. I could be going to jail. Real jail. Not *Orange Is the New Black* jail. Bad stuff happens in real jail. I don't want anybody calling me Sparkles."

"Why would somebody call you Sparkles?" she asks with an adorable look of confusion.

Sighing loudly, I answer, "Never mind."

"You're not going to jail," Ethan announces as if he's judge and jury.

"Thanks, Nostradamus, but you can't say that for certain, can you?"

"Do you trust me?"

My irritation crumbles in the face of that sweet, earnest way of his. "You know I do," I mutter sourly.

"I won't let that happen." Underscoring his promise, those devastating eyes hold mine.

"This is sooo cool. I'm so happy you're my sister." I glance at Audrey and find her mid-swoon, licking fancy hot chocolate off her top lip. I take in the happy expression and metallic grin.

"Time to let your parents know where you are," I say, holding my hand out for her phone.

* * *

As if our differences weren't already glaringly obvious, where we shop for our food is another perfect example. He's a hardcore Whole Foods fanatic where as I'm more likely to shop at the corner Seven-Eleven than walk ten blocks to go to a real grocery store.

"There's nothing for me to eat here," I whine while I push the cart loaded with a bunch of healthy crap down the grain aisle. "Everything's brown. I'm not a fan of brown food. I prefer food with color. Specifically Blue #1 and Red #40."

He caught me as I was stepping out the front door to go to the corner market and summarily steered me in the direction of his favorite place.

As usual, Ethan's busy ignoring me. He grabs a box of quinoa and holds it up for my edification. "You're not getting any younger, Jones. Time to start watching what you eat."

Not getting any younger…same thing Marty keeps telling me.

I randomly pick up a small box of rice. "12.99 for a tiny box of brown rice? Was it harvested by the fingertips of angels? Did a fairy fart gold dust in here?"

Ethan's quelling raised eyebrow does not *quell* me. A beat later his expression changes to surprise.

"Jane?"

My gaze tracks Ethan's over my shoulder. A woman wearing a bright smile stares back at us. She's the girl next door, pretty in a wholesome way. Pin straight brown hair, delicate features. She's even wearing pearls with her cashmere sweater. I've got a bad feeling about this, and the pit in my stomach agrees. Ethan has a smile on his face, the genuine kind. The pit gets larger.

"Jane? What are you doing in New York?"

The two of them hug. It doesn't take much for me to infer that this is some kind of long lost lover, or maybe an unrequited love. Whoever she is, Ethan seems to genuinely like her in an unfriendly like manner. As far as I'm concerned, *Jane* sucks.

As they exchange pleasantries, I'm forgotten. That doesn't bother me. What does, however, is that Ethan's face lights up every time he looks at *Jane*.

"And you said you'd never move to New York," he says, beaming sunshine and rainbows at her. The fire-breathing dragon that lives in the darkest nook of my soul rouses from deep sleep.

"Yeah, lesson learned. Never say never," replies *Jane*, with a lilting chuckle.

Her attention shifts and finds me looking bored. She smiles. "We're being rude," she tells Ethan, who looks at me like he suddenly remembered I exist.

Yeah, jerk, you're being rude, my eyeballs say while my mouth stays shut.

"Jane this is Amber, Amber Jane." The way he says her name makes me want to stab him in the neck with one of those overpriced, wooden spoons made from the hands of blind little old Peruvian ladies I saw in the kitchenware aisle. I slap on a super fake smile.

"Nice to meet you, *Jane.*"

Her rosebud mouth quirks at the inflection in my voice.

"Likewise." She turns her bright smile on Ethan. "Well, I should get going. Scotty's waiting for me."

This does nothing to appease the fire-breathing dragon. For all I know, Scotty could be a Scottish freaking Terrier. I immediately look for a ring. No such luck. *Jane* is wearing gloves.

Ethan watches her walk away with a soft smile on his obnoxious face. I'm pretty sure if I open my mouth I'm going to start saying stuff I'll regret, inappropriate stuff, stuff that I have no right to say. Therefore, I keep my lips locked tight, only allowing for an occasional 'yes' and 'no' for the rest of our shopping expedition. Given my propensity for saying inappropriate stuff on the regular, I give myself major kudos for that.

As soon as we get back to the house, I plead a headache and bolt to my room. The perplexed, semi-hurt look on Ethan's face elicits not one drop of sympathy from me. This experience only cements the fact that I need to keep some distance between us. We've been getting way too chummy lately. It is madness to have any feelings, proprietary or otherwise, for this man, pure madness for a multitude of reasons.

My cell phone signals.

Fancy: I made buckwheat noodles with pesto. Want some?

I've barricaded myself in my bedroom like a moody teenager.

Me: No thanks.

My pride won't allow it even though I'm starving and the noodles sound utterly delicious. *Don't you fucking dare, you spineless pathetic excuse for a female,* she whispers in my ear. My pride is a vicious bitch. She scares me. I don't dare cross her.

Fancy: I'll leave some for you anyway.

By nine, I've managed to distract myself from sulking with a couple of episodes of *The Affair.* The door to the bathroom swings open and Ethan is standing in the doorway in nothing but a pair of pajama bottoms hanging low and a toothbrush hanging out of his mouth. And by the looks of the V taunting me over the waistband of his bottoms—no underwear. God almighty, what does he have against underwear?

A deep flush starts at my scalp and moves all the way to my toes. Actually it feels more like I'm being roasted at the stake. I'm chalking this up to my cooch being lonely. You can't blame her. She hasn't had a visitor in a really long time.

Grabbing the toothbrush, he says, "Are you mad at me?"

My attention darts back to the television screen. "What makes you say that?"

"You haven't said a word to me since we left Whole Foods."

"I have a headache." The quiet provokes me to steal a glance. His eyes are on the script I'm holding, his brows drawn together.

"Can't be that bad if you're reading and watching TV."

Note to self: you're an idiot and for future reference, stay away from lawyers.

"Thanks for the brilliant analysis, Sherlock, but it is—and you're making it worse."

"You're definitely mad at me."

"I'm not mad at you," comes emphatically rushing out of my mouth. "Why would I be mad at you?"

"Exactly. Why would you be?"

"I wouldn't."

"And yet, you are. Why?" His expression says I may as well be the Sunday Times crossword puzzle. He can't make heads nor tails of me.

"I'm not mad at you, damn it," I bark. "Do I need to draw you a happy face?"

Crossing his arms, he cocks his hip and casually leans against the doorframe like he hasn't a care in the world—not a care. Which only serves to fuel my rage. "You're downright furious."

"I am not mad!" Popping up on my feet, I'm standing on the bed I'm so freaking mad. "God! You're such a megalomaniac! Everything isn't about you. Sorry to disappoint, but I haven't sucked down the Jonestown brand of Cool-Aide! I don't think you're the sexiest thing since Bieber hit puberty! My panties aren't about to start a five alarm fire by *exploding* or *disintegrating* or *combusting* every time you bat your eyelashes. My panties are just *fine*. So save it for *Jane* and the rest of the pussy parade!"

His expression morphs from surprise to...what's he smiling about?

"Now if you don't mind, can I have some privacy?" Pointing to the door, I fall back down on my ass. He doesn't budge, though his smile grows increasingly wider. "Vaughn, if you don't stop smiling, I am going to throw something at you."

Unfazed by my threat, he stands, extends his arms, and then proceeds to stretch from side to side. True story.

"Go do your little aerobic stretches elsewhere please."

"I'm going."

"Good."

He's still stretching. I can see him from the periphery of my vision. My blood pressure must be at three thousand. I'm ready to bust a vein.

"I left a bowl of noodles on the counter in case you get hungry." With that, he closes the bathroom door behind him and I flop onto my back.

I'm so hungry I'm ready to chew my arm off. As I stare at the ceiling, my stomach growls at me. I'm pretty sure it's saying that the last thing I should be doing is listening to my damn pride which is not to be trusted with our welfare. I give it a respectable fifteen minutes before I sneak downstairs and inhale the delicious noodles. My pride and I are no longer talking.

CHAPTER FIFTEEN

"I'M DOING A *BLACK SAILS* marathon. These bitches are badass. What I wouldn't do to get on a show like this," I say into the phone, the one squashed between my shoulder and ear. After which, I shovel a spoonful of rocky road ice cream into my gapping pie hole. The lounge being closed for a private event, I'm making good use of a rare Tuesday night off by binge watching my favorite shows in the newly renovated den.

It's been two days since Audrey's impromptu visit and Ethan's been acting strange. Strike that, *stranger*, ever since. After we let Dan and Eileen know that Audrey was not chained up on a rack in the dank basement of some nice man who likes to experiment with knives, Ethan made dinner. He's actually an amazing cook when he's not trying to poison me with his kale concoctions. Since then I keep catching him looking at me with a puzzled frown. Well, no, not quite a frown, but a look that says he can't figure something out and it's frustrating him. To that I say join the club.

In the meantime, David has been making progress with the case, trying to negotiate with the Gregorys some kind of settlement that doesn't entail me draining whatever money my Grandmother leaves me so I can stay out of jail.

"What I wouldn't do for the time to watch a single

episode," Camilla whines. "The traveling gets old fast. I'm actually excited that I'm not allowed to fly anymore."

"Stop complaining. At least, you're getting some on the regular. If something doesn't give soon, I could wind up on a sexual offender list and the first victim may very well be my roommate. He has no idea what kind of danger he's invited into his life."

"What about Kurt? All that ink..."

My mind shoots straight to Kurt, one of the security guys at the lounge, and a shiver crawls over me.

"Nope. Mouth breather. We made out once. I wasn't sure if he was trying to kiss me, or practicing CPR."

"That's not good," she says, stifling laughter. "What about that cute bartender that only works on Thursdays?"

"Shane?"

"Yeah, what about him?"

"I slept with him after Parker the Penile Implant dumped me."

"*That's* the guy you had revenge sex with?"

"Yeah, except the revenge was on me."

"I'm scared to ask."

Hunting for a stash of marshmallow, I pick through the ice cream and hit pay dirt. "Porn sex."

"Oh, God. What does *that* mean?"

"Ass slap, hair pull, pump, pump, pump, ass slap, hair pull, pump, pump, pump. Turns me onto my back. More of the same. Porn by numbers."

"Ugh."

"Besides, he's bare down there. Not my jam."

"Bare? As in totally bare? Men are doing that?" she says, practically gasping.

"Welcome to twenty first century. How was your trip?"

"How the frig am I supposed to know this? I've only seen two in my entire life."

"Anywhatever, now do you see why I prefer dicks of the plug in variety? He managed to put me off sex with another human being since then."

Speaking of humans. A man suddenly appears in the doorway of the den. Tie and jacket discarded, hair messy from running a harried hand through it. He ambles into the room and heads straight for the couch.

"Somebody just stepped into my den of iniquity," I whisper into the phone. My eyes commit a lecherous perusal of his person. "He wouldn't even have to do any work. He could just lie down and close his eyes."

Camilla chuckles. "Don't leave any evidence. You know I can't lie for shit and I don't want to raise my child in jail."

"Call you later," I mumble and hang up.

He drops onto the opposite end of the couch with a tired sigh.

"Long day, counselor?" I place the spoonful of ice cream back into the container, and before I know to protect my booty, he snatches it out of my hands. That's booty as in treasure, not as in my nonexistent ass. I wouldn't be upset if he snatched my ass—the ice cream is a different matter altogether.

"Heeeyyyy."

Ignoring me, he starts eating, slowly bringing the ice cream laden spoon to his lush mouth. Yes, I'm staring again. Sue me for having ovaries. If I didn't know any better I would think he's trying to seduce me with the way he's sucking on that spoon. Except, I do know better.

Blindly, he stares at the television screen as he eats—the new television screen that is.

"Hmm, the draft."

"You've officially hit your quota on that word. Unless you want to see me on the evening news mowing people down with a BB gun, you will refrain from using it ever again." That's all he's been talking about lately. The draft this, the draft that. Every time someone orders a draft beer at work I get a nervous twitch of the eye.

A lazy smile brightens his face. "Occupational hazard. What about you?" His eyes drop to the script I'm browsing, and as he's looking down, I'm looking at him. A smear of ice cream on his top lip taunts me. For the love of lips, I'm human. How much temptation can one woman resist?

"You're doing the spacing thing again."

Right, if he only knew.

"Second call back tomorrow for a play. It's a small part, but it's juicy."

"You'll get it," he says with absolute conviction. My insides feel fuzzy. I don't know whether it's the way he's looking at me that's causing it, or his unwavering belief. No one other than Camilla has ever had belief in me of the unwavering kind. Some belief? Sure, my grandmother. Waning belief? Marty, as of late. But unwavering? Nobody else.

"Why would you say that?" I ask, my tendency to be suspicious of anything good cropping up. I'm simultaneously starving for his good opinion, and ready to discredit it for no-good reasons whatsoever.

"Because I know you'll give it everything you've got and leave nothing on the table."

His words hit me in a soft spot, part of me embarrassed at his unabashed praise because I'm not sure I deserve it. At one time, I did. I was that person, no holds barred, balls to the wall. I was born that way. Except I've spent so much of my life trying to make myself small to please other people, or rather not to aggravate them, that I forgot who I was along the way.

Sincerity. That's all I see in Ethan's eyes when I look over. And as I stare into them, an epiphany hits me with the force of a speeding car. The decision I've been hemming and hawing over for years suddenly seems so clear. And I'm pretty sure my face is wearing my thoughts because Ethan tilts his head and regards me curiously.

"I'm going to do it," I blurt out.

"Do what?"

"Move to L.A. as soon as I legally can. You're right. I can't have it both ways, and time is running out for me. I have to give it an honest shot—" I'm nervous, talking quickly, this revelation suddenly so clear my heart is racing. "Leave nothing on the table."

He slow nods in understanding and takes another bite of my ice cream, his eyes glued to the bottom of the container. And as I watch him something tender and fragile unfurls in my chest. Something that scares me.

"What's with all the women you're always running from?"

He turns to face me with one of his signature cocky smiles, but there's something missing. Something he would have no problem hiding from someone that isn't as adept at pretending and hiding as I am.

"Believe it or not, I'm considered a catch," he replies

without looking at me, his tone irreverent. Though I detect a sour edge.

"I don't doubt it," I murmur. "I don't doubt the women of Manhattan would find you the crown jewel of bachelors."

He's gorgeous, smart, a decent human being. On top of that he's also wealthy and successful. What's not to like? Not my thing personally—hard not to look like *Igor* standing next to him. However, I could see how other, more ambitious women than myself would welcome the challenge. He would make quite a trophy.

And that's when it dawns on me.

"You don't like it. You're not interested in women that are attracted to *this*," I say, motioning up and down the delicious body draped on the couch with legs spread apart. The spoon pauses halfway to his mouth for a moment, then continues its journey to its sexy destination.

"You're not."

Maybe abstinence has robbed me of the ability to decipher all things male because I have no clue want he means. Is he bummed that I'm not into him? I sense a hidden question lurking beneath the surface, but who knows—maybe I'm imagining it.

His eyes are still fixed on the bottom of the pint of ice cream. Annoying. I desperately want to see what the windows of his soul are telling me and I can't from this vantage point on the dratted couch.

"No. Nothing about you is appealing to me. Not even a lil' bit."

Heavy lidded eyes peer back at me, a smirk decorating his mouth. "I've caught you staring at my ass, Jones."

He thinks he can shake my confidence with this? This is

child's play to me.

"That's because it's so big. How exactly does one get a butt to bubble like that?"

His lips purse, pink blooms on his high cheekbones. I smother the urge to laugh in his face. It's about time I had some fun at his expense.

"Skating. Lots of ice hockey when I was a kid. Tennis."

"I've been to a couple of Rangers games and I have yet to see one that looks like yours," I say, head shaking. "Yours is abnormally bubblicious."

A coughing fit ensues, a lot of pounding on his chest. "I think you've made your point."

"Besides, I'm not like other women—" For this, I get a snort. I go to lightly shove his hip with my foot and he grabs my ankle, wrapping his long fingers all the way around it, and squeezes.

That feels...crap, that feels good. Too good, in fact. I retract my leg and he lets go. "I'm done with relationships, and marriage is dead to me. It *sleeps with the fishes*. I never want to hear the word ever again. Besides I've got Garrett and Gabriel and the rest of the boys to keep me company." If that doesn't shut this topic down for good, I don't know what will. I watch the corners of his lips creep up around the spoon in his mouth. "But enough about me. Why no girlfriend—or wife, for that matter?"

"Getting the job with the Titans is the only thing on my radar right now."

"That savors strongly of bitterness," I respond, quoting *Pride and Prejudice*. He doesn't get it because, poor thing, he's male. The confused quirk of his brow impels me to continue. "What happened? Did you get dumped in the tenth grade by

Whitney the WASP queen for Chet the king of the yuppies?"

His expression turns pensive.

"Her name was—is, Hope. She's a professional tennis player. And she didn't dump me for Chet, she dumped me for Jake—my older brother."

My face falls, all humor wiped away. I didn't expect him to answer, which is why I'm surprised. My surprise, however, is quickly overshadowed by shame. All of a sudden I feel an inch tall. This has got to be tender territory, and with my mouth's tendency to run as rampant as a bull in a china shop, I may have trampled it, as evidenced by the look on his face.

"Fancy—" I sigh.

"It was a long time ago. I'm over it." He shrugs, shoveling more ice cream into his mouth. Eyes still ahead, not a single glance in my direction. After which, he licks his bottom lip and I'm back to ogling him...somebody save me from myself.

"Did you beat the snot out of them? Was there a nice spinning hook kick to the face?"

His chuckle is low and husky. The vibration travels through the air and lands between my legs. I grip my knees together and pray he doesn't notice.

"Only in my mind. Everyone was very civil. I even went to the wedding."

"Do NOT tell me you were the best man."

He gives me a one sided smile that I know is hiding some leftover pain. "No...he asked, though. We were close once, really close."

For some incomprehensible reason I want to go Hulk right now. I want to turn green, stomp off to find his infernal brother, and beat some sense into him—for Ethan's sake. I don't want Ethan to be hurt. I don't want him to have that look on his face. He's a grown man and yet I want to pet his pain away. To be clear, this is bad.

"Then what? They ride off into the sunset of their epic love story and you skulk away quietly?" I do my best to temper the anger in my voice, though apparently my best is not very good at all. I can hear myself shrieking and it's not pretty.

"Then..." He sighs, gazing blindly at the television. "Then, I went back to school, partied too much, got kicked off the tennis team, slept my way through the female student population, and wound up in the ER with meningitis." His gaze flickers to mine, searching for a reaction, maybe looking for judgment that he won't find.

"Impressive."

"Cal saved my life. If it wasn't for him, I'd probably be dead."

Wait a minute...*dead?* I try to imagine never having met him, not having him in my life, and a pain grips me, the likes of which I've only felt one other time in my life—when Eileen sat me down and said I wasn't going to live with her anymore.

"He took me to the ER when I refused to go...even got a black eye for it."

He's rendered me speechless. We sit in silence as I process all the stuff he's lobbed at me.

"Why on Earth couldn't you leave that part out?"

"Pardon?" He looks confused.

"I have to be nice to him now. Like all the time. Do you have any idea how difficult you've made my life?"

He takes a long, hard look at me, his lips twitching in repressed mirth. "I'm flattered, Jones. If you're even considering being nice to Cal, you must like me a heck of a lot."

"Slow your roll. It's not a done deal yet. Being nice to Cal requires a serious amount of like."

A huge, white grin spreads across his face. A real one, the kind with the capacity to halt trading on the DOW and cause a power outage in lower Manhattan.

"It's an embarrassing amount, isn't it?" He adds. "You hate yourself for it."

All evidence of the humor that was on my face seconds ago is gone. Boy did he hit a nerve. That's what it feels like. Part of me does hate that I like him so much. And that's the last thing I need, or want.

He sees the look on my face and the smile melts right off of his. "I didn't mean it, Jones. I was teasing."

"I have laundry to do," I mumble, shooting up off the couch. I don't get far though, because I'm suddenly tackled to the ground, sandwiched face down between the wood floor and two hundred plus pounds of muscle. I struggle for about a half a second before I give up.

"Get off of me, you load."

His low chuckle tickles my ear and makes me shiver. "Not until you accept my apology."

"Ever consider going on a diet?"

He flips me onto my back and secures my arms over my head with scary ease, his hips holding mine down, a slow heat working its way along my body. The weight of him alone is giving me enough pleasure to drive a loud sigh up my throat. And by the smug grin he's just given me, he noticed.

"I was teasing you. I know you don't like me. You've made that very clear."

I struggle some more. I huff. I refuse to look at him. I do everything to avoid giving him even an ounce of satisfaction. "This is funny to you?"

"A little."

That's when I feel a very, *very* hard protrusion against my leg. The smirk that overtakes my face is downright evil. "Who likes who now?"

"That's biology. A reflex. I could rub up against a lamppost and it would happen."

Umm, really? Because I'd be interested in seeing that.

"It's biology alright, it's a freaking anaconda!" I shout, feigning appall. "I'm reporting you to PETA for animal cruelty." *Is he blushing? Oh good, he's blushing.* "I'm telling them you keep that thing in inhumane conditions."

His mild blush turns fire engine red. So naturally, smelling blood in the water, I go for the kill.

"How many unsuspecting women have you maimed? How many stuck their hands down your pants and drew back a stump?"

"Shut up, Jones."

"Or what?" Incredibly immature of me, but also— incredibly satisfying.

His eyes spark with challenge. "Or I'll make you."

Something in his tone quells my laughter. I look into determined brown eyes and ignore all the warning signs. "Very cute, counselor. No one's managed it yet, but I'd like to see you try."

His lids drop, heavy with what looks like...lust. Burning brightly, his gaze falls on my lips and my smile falters. *Oh crap.* Too late. I realize much too late how I played this all wrong, how badly I've misjudged him. My wide-eyed gaze meets his. That's all it takes for him to make his move, for his lips to crash into mine.

At first the kiss is hard, as if he miscalculated in his excitement. Just as quickly he pulls back and softens his touch, brushing his lips back and forth on mine, testing me. In the meantime, I'm frozen. Partly in disbelief, partly because I'm afraid I'll wake up to find I'm dreaming.

One large hand cradles my face and I'm completely swept away by the tenderness of his touch. Gentle. Reverent. Magic. He slants his mouth and fits it onto mine. And it fits. It fits perfectly, as if he's tailored just for me.

His tongue sweeps the seam of my lips and God help me with a dazed sigh I open for him. He tastes sweet, the ice cream we shared minutes ago still on his tongue, on his pouty bottom lip. He's ruined rocky road ice cream for me. You can bet that every bite I eat from now on won't taste nearly as good.

He hums and I hum right along with him. Because this feels right. *He* feels right. Everything about him does. The taste of his lips, the weight and warmth of his body, the smell and feel of his skin.

My hands skate over the tense muscles of his glorious back. Under my fingertips, I can feel the energy coiling tightly within him pulsing, his bare grasp on it. And in the back of my dirty as dirt mind my inside voice keeps telepathically willing him to let go, cut it loose, unleash whatever it is that's holding him back.

Do it. Do it. Do it, the devil inside my head chants.

He shifts his hips and the head of his erection hits me right where I need to be hit—and hit *hard*. Instinctually, my body bows into him, desperate for more, longing for everything.

A moment later I feel a cool rush of air as he rips his lips off mine and vaults up onto his feet. I watch him walk away, rubbing his face, his gait awkward as he adjusts the log that's jutting out between his legs.

"Can't," I hear him mumble.

This blows.

CHAPTER SIXTEEN

"HER NAME IS CHEYENNE. SHE'S a twenty-two year old model from St. Petersburg—Russia that is, not Florida—and her name is *Cheyenne*. How much you wanna bet she doesn't have a drop of Native American blood in her veins?"

We're both crammed in the Bloomingdales dressing room. Camilla is busy examining the navy dress she has on, pushing her gigantic boobs around as if she could knead them into getting smaller while I sit in the corner doling out orders. Straightening and smoothing the lower part of the dress, eyes still trained on the image in the mirror, she says, "How's that? How do my boobs look? Be honest."

"Like you're hiding two pot belly pigs in your bra."

She tears her gaze away from the floor length mirror and levels me with a glare I've seen her use on her rambunctious third graders. Her lips twitching in repressed mirth, she says, "You know what I'd like to hide? My fist in your eye socket."

I take a big bite of the Swedish fish I bought at Dylan's Candy Bar. "Get in line. And you said to be honest." Pointing my headless Swedish fish at a cream colored dress with dolman sleeves, I say, "Try that one on." With her skin tone, cream always looks amazing on her.

"I don't have a single thing that fits me anymore," she

huffs. "If I can't find something today, you'll be seeing me in a Hefty bag next." She strips down to her underwear again. Her body is stunning, big belly and all. Left and right she turns. She turns again, checking herself out in the mirror. Her lush mouth creeps into a frown.

"Stop showing off," I snap. "Your mother called me about a baby shower."

Camilla's attention whips back to me. There's violence in her eyes. "I'm only going to say this one more time. I do NOT want a baby shower. I'm fat. I'm mostly in a bad mood. And nothing fits me. My husband keeps buying shit we don't need. We have so much shit I'm not even unpacking half of it; I'm sending it directly to the Red Cross and some other children's charities. Which is only making more work for me and Mercedes. So help me God, if someone organizes a surprise baby shower, I will commit bloody murder."

I chew my candy slowly, my brows halfway up my head. "So you don't want a baby shower?" Her nostrils flare and I know not to push her any farther. "No wedding and no baby shower. You're no fun. For the record, I want you to make a big deal out of mine—unless I'm forced to marry my prison mistress, in which case let's never talk about it."

"No one is becoming a prison wife. At least, no one I know." She gives me one of her signature side-eye smirks. "And I had a wedding."

"City Hall does not count. Speaking of weddings, Parker's getting married at the botanical gardens."

Camilla's large brown eyes widen then narrow. "That's where you wanted to get married—how do you know?"

"Facebook."

With a disapproving frown, she says, "I thought we

agreed you were going to stop using."

"It's either Facebook, or flog myself."

"I hope he gets gangrene of the testicles." She says this with a look of pure disgust on her face. This pregnant version of my best friend is proving a lot of fun.

"I like where your head's at. Speaking of testicles, my roommate is giving me blue balls." She seems unimpressed by my prior statement so I up the ante. "He kissed me."

Her eyes cut to mine again, this time sparkling with interest. "He did?"

I slow nod. "It was good, too."

Good? The understatement of the year. More like burn the house down good, no chaffing dishes required.

"And?"

"And nothing. Nothing can happen. He could get disbarred. *Apparently* it's unethical to sleep with your prisoner, or ward, or whatever I am."

"Imagine that," the wiseass drawls.

"My book boyfriends aren't even cuttin' it anymore." I point my fifth Swedish fish at her. "This could get ugly if I don't get laid soon."

She slips the cream dress over her head. "I'm still processing that you aren't sleeping with Justin."

Time for the obligatory eye roll. "Why is that so hard to believe?"

"Oh, I don't know—maybe because he was always coming over and hanging out in your bedroom when I lived with you. What else would you be doing in there?"

"Talking. He's a big talker. There was a small window of opportunity in the beginning. Until he told me I reminded him of his older sister, the one who raised him, and that window closed in a New York minute."

"Nooo," she says, choking back laughter as she zips up the dress.

"Yep." I shove a handful of the gummy bears in my mouth. "Young men. Gotta love 'em. Be glad you dodged the dating bullet twice."

Camilla turns toward me, the cream dress hitting her in all the right places.

"What do you think?"

"I think we have a winner."

* * *

Audrey has been texting with alarming frequency lately. Three nights ago, as I was going through my lines for yet another commercial I found out this morning I did not get a callback for, I got this at eleven pm.

> **Funsize: what's your favorite type of food?**

> **Me: Italian. Shouldn't you be asleep?**

> **Funsize: me too!!!!**

> **Me: Easy with the !!!!**

> **Funsize: who was your first kiss and how old were you?**

Oh shit sticks.

> **Me: I was 26 and it was at my engagement party.**

Funsize: :(((((((

Me: :/ fine it was Robert Winchell and it was a spin the bottle situation. I was 14.

An egregious lie. I was barely thirteen, but she doesn't need to know that. The texts didn't stop there.

Funsize: what's your favorite color?

Funsize: If you were a *Game of Thrones* character, who would you be?

Me: You're allowed to watch GOT??!!

If this is anything like what I put my grandmother through, I would've gotten rid of me. The texts eventually graduated to phone calls. This happened last night at...you guessed it, eleven pm.

"What do I do to get a guy I like to notice me?"

Not even a hello. What happened to hello, please, and thank you? My grandmother would have a conniption if she knew.

"Nothing—until you turn seventeen."

"Come on."

I chew on her question for a long while. "I don't think anyone can answer that question, Audrey—Oprah can't even answer that question."

"Please, Amber," she whines.

"Who is this boy?"

"His name is Grady and he plays baseball and draws his own comics and he's a really good artists."

"He's in your grade, right?"

"Yeah. We sit next to each other in art."

Thank God for small favors. "Well, the short version is that boys are dense and they only see what they want to see. The long version is that sometimes it takes a grand gesture to get their attention."

"A grand gesture?"

"Yeah, something that puts you under the spotlight and shows them how awesome you are and that they've been missing out." I can't believe the bullshit coming out of my mouth. However, I suspect she won't stop until she gets something out of me.

"So...what do I do?"

"Since you noticed how talented he is, maybe you can find a way to show him how talented you are."

A long pause tells me she's mulling this over.

"Okay, yeah, I can do that."

"And Audrey—"

"Yeah?"

"No more eleven pm strategy sessions. Get some sleep."

"K, bye."

That's why I'm not at all surprised when I received a text from her half an hour ago as I'm on my way to work asking if I'm busy. What I was not prepared for was this—

> Funsize: I'm at the Manhasset mall and mom and dad aren't answering. Phone almost dead. Come and get me.

In a panic I called Fredo for a ride to Long Island. He was at the townhouse not fifteen minutes later, God bless his heart.

"Don't worry. We'll be there in no time," he tries to assure me.

Yeah, it's not working. I nod as I blindly stare out the passenger side window and rub my sweaty palms on my jeans. Rationally, I know he's right. And yet I can't seem to stop my stomach from churning. I've never felt this kind of anxiety. And quite frankly, if this is what being a parent feels like, then sign me up for tubal ligation surgery, stat.

"Do you have kids?"

"A son. He's sixteen." Fredo throws me a brief smile. "I'm blessed. He's a really good kid."

"Did he ever pull any teenage nonsense on you?"

Fredo's expression grows thoughtful before he answers. "He didn't have it easy growing up. I was going through some stuff." With a sideways glance, he gauges my reaction. "Being unemployed for so long gets to you. I went through a bout of depression."

If bartending has taught me anything, it's that each and ever one of us has a little red wagon of issues we drag around. Sadly, nothing surprises me anymore. "Are you doing better?"

He nods, a small smile softening his blunt masculine features. "Every man needs a purpose, and being able to take care of his family is an important one."

"Her friends ditched her at the mall and she has no money for a cab. How would you handle it?"

"My two cents. Don't say or do anything impulsive. Hear her out first. Take it from someone who's learned how to parent by trial and error."

By the time we reach the mall I've lost half my body weight in sweat. I once drank three Monster drinks in a row and felt nowhere near as jittery as I do now. The car hasn't even come to a full stop and I'm out the door, yelling at Fredo to meet me inside and to keep his phone close. The weather still being on the chilly side I warned him that she could be wearing purple Uggs and most likely carrying a purple backpack.

In the food court, I spot her sitting by herself, chin in hand and staring at her phone. Relief spreads through me, the sweat on my back and forehead cooling. Shivering, I wipe the sweat on my forehead with the back of my hand. As I walk up, I notice that she's flipping through her Instagram account and a pickle of unease crawls up the back of my neck.

"I thought your phone was dead?"

Startled, she looks up with big wide eyes. Something stinks and it's not the fast food.

"Tell me you didn't lie. Tell me you actually called your parents." Anger bubbles up from my gut because I already know the answer to that. Her gaze falls to the floor, her bony shoulders curving.

"Audrey!"

Suddenly, she stands. "I'm sorry!" she wails. Some of the mothers and kids sitting nearby turn and stare at the commotion. I tell them to mind their own business with a glare.

"I can't believe you!" I grind out, jaw in jeopardy of snapping in two. "Get your things and let's go."

"I'm sorry, okay." She ducks her head and shoves her backpack over her shoulders, pulling her sleeves over her hands. Oh please, is she crying? Of course, dramatic streak a mile wide in this family.

"You're crying? Really? I'm losing about 400 bucks in tips tonight and you're crying? I'm the one that's crying, Audrey. On the inside. I'm inside crying for being so goddamn stupid."

With that, I turn and start marching through the mall. In the meantime, I shoot Fredo a quick text that I've found her and to meet us out front.

"Why did you come?"

"Because that's what I do, I chase after things," I say, yelling my response while ironically walking away. Audrey picks up the pace, staying right behind me.

"Things, or people?"

"Both."

"People you love?"

My feet come to a hard stop and Audrey bumps into my back. "Yes."

"Does that mean you love me?"

I turn and find her peering up at me with nervous anticipation, her eyes still wet, her cheeks pink. Why doesn't she just drive a stake through my heart? Maybe dangle some garlic under my nose.

"Yes. And Audrey, here's a serious warning. I *despise* manipulation. Manipulating me will only make me love you less, so don't do it again."

Lying and subterfuge are tedious and time consuming. I don't possess the requisite energy or desire to keep track of lies. That is why I always go with the truth—no matter how painful, ugly, or savage.

Without missing a beat, she throws her skinny arms around my waist and hugs me tightly. My arms hover over her shoulder, unsure where to land.

I don't know why I'm surprised at her open display of affection. I remember all too well how much I craved it when I was her age. I would do anything to get attention, which means I was often obnoxious, which also means I usually received none. It was a vicious cycle. One I don't want Audrey falling into.

My arms fold around her, my hands running up and down her back as she presses closer. "Let's get you home."

"I love you, too. In case you didn't know," she blurts out, her voice muffled by my clothes.

"I know."

"Are you gonna tell Mom and Dad?"

I give her the old suspicious eyeball. "Not this time. This is your one get out of jail free card and you just used it."

She nods. Keeping my arm around her, we make our way to the parking lot.

CHAPTER SEVENTEEN

"WANT TO GO TO THE gym with me?"

I rip my eyes off a very good episode of *The Affair* and level the man that has just spoken with a disbelieving expression. He's standing in the doorway of my bedroom in track pants and a hoody. Ugh, he even manages to make a hoodie look sexy. Who does that?

I've been avoiding him. There, I said it. The first step in recovery is admitting you have a problem. I've been avoiding him for this exact reason—I can't be around him without conjuring up the lewdest, filthiest images. The shit I want to do to him is illegal in approximately 50 states. I'm not sure about Massachusetts and North Dakota, and I can't Google it in fear that should something happen to me, someone would find it on my browser history. It's not his fault that I've acquired the worst case of puppy lust since the creation of puppy lust. He's a witless victim. In mind only, as of now. If I keep hanging around him, he'll be a victim for realz.

I tuck the French fries I was diligently shoving into my mouth a second ago into the side of my cheek. "This may come as a shock to you, but all this awesomeness—" I motion to said awesome body, "is *au naturel*. I do not work out."

That said, I resume chewing.

"I'm going to Chelsea Piers to do some rock climbing. You should come." He lifts his arms and stretches from side to side, which causes his t-shirt to ride up, exposing his ridiculous abs and happy trail. I stop chewing.

"I'm busy," I say, my eyes glued to that freaking trail of happiness. The one I'd happily trace with my tongue if it wasn't grossly inappropriate.

"You don't look busy."

"Well, I am…busy…eating."

"I think you should come with me."

I look up and find a knowing smile on his face. The hell is he smiling at? My eyes narrow. "No, I don't think I want to," I respond and shove another French fry in my mouth for good measure.

"Yeah, you do. I'll feed you. I'll take you to Sarabeth's for brunch after."

"Tempting, but—no."

"Unless you're scared to break a nail."

After a full two minutes of silence, I find my voice. "Did you just say scared?"

Twenty minutes later, hands on hips, I'm staring up a forty-six foot wall, cursing my pesky mouth. It's a ninety degree angle of death. This place must be a freaking graveyard. It must be.

"Where are the bodies buried?"

"Excuse me?" says Shaggy of the Scooby Doo gang, also known as the safety instructor. He looks confused. And clearly feigning stupidity because, let's face it, what's he going to do once the harness breaks and someone plummets forty-six feet to the ground? Nuf said.

"How many people have died here?" I annunciate

carefully and loudly.

"Uh, none." His eyes fill with worry. They flicker in Fancy's direction, searching for a lifeline. News flash: there 'aint one. Fancy is much too concerned with checking his harness for his K2 ascent.

"Our odds are shit," I say to Ethan. The lack of response prompts me to glance his way. Where I find him very busy ignoring me. "According to the Law of Averages—and Malcom Gladwell—had someone fallen to their death recently, we would be okay. However, if what Shaggy here says is true, then the next person to climb could very well be the first fatality."

"We happen to have a perfect safety record," interjects the safety instructor who sounds a bit put out.

After pinning Shaggy with a weighty glare, I dismiss him. Still prepping, Fancy has yet to come up for air once. "Ethan."

His head jerks up. The sharp look in his eyes takes me by surprise. "Say my name again." His voice is low, huskier than usual—and does strange things to my female parts. A hair singeing flush starts at my feet and shoots straight to my scalp. The intense scrutiny makes me nervous, makes me want to hide.

"You're my get-out-of-jail-card, Fancy Pants. If something happens to you, I'm going to have to pull a *Romeo and Juliet* and follow you to the grave."

The spark that was in his gorgeous eyes only a minute ago dissipates, which makes me feel like garbage. I'm a coward. I'm a bloody coward and fully admit it. I can't say it. Because in that one unspoken word, his name, a thousand unrequited sentiments lie behind it. Yearning, lust, friendship, respect. Pick one—they're all there. It's an effing smorgasbord of feelings that I vowed to avoid like the black plague until my career was off the ground. And yet here I am, having them for a person that is unequivocally off limits to me. Add insult to injury, he's much too perceptive for his own good. I can't let him see how I feel about him. That would be beyond mortifying.

"Hold my crown while I do this," he says, a blinding white grin on the tail end of it. Another one of his unique gifts. Like he has a clear line of sight into my thoughts and knows when I feel cornered, when I've been pushed too far.

"Yeah, yeah. Stop flapping those lips and focus on staying alive."

"Watch and learn, Jones."

He begins climbing as he does everything else in life— carefully, thoughtfully, methodically. He finds a hand hold, grabs it, testing it before proceeding. Then he finds the foot hole and does the same.

He shucked off his track pants before harnessing up and is presently in his shorts and a v neck t-shirt. Long, sinuous muscles outlined by the sweat soaked t-shirt band across his back. The power of his shoulders on full display as he pulls himself up. And that hiney? Goodness sake, have some mercy. Have some freaking mercy. I want to take a bite of it. I want to sink my teeth into each juicy, muscular globe. I want to…

There's a dude standing next to me. And he's busy doing the exact same thing I'm doing—violating Ethan with his eyes. An immediate impulse to defend my turf steals over me. I perform an open inspection of my competition. Tall, bald, and muscular. I stare at his closely shaved head in the hope that he'll feel the heat shooting out of my burning gaze. For my effort, I get nothing.

"Yo." A minute passes, two. "Hey," I go with this time, a little more force in my voice. Finally, he deigns me with his attention. "You're barking up the wrong tree, bud. He's into hot pockets, not corndogs."

My so-called competition crosses his arms and performs a pointed inspection of my person. It's all very *National Geographic*, two opponents sizing each other up. And since I'm practically a professional at this, I do not blink. After a full two minute stare down, he walks away. I'm getting a pretty good idea of what Fancy has to go through every time he steps out the door and I do not like it one bit.

My attention returns to the man in question. He's only one more foot hole from the top. As soon as he reaches it, he looks down at me, over his shoulder, and smiles. Somebody start thumping on my chest. I think my heart just stopped. After that, he rappels down, taking with him my eyeballs, which seem to be glued to his ass. Don't judge.

He walks up beaming that same unguarded smile.

"What? That's supposed to be impressive? I'm supposed to be impressed? A monkey could do that in half the time."

Hands on his hips, breathing deeply, he says, "It's not as easy as I made it look." Then, he grabs the bottom of his t-shirt and wipes his sweaty face with it, a six pack I could shred cheddar cheese on in my face.

"Don't you have a towel for that?"

When he drops the t-shirt, his expression is a combination of amusement and confusion. He steps closer and I automatically take a giant step back. He barks out a laugh, and puts his hands up.

"Easy there, jumpy. I'm just checking your harness."

"Fine. Do it. Just 'cuz I don't want to die." I hold my arms out while he checks the tightness of the straps. He's so close I have to hold my breath in fear I'll get woozy from the pheromones pouring off of him. Head down and expression hyper focused, he tugs and pulls on the straps, the backs of his hands brushing against my stomach and hips. Thank the good Lord I wore leggings and a long sleeve shirt.

"Okay, that's good. I got this," I say, scooting away. Grabbing some chalk, I clap my hands together, making a big show of it, outwardly exuding confidence while a larger part of me wishes I was wearing a diaper.

Whatever. It'll be fine. I'm athletic and very nimble. I took years of modern dance and some gymnastics when I was a kid because it was the only way to burn off all the energy I had. How hard can this be? I look up again and my stomach plummets.

"Are you sure? Because we can do it together. I can talk you through it."

"Shhh, quiet. You're messing with my mojo."

Ethan's lips quiver while I'm all business, zoned in and focused on recalling the path he traveled.

The first half of the wall is easy. I'm getting the hang of this rather quickly. This rock climbing thing is fun. I never doubted myself, not for a minute.

As I make my way up the rock, I can hear Ethan shouting words of encouragement. Right, like I need him to play cheerleader. Before I know what's what, I reach the top. Much faster than I anticipated. And now...

Huh? Now what? Now what? Now...what? At this point I am desperately trying to recall what Shaggy said while I was busy making googley eyes at the man I live with, my friend, who I have less than zero business making googley eyes at.

A million scenarios run through my mind at once. In the meantime, I begin to sweat a little, my heart beating a little bit faster. Then I look down. I shouldn't have done that. I definitely should *not* have done that.

The blood rushes out of my head and goes straight to my feet. My mouth is so dry I can't even lick my lips. My hands are shaking. The shaking spreads, infecting the rest of my body parts.

"Are you okay?" Ethan shouts.

No, I'm not okay. I am so far from okay, I can't even see okay on the horizon. A screechy wail reverberates in my head. Sounds like one of those howler monkeys on *Animal Planet*. Then I realize it's me. I'm the one screaming. Except nothing is coming out of my mouth. I can't even feel my tongue.

"Hold on. I'm coming to get you," a deep voice shouts.

I'm paralyzed, clinging to the wall by fear alone because my limbs are jelly.

"Amber. Hold on." His voice draws closer. "Be there in a minute...almost there."

As soon as he reaches me, I go to grab him.

"Easy," he says in a low, soothing voice when I almost dislodge the both of us from the wall.

"Ethan." My voice is reed thin. Trying not to hyperventilate, I focus on soft, brown eyes.

"Ethan."

"I'm here."

"Ethan."

"I'm going to talk you through it and we'll rappel down together."

"Ethan."

His lips twitch. "That's the fourth time you've used my name since we've met. We may have to stay awhile so I can hear you say it again."

If I wasn't about to faint, I'd deck him. "Get me down."

"Look at my legs," he orders. "See how they're spread and stiff against the wall?" I nod vigorously. "Do it." Without delay, I do as I'm told . "We're going to bounce gently off the wall as we rappel down together. Slowly. Keep a firm grip on the line but not too firm." With that, we begin our descent.

The minute my feet hit solid ground, the adrenaline drains out of me, instantly replaced by two things: a bone deep weariness and out and out fury. I don't think. I just react. I cock my fist back and punch him in the gut...and hurt my hand in the process because I may as well have hit a brick wall.

"Ouuuuuch. You asshat!" I scream. I shake out my hand and cradle it. "All I wanted to do was binge watch *The Affair* and eat French fries!"

Before I get a chance to say another word he wraps me in a bear hug, my face smothered between his pecs while his arms hold me securely. I have no fight left in me, my limbs sapped of all strength. Instead, I burrow closer and let him hold me up. And then I get a giant whiff of him.

What is it with this guy? He's like catnip, or crack cocaine—totally intoxicating, completely irresistible, and most importantly, a *very* bad habit. Not only does the man stink of virility, but there's something so darn comforting about his scent. That's the dangerous one. Virility, I have no use for. As a matter of fact, he needs to keep that shit as far away from me as possible.

"Athhhat," I half shout, my voice muffled by the hills of

muscle I'm squashed between. His chest heaves from the laughter he's trying to contain.

Gripping my shoulders, he holds me away and inspects my face. "Are you hurt?"

"I'm fine," I snap, indignant as all get out.

"Right there," he says, pointing to a spot on my shoulder, his laser focused stare on it.

"What?" I grumble sourly.

"A dent in your pride—"

He barely has time to finish the sentence because I launch my fist at him again. Except this time he's faster. He catches it in his hand and brings it to his lips, placing a quick kiss on my knuckles.

I shouldn't be smiling. I really shouldn't be. But I am.

* * *

I can never, *ever* show my face at Chelsea Piers. We step outside. The river walk along the Hudson River is jam packed with women pushing strollers, cyclists, runners barely avoiding us.

"Ethan?"

My eyes rise off the sidewalk to find the owner of the feminine voice. Dressed in workout clothes, she's tall and super fit, pretty in a 'I'm too sure of myself and naturally beautiful to care what I look like' way. *Hate her.* Her platinum blonde head tilts, her long ponytail swaying in a disgustingly adorable manner as she studies me with a quizzical expression. It's then that I realize Ethan has yet to say a word. One quick glance reveals he's stiff as a corpse and just as pale. His jaw is locked and his usual crooked grin absent.

"What are you doing here?"

Wow. Fancy Pants rude? Never would've imagined it. A

second later, a near carbon copy of Ethan walks up to the blonde and hooks a wrist onto her shoulder. This man's features aren't nearly as refined. He's a bit rougher around the edges, and older by the look of the lines fanning out from his eyes. Though, in his own way, just as handsome. My CSI skills lead me to deduce that they must be somehow related.

Four sets of eyes bounce around. We all stand there quietly for far too long, pretending it's not awkward when in truth it is awkward as fuck. No surprise that I'm the first to lose my patience and decide to take care of business.

"Amber Jones, nice to meet you," I announce, sticking my hand out to the handsome stranger.

His smile is genuine, reaching his eyes—if not a little tempered. "Jake Vaughn, nice to meet you, Amber. This is my wife Hope."

Holy mother of all mothers. The brother and the infamous ex. Ethan's dodgy behavior makes sense now. The ex extends a hand and we shake.

"We're in town for a photo shoot so we thought we'd stay for Norma's birthday party," Jake offers.

"She didn't tell me you were coming." Ethan's voice is almost unrecognizable, low and angry.

Eyes crinkling at the corners, Jake looks off into the distance, clearly uncomfortable. "That doesn't surprise me."

Another eternal three minutes passes in silence. I can't take it anymore.

"Anywho, as much as I'd love to continue this *riveting* conversation, someone—" I hook a thumb at the stiff standing next to me, "—promised to feed me." I turn to find Ethan looking back at me with...relief. He's relieved, his crooked grin back on his beautiful face. The same smile that makes my heart lurch inside my chest...*crap.*

Time to redirect this very self-destructive train of thought. "Sugarpuss, you know how unbearable I get when I'm hungry."

Ethan's lips twitch up before he manages to press them into a tight line. He can't keep the smile out of his eyes, though. "I sure do, babe."

Babe? I need to not like that as much as I do.

Something in his eyes draws me in and holds me captive. I'm momentarily flummoxed, my world narrowing until there's only him. Only us. I don't know what kind of voodoo this man practices, but it needs to stop.

Someone clears their throat. "I guess we'll see you at Norma's," Jake says, while Ethan and I continue to stare at each other.

"Guess so," Ethan absently answers. Then he threads his fingers between mine, and yanks me away from sporty Ken and Barbie. As we make our way up the riverwalk, he raises our joined hands up and takes a long measured look.

Judging by his expression, he's as confused as I am. I would give a kidney to know what he's thinking right about now. I don't have long to wait, however, because he shakes his hand loose and wraps his arm around my neck, tucking me onto his side.

Gasp. That feels amazing. So amazing I press even closer and indulge in another covert whiff of his scent, my eyes practically rolling to the back of my head. And as I'm doing so, I catch sight of Ken and Barbie. They're still standing there, watching us. My hand glides down from Ethan's waist to his perfect booty, where I manage to get a nice handful and squeeze. A strangled cough comes from my human grope toy.

"Have a nice trip back to wherever you came from," I shout over my shoulder. Jake smiles while Hope frowns.

Ethan looks down at me. "Sugarpuss?"

"Better than Fancy McButterPants?"

The amusement is still there, on the face I've come to know so well. "Not by a long shot."

I'm almost certain he's going to let go, but he doesn't. Instead, he holds on tighter. For another ten minutes we walk in comfortable silence, millions of people all around and I barely notice because I have the object of all my dirty dreams touching me. Not because he has to—because he wants to.

The world starts to melt away. People all around us, running past us, riding their bikes, walking their dogs. And yet it feels as if we're the last two people on the planet, enjoying each other's quiet company on a lazy Sunday afternoon. I close my eyes and soak in all the feels, letting his steady presence be my guide.

"Thanks," he says, a pronounced rasp in his voice. Something about it garners my immediate attention. My eyes slow blink open, narrow at the sunlight flooding in.

"For what?" I glance sideways and find him staring straight ahead, as serious as I've ever seen him.

"For being awesome."

My stomach sinks. My heart stops beating. Boom. I'm dead. Or something like it.

CHAPTER EIGHTEEN

IT'S THE SECOND TIME THIS week I made the trek to New Jersey. Lately, I find myself wanting to see my grandmother any chance I get, as if we're on borrowed time, which in all likelihood we are because of her disease. Or maybe we're not. Maybe time has already run out.

"Margaret?"

My grandmother turns and takes me in. I look for a sign that she recognizes me—a spark, a furrow of the brow, any glimmer of hope—but nothing, she may as well have laid eyes on me for the first time in her life. I'm a stranger to her.

"Do you remember me?"

Her expression is flat, at best a touch inquisitive, if that. She gives me one of her polite smiles, one I know well from my time working at the funeral home with her. It's the same one she would give to grieving family members while she explained how much a funeral was going to cost them. You'd be surprised to learn how expensive it is to die.

"How are you?"

She smiles again, her gaze moving over my face as if she's trying to figure out who I am. I'm momentarily excited that she's on the brink of remembering me.

"I'm fine. How are you?"

"Good...good." I struggle to come up with something that won't confuse or frustrate her. "I'm Amber," I say, continuing with caution.

"Right, Amber. I thought you looked familiar." She grips and releases the arms of the chair, a gesture I know means she's a bit nervous. "You remind me of my daughter."

My heart leaps. This is more than she's said in the last few weeks.

"Really? What's your daughter like?" I'm on the edge of my chair I'm so excited.

"Oh, she's wonderful. She's a great daughter. She comes to visit me all the time. Brings me gifts."

Uhhhh, no. No, she doesn't. *I'm* the one that comes all the time. *I'm* the one who brings gifts. My mother comes to visit her maybe three times a year. And that's only because it's on her way to the Short Hills Mall to shop.

"What's your daughter's name?" It's dangerous for me to ask questions. I know this. And yet I can't help myself.

Her paper thin lips, ruffled on the edges by time, press together in deep thought. Something sparks in her eyes. "Eileen," she says. Overjoyed at the recollection, she beams a smile at me. The only smile I've seen on her face in months.

Even though I want to laugh and shout and hug her, I'm simultaneously crestfallen. Because although I'm glad she remembers Eileen, a daughter she was never close to, a daughter that has never lifted a pinky to help her, I'm a stranger. Me, the person that gave up everything to help take care of her. That has always been there for her. I'm the stranger.

"You remember Eileen?

"Of course, dear. Why wouldn't I?"

This of course compels me to continue—against my better judgment. "What do you remember about her?"

"She's a real beauty. I'm very proud of her. She won Miss New Jersey." No she didn't. She partied hard and passed out in front of her hotel room door the night before the second day of competition and was immediately cut from the pageant. It's one of my favorite Eileen stories. "And she's a good daughter." My grandmother grows serious, a slow to develop frown replacing the soft smile she wore not a second ago. "Unlike my granddaughter."

Her words hit as forcefully as a physical blow to the solar plexus, knocking the wind out of me.

"What do you mean?" I croak.

"She's a whore."

I struggle to keep my emotions hidden as hard as I struggle to breathe. "You don't mean that."

"No other way to say it, dear. The girl is easy. She spreads her legs for any loser that smiles at her. She was always trouble, that one. Right from the start." She waggles her index finger. "Staying out late...the short skirts." Leaning closer, she whispers, "I don't think she wore undergarments half the time." After which, she purses her lips in a disapproving look.

I'm stunned. I'm stunned and shaking. In my mind I'm screaming, *You mean your daughter! You mean Eileen!* But I keep it to myself. I can't argue with her.

"What's your granddaughter's name?" I dare ask, my voice raspy and raw from bitterness.

She frowns, her thin, gray eyebrows drawing together in deep thought. Her index finger on her lips, she stares out the window looking for answers. "I...hmm...I...her name is...her name is..."

She huffs out a sharp breath. She's getting upset, working herself up into something that could turn into a fit. With that in mind, I rush to distract her.

"It's okay. It's okay, Margaret. You're daughter sounds wonderful. You're very lucky to have her."

Her pale blue eyes clear of the confusion and meet mine. "Why are you crying, dear?" Her brow puckers—in worry this time. Her hand presses over her heart. "Is it something I said?"

"No," I tell her, head shaking. I wipe my cheeks with my palms and conjure a smile I'm not feeling. "I'm just thinking about how much I miss my grandmother."

"Is she gone, dear?" she asks with a sympathetic smile.

Nodding, I answer, "Yes, she is—and I really miss her."

* * *

"Jones?"

I don't answer, hoping and praying he goes away. I can't face him right now. I've got nothing left in me. No jokes. No easy words. No energy to keep him at bay. And I'm tired. So damn tired I could sleep for a thousand years. None of me is soft. I'll admit it. I'm all sharp angles and sharper words, but am I really that hard to love?

"Amber? Are you okay?"

I should've known that stubborn streak of his wouldn't allow him to walk away. "I'm fine." I hear the squeak of the wood door creeping open. "I said I'm fine."

"You're sitting in the dark—listening to Alanis Morissette. You're not fine."

That I Would Be Good plays in the background. I didn't realize it was still playing. I'd lost track of the music, lost track of the time, lost track of my will to fight.

He pads to my side of the bed. "And you're sitting on the floor."

"I'm not in the mood to talk." My voice cracking, it's all I can muster out. I rarely indulge in feeling sorry for myself. I'm not prone to bouts of tears. Everyone has a hard limit, however, and today I've reached mine.

Standing a few feet from me to the left, all I can make out is Ethan's silhouette as he removes his jacket and tie, and throws them on the bed.

"I…" I sigh, the sound brimming with defeat. I've never been so thankful for the cover of night, grateful that I can't see his expression because I'm ninety-nine percent certain that if I see pity on his face I will erupt in a flood of tears. "Really Ethan, I'm not in the mood for company."

"We don't have to talk. I've had a long day, too. All I want to do is sit in the dark and listen to Alanis. And here you are— doing that exact same thing." He sinks down to the floor next to me, back against the bed, long legs hitched up and his elegant wrists resting on his knees. His body heat soothes me. Radiating from his upper arm, where we touch, it spreads like an antidote to the sadness infecting me.

He is so good. This man is as good as it gets. Strange how someone you think you have nothing in common with could turn out to be someone who understands you implicitly. Never in a million years did I suspect that he would turn out to be someone I could say anything to and feel accepted. And yet here he is before my very eyes.

"Nothing like some angry chick music to help me decompress," he deadpans.

My smile turns into a chuckle, which turns into tears. In seconds I'm sobbing, curling into a fetal position and sobbing like I may never stop. Ethan wraps a heavy arm around me and pulls me onto his lap, his strength absorbing the awkward tremors and jerks that for the life of me I can't seem to get a handle on. The vibration of his soft murmur, words I can't make out, makes my skin tingle. The fingers he pushes into my hair, raking it back and massaging my scalp, make me shiver.

I'm so tired of fighting this thing between us, tired of trying and failing on a daily basis to keep him at arm's length. It's not only the physical comfort he gives me willingly, it's understanding, it's lack of judgment. He takes me as I am, sharp angles and all.

We sit like that for a long time. Long after I've drained gallons of tears onto his dress shirt, and wiped my snots on his shoulder. Long after the hiccups stop.

"My ass is killing me," he quietly admits. We both snort and chuckle.

I'm about to get off his lap when he grips me closer. Tucking me securely against his chest, he stands with no effort whatsoever. When he places me on the bed, I have no choice but let go of his neck and instantly feel the loss of him.

I can't remember ever letting anybody other than Camilla catch me in such a vulnerable state. Face wrecked and raw, soul laid bare, emotions delicate, and ego battered. And yet my natural instinct to protect myself, to put a brave face on it remains quiet. The dragon sleeps peacefully.

For a moment he doesn't move, only stands there watching me while the moonlight spilling in through the open curtains traces his features in blue, his expression serious. I'm too tired to try and decipher what it means, or what he's doing when he strips off the tear soaked shirt and gets into bed next to me. I don't even make a peep when he hauls me against his side and wraps me in his arms again.

"Want to talk about it?"

"No…it's embarrassing."

"More embarrassing than looking like road kill on New Year's Eve?"

I snort and pinch the non-existent fat of his waist. "Ouch."

"You deserved it. And yes, more embarrassing than that."

"I think you'll feel better if you talk about it. We're friends. Isn't that what friends do for each other?"

Friends. He's turned into the best friend a girl could wish for. That alone makes me want to get hysterical again. In the silence, I listen to him breathe, feel the steady beat of his generous heart under my palm.

"I went to see my grandmother today." When I don't continue, he squeezes me closer and waits. No platitudes, no easy assurances, no junk––just patience and gentle persistence. In the end that's what persuades me to tell him everything.

"My grandmother's the one who raised me. My grandfather died shortly after I moved in so I never got a chance to know him. My grandmother was old school." I catch my mistake. Was…is. Is she anymore? "I mean she's old school. You know, children should be seen and not heard and all that. When I was in high school, I had to harass her to buy me jeans. If it was up to her I would've been wearing skirts and dresses to school. I wasn't allowed to date, so of course I was always sneaking out and getting grounded. My curfew was always much earlier than everyone else's. But over the years we learned to get along.

"My sophomore year at Yale I got a call from the police.

She'd forgotten how to get home from the grocery store. That's how I discovered that she had Alzheimer's. She'd been keeping it a secret for a while. Anyway—I dropped out of school and moved back home."

"Hmm."

"She knew she could count on me. The only reason she insisted on making my mother power of attorney was because she wanted me to finish school and pursue my career. She didn't want her illness to hold me back."

"She loves you."

Memories barge in uninvited, dragging me back to my childhood. "I used to think she hated me. She was always correcting me, criticizing me. She thought that changing me would make my life easier."

"What happened today?"

I burrow closer to him and still I'm not close enough. I want to get so lost under his skin that they have to send a search party to find me.

"She's getting worse. She doesn't remember me." Disembodied, my voice sounds far away, as if it doesn't belong to me. "She said some horrible things."

"She's sick. She doesn't mean it."

The weight on my chest is too much. It's crushing the air from my lungs.

"I know. But it's hard…she's the only person in my family that's ever been in my corner, that's ever…" My voice fades out of existence. I can't say it out loud. I can't. It's too humiliating.

"Ever loved you."

All I can do is nod, my face brushing against his undershirt while his fingers run through my hair, combing it back.

"She might've been the first person to love you, but she won't be the last."

Madness comes on. The lyrics *'inadvertent hero, an angel in disguise'* rise above the rest. I can't disagree with Alanis.

CHAPTER NINETEEN

THE TIME HAS COME FOR the dratted birthday party.

Me: I can't go. I have nothing to wear.

Needless to say I am decidedly uncomfortable with the idea of not only meeting his entire family, but worse yet having to pretend to be his date because he can't manage to convince one little old lady that he is in fact *not* gay. I've never witnessed anyone coming out as straight. I'm not even sure it's a thing.

Fancy: I'll have my personal shopper at Bergdorf send something over for you to choose. Problem solved.

Me: I can't afford Bergdorf!

Fancy: I can.

Me: Never mind. I'll find something at the second hand stores.

Fancy: No second hand stores. Stop fighting this. You

wouldn't want to look ungrateful after everything I've done for you, would you?

I suck in a horrified breath. Man, he went straight for tender bits with that one.

Me: You fight dirty.

Fancy: Always. Don't ever forget it.

I step out my bedroom as he's stepping out of his. Simultaneously we do an open inspection of the other. I have on the J Mendel mini dress the personal shopper sent over along with a pair of black high heeled Manolo Blahnik pumps. The dress is simple and stylish and all kinds of amazing. Audrey would approve; it's purple. God knows what this thing costs. I've never worn anything this beautiful and expensive.

Fancy looks like his usual hideously gorgeous supermodel self in a lean blue suit with a black tie.

"You clean up nice, Vaughn."

"You're not so bad yourself, Jones. You have your overnight bag ready?" I motion behind me and he moves past me to grab it.

It feels like a date. It does. There, I said it. The whole dang thing is weird. I'm acting weird. He's acting weird. We're acting weird together. And yet, as weird as it is, it's still the best time I've had in a decade and we haven't even stepped out of the house.

If we weren't headed to this Vaughn family reunion I would actually be giddy with excitement. The night sky is bright with an infinite amount of stars. A beautiful man is opening all my doors. What more can a girl ask for?

I slide into the passenger seat of his Audi while he watches me with a look of confusion, his hand poised to shut the door.

"Christ, Jones, you're an actress. How hard can it be to act like you're interested in me."

What? Wait, what? Whatever he's trying to communicate is not computing. "I have no idea what you're talking about."

"That look on your face."

"What look on my face?"

He closes my door and gets behind the wheel. "The one that says you don't want do this. Look at it this way, if you can't convince my eighty-five year old grandmother that you're into me, then what hope do you have of making a career out of acting?" He starts the car and pulls out onto Madison Ave.

"You better watch it, McButterpants, or you'll get exactly what you're asking for," I warn with narrow eyes. "And I wasn't looking like I don't want to do this. I was just thinking that if I didn't have to meet your entire family tonight, I would be having a great time already...and this dress makes me nervous. It's too expensive."

There's that baby v again, sitting smack dab in the middle of his brow. "You were?" He sounds suspicious.

"Yes—I was." Okay, maybe that came out a little churlish. At the deafening silence coming from my left, I'm forced to look over and I find him wearing one of his panty exploding crooked grins. Which of course makes me begrudgingly smile back at him.

"The dress looks great on you."

My gaze swings out the passenger window to hide the

flush scalding my neck. "Getting a stalkery vibe from you again."

Half an hour later the Audi pulls up to an elaborate wrought iron gate. He punches in a code at the security box and the gate eases open to reveal an honest to goodness estate.

I can feel the corners of my mouth turning down. "Come on. Seriously?"

"It's just a dinner party, low key for her," he explains with a smirk.

I don't really give a fig about money. Other than for the purpose of it buying fantastic legal representation if you should so need it. Nor do I care either way about people that have money. Parker's family has money and it never mattered to me. However, this…this is intimidating.

The butler meets us at the door. My eyeballs are going to get a serious workout.

"Hello, James. Everybody here already?"

"Good to see you, Mr. Vaughn. Not yet." James takes our coats and we climb the marble stairs to the living room. Ethan's hand has been on the small of my back since we got out of the car, consuming enough of my attention that I don't have time to be nervous.

"What does one usually discuss at these things? Whose great granpapy came over on the Mayflower?" His eyebrow twitches but that's about it. That's all I get from him. "I'm going to stick out like a sore thumb. I don't know where my great granpapy came from. I wouldn't be surprised to find out he was a convicted criminal transported to the colonies."

As usual, Mr. Perfect is unfazed by my rant. "Just be yourself and you'll be fine," he nonchalantly states as we enter the room.

Be yourself? Be yourself? Most of my life people have been telling me *not* to be myself—and this man wants me to *be myself?*

Before I can give this epic event the thought it deserves, he pushes me into the massive living room. Thirty or so people mill about, talking and sipping cocktails. Every one of them turns to look at us.

"Come on, I want to introduce you to my father."

"No, no. Fancy, wait," I whisper shout.

Little good that does. Removing the hand he has on my back, he laces his fingers through mine and drags me toward a group of men in a corner. If it wasn't for the impeccable Turnbull and Asser suit, one of them could be mistaken for Paul Bunyan.

"Dad."

Paul Bunyan's smile is broad and bright. "Ethan, my favorite son."

Ethan smirks and embraces his father. Two stuffy looking middle aged men standing with Mr. Vaughn greet Ethan before they peel away under the guise of refilling their drinks.

"I want to introduce you to someone."

Ethan moves aside to reveal me. With an outstretched hand I step forward and Mr. Vaughn takes it, his hand dwarfing mine.

"Amber Jones, nice to meet you, sir, I mean, your Honor."

His warm brown eyes turn into crescents, the only feature he and his son seem to have in common. "Lovely to meet you, Amber, but please, call me Harry."

No chance of that happening.

"What time is dinner starting?" Ethan asks his father.

"Norma's still getting ready." Father and son share a knowing look.

While the two of them quietly converse, I'm happy to be forgotten, taking the opportunity to study the indigenous species. My favorite past time after watching movies is watching people and this scene is rife with entertainment.

"We met through Calvin—"

That garners my immediate attention. I find Ethan looking down at me with an amused twinkle in his eyes. He squeezes my hand. The one, I now realize, he never let go of.

"You'll have to introduce her to your brother," Mr. Vaughn says with an equally mischievous twinkle in his eyes.

"Jake and Hope already met her."

Is that pride I detect in his voice? Probably imagining it. Probably.

"Really?" Mr. Vaughn takes a sip of his whiskey.

"Yeah, we ran into them last weekend at Chelsea Piers. You didn't tell me they were coming."

"Didn't I?"

"No, Dad, you didn't."

"My bad."

My bad? The Honorable Harrison Vaughn says 'my bad'? This species is very interesting.

"Hello, friends and family," a whiskey roughened voice drawls. A woman's voice. Everyone turns. And there she is, standing at the foot of the stairs—the birthday girl.

This is not what I was expecting. I was expecting snooty elegance, a tight face in a Chanel suit. That's not what's floating into the room however. Nope. Norma Ellington is a hardcore hippie.

* * *

"So, no love match with Daryl? And I was so sure you two would hit it off." She pats Ethan's face and I draw blood biting the inside of my cheek to keep the laughter from exploding out of me. Shortly after Norma appeared and greeted her guests, she made a beeline for Ethan.

"There was never a chance of one because I am *not* gay."

Her curly white hair, swept back in a colorful silk scarf, dances as she nods in understanding. Or more precisely, feigned understanding. "There's no need to hide anymore, Darling. It's 2017, everyone's coming out of the closet. And not only do I accept you for who you are, but love you even more for your bravery."

"Mrs. Ellington, I can assure you that your grandson is not gay," I feel the need to say in his defense. I've never seen Ethan this close to losing his shit, but he is definitively almost there.

"It's okay, Dear, no need for you to continue the charade. I have you in two separate rooms. Just in case Ethan hits it off with Thaddeus, my hairdresser." She wiggles her bejeweled fingers at him.

And people think I'm too much.

"I'm not gay, Norma. Don't know how many times I have to repeat myself before you accept it."

"What makes you think he's gay, Mrs. Ellington?"

"Call me, Norma. Mrs. Ellington makes me sound old. Well, it's been years since he's dated anyone. We haven't seen him with a woman since that unfortunate incident."

"You mean the incident where I brought my girlfriend home for Christmas and she broke up with me to marry my brother."

"Yes, Dear, that one. But in the end, it all worked out. You were free to explore your sexuality, and your brother is happily married." Norma waves at someone in the distance, her gold bangles clanging. "Connie Sawyer is hitting the tequila hard. God help us all if she starts singing. She sounds like a pig in the midst of a death rattle." With that, she departs, leaving behind the scent of sandalwood and vanilla.

Hands stuffed in his pants pocket, Ethan watches her float away while my attention remains on him.

"How much weed does she smoke?"

"She grows her own," he says in a flat voice.

"And I thought my family was kooky."

Fifteen minutes later we're escorted to a large dining room that holds a very long table. It's lavishly decorated with heirloom quality crystal and china. The flower arrangements alone probably cost as much as my rent. Ethan pulls out the chair next to his for me.

Jake and Hope who walked in only minutes prior take the seats directly in front of us. This should be all sorts of fun. Hope's eyes dart back and forth between me and Ethan. After the quick examination, she's done with us, not sparing us another glance. Jake says his hellos, his eyes turning to familiar crescents when he addresses me.

Norma taps her glass with her fork and the entire room grows quiet. Raising a wine glass, she thanks everyone for coming and in return everybody wishes her a happy eighty-fifth birthday. Everything's groovy, until this…

"We're pregnant!" Hope gushes. Jake smiles. The congratulations start. Cousins and long time family friends get up and start slapping backs and kissing cheeks. At some point they all direct awkward, tight-lipped smiles our way, coupled with shifty eye contact. Impulsively, I reach under the table, take Ethan's hand and squeeze.

I don't know if he's still in love with her, and frankly, I don't want to know. Because if he is, that would mean that while I've been fostering the world's dumbest crush on the sweet guy sitting next to me, he's been pining after his brother's wife. Which would also mean that I've made the same mistake yet again—that I haven't learned a damn thing.

One glass of hemlock coming right up.

My gaze slides over, and finds him watching me with a gentle smile on his face and what is indisputably affection in his eyes. Although I've caught glimpses of it before, I've never seen it living out in the open like this. The fire breathing dragon yawns and goes back to sleep.

He lets go of my hand. Except he doesn't really. Instead of dropping it, he places it on his thigh and covers it with his own. My heart gets a little bit bigger, swelling inside my chest till it hurts.

The good times don't stop with the baby announcement. No siree. The baby announcement serves as a springboard for all kinds of jokes at Ethan's expense.

"Remember when E took Jake's fishing pole without telling him," cousin number one serves up as fodder.

"Yeah, E, remember the ass kicking you got for that," cousin two adds, his inflection riddled with delight.

"How 'bout when E crawled through poison sumac to spy on us in the woods," family friend number one feels the need to insert.

"I nailed Pam Simmons that night. That was a great fucking party," cousin number two cheerfully responds.

Classy. This is a classy bunch. And all the while, I can feel Ethan stiffen, the muscle under my hand rock hard with tension, his grip on me tightening with every jab.

"What about the Christmas party in Sun Valley when Ethan brought Hope and she dumped him the minute she got a load of Jake?"

The last one came from cousin number two. Brett, I believe this joker's called, who happens to be conveniently sitting next to me. I'm ready to stab this dude in the throat with my dessert spoon. In the meantime, Ethan remains as stoic as ever, noble in the face of all the asinine ridicule directed at him.

"Brett, stop. That's enough," his wife, Jennifer, chimes in. The voice of reason. I am *this* close to asking her if she needs me to alert the authorities because there's no chance anyone would willingly marry Brett.

I excuse myself for fear of shedding blood all over the Irish linen tablecloth and go in search of a bathroom. On the way I find the french doors that open onto a patio and decide that a little fresh air may be in order, more helpful in calming the firestorm that's brewing. I would love nothing more than to wipe the floors with this merry band of douchbags. The reason I don't, however, is that I wouldn't want to embarrass Ethan in any way.

Outside the air is crisp, winter making a last stand. There's a full moon out, the clear night sky littered with stars. I get a whiff of cigarette smoke and glance to my left to find a shadowy figure taking a drag. He blows out and shifts under a slash of moonlight, revealing his face.

"I promised my wife I'd quit," Jake admits, not in the least bit ashamed. "Can I count on you not to rat me out?"

"Absolutely not," I reply, while thinking, *lying sack of shit.* "I'd love to rat you out, but she'll smell it on you first."

"Probably." He follows that with a crooked grin that's almost identical to his younger brother's—not nearly as beautiful, though. "I'm ready to pay the consequences," he adds, flippantly.

Like the loud and proud bitch that I am, I see my opening and take it. "Speaking of consequences."

"Uh oh—"

"Your bother misses you." When that's met with silence, I decide to go for the kill. "I sympathize. I really do. It must be awful to know that your little brother was balls deep in your wife over and over and over—"

"Okay. Okay," he says, and follows it up with a dry chuckle.

"—long before you were," I continue, talking over him. "But you knew that when you started something with her, didn't you? I would think that family would mean more to you that your ego."

He continues watching me with a carefully neutral expression. The half finished cigarette drops to the stone patio under our feet and he steps on it. "You're right. I let it get weird."

"It's not weird, Jake. Everyone's moved on but you. You're the weird one. Hope seems fine with it. Ethan's fine with it. He just misses his brother."

That said, I turn to make my way back to the dinner party. I get as far as the door when I hear, "Hey." Stopping, I glance over my shoulder. "I'm happy for Ethan. Really—he deserves the best."

"Your opinion means nothing to me. How you treat Ethan does."

CHAPTER TWENTY

IT'S OFFICIAL I WON'T BE getting any sleep tonight. I'm too bent out of shape over what happened at dinner. It's my trigger. No mystery there, I recognize it for what it is. I can't stand watching someone being systematically taken apart by the people that are supposed to love them most. Granted it was done in jest, but it still ignites an indescribable rage in me. He's a grown man. And a lawyer, an accomplished one. Let's not forget that. He can handle his own defense without any assistance from me. However, watching his discomfort set me on fire.

I glance at my iPhone. Ten past midnight. Throwing off the covers, I march out of my room and head for the one two doors down without bothering to put anything else on. I'm in my shorts and tank top and too mad to give a damn. At my quiet knock, he says, "Who is it?"

"Your beard."

Without waiting for a response, I enter and find him in bed—naked. By the look of the sheet barely covering his privates, the only thing he seems to be wearing are his reading glasses...I think I just felt an egg travel down my fallopian tube.

He places down the book he was reading, and regards me

curiously. His brow quirks up.

"I can't sleep," I huff.

"I see that."

"Because I'm fuming."

He sits up in bed, clutching the sheet to that winning six pack, his expression alert. "What's wrong?"

"I don't like the way they treated you at dinner." The tension on his face eases. Mine doesn't.

"That's what they do. They don't mean anything by it."

I couldn't care less what they mean by it. I. Don't. Like. It. Their casual ribbing resulted in me watching a man I respect and care for, a good man when everyone knows there aren't a lot of 'em out there, a man that is most of the time good humored and upbeat, turn into an ice sculpture. Fuck that. Not on my watch.

"Get out of bed."

"What?"

"Get out of bed."

"You're starting to worry me, Jones."

"Do I have to ask again?"

He breathes out a tired sigh. "Turn around."

"Why?"

"Because I sleep naked." *Oh sweet baby Jeezus.* "My pants are on the chair." Instantly, I'm picturing the monster that lives between his legs in all its glory. *Triple sigh with a back flip.* Heat flares up my neck and south of my waist. Time to implement my plan before I forget what I came here for.

"Oooohh. Ooohh, yeah."

"Jones?"

"Ooooohh, oh, God. Ethan don't stop," I moan a ton louder this time. Then whisper hiss, "Are you decent?"

I get a cough, a clearing of the throat, and a muttered, "I guess."

As soon as I turn, I'm confronted with the reason for the strange reply. Ethan is standing at the foot of the bed, pajama bottoms hanging low, with an enormous hard-on he's trying and failing to hide under his hands.

"Ignore it," he mutters.

Right. Like traipsing through the desert and trying to ignore the oasis in my freaking face. Welcome to my theater of pain.

I walk over to the foot of the bed with my eyes aimed above his neck. And he's not fairing any better. Eyes wide, jaw locked, a streak of color across his cheekbones, he presses down on the kick stand in his pants and it bounces back—with force.

"Ooohh, God. Oooohh, God. Ethan, don't stop. Whatever you do, do not stop, baby."

I push the bed and it makes a loud thump. Eyebrows raised, he smiles and I smile back. Then he helps me shove the bed against the wall.

Thump. Thump. Thump.

"Ethan. Yes, like that! Yes! Yes! Yes! I'm coming so hard, baby!" My throat will definitely be sore tomorrow. "So hard. I'm coming. I'm coming. Yes! Yes! Yesssss!"

Falling backward on the bed, I say, "And the Oscar goes to...you think they heard?" I pick my head up off the bed to get a load of his reaction.

"The neighborhood heard," he says, chuckling, his bright grin stretching from ear to ear. My heart keeps doing things it's not supposed to at the sight of that smile.

"I'm sleeping in here tonight."

"Okay." His smile broadens.

Ugh, be still my stupid heart.

"But you're keeping your bottoms on."

"Okay."

"And your man parts on your side of the bed."

"Okay."

"Okay," I say as I crawl into bed.

He turns the lamp off and the room descends into darkness, his features outlined by a dim nightlight. I tuck my hand under my face and watch him get into bed, his eyes steadfast on me. This isn't the first time we've shared a bed. It's the first time I've been genuinely nervous, though.

"Is it hard for you to see them together?"

He gets comfortable. Barely twelve inches separate us as we lay face to face. "No," he answers without hesitation.

"And the baby?"

He shrugs. "I'm happy for them."

Nothing in his demeanor tells me he's dissembling. "Did she break your heart?"

I'm pressing. I know I am. Part of me hopes he says yes, that if I can torture myself enough for it to be really painful it will put an end to this ridiculous crush I have on him.

Slowly, he reaches over and tucks a loose strand of my hair behind my ear as if it's the most natural thing in the world, as if he's done it a million times. My breath hitches and my stomach feels weightless, suspended in the moment. I want to touch him too. I want so badly to reach over and touch him that I grip my pillow to stop myself.

His gaze lingers on my ear. "She didn't."

"But you were in love with her when it happened?"

His long lashes lower as he thinks it over. "At the time, I

thought I was."

"What do you mean?" I say, when what I really want to say is, *Why did you love her? What made her special, and why didn't she break your heart?* A thousand questions are begging to be asked. I keep them all to myself.

His gaze moves between my eyes and mouth. "She was my first girlfriend…in hindsight it was more like puppy love. I was in awe of her. With her relentless drive to achieve her goal of turning pro and ranking." In the pause, his unguarded eyes seek mine. "She didn't break my heart. My brother did."

"You guys didn't talk at dinner."

The hurt and frustration in his eyes is hard to miss. I send up a silent prayer for Jake to get his shit together and reach out to his brother.

"No," he says with unmistakable longing in his voice. "When we were kids, I worshipped him. Remember when I told you how sick I was?"

All I can do is nod. The way he keeps playing with the loose ends of my hair puts me under a spell, quiets my mind and soothes the frayed edges of my emotions.

"I didn't have any friends because I was always in and out of hospitals. My mother was always pulling me out of school. And because I couldn't eat without getting sick, I was small for my age."

Stop. Please stop, my mind keeps saying while my poor heart bleeds in silence. I can't take much more of this. One more sad story and I'll start to cry.

"By the time I started feeling better I was around eleven… Jake was fifteen so, yeah, I was eleven," he repeats. "He was always popular. Always had friends over. I would follow them around. It used to annoy the shit out of him," he adds with a small chuckle.

"They would party in the woods behind our home in Westchester. And I would follow and get him in trouble with my father. Eventually he got tired of getting busted and let me stay. After that, we were tight."

"Until you brought Hope home for Christmas."

His gaze moves to my lips. He looks lost in the memory. His mouth curves up on one side, the smile sad. "I should've seen it. He never acted that way with a woman before, and he went through a lot of them."

"Hmm, what a shocker." In understanding, he gives me a brief smile. "Why haven't you dated anyone since then?"

The pause is heavy. As if we've reached a critical point in the conversation—and our friendship.

"I haven't met anybody I want to spend my life with." *Life? Err, I said date.* "I've dated. Nothing serious, though... remember Jane?"

Ugh, *Jane.* I knew it. I knew it. Rolling onto my back, I stare at the ceiling. Anything is more appealing that watching hearts appear in his eyes for *Jane.*

"Yeah, I remember how you gushed and preened."

His laugh is low and soft and makes my heart hurt. I love hearing him laugh. It's on my list of favorite things.

"I did not preen, or gush."

I sense amusement even though I can barely make out his features. He gets up on an elbow and stares down, the space between us crackling with sexual tension.

"Did you sleep with her?" I sound bitchy, I know I do. But I can't manage to hide my feelings anymore. I am downright exhausted from hiding my feelings. Exhausted.

"Yes. On and off over the years. We were both busy with

our careers." I sneak a quick peek and find him watching me with a soft smile on his face. "We saw each other when we could—no questions asked. She's a good friend. We met in law school."

Good friend, my ass. Justin is a good friend and I have no desire to play hide the salami with him. Not even for convenience. Not even out of desperation. I'll shut up now. I'll shut up because if I open my trap I'll say stuff I shouldn't.

"She's also happily married."

"So she broke it off. Otherwise you'd still be with her." I refuse to look at him. I refuse to see the longing on his face for *Jane*.

He remains quiet. Which of course compels me to look at him. He's wearing that lopsided grin I hate to love. But it gets worse. He rakes my hair back and I almost scream from the pleasure, from the sense of connection a mere stroke of his fingers in my hair invokes.

"Don't be mad."

"Mad? Why would I be mad?"

"I know when you're mad...I know when you're trying to be mad and failing. I know when you try to hide that you're mad. I know every single one of your countless emotions."

This is not going to end well for me. Every word he speaks makes me wish for things I can't have. Not with him.

All of a sudden he grabs me and pulls me closer, my back to his chest. I don't move a hair, or utter a word. For a second I contemplate asking him what's gotten into him but change my mind just as swiftly. I don't want to discourage whatever has gotten into him. I whole-heartedly approve of whatever has gotten into him.

"She works in tech and lives in Silicon Valley," he

murmurs in my ear. I shiver at the feel of his breath on my skin, at the feel of him wrapped around me. "At least, she did. The flying back and forth got to be too much and we decided to take a break. She met Scott a month later and they eloped shortly after that."

"Sounds rash."

"When you know you know."

"That's ridiculous. How could you possibly know if someone is right for you in such a short amount of time?"

"Some of us know right away." The determination in his voice causes me to look over my shoulder. The gaze that meets mine is committed, unwavering. For a minute I think he might kiss me, that he might actually do it this time.

"Don't look at me like that," he murmurs with a rasp that says given half the chance he would fuck me dead. And I am *this* close to begging him to do just that.

"Like what? I barely looked at you."

"Like you want me to kiss you." Before I can start to argue, he holds me closer, his lips on my ear, his nose in my hair. "When I kiss you, it won't stop there…and that's not happening here." Grabbing my hips possessively, he pulls them back into his groin, my ass crashing into his raging hard-on, while I suck in a shocked gasp.

"I should probably go back to my room."

He shakes his head.

"Ethan," I say, desperation ringing loudly in my voice.

He snuggles closer, his nose in my hair, the steady beat of his gorgeous heart against my back. Tucked into the safe harbor of his body, I breathe out a sigh of relief and breathe in a sigh of contentment. I'm content for the first time in forever.

"Go to sleep, Amber."

Seconds later, a sense of peace steals all my apprehension away. I sleep like a rock through the night. No battery operated book boyfriends required.

CHAPTER TWENTY-ONE

THE NEXT MORNING I WAKE to an empty bed. By the looks of the clothes on the floor, Mr. Perfect went for a run. I get ready and head downstairs only to catch him on his way up to get me. I try my best to *not* look awkward considering the turn of events last night while he looks...blank. Judging from his expression, it never happened—except it did.

His eyes do the slow crawl from my vintage *Rolling Stones* t-shirt, to my black jeans, down to the black Gazelles. His eyes settle back on the *Stones* t-shirt.

"Favorite song?"

I give him a look of serious disappointment. "*Sympathy for the Devil,* obviously."

"Obviously," he responds with a slight lift of a sexy brow. "You?"

"A tie between *Start Me Up* and *Beast of Burden.*"

"Figures."

"Come on. Let's go home."

Home. Something in the way he says it sticks in my craw. I shouldn't like hearing him call it that, and yet...

We find his father, Jake and Hope, and a few more family members on the patio having brunch. Every single one of them gives us a queer look. Except for his father—his father smiles broadly. I'm guessing my little ploy worked. Ethan kisses Norma. I get a suffocating albeit nice hug from the Honorable Judge Vaughn. We say our goodbyes and depart.

"Why don't you know how to drive?" Ahead of us, traffic crawls to a stop.

Talk about a loaded question. I'm riding the crest of a good mood. The last thing I want to do is talk about my childhood. After last night, however, it feels petty to hold out on him.

"Yeah, driving around in a hearse would've done wonders for my popularity."

"A hearse?" That got his attention. He's watching me now.

"Eyes on the road, Fancy Pants. Traffic's moving. It's the only car my grandmother owned."

"Why would she own a hearse?"

"Because she owned a funeral home. We lived upstairs."

He side-eyes me, assessing whether I'm messing with him by the looks of it. Whatever he finds convinces him. "Holy shit," he says with a bark of laughter.

"Can I ask you something?"

"Hmm."

"What's up with Norma? Why would you agree to have her set you up?" Then it dawns upon me. "Unless you're fine being set up with women."

"No," he says, before I even finish. He sighs, his eyes shifting back and forth from me to the road. "My mother was her only daughter, and the baby. Norma took it the hardest. Sometimes I think harder than my father." He shrugs and squirms in his seat. "I started spending a lot of time with her because I was scared she would...she was really depressed. Since then, I've always been closer to her than anyone else."

"Hmm. You think she would've hurt herself?"

"I don't know…at the time it sure seemed that way. We helped each other. She kept my mind off my mother, that's for sure."

"So you indulge her."

He shrugs. "It makes her happy, and it wasn't a big deal when she was setting me up with women."

The thought of him going on dates makes me cringe.

His phone starts ringing. Glancing at the screen, he frowns and answers it. I listen to him bullshit with one of his client's family members, a brother or uncle or something, for a time I deem far too long. He hangs up and briefly glances at me.

"I'm leaving in a couple of days for the draft."

"How long?"

"Two weeks. Try not to miss me too much."

Glancing sideways, I catch him wearing a shit-eating grin. I can't keep from returning a smile of my own. "I'll try my best."

* * *

"Get dressed."

"No." I burrow deeper under the covers and shove my head under the pillow. Two bartenders called in sick last night, leaving me to man the bar on a Saturday with only one other fellow bartender. Practically crippled, I stumbled in the door at three am.

"Get dressed now." I feel the bed dip beside me. With a whoosh, my pillow is gone.

"Hey!!!" I screech and cover my head with the blanket. That's when I feel a large body straddling me. The blanket is ripped down and I'm staring up at the determined expression of a soon to be dead man. "Do you have a death wish?"

"Get dressed."

"You're a New York minute from being murdered by dragon breath," I growl.

He hops off the bed and before I know what's what, he rips the cover away, grabs me by the arm, and throws me over his shoulder. I scream. He slaps my ass, throws me into our newly remodeled bathroom, and slams the door shut, holding it closed from the other side.

"Have you lost your ever loving mind?!" No answer. Not even a peep. "I guess that's a yes!" I turn on the shower and begrudgingly divest myself of t-shirt and underwear.

"I don't have time to sweet talk you into it. Get going."

"Sweet talk me? When have you ever—"

"That's my point, Jones," he says, interrupting. "You're so clueless, you don't even notice when I'm doing it. That's why the change of strategy. *Art of War* and all that."

"*Art of War*, my ass. I wrote that book, Vaughn. And you'll pay for this."

He won't. But I'm having too much fun. I get under the hot jet spray of the new shower. I shouldn't be smiling like a loon. I shouldn't be. But I am.

Twenty minutes later I'm riding shotgun in Fancy's Audi headed who the heck knows where. The sun is out. A dust of green coats the trees, signaling that spring is finally here. Despite that I'm a total train wreck, I'm enjoying myself. However—I'd flay myself alive before I'd ever admit that to him.

"Do you derive some kind of sick pleasure from torturing me?" I mutter with my head in my hands.

"What a stupid question, Jones. You know I do."

"I need, like, three more Monster drinks right now just to hold my head up. I hate you."

"You love me. You can't stand how much you love me."

If he only knew how dangerously close to the truth that is. Lifting my black wayfarers, I get a good look at the man inflicting the pain. White shirt, super stud sunglasses, worn jeans and some kind of bullshit limited edition sneakers. I shamelessly inspect each and every article of clothing he's wearing, and as I do, I can feel my face twisting into a smirk.

"What?"

"It's like a cry for help every time you get dressed."

"You can't keep your eyes off me. Man up and admit it."

"I'll admit you're annoying. That's what I'll admit. And stop being so cheerful. That's annoying, too."

"I didn't even shower this morning. The pheromones I'm giving off are especially powerful."

"Lovely. Is that what that smell is? I thought you forgot a salami and provolone sandwich in the back seat."

"You can't help yourself. I get it. I'm irresistible to women and you're—" He looks me over with a provocative smirk. "—definitely a woman."

"I'm glad we got that cleared up."

"It's simple math," the sexy bastard continues without a pause.

If I thought for a minute there was any real arrogance behind those words it might have earned him a smack down. The thing is, I get the distinct impression that he truly doesn't know the magnitude of his appeal. My gaze swings out the window as I wrestle with a smile that won't stay down.

"Here's some simple math for you—two minus one equals this." I flip him the bird.

A deep chuckle draws my attention back to him. He's smiling again, the genuine kind, the kind that makes me want to simultaneously pick out baby names and insert a gun in my mouth.

Pulling off the road, onto a deserted parking lot, he parks the car. "Oh my God, it's finally happened. I've driven you to murder and you're too lazy to transport my body."

"Get out of the car."

"I am not going to walk into the woods and make this any easier for you." I open the door and get out. Hands on hips, toe of my black sneakers tapping, I wait as he walks over to my side. When he reaches me he stands awfully close. Close enough that if he bends down, his mouth would be directly...

He pries my hand open and places something in my palm. I stare, and stare, and stare. Car keys. Then I look up and stare at him some more. One side of his mouth hooks up. I don't know why, but he looks a little unsure and a lot serious.

"I'm going to teach you how to drive."

My stomach sinks, the smirk melting off my face. My pride keeps telling me he's too good to be true. That I couldn't possibly have gotten this lucky. I should know better than to listen to my pride where my heart is concerned.

We spent the rest of the afternoon driving around the empty parking lot, a stupid smile permanently tattooed on my face while Mr. Perfect pretended to sleep through it all. Ethan left the next day, taking a piece of me with him.

* * *

Fancy: What are you wearing?

Me: Nothing.

Fancy: ...

Fancy: ...

Fancy: Really?

Me: He he he.

* * *

Funsize: Grady is moving. He's going to live with his father.

How to handle this? I'm probably the last person she should be seeking advice on Love from. That's why I type and delete four different responses. And in the end, go with the only one that is true.

Me: I'm sorry kiddo.

* * *

I don't know what I was expecting, but it isn't this. I check the address on my cell phone one more time. Yep, I'm definitely in the right place. When Cassandra said sex shop, I thought— sex shop. I didn't expect it to look like a Madison Ave boutique. The lingerie in the store window is stunning, a little more racy than Agent Provocateur, though not by far. I'm almost intimidated to walk in.

Inside, I am immediately met by the soft, seductive sound of Astrud Gilberto. The lavender walls, the deep purple shantung silk accents scream sophistication. As I walk further into the store, I can't resist running my fingers over the silk of the teddies, the Chantilly lace of the garters, the butter soft leather of the...*what in the precious fuck is this thing?*

"Can I help you with something?" a deep, smooth voice inquires. Glancing past a display case of baffling sex instruments, I spot the owner of the voice. Dressed to the nines in a Narciso Rodriguez dress that slays on her tall, lithe frame, Cassandra arches a well groomed brow.

"I sure hope so," I answer with a smile.

"Took you long enough," she says, her open arms ready to wrap around me.

"I've been busy trying to stay out of trouble." Walking into her embrace, I hug her back.

"By trouble I hope you mean that delicious lawyer you had bail me out."

"He is delicious, isn't he?" I grumble sourly.

"Cinder, that's some prime beefcake you've got yourself there. What I wouldn't do to wrap my lips around—"

"Whoa." I hold up a hand, putting the brakes on whatever she was about to say next. Looking around, I say aloud what I've been thinking since I walked in. "This shop is beautiful. How can you afford this?"

She smiles knowingly. "Hmm, old boyfriend."

"The one you moved to New York for?"

"Yeah. He left it to me in his will."

Oh, poop. I stepped in it now. "I'm sorry. I didn't realize he'd passed."

"That's alright. It's been years." She looks me up and down. "Come on, you look like you could use a drink. Tammy," she shouts over her shoulder, "You're closing."

Happy hour is underway by the time we reach the Gansevoort Hotel in the meat packing district. The bar is jammed full of hipsters and suits. I recognize one or two from One Maple.

"Are you, or are you not fucking him?"

Two suits sitting at the next table turn to stare at us. Cringing. I'm cringing. "Don't say it like that."

"How would you like me to say it? With an accent?"

That elicits an unwilling smile out of me. "That's not the point anyway."

"I beg to differ. That's always the point."

"I'm moving. If I start something with him, then what?"

"Oh…" Her dark eyes perform a thorough examination of my face. Elegantly, she crosses her long slender arms. "You're in love with him."

"I'm not in love with him." My eyes dart to the skull themed art on the wall.

"You're in love with him," she repeats, disappointment in her tone.

"I may have developed an affection for him. Small, tiny little thing."

"That was stupid."

"I know," I say morosely. I'm cringing again. She keeps echoing back all my concerns.

"Don't sleep with him."

"What??" My eyes full of surprise cut back to her. Needless to say, this is not what I was expecting.

"You won't move if you sleep with him."

My heart sinks. Feels like she just hit a nerve. "You think?" I say, and suck down my vodka gimlet.

"Cinder, face the facts, you're a romantic. And from one

recovering romantic to another, I can say beyond a shadow of a doubt that if you sleep with him, you'll eventually give him everything else as well. In other words—you'll give up your career."

CHAPTER TWENTY-TWO

ANTICIPATION IS A TWO SIDED blade. The butterflies, the giddy rush, all good things. The waiting? Mmnot so much. Since he left, I've been wavering between elation every time the phone rings and bone deep loneliness when it doesn't. In other words, I miss him something terrible.

It's your typical Saturday night at One Maple. The bar jammed three rows deep, the customers demanding, the money rolling in. Until I spot an obscenely handsome man walk in. Then it's no longer typical because Ethan has never come to visit me at work before. Just being in the same room with him makes me feel better.

I take good measure of the man. Navy suit, impeccable white shirt, no tie. Then again he could make a dishrag look sexy. His almond shaped eyes roam until he finds me, his lips mirroring mine curve up. Walking through the room, he catches the attention of every pair of female and some male eyes in the general vicinity.

At the bar, he pushes his way past the crowd to the front, never breaking eye contact.

"Of all the gin joints in all the towns in all the world," I say, openly beaming.

His smile fades, his expression   suddenly grave—the

happy vibe we were sharing a minute ago dead on arrival.

"Hey? What's wrong?"

"I missed you."

My stomach bottoms out and my throat closes up. It was a direct shot to the heart. "I missed you, too." The words tumble out of my mouth without any thought to the consequences. Something is happening. The question is, what?

"Abby! Can we get some drinks here?" someone shouts over the ruckus of the crowd.

Ethan's face darkens, adopting an expression I've never seen on him before. His narrow eyed death glare turns in the direction of the screamer.

"I'll be right back," I tell him, though it doesn't look like he's heard me; his attention still glued to my two favorite customers.

I make my way over to them wearing a fake grin. "Howdy, fellas," I cheerfully chirp as I wipe down the bar. "What's going down? I mean—besides you two on each other?"

The dark flush running up jerk number one's neck tells me he finally gets it. The daggers his eyes are throwing tell me he won't be going away quietly. Whatever. Nothing I can't handle. "What can I get you?"

"Two Macallans," jerk number one answers. I turn to grab a set of clean glasses and hear him as clear as a bell say, "I'd like to bend that bitch over the bar and teach her a lesson."

My gaze flickers to Ethan. He couldn't possibly have heard. Except that his expression goes suspiciously flat. Nasty insults from narcissistic egomaniacs are nothing new to me, barely warranting my attention, thus I resume my work without a second thought.

Mistake. That was a mistake.

Not a moment later, I hear shouting and screaming erupt behind me. I judged wrong apparently because I whip around to see Ethan on top of jerk number one, pounding away at his face.

Holy hell.

Kevin, one of the bartenders, is a step ahead of me, jumping over the bar before I can get there. Dave, a member of the security staff, pushes his way through the halo of people surrounding the assault in progress. He grabs Ethan under the pits and lifts him off jerk number one, who bloodied and bruised, still manages to scramble to his feet. Kevin grabs him before he can lunge at Ethan.

Grabbing Ethan's arm with both hands, I tug. "I got him," I tell Dave. After a pointed look at me, which says *get him under control*, Dave releases Ethan and I drag him away, headed for the employee locker room.

He follows willingly as I pull him inside the empty room and push him down onto a bench. Cut lip, shirt ripped and bloodied, hair mussed, he stares up at me with fathomless eyes, his breathing still rough.

"Seriously?" I shout, staring at his bruised knuckles. "What is wrong with you?"

I leave him to grab the first aid kit and when I return, find him still staring up at me with the same expression. One I can't even begin to understand. And by the looks of it, he isn't about to explain. The cotton gauze doused with alcohol, I dab the cut on his lip. Gently. Tenderly. He hisses at the sting and my eyebrows crawl halfway up my forehead. "You start a barroom brawl and now you're going to be a big baby over a little alcohol?"

It happens in a blink. He stands, grabs my face in both hands, and slams his lips onto mine. Then he pushes me against the wall, and stooping, pins my hips in place with his. The first thing I feel is relief. So much damn relief I could cry. Like my head was underwater and I'm finally allowed to take a huge breath. The second thing I feel is him. I feel every hard inch of him.

Thank you, God. Thank you for this man. Thank you. And the thank yous keep coming because you can never be too grateful.

He devours me, kissing me as if time is running out. And in return, I grab the lapels of his now rumpled five thousand dollar suit and kiss him back—no holds barred. His lips gentle. With my face cupped in his hands, he takes his time tasting me, relishing the moment, encouraging every sigh that rises up my throat. His tongue plays with mine. He nips and sucks on my bottom lip. I taste blood and alcohol and still we kiss and kiss and kiss with his body pressed against mine, like he can't get close enough. I wasn't imagining it the first time. Nothing has ever felt so right.

The door bursts open and we jump apart, startled as one of the bus boys walks in. Hands on hips and breathing heavily, Ethan drops his head, sucks in a deep breath, and when he raises his chin again, the look on his face is saying everything at once. Questions, answers, feelings—which neither of us voices out loud.

"I'll ask Kevin if I can leave early."

It's already close to the end of my shift. Once Kevin tells me it's okay to leave I meet Ethan in the back alley. As soon as I step out the door, he takes my hand. He has yet to say a word—and God knows I'm not about to say something and ruin the moment.

He leads me to where Fredo waits for us. In the meantime, every scenario imaginable is running through my mind. Fredo gets out of the driver's seat but Ethan reaches the door first, holding it open for me. I slide in with Ethan right behind me. Looking straight ahead, he stares out at nothing while my eyes fall on my hand, the one he has yet to relinquish.

* * *

Once we get back to the townhouse, we make our way upstairs to the bedrooms on autopilot. Not one word is spoken, the tension growing with every step we take. Ethan looks completely lost to whatever is going on inside his skull. Maybe he's regretting that life-altering kiss. The thought eats away at me.

I can say with absolute certainty that I've never been kissed like that before, with an all-consuming need that couldn't be denied if lives were at stake. And if you would've told me five months ago that I would have this kind of chemistry with this particular man I would've laughed in your face. Then again given my life, that's par for the course.

At our bedroom doors, he stops.

"I have a suggestion."

He slowly turns to face me, his shoulders squaring, his eyes huge, boring into mine with super human intensity. I can sense the charge around him. His expression shifts, growing a little…predatory? Yep, predatory. He slowly steps closer with his hands raised in a sign that could be construed as surrender. *Could be construed,* I said. This man does not surrender.

"Offer, if you will." In a spell, I watch him stalk closer. "I propose that…we have sex."

I'm a deer caught in headlights, frozen and ready to bolt—onto his erection, the massive one pushing against his slacks. My eyes drop. I've done a great job of ignoring it until this very minute. Now, I can no longer ignore it. For the love of erections, I'm human, a sexually frustrated one—a very important part of this equation.

"With each other?" I mumble, way too excited for my own good.

He nods at this. "For the sake of our mental health. You don't have anyone. I don't have anyone, haven't for a long time—too goddamn long by the looks of my behavior lately. We should have it together."

I stare back blankly. On the outside I'm a mummy. Where as on the inside…heck, on the inside, I'm shooting guns off and singing *Yankee Doodle Dandy* at the top of my lungs. I'm doing cartwheels and kissing my biceps. I slow nod in agreement, a ready and willing accomplice to this ridiculous plan that has disaster written all over it. "For medicinal purposes," I suggest.

He takes a couple more steps, his heavy lidded eyes dropping to my lips. "Exactly."

I watch his Adam's apple rise and fall as he swallows. "Abstinence is a dangerous thing. Could make a person do things he or she wouldn't normally do."

"Like get in a bar brawl when one can't afford any negative press," he adds and gets even closer, close enough that I take in a lung full of his intoxicating scent. "But on one condition."

I stiffen, nervous that there's some outlandish request

coming. Sorry, but I don't do threesomes. There may have been a small window of opportunity where that could've happened in my early twenties, for shock value more than anything else, but that window closed a long, long time ago. "Yes?" I summon the courage to ask.

"I don't share."

Praise Jesus. Thank you, tiny, adorable, newborn, baby Jesus. "Me neither."

"That means not even with Jacob, or Gary, or whatever the hell you call those things."

It takes me a minute to figure out what he's talking about. An irrepressible grin stretches across my face. "I don't know. Those guys do a heck of a lot of heavy labor."

"I'm willing to do just as much, if not more."

My eyelids are pinned to my forehead, my heart racing. "Promise?"

"Fuck, yeah." With that, he grabs my face like he has a right to it and cradles it possessively. He's not tender. Not even a little bit. His mouth crashes into mine, kissing me like a man sentenced to life, a man deprived of something essential. And I am gone, my body and soul humming with a sense of right time, right guy, right everything.

"I trust you won't poke holes in the condoms," he mutters in between his relentless kisses.

As quickly as he picks me up, I wrap my legs around his waist. Stumbling, we crash into the wall. Without a doubt there will be bruises tomorrow. His hips press into mine. He wants me to feel him. The baseball bat he carries in his pants presses against every part of me that loves baseball bats. *Sigh, triple sigh with a cherry on top.*

"Wouldn't dream of it," I mutter. "I take it you won't be

giving me pube fleas."

"Not a chance."

My fingers dig through his thick, soft hair and close around a fist full. He moans and thrusts his hips, the pleasure edged with a touch of pain. I tear my lips away and place a hand on his chest to stall him from plundering my mouth again. "I have an amendment to our agreement."

"Which is?" There's wariness in his voice. He's scared I might back out. Little does he know. Nothing, and I mean nothing could stop this from happening.

"There will be shagging, banging, boning, even humping. There will, however, be no lovemaking. We good?"

His face stills. The excitement he was wearing a minute ago dims. His eyes search mine but I don't let him in. I keep my thoughts to myself. Because I'm scared he'll see how much I want this, how much I want him in particular. I can't let this be more than a physical thing. Anything more than that and it will destroy me for good. *Finito*. Annihilation complete. Everything before him was junior league in comparison, and I can't let him have that kind of power over me.

He gives it a minute of thought before acquiescing with a curt nod. Not very convincing, but I'm too worked up to care at this point. "Good. Are you hydrated? Because I have a lot of time to make up for and I can't have you fainting on me."

His smile is back in full force. Without further delay, he tears me away from the wall and kicks open the door to his bedroom. He drops me on the bed, and I fall back with a sigh of relief. I thought this day would never come. Grabbing the waist of my skinny jeans, he rips them down to my ankles without even bothering to unbutton them.

"Ouuuch."

My nice guy likes it rough? Didn't see that coming. I check for burn marks down my thighs with a stupid smile on my face.

"Man up, Jones." His voice is deeper than usual. Hearing it makes goose bumps break out over my skin. My Gazelles are next. He tosses one by one over his shoulders.

"Okay, but—you know I'm not really a man, right?" I say giggling like a loon.

"Thank fuck for that," he says, yanking my jeans off for good. "Otherwise I'd have to go gay for you."

My giggles come to an abrupt stop. Pain and pleasure expand in my chest. Eyes watering, I pick my head up off the pillow and stare at the gorgeous specimen kneeling between my thighs. Hair all mussed, lips swollen, and sexier than any one man has a right to be.

"Fancy—"

At the wobble in my voice, he looks up. "Yeah?"

As he watches me his soft lips descend onto the sensitive skin on the inside of my knee. Kiss after delicate kiss the tension grows. My lady parts throb, desperate for some attention as the kisses travel north.

"That's the nicest thing anyone's ever said to me."

He takes my face in one piece at a time. My lips, my eyes, my clenched jaw. A wolfish grin spreads across his face. "It's true. Now shut up so I can *bone* you properly." He cups me possessively and my eyes do a full roll to the back of my head while my head drops back onto the mattress.

Tender moment over, he gets back to work, taking his time feasting on the insides of my thighs while my prone form tenses in eagerness for what's to come.

When he reaches my panties, strong fingertips curl over

the edge of my boy shorts and pause. Curiosity forces my head up. Almost an impossible task but I manage. I find him looking up at me with a heated gaze that could very well send me up in flames all by itself.

"This—" he says. Extending his long blunt index finger, he taps me twice on my poor neglected clit and I nearly shoot off the bed. "Belongs to me now."

"Oh Gawd," I half screech, half pant.

He drags my underwear off slowly. Anticipation is a heartless bitch. I'm squirming from it. A moment later his mouth is finally on me, hot, direct. No messing around, he knows what he's doing. For a second this bothers me. Only for a second though because he swipes his tongue over my sweet spot and follows that up by sucking on it. My body practically levitates off the bed. I'm on the brink of an O and we've barely started. Either I have a crappy memory, or sex has never ever been this good ever for anyone ever...ever. And we haven't gotten to the main attraction.

He lifts his head while his arms pin my spread thighs to the bed. "This beautiful pussy is all mine to lick, suck, and fuck—" My eyes slam open. *'Scuse me? My nice guy is a dirty talker?* "Whenever I feel like it. And I'm gonna feel like it a lot."

Omg—my nice guy is a dirty talker. I can't wait another minute. Not a second longer. I have been drowning in lust for this man for months. They say that the word hysteria derives from some sketchy history of it being specific to women, from the Latin root meaning "of the womb". Yes, yes, a thousand times yes. My womb is crazy for him.

"Ethan, I need you." Begging is not beneath me. I would happily crawl over a bed of hot coals if he were to ask. At the sound of his name something sparks. Some of the blatant lust on his face fades, changing to something softer, something affectionate. He gets up, never once breaking eye contact.

"Get naked."

The bossy type is not my jam. However, by the way my body is responding, getting even more aroused, I approve. Then again, I'm pretty certain it's the man doing the bossing.

In one fell swoop, I rip my t-shirt and bra off. He's seen the goods already, or rather lack of goods. No need to be shy. And in return I watch him slowly unbuttons his white dress shirt. I've never seen anything sexier—never. I can't even imagine anything sexier than Ethan standing with his legs slightly spread apart, gray slacks tenting from the massive hard-on he's showing off, look of utter hunger on his face— and I have a very vivid imagination.

His burning gaze turns my pale skin pink. His jaw pulses as he finishes unbuttoning his shirt and shucks it off, unzips. Pants gapping open, I can see his erection twitching as I stare at it, a wet spot on his boxers. He pushes his pants down and drags his underwear along with them.

Sigh. Double sigh with a back flip.

There are no words. None. I didn't exactly get a good look last time I saw him in all his naked glory. You know, with him bleeding all over the place. But I am looking my fill now.

"Like what you see?" he murmurs as he opens his bedside table drawer and pulls out a condom. He watches me as he rips it open with his teeth and suits up.

"Like?" I rasp, my throat bone dry. "Yeah, you could say that."

His mouth hooks up. Thank God I'm lying down because if I was standing right now, I'd faceplant.

"Good," he says, moving towards me. He crawls up the bed, and over me. "Because I love what I see."

As soon as the words are out of his mouth, his smile falters, the mischievous sparkle in his eyes replaced by something significantly more serious. I see more than lust and need, more than a physical attraction that will not quit. I see everything, and he lets me.

Panic starts to overshadow the lust. *This is about sex! Just scratching an itch!* I remind myself. He must've sensed my flight instinct kicking in because he kisses me. So soft and sweet. The panic turns into unbridled excitement of the earth shaking sex I'm about to have.

With his face above mine and his hands bracketing my head, he holds his upper body suspended while his lower body settles between my thighs. His hot length presses against me, sliding. I moan and whimper and struggle for more. I need to feel him over every square inch of my skin. I need to feel the weight and strength of him pushing me into the mattress. I cup his face and bring it closer, our lips a breadth away. "Stop teasing me."

"So impatient," he murmurs in a voice that speaks to the basest part of me.

Bring it on, my mind screams, *bring it all on*. And he does. He gives me what I need. His tongue slips into my mouth and makes love to mine. He cups my breast and rubs his calloused thumbs over my sensitive nipples and I arch closer—the calluses only I know he gets from pounding away at that sheetrock. Rocking his hips, he swallows my moans. We've been dancing around this for far too long, the slow burning foreplay serves as tinder to the fire inherently burning between us—no app necessary.

On the next rock, he pushes inside of me with a force that makes me gasp and dig my short nails into his back muscles. His fingers threaded in my hair, he tugs on it to look at my face. "You okay, baby?"

Baby? Oh God, I actually like that. I give him a short nod and he rolls his hips again. And just like that I'm on the verge of coming.

"You feel so good, Amber. Nothing has ever felt as good." One big hand grips the back of my knee and hikes my leg up, hooking it around his waist, sinking even deeper into me, sinking all the way to the root. His grip on my hair tightens possessively and the prickle of my scalp translates into a throb between my thighs.

My nice guy—a hair puller. I'm grinning from ear to ear. This man is full of surprises. Sensing my amusement, he looks at me. "What's so funny?"

"I'm happy. And I want you." His hips have mine pinned down. "Move."

I cup his ass and squeeze. His eye lids drop, gaze filled with lust. "I want you too. I've wanted you for so long."

"Well then, stop talking and get to work."

He smoothly pulls his hips out and slams into me. I cry out and dig my fingers into his ass muscles. "It's been a while so this may be quick. But it's just the start, baby," he murmurs, his pace as steady as his words.

He swivels his hips, tests the angle until I gasp. His teeth scrape my neck. The pads of his rough fingertips play with my nipple while he drives into me. The pleasure builds quickly. Almost too quickly—I need it to last. As soon as he senses my impending O he picks up the pace.

Uncorked, my orgasm explodes through me. But Ethan

doesn't stop. He keeps driving, prolonging my pleasure. His breath tickles my ear as he murmurs words I can't make out. Words of encouragement, I think. I am fighting not to lose myself in this feeling of completion, of wholeness of body and spirit. Sweat beads on his forehead and he bites his bottom lip, staving off his own release for my benefit.

"Ethan," I whisper. That's all it takes for him to come, for his back muscles to turn to stone under my hands, for his eyes to slam shut as he savors every minute of it.

CHAPTER TWENTY-THREE

THE TOUCHING DOESN'T LET UP for a minute. He's mapping me with his hands. I went to bed with a sexual beast and woke up with Helen Keller—if Helen Keller were a six-foot-two gorgeous slab of man meat. Gripping my hips, he grinds against me.

"You're full of surprises."

He kisses my neck and murmurs, "Hmm, how?" on my skin.

"Why tonight? What happened?"

A weighty pause follows.

"I'm so damn tired of fighting it...aren't you?" The last few words are tentative, vulnerable.

"Yeah, I am. But I don't want to get you in trouble."

"We'll be careful."

"Living dangerously, counselor. I might have to revoke your Mr. Perfect card."

"Mr. Perfect?" he parrots. "Hardly. Far from it, in fact."

I turn onto my back and peer up at him. "Right."

His eyes roam over my face while his remains inscrutable. "But I wouldn't mind being perfect for you," he says quietly with a half-smile that's tentative and shy and makes my insides fuzzy, makes me want to be perfect for him. And that is not what this is about.

His gaze sharpens on me. "I want to show you something."

Before I can respond, he's out of bed and walking naked to his dresser and holy moly is the view spectacular. A minute later he's back, walking toward me all easy grace, his heavy erection bobbing with every step he takes, the dark hair surrounding it neat and tidy—of course. Time for an obligatory eye roll.

"I've seen it and I approve."

A slow grin spreads across his face. "I mean these," he says, motioning to the stack of pictures in his hand. Pictures? Who gives a crap about pictures when I have an interactive feast for the senses before me. He slides back into bed, and my face turns into sad Emoji. Jeez, I'm worse than a kid with a new toy.

He sidles up next to me and wraps his muscular arm around my neck—touching me, needing the connection as much as I do. The pictures he hands me look old, weathered on the edges. They've been handled a lot. I sit up, to get a better look, and Ethan's hand spontaneously falls on my lower back. The warmth radiating from his palm sinks all the way to my bones. A lazy warmth spreads through me. It feels so good my eyelids get droopy. There's only one thing that feels better and that's his magic d—

"Amber?"

"Yeah," I say, shaking off the daze.

My interest perks up at the first picture. A healthy looking boy with a very deep tan and an amazing grin peers back at me. Around eleven or twelve, he's already incredibly handsome. He's also holding up a fish half the size of his torso, and looks quite proud of himself.

"Very cute." I trace the boy's features with my fingertip. "I see promise of perfection in your smile. Where was this taken?" My question is met by silence, compelling me to look over my shoulder. My smile slips when I realize the one Ethan is wearing is fixed in place, held up by sheer force of will.

"Sun Valley, Idaho. And that's not me." Sitting up, he gently takes the picture. "That's Jake." Pointing at the figure in the corner, he says, "And that's me."

In the background, a skinny kid sits on a rock. He's wearing a crooked baseball cap, glasses, and he's holding a book. He also looks incredibly sad. "We took that trip shortly after the cancer went into remission...the first time."

Fuck, fuck, fuck, fuck. This is not the time to be stingy with the fucks. There's suddenly an elephant sitting on my chest. An overwhelming urge to cry for that little boy hunched over with his chin resting on his hand takes hold of me.

"I was a late bloomer."

Ethan pulls the next picture out and it's the same little boy standing next to the much huskier one, an enormous Christmas tree behind them. Jake is smiling, his arm hanging around Ethan's neck. Ethan, however, is not smiling.

I glance up at him and the brief smile he gives me doesn't reach his eyes. The sad little duckling became a swan. *Do not cry. Do not cry. Do not freaking cry.* He squeezes my hand, trying to make me feel better. Me. Here I am, staring at the source of the most profound pain a child can experience and he's trying to comfort me. My eyes flicker away from his, back to the pictures. I'm barely holding it together, and if I look at him I will lose it.

He pulls the third picture out and my eyes go straight to

the gorgeous woman standing between the two boys. She has a colorful scarf wrapped around her head, and although she's wearing a huge smile that's almost a carbon copy of Ethan's, she's so tall and thin it looks like a light breeze could push her over.

"So beautiful. You look like her." My voice sounds far away. I can barely make it out I'm so overwhelmed with emotion. "Do you carry these on you? They look really worn."

His long lashes cast shadows on his cheekbones as he looks at the pictures. "Touching the paper somehow…" He shrugs. "I don't know."

I get it. For some strange reason I understand him. It seems as if we've been in lockstep since the day we met. Never pushing each other too far away, or pulling each other too close—dancing around this inevitable outcome since the start.

"Come back to me, Jones."

I look up into his open face and see only the tiniest glimmer of that pale skinny kid, the one that grew into such an amazing man. Because he is amazing. Kind, smart, thoughtful, generous. Basically he's a unicorn. My unicorn. Wait, he's not mine. He's definitely not mine.

This is all kinds of terrible. I can't be having these feelings for him. I'm leaving soon—with any luck. I'm taking my foot off the brake pedal and charging full steam ahead with my career. And so is he. There's no place for "feelings" in this arrangement.

"Where'd you go? You looked like you were a million miles away." It's his smile that's my undoing. This time it's relaxed, guileless…happy.

"You are."

"I'm what?" he asks, his voice quiet. Cupping my face, he traces my bottom lip with the rough pad of his thumb.

"Perfect for me." My stomach clenches, my pride screaming in outrage that I've handed him the weapon of my destruction, that I may have authored my own demise with that admission.

His eyelashes flutter for the barest of seconds. When those almond shaped eyes find mine again, he's wearing a frown. I'm about to pull away but he's one step ahead, pinning me to the mattress with the weight of his body. He brings my arms up over my head, slides my hands open with his much larger ones and laces his fingers through mine. He's holding my hands.

I am toast. I am utter toast.

His kiss is sweet, coaxing, as if he doesn't want to scare me off. In a spell, I kiss him back. He spends the rest of the night convincing me with his body just how perfect for me he is.

* * *

"I've got fantastic news," Marty announces as soon as I walk through the door of his office. He's got an enormous pastrami sandwich between his meaty paws—and by the smell of it, with onions.

Pinching my nose shut, I plop down in the arm chair across from him and put my kicks up on the desk. "Scorsese cast me as the lead of his next flick."

"I said fantastic, not fantasy."

Shrugging, I say, "A girl can dream."

"Forget the dream. The casting director for that time travel show you were crying about called."

Every hair on my body stands upright. "And? You're

killing me Marty!"

"The sister of the lead is now available." He takes a big bite.

"The Carinne character, the bitchy one?" I query, sitting upright in the chair.

"The Carinne character," Marty mimics with a mouth full of food and nods.

"That sandwich stinks, my dear Martin."

"I've been looking forward to this since breakfast. Deal with it." He takes another bite of his sandwich. "The one they cast was pregnant and neglected to tell the producers. It's a physical part so she's shit out of luck." He smiles broadly, a piece of pastrami stuck between his teeth.

And then it hits me like a freight train. I can't go anywhere. Certainly not to Canada, where the show films.

"I can't take it," I say on the verge of crying. "My case hasn't been settled."

"What?? What the hell is taking so long?" Marty looks as crestfallen as I feel.

"It's complicated. She wants a lot of money for the repairs. Money I don't have." Elbows on my knees, I rub my temples in a vain attempt to stave off a tension headache.

"Jesus Christ, kid. Get your shit together. Life is happening and you're missing it."

CHAPTER TWENTY-FOUR

"HOW DO YOU WANNA PLAY this? I think we should tell our friends."

I knew this conversation was coming. I've been dreading its impending arrival. My gaze steers out the car window, anything to avoid eye contact.

"Where is this thing?" I ask, deftly avoiding the question as I press my palms on the bare skin of my thighs. I'm wearing a simple black mini dress, sleeveless, mock turtleneck while Fancy McButterpants looks ready for the cover of Men's Vogue in a closely tailored blue suit, white shirt, and black tie.

"Metropolitan Pavilion."

The Titans organization is hosting a party to welcome the new draft class. I only agreed to attend because my best friend is a conniving mafia bitch. Camilla threatened to post pictures of me on Facebook. Intimate pictures. Of a moment no best friend should ever black mail a best friend with. Pictures from when we were in the eighth grade and I got it in my head that I wanted big curly hair like Julia Roberts in *Pretty Woman*. My grandmother refused to take me to a salon, no surprise, so I took matters into my own hands, no surprise, and bought one of those at-home perm kits with my babysitting money. You can follow that thread to its logical conclusion.

The mafia bitch decided to document this disaster in Polaroid. The same mafia bitch saved those pictures on her phone and routinely likes to taunt me with them. Whenever she wants me to do something I get a text saying, *remember this?* with an attachment. Needless to say, I am currently on my way to the draft party.

In the periphery of my vision, I can see Ethan's eyes shift back and forth to me.

"Amber?"

My name in that deep voice, that voice that feels like velvet with a touch of rough around the edge, is my kryptonite. But I can't give in, for a multitude of reasons. I won't allow my feelings to dictate how I do business anymore. For the first time I stick to my plan and quiet the distant voice in the back of my mind that's telling me to give in and fall. Being a grown up sucks. *"First rule of fight club. You do not talk about fight club,"* I say, quoting one of my all-time favorite movies.

The silence prods me to steal a glance. His face is tight... he's upset.

"I disagree. We can't hide this from our friends. They'll figure it out anyway. Might as well tell them we're—"

"Benefriends," I say, cutting him off. "If you say fuck buddies, I will hurt you."

"Benefriends?" He can't decide whether to be angry or amused.

"Friends with benefits," I explain, one he doesn't care for. His sexy lips press together, irritation etched around his eyes, the quiver of his jaw. I can see the wheels turning, strategizing. He's formulating a plan of attack.

"Remember that little detail about you getting disbarred if

you get caught playing naked Twister with the prisoner?" I feel the need to remind him. "We need to keep this under wraps."

He blows out an exasperated breath and runs his fingers through his hair. "Yeah, I know we have to keep it quiet until your case is closed but—"

"Ethan—I'm leaving as soon as the case is closed. I went to see Marty today. I'm missing out on a really good part, a great part, because I can't travel out of the area. These opportunities don't come around often. It broke my heart to say no."

"You turned it down?"

"I had to. And let's not forget I may have to go to jail."

"You're not going to jail," he says, speaking over me.

"And if not, I'm moving to L.A. Telling anyone only complicates the matter."

After that, a black cloud descends in the back of the town car and lasts until we reach Chelsea.

* * *

Inside, the loft type venue is packed. Most of the players and their families are in attendance, the room decorated in team colors. A very large redhead makes his way to us. And when I say large I mean the man is the size of a baby grand piano. Red is wearing a tartan bowtie that looks sharp on him. He reaches us, slaps Ethan on the back, and shakes his hand. "'Sup, boss." He rubs his full red beard and gives me a dimpled smile that makes him look like a little boy up to no good.

"Amber, this is James Popovitch. Pop, Amber."

"Hello there Amber," he singsongs, which makes me chuckle. His attention returns to Ethan. "Fuckers drafted a nose tackle," he mutters conspiratorially.

Ethan shakes his head. "Kid's green. Really green. His footwork needs a lot of work. You've got nothing to worry about."

I spot Justin across the room. I wave and he blows me a kiss. What a goofball.

"If you say so," Pop says in a low voice.

"I do."

"Excuse me, gentleman. I have a friend to see." Ethan frowns. Before he can make a move I sense his intention to reach for me, to make some gesture that would imply intimacy, and before he does I check him with a wide-eyed glare.

"I'll see you in bit," I warn. After which I smile at Popovitch and go in search of Justin.

On my way to Justin, I run into Calvin coming from the buffet table. In one hand is a dish filled with food, in his other a chicken skewer. He takes a big bite.

"Hey." His mouth full, he nods his greeting. "Where's the woman who blackmailed me into coming to this thing?"

Before Calvin can answer Ethan walks up, standing much too close to me. Cal continues to chew on the chicken skewer while his shrewd gray eyes bounce from me to Ethan and back again. No sweat. I am a stone cold killer, a vault, Fort Knox as a matter of fact. I got this thing on lockdown.

"You two are sleeping together."

Mmmkay, maybe not entirely on lockdown. It's not even a question. Regardless, I'm prepared to deny, deny, deny.

"First rule of fight club. You do not talk about fight club," says the man that gave me more orgasms in one night than is healthy. It obviously damages gray matter otherwise the same man wouldn't have such a hard time following one simple fucking rule. My eyes roll so hard I can see the back of my skull.

Cal stops chewing and swallows. "I knew it."

"Ethan," I snap, eyes wide and accusing. He's not even a little bit remorseful. Nope. He's smiling, the sexy turkey, is smiling proudly at me. My attention returns to Calvin. "It's for medicinal purposes."

Cal arches an eyebrow. "This is a bad idea. And that's all I'm gonna say on the subject." His attention swings back to Fancy. "Anything from Phil?"

Ethan's eyes flicker to me, then back to Calvin. "You want to talk about this now?"

Calvin takes one look at me and gets the gist. "Her? She's family."

Three words, two if you go with the abbreviation, trigger a seismic event. He thinks I'm family. My eyes slam into Calvin's. He's dead serious, no sign of anything other than total honesty. This does not surprise me. Calvin's way too arrogant to be anything other than honest.

Family. Maybe it's been staring me in the face this whole time? Maybe family isn't something you're born into but rather something you create for yourself. I hear people saying all the time that you can choose your friends but you can't choose your family. Maybe we should choose our family.

"Phil isn't stupid. I'll let him save his pride and drag it out only because we know, in the end, you're getting everything you asked for."

"And if he gets stupid?"

"It's handled. Gladiators already have an offer in. They know you want to finish your career in New York."

Their voices fade into the background of my thoughts. So much has changed in the last five months. I've made decisions, claimed a sister, found a lover and best friend, and now discovered family in the least likely of places. Am I ready to leave all this behind?

To Calvin's left, I spot a woman vigorously waving at me from her seat at a table. Deep in conversation, the guys don't notice me move away.

"Jesus, Mary, and Joseph. I've been texting you since you walked in the door," my very pregnant best friend semi shouts.

"I don't have a bag. I didn't bring my phone."

"I'm miserable."

I want to laugh. I really do. But I can't. She's two weeks from her due date and hella irritable. "How's the bun cooking?"

"He's overcooked! His cute ass needs to vacate the premises."

"But he loves it in there, Fiona," I say, annoying her further by rubbing her gigantic belly. Seems only appropriate to call her Fiona when I keep insisting that she married a real life Shrek.

"Look at my feet." She moves the tablecloth aside so I can check them out.

*Wut in the ever loving...*I give myself major props for not gasping in horror at the size of her feet.

"They're ruined forever," she whines. "They will never go back to being as cute as they once were."

I can't argue. "I don't understand. Is that where the baby comes out?"

"Scary, right?"

"Why are you here? Why aren't you at home with your feet up?" I inquire, my expression terrified.

"We had to make an appearance. You know, remind Phil that if he doesn't make a decision soon he'll be left with two third round rookies and a career back-up QB and that I will send a squad of hit men after him. Besides, between the baby and the stress of the contract I'm ready to murder my husband in his sleep."

"Wow, this pregnancy has made you a little testy."

"Hello ladies," a familiar voice drawls from behind me. Justin kisses us both on the cheek and takes the chair next to me. "What's up?"

"Camilla's feet look like baby hippos. And by the looks of her feet. I'm never having children. What's up with you?"

"You still haulin' that baby around?" Justin says to Cam.

"Not much longer," Calvin answers. He's standing next to Ethan, whose eyes narrow when he sees Justin's arm draped around my shoulders.

"Can I have a word," he says in a low voice. Everyone turns to stare at me.

Umm. "Can it wait?"

"No, it can't wait." My eyebrow nervously twitches up. The turkey is going to blow our cover. I can see it in his eyes.

"Really?"

"Really."

Heavy sigh. Heavy freaking sigh. I stand slowly, very slowly, and say to our curious looking friends, "Be back in a jiffy," with a tight lipped smile.

As soon as we begin to walk away, I hear Justin say, "They're sleeping together," and a combined, "Yep," from Cam and Cal.

Dandy. Just dandy.

I follow Ethan along the edge of the dance floor, past the many tables filled with people giving us dubious glances, and down an empty hall. He opens an unmarked door and pulls us inside, pinning me against the back of it. It's dark. An emergency sign offers the only light, tracing his features in blue.

"What are you doing?"

"What does it look like I'm doing?" Bending his knees so that our hips are aligned, he grinds into me and I nearly lose it there and then. He kisses me then. Hard. Possessively. Ripping his lips away, he pants and says, "He can touch you, but I can't?" One large hand cradles my neck, the other shoves through my hair. There will be no doubt about what we were doing once we rejoin the party.

"Really? You pulled me away for that?" I reply as breathless as he is.

"He's all over my girl and I'm supposed to stand there and watch him. He needs to get his own goddamn girl. What's so funny?"

"Your girl?" The giggles won't stop. "You sound like you stepped out of a bad romance novel."

"You're my girl," he repeats, his voice projecting the Neanderthal brand of steely determination. "This is mine," he says and plants a tender kiss on my lips. "This is mine," he says and yanks my dress up, exposing my lace thong. He pets me over my underwear and my eyes flutter drunkenly. "This is mine," he says and pulls my underwear aside, rubbing my clit with the rough pad of his thumb.

Sure. Whatever. It's yours. All yours—just keep doing that! I'm screaming on the inside. I'm also pretty sure that at some point the same words came out of me loudly and an incoherent mess.

"And this is definitely the fuck mine," he says as he slips his fingers inside of me. The impatient sounds coming out of me are downright embarrassing. "Now do I sound like a bad romance novel?"

"Oh no, no, no," I whine, clutching his arms. His fingers are working magic, stroking me with a certainty that has me on the verge of coming in seconds. The man's got skills, he really does. "No, you sound like one of the really, really good ones."

"You think you can walk away from this?" he whispers against my lips. "I'm going to make it impossible for you to leave me."

Our eyes meet and what I find gives me pause. I see need, desperation—and a dash of something tender. For the first time he can't negotiate for what he wants. His easy smiles and Prince Charming act, all the tools in his arsenal, the ones he's always relied upon, won't do him any good. They won't work on me and he knows it.

"Fancy—" I stroke his cheek. "That's not going to happen."

As soon as the words are out of my mouth, I regret them. This happens to be an almost daily occurrence for me, hence it doesn't warrant alarm. What does, however, is how quickly Ethan's demeanor changes from vulnerable to lethal.

"Watch me." Maybe it's the determined look on his face. Maybe it's the conviction in his voice. Whatever it is, nothing raises my hackles more than the idea that he may accomplish it. He smiles then. One of his sexy smiles. One that promises to be my downfall.

His strokes grow steady and sure, his thumb drawing circles on my sweet spot exactly the way he knows I like it. I come so hard I have to bite down on his shoulder to muffle the scream. Weak kneed, I sag against him while he holds me close. Then he pulls his fingers out and licks them, his eyes never leaving mine.

"Get on your knees. Let's put that pretty mouth of yours to good use."

Any other time in my life, with any other person, that would have earned a punch to the nut sac. But with him? Without having to be asked twice, I drop to my knees at the altar of Ethan.

He pushes his suit jacket out of the way and plants his hands on his hips. "Take it out." Even in the dim light of the utility closet, I can read the undisguised hunger on his face.

Eagerly, I do as I'm told, unbuckling his belt and dragging the zipper of his trousers down. I'm so giddy it feels like I'm unwrapping a present a day before Christmas. They drop to his ankles. I rub my mouth and nose over his hard-on, the one begging to be released from the confines of his boxer briefs. The musky scent of him mixed with laundry detergent and soap is crack cocaine to my libido.

The deep moan coming from above forces me to look up. His eyes beg me to continue. And I do. I drag his underwear halfway down his muscular thighs, cup and squeeze his sac, his erection jerking in response.

"Perfect," I murmur. Because he is. God help me, he is. I wrap my lips around the tip and grab him firmly at the base. His knees wobble, and his body sways. I lick and suck, pumping my hand in rhythm.

"Holy shit," I hear him mumble between short burst of

excited exhales.

"Hold on to something, Fancy McButterpants. I'm about to blow your mind." And I did. I don't make promises I can't keep.

* * *

"You're quiet." Ethan brushes the hair off of my face with one hand and pulls me closer with the other. I throw my leg over his naked lap and straddle him, head resting on his chest and wrapped in his arms. No better place in the world to be. Needless to say, after our session in the broom closet, I looked like I was jumped by a heard of horny adolescent bull elephants. No way was I going back to that party looking like that. Ethan texted Cam and Justin that we'd decided to make an early exit. And truthfully, I wasn't ready for the third degree from our friends.

As soon as he unlocked the front door, we stumbled inside with our mouths fused together and began to tear each other's clothes off. The kisses out of control, greedy. By the time we reached the top of the stairs there was a long trail of discarded clothing left in our wake. Naked, I was unceremoniously thrown over his shoulder. He got a smack on his ten star bubble butt for that. After which, I got a slap on mine. Can't say I minded it, though.

"Hmm." I lean in, burying my face on the side of his neck, and suck in a big whiff of him. It's one of my favorite things to do now. Which, I've determined, should be a thing—a legit hobby. I don't know what it is about his scent, but it quiets the crazy and that is something that should always be encouraged.

"Should I be worried?" He sounds more amused than curious.

"No," I say head shaking. "I was thinking about what Cal said."

"That you're family?"

I lift my eyes to take in Ethan's reaction and nod. He picks up my hand, the one that's brushing back and forth over his chest, and places a kiss on my knuckles, on my palm.

"My grandmother doesn't know who I am, my mother is a stranger I can barely tolerate...all I have left is Audrey, and I'm still getting to know her."

"You forgot one other person."

"Hmm, who did I forget?" I ask, the words garbled by the irrepressible smile spreading across my face.

"The naked man under you."

"That's sweet," I say planting a kiss on his chest, on the side of his neck. "But one day you'll meet someone and fall in love and she, rightfully so, would take issue with a *benefriend* being in your life."

"What if I make you fall in love with me?" His voice sounds strange, rushed, lacking the self possession he's famous for. Beneath me, I can feel him holding his breath. A staring contest ensues. Which he wins when my smile breaks free.

"You think you can make me fall in love with you?" I echo, half chuckling at his audacity. If I didn't know how hard fought his confidence was, it'd be a major turn off. However, knowing where he started makes my throat burn with pride for him.

Dancing with wily mischief, lids heavy, those eyes move back and forth from my eyes to my lips. "Hmm."

"It's like that, is it? You decide to make me fall in love with you and it's a done deal? You're calling your shot? Eight ball in the corner pocket."

"Hmm," he says with a cute little nod.

"A little full of ourselves aren't we? And when I say ourselves and we, I mean you."

"When I put my mind to something I usually get what I want." His arms tighten around me, hands brushing up and down my spine.

Falling in love, loving someone, never felt like a risk to me. Exhausting, yes. Time consuming, mostly. But not risky. Because I was always prepared for pain and rejection, for the inevitable demise of every relationship I've ever been in. What felt risky was allowing myself to be loved, to let someone else take care of me. I've craved it my whole life. And like any reformed addict, I know my limits. If I let myself be loved, then what? What becomes of me once they leave? And judging by how terrified I feel right now, it's the first time I've ever wanted to risk it.

"Not this time." Before I know what's what I'm on my back, pressed between a soft mattress and hard muscles. He shifts his hips and makes room for himself between my thighs. "Are we starting? Is this part of your strategy? *Art of War* and all that?" I say, holding back a throaty laugh.

I feel his body grow thick and hard at top speed and an electric jolt zips up my spine in anticipation of what's to come. Shifting higher, he rubs against my sweet spot and I nearly come undone, my body revved and ready to go, in a constant state of pending orgasm around him.

"More like Art of Love," he murmurs, his voice husky with desire.

"Cute. Very cute. Adorbs, really." My voice is thin. I'm hanging on to rational thought by my fingertips. "No one's managed to make me do anything I don't want to yet, but I'm breathless with anticipation to see you try."

A wicked smile lights up his face. A half opened condom wrapper is ready to go on the nightstand. He grabs it and rolls it on. Then he lowers his firm lips onto mine, peppering them with soft biting kisses, kisses so tender and distracting that I barely notice him sliding his palm from my hip to the back of my knee, hardly notice him hitching that leg high around his waist. But when he thrust his hips and buries himself inside of me, fusing us as one, then I notice. When he looks into my eyes as if I'm the only thing in the world worthy of his attention, I notice. Every smartass comment I'm about to taunt him with dies on take off because I am left speechless from the feelings passing between us.

"Ethan," I murmur as I reach up and cup his face. He kisses my palm, then rubs his prickly cheek back and forth. Just a name. It shouldn't mean so many things. And yet it does.

I can't hold his determined gaze a second longer. I'm lost to the pleasure moving through me as he slowly rocks his hips. "Hold on tight, baby. I'm about to wreck this pretty little pussy," he murmurs in my ear as he drives his body into mine. Harder, more demanding now. "You're gonna hang a condemned sign on it when I'm done."

Seriously? I bite down on my lips to stave off the grin, the laughter, the pure joy. He's the most fun I've ever had. Seeing my amusement, a slow smile lights up his face.

"Too much?" he murmurs.

All I can do is shake my head as my tightly coiled body gets ready to cut loose another epic O. My dirty talking nice guy... too cute. Too damn cute. There were no declarations of love that night. Though I can't fault the man's strategy.

CHAPTER TWENTY-FIVE

THE NEXT WEEK FLIES BY in a blur of sexual experimentation, some that will have to be added to the Kama Sutra I'm pretty sure. It's kind of troubling, how neither one of us seems to be satiated—ever. I can barely walk and yet the man looks at me funny and I'm ready to go. I chalk this up to abstinence being a dangerous thing.

"Ethan—" Strong fingers press into the insides of my thighs, spreading them open and holding them down. He came home early this afternoon on some ridiculous pretense that he wanted to work in his newly renovated home office. As soon as he walked through the door he grabbed me and began peeling clothes off. I was naked before we even made it to the stairs.

"These are the most beautiful legs," he mutters, placing a string of kisses on the inside of my thigh. "And this is the most beautiful pussy—"

"Eth—" My voice is strangled, breathy. Which is no surprise since the man in my bed has been torturing me with his hands and tongue for the past twenty minutes. It's the other body part, the one he wants to keep to himself, that I'm interested in.

"Hmm."

"Eth—"

Then, a low chuckle. "Hmm."

My clit has been teased so mercilessly it's seconds away from crying, throwing its toys on the ground, and going home.

"If you don't stop torturing me, I will rip off your dick and pleasure myself with it."

A burst of hot breath hits the bulls eye, the deep chuckle that follows it vibrating to the rest of my lady parts. I nearly shoot off the bed I'm so sensitive.

The man doing the torturing lifts his head and gives me a sultry look, his sensual mouth curving into a grin that promises retribution. "Since you asked so nicely." His expression turns aggressive. "Get on your elbows and knees—ass up."

My eyes widen in sweet, salacious joy. "Aye aye, sir," I chirp in glee, scrabbling to do as I am told.

"Amber—" The inflection in his voice gets my attention. I turn to examine his face. "I'll use a condom if you want me to but—I know you're on the pill." With uncertainty in his eyes, he holds my gaze. I saw him watching me take it two nights ago. And it's not like it was a secret; I keep them in the bathroom we share.

"You know I'm clean," he says.

Nothing about this affair feels casual anymore. Definitely not if we're ready to cross this line. Cassandra's word's are always there, scratching at the back of my mind, telling me I'm losing control of the situation—and more importantly, of my feelings.

"I am, too. No condom."

His eyes first brighten, then fill with raw desire. He's the sexiest man on the planet full stop. It seems inconceivable that a man could be this good—the kind of good that's bone deep—and be just as beautiful on the outside. I almost look around to see if anybody else sees it, or if it's all in my head.

"Face down," he murmurs with a pronounced rasp. A hard slap on the ass makes me yelp and smile into the mattress. Nope. This is real, thank heaven. "And, Jones—" New discovery: he calls me Jones whenever things are about to get really good. "You might want to bite down on that pillow."

The *Monday Night Football* theme starts playing and I almost go apoplectic. Somewhere in another room, I simultaneously hear my phone ring.

"Ignore it," I bark.

When the ringing continues, Ethan breathes out a tired sigh. He leans over my body, his chest draped over my back, and reaches for his phone on the nightstand. A moment later, I feel cool air hit my skin when he springs off the bed.

"Get dressed. Camilla went into labor."

* * *

Once baby Shaw decided to vacate the premises, he did it post haste. Calvin barely made it to the hospital in time, the baby delivered into the capable hands of his papa only an hour after rushing through the doors of the emergency room. Knowing that mother and child are safe and healthy, Ethan and I stop at the nursery first to get our first glimpse of young Connor.

Plastered to the glass, we gaze out over a large swath of babies. One of the young pediatric nurses smiles at the handsome man standing next to me.

Slut. Defiler of the innocent. I give her the evil eye and her brow quirks in confusion. It's official, I've turned into *Gollum*.

"Where is he?" I ask, while I subtly shuffle closer to him.

"There." Ethan taps the glass. "Third baby from the left, in the middle—Connor Shaw."

I've never fallen in love so hard and fast. The second my eyeballs find him I'm gone. Amazing how you can feel so strongly about someone who's basically a small lump of meat with no thought process.

"Oh, he's umm, he's..." I can feel my face melting into a frown. "He's kind of small. Don't you think? Doesn't look like Cal got a lot of bang for his buck," I mutter. "I'd ask for a refund."

"Hmm."

At the absent reply, I glance sideways and find him staring at the babies with a soft smile curving his lips. For whatever reason, this motivates me to continue. "That girl baby is twice his size." More humming from the man standing next to me. I brave another furtive glance, and yet again, find that dreamy look on his face. Which is bordering dangerously on longing.

"Kind of an ugly spud, too."

No joke, baby Connor looks like he went thirteen rounds with Manny Pacquiao and was on the losing end of that tussle. His eyes are swollen shut and the color of his skin angry.

"Do you like kids?" His voice is lower than usual, also a tad husky. He's working hard to sound casual but his voice is betraying him.

I, however, am not faring much better. Calling me surprised is putting it lightly. My throat closes up. Swallowing has suddenly turned into an Olympic event, the most difficult thing I've ever accomplished. Something seems to be messing with my motor skills.

"I mean...they're kind of messy. And a lot of responsibility. But I would be genuinely upset if *The Hunger Games* was a real thing. That wouldn't be okay with me. I would probably...I don't know, sign an on-line petition or something. Maybe write to my congressman."

Silence. Which prompts my attention to slide over to him once more. He's no longer watching the babies. This time I find him staring straight at me. His unblinking gaze is hyper intense.

"How about you?" I have no idea what prompted that question and regret my idiocy the moment the words fall out of my loose lips.

A glimmer of excitement sparks in his big eyes. "I want a whole bunch. Enough for Thanksgiving football games on the front lawn."

Good grief, he's a freaking Duggar.

Instantly, I get a clear image of a passel of beautiful brown eyed babies hanging onto Ethan's legs while he tosses one up over his shoulders. And now I want to go ahead and retch because...well, because I like it. Why would I *like* it? That's just not me. No way. I'm not fit to be anybody's mother. I'm not even fit to own goldfish.

In my mind's eyes, Ethan is smiling broadly at someone, someone walking next to him. A woman. I hate her. Even though I can't see her face I know that she's as perfect as he is. Hanging onto the legs of the kid dangling on his shoulders, he leans down to kiss her. And that's when it happens. I bend over and vomit all over his shoes.

Half an hour later I emerge from the ladies room

clutching my stomach to find Ethan standing in the hallway, waiting for me. I look a touch less like a character in the *Walking Dead,* and his Tod's loafers don't entirely smell like the lox and cream cheese bagel I had for lunch.

"I'm pretty sure I was poisoned. The kid making my bagel didn't like me. I could sense it." I catch Ethan pushing down a smile.

"You weren't poisoned. The fish might've gone bad, though." He brushes a piece of hair that I hadn't noticed hanging in my face back behind my ear and I get nauseous all over again. The urge to nose dive into the crook of his arm is overwhelming.

Moments later, we step into Cam's room and are immediately met by a chorus of hellos. Camilla's parents, Angelina and Tom DeSantis, one by one throw their arms around me and kiss each cheek. I'm squeezed and prodded in the process, told I'm too skinny, and ordered to eat more. This is nothing new. They've been doing it since I was eleven and their daughter brought me home for dinner.

In the meantime, Mercedes—Calvin's estate manager, but also much more since Cam and Cal consider her family—hugs Ethan, who then gets his cheeks pinched by Mrs. DeSantis. The only people missing are Calvin, Amanda, and Sam.

"Whatever you do, do *not* bring up the delivery room. He's—" Craning her neck, Camilla furtively checks the doorway. "He gets very emo."

As if summoned, Cal walks in carrying two shopping bags filled with food from Citarella and wearing a face-breaking, white grin. I've never seen him smile. Like—ever. I wasn't even certain he had teeth before this very day. He actually looks weird smiling. Kind of reminds me of Bruce, the big shark in *Finding Nemo,* and it's creeping me out.

"Congratulations, buddy," Ethan is the first to offer.

"Hey, Cal."

"Did you see my son?" Cal asks, pride gushing from every pore.

Oh how the mighty have fallen. I remember a time not too long ago when he wasn't so stoked to claim him. And now he's, *my son.* Men, need I say more?

"What's most important is that he's healthy," I toss out.

All the attention in the room swiftly turns on me with expressions ranging from curious to confused.

"He's beautiful," Ethan quickly adds with a straight face. Always the loyal friend. His eyes hold mine.

For a second it feels like it's just the two of us in the room, connected by some invisible apron strings...or is it heart strings? Whatever, some kind of goddamn invisible string. The corners of his firm, pink lips tip up and I answer with deliberate roll of my eyes. What a sap. A cute one.

"We came straight from the airport," Amanda, Calvin's sister, says as she rushes into the room.

"Cam!" Sam, Amanda's eight year old son, shouts. He heads straight for Camilla and throws his long, skinny arms around her neck.

"Easy, Sam. Your aunt just had a baby," Calvin tells him while Camilla hugs Sam even tighter.

"I'm so happy you're here. I missed you," she whispers in Sam's ear and breathes him in. These two have had an ongoing love affair since the day they met, and if I didn't already know that Camilla was going to be an amazing mother, watching her with Sam convinced me that she should have ten. Unlike yours truly, some people are born for this.

Amanda wraps an arm around her brother's waist. "Where's the baby?"

"Sleeping, finally," Camilla answers with a smile, though the exhaustion is clear in her voice.

The quiet turns to chaos, the sound of joy and celebration filling the room. There's so much love here. So many people holding this extended family together. I notice Camilla watching the chaos with a soft smile on her face. Her eyes meet mine and a bottomless depth of understanding passes between us. This is all she's ever wanted.

"Happy?" I mouth.

"Just a little," she mouths back, gesturing with her thumb and index finger.

I turn my attention to the tall, gruff man that's made my best friend's dreams come true. "How was the delivery, Cal?"

The room goes silent, the only sounds are the ones coming from the hallway. Calvin's face goes flat. A short while after that his nostrils flare and the side of his eye twitches. This is a master class in control. Until he loses the battle and his face starts to fold. Eyes glazing, he looks around once more and mumbles something that sounds like, "Be right back", turns on his heels, and walks out the door.

Sorry, not sorry.

CHAPTER TWENTY-SIX

BY THE TIME I WALK into the townhouse the following evening it's already past seven. The banging of the sledgehammer tells me something's up with Ethan. I would have to be blind, deaf and dumb to not have figured out that he takes to beating the life out of that wall when something's bothering him.

Before making my way to the living room, I detour to the kitchen, put the groceries away, and grab a bottle of water. He didn't hear me come in. I know he didn't because he goes about his business while I stand in the doorway and watch him like the filthy pervert that I am.

"Whatever that wall did to you, it's ready to apologize."

The sledgehammer raised above his head, he stops, then slowly lowers it to the ground. Even from across the room I can feel the bubble of emotion surrounding him. He turns and our eyes meet, the sparkle and good humor he often wears missing. I can't decipher the look on his face. Though, if I were to guess, I'd say equal parts sadness and longing, as if he's lost something that matters. Beneath all those fancy clothes, he's just a man. Albeit a beautiful one. But still, just a man made of bone and flesh and tender parts.

Panting and sweating from the exertion, he leans on the hammer for support as he watches me walk up and hand him the bottle without a word. For a brief moment he stares at the bottle with a funny look. Then, opening it, he takes a big gulp.

"Wanna talk about it?" I plant my butt on a wooden workbench left by the construction crew and patiently wait for him to answer. In the meantime my gaze flickers to the sweat dripping down his chest, the sweat he makes no move to wipe away.

"You know my second rounder?" His gaze slides to the handle of the sledgehammer.

"The running back from Alabama?"

Ethan nods. "He went to a house party last night. Somebody in his group was carrying. They got into it with another group—haven't gotten the full story yet...bottom line, somebody's dead." At my silence, he continues, "The team cut him an hour ago."

"How bad is it?"

Ethan takes another long pull of his water. "Bad. There's video. Two guys were gang affiliated. Old friends from home." Shaking his head, he places the bottle down and takes the hammer in both hands. "Everything was riding on that draft money. That kid has at least twenty-five people to carry on his back."

"I'm sorry. I know how much time and effort you put into cultivating their careers." At this, he nods, his brow doctored with worry. "Is it over? His career."

"If they don't charge him, which looks like they won't right now, he'll get a suspension and a fine from the league. I may be able to get a team to pick him up afterward...depends how bad injuries are during the season...but after Ray Rice and Hernandez—" Ethan shakes his head. In frustration, I gather. "It's zero tolerance. He'll have to work ten times as hard to prove himself." For a moment, I lose him to his thoughts, his absent gaze fixed on the torn up wall.

"You're a good man, Ethan Vaughn."

Surprise, wonder, something akin to longing—it's all there when his attention returns to me. He smiles but it's small and sad, weighed down by all the responsibility he carries on his shoulders. Bending closer, his lips meet mine and brush back and forth until I kiss him back. Until I stand and wrap my hand around his neck and feel him shudder, his frustration tangible under my fingertips, trying to remain stoic in the face of adversity. My fingers knead his neck, working the tension out.

He exhales harshly and I know he's given up resisting me. Seeking comfort, he places his forehead on the curve of my shoulder and I almost stop breathing, a familiar ache under my sternum. All I want to do is hold him and make him feel better, take all his concerns away. And that terrifies me. I didn't sign up for this. I signed up for mind blowing sweaty monkey sex. Not tenderness. Not affection. Not heartache and understanding.

"I got an email from Parker. He wants to talk," I say, bringing the tender moment to a sudden end. His head comes up, expression unreadable. "Why is this case taking so long?"

"David is negotiating. What she's asking for is extortion."

"I'm ready to borrow against my inheritance to be done with this. It won't be much, but—"

"The hell you are," says the ruthless lawyer, cutting me off. "Did you write him back?"

"No. Whatever it is, I don't want to hear it." That part of my life is dead and buried. For good, once the case is closed. "He must take me for an idiot if he thinks I have any intention of hearing him out. Last time we spoke—" Embarrassed, I glance up and find Ethan watching me. "He called me abrasive. Said it would be *career suicide* to work together."

Maybe I said too much. It certainly wouldn't be the first time. A lot of mental handwringing ensues while I wait for him to say something. Instead, a slow smile grows on his face.

"What are you smiling at? You think I'm abrasive too? Great," I mutter.

His smile fades. "I don't think you're abrasive."

"You don't?" I do nothing to keep the suspicion out of my voice.

A silent moment passes, two, his eyes fall on the handle of the sledgehammer. I watch his hand grip and release it over and over. "You're like this sledgehammer."

And the bud of hope I was nurturing a moment ago shrivels. "Loud and destructive? And here I was thinking you liked me."

He shakes his head, his eyes search mine. Serious. So serious. The silence lasts for an amount of time that tells me this moment is important, that I should pay attention to what comes next.

"A force to reckon with."

Gravity ceases to exist and all the hair on my body stands on end. His gaze pulls away from me, returning to the sledgehammer. "The type of woman a man holds onto with both hands and never lets go."

This is it. This is the moment when everything changes. The moment when that restless feeling in the farthest reaches of my soul quiets. The moment I fall off Cloud Nine and land on a rainbow made of cotton candy. The moment I fall irrevocably in love with the man standing before me.

* * *

We're at family Shaw's house for a barbecue. Last night, after the revelation landed on my head as gently as a piano, I pleaded a headache and hid in my room. Around midnight, as I was staring at the ceiling in total darkness, I heard him enter, get into my bed and wrap himself around me. It took everything I had not to cry like a little bitch. Somebody revoke my badass card.

My inability to string words together continued. I didn't speak a single word on the car ride over. Every time I glanced over at Ethan, I found a soft smile on his face. Why he was smiling is anybody's guess. I'm chalking it up to him being blissfully ignorant to the shit floating around in my head—and more importantly, my heart.

"Would you look at the gorgeous man holding that baby," Camilla says wearing a stupid grin. I lift my sunglasses and squint at the men standing under the shade of the patio awning. They're far enough away from the pool chairs we're occupying that we can have a conversation without masculine ears eavesdropping—by design of course.

Ethan gently bounces on his feet with the baby safely tucked in the cradle of his arms.

"Yeah, he loves babies, miniature horses, and glitter," I mutter sourly and drop my wayfarers back down.

I'm pissed. Actually, I'm beyond pissed. Love was not part of the plan. As a matter of fact, it was the opposite of the plan. And yet here I am, staring at the *gorgeous man with the baby in his arms,* my heart tripping over itself every time our eyes meet. I'm ready to poke them out of my head just to get some relief.

"You need to have one soon so our kids can grow up

together."

If this doesn't deserve an eye roll, I don't know what does. "I'll get right on that for you. Speaking of kids, when do you think yours is going to grow out of this ugly stage?"

Her loud bark of laughter gets everyone's attention. Cal and Ethan glance our way. Finding us uninteresting, their attention returns to the baby.

"Reginald," she shouts. "Ethan has the baby. Are you going to check the hamburgers, or do I have to do it?"

Calvin's black brows lower in a squinty scowl that could be seen across a football field. "I'm handling it," he informs his wife.

With a fake grin, she mutters to me under her breath, "He's driving me caaraazy. The worst mother hen." After which she shouts, "Thanks, Boobear." Then she pokes my arm. "Look at Ethan. The man's a frigging fertility treatment. He would seriously cause a stampede if the women of Manhattan could see this." Then she snickers.

Yes, hilarious. I can't even muster a smile.

"Calvin's dying to take the baby back," she adds.

Calvin's eyes dart between the grill he should be manning and his son, eyeballing the situation as if he expects Ethan to drop the kid any minute.

Denying it is pointless. In hindsight, it's clear I've been stumbling towards love since I sat outside that courtroom with everything at stake, and him by my side telling me I could count on him. How could I have let this happen? Every time I think about moving to L.A. I get a chill up my spine and a cramp in the gut. Cassandra's words keep haunting me.

"Hand me the potato chips," I say. The need to drown my sorrows in food is strong.

"No. I'm still mad at you for ditching me at that shitty draft party," says my so-called best friend. Her stare-down has Sicilian vendetta written all over it. She tucks her bare feet up, her normal size feet that is, on the oversized lounge chair and raises a well groomed brow.

"I've already apologized a million times. I had jizz in my hair. There was no good choice."

Camilla grabs a handful of potato chips and makes a big show of popping one after another in her mouth. "Being a hoochie is no excuse."

Night has fallen by the time we finish eating and I clean up while Camilla feeds the baby. Ethan and I are about to leave when he gets a call, the Titans logo flashing on the screen of his cell phone.

"I have to take this," Ethan says.

I smile, knowing full well what this could mean. "Go," I say running a hand up his arm. He walks into Calvin's office and shuts the door.

In the kitchen Camilla finishes feeding the baby while I watch. "He's the perfect man," I say as I stare at Connor. "Naked and defenseless."

Camilla smiles down at her son, then eyeballs the container of gelato I pilfered from the freezer. "Do you want to hold him?"

"Too soon," I reply with a face-scrunch. "I'm loving him too much right now. I could squeeze him to death, or eat a couple of toes in my excitement. Those have got to be the cutest big toes in the whole wide world."

"They are, aren't they?" his mother says, beaming. "He gets them from his father."

I vomited a little in my mouth. "You had to ruin the

moment."

While I take a bite of the hazelnut gelato Ethan and I brought over, Camilla watches me with undisguised longing. "Is there something you want to tell me before male ears return?"

"Nope."

In response, I get an arched brow and a knowing look. She gently places the baby in the basinet. After which, without warning mind you, she snatches the container out of my hand, then the spoon.

"Fine. I'm in love with him, okay?" I whisper and close my eyes, bracing for the impact of her opinion. One minute passes silently, two. By the third, I crack open one eye, then the other. And find Camilla digging into the ice-cream. She stuffs a big spoonful in her mouth, and smiles drunkenly.

"I launch a hand grenade at you and you're eating?"

"Am I thupposed to be thurprised?"

"Aren't you?"

She swallows. "I've been waiting for you to figure it out. Aaand waiting. Zzzzzzz. This hazelnut gelato is some powerful sorcery, by the way."

"Whatever."

"What are you going to do about it?"

"A big fat nothing. I'm leaving for L.A. as soon as the case is closed, depending on whether I'll be spending any time in a New York State gulag—and he'll get the job with the Titans."

"I can't talk about you leaving, or I'll start to cry."

"I know. But you know I have to give it a shot."

"I know you do. Still, sucks for me."

"For both of us."

Her large, dark eyes hold mine. "He's in love with you,

too."

Head shaking, I say, "He's never mentioned the L word. Not once."

Except to promise that he'd make me fall in love with him and dang but he was right. Score one for team McButterpants.

"Puhleeze. I've seen the way he looks at you when you're not paying attention."

My ears immediately perk up, my curiosity piqued. I really shouldn't care. I really shouldn't. But I kind of do. "Like what?"

Her face twists into a smirk. "Like a toddler that's been handed a cell phone." The confused look I return prompts her to continue. "He doesn't have a clue what to do with you, but he's willing to spend the rest of his life trying to figure you out."

Huh.

"What are you girls up to?" a deep baritone calls out, interrupting what was sure to be a serious episode of me dissecting this information ad nauseam. Calvin leans against the massive kitchen island. Seeing the baby in the basinet, he swoops him up in his arms.

"We're about to shoot a low budge, girl on girl porno. It's either naughty Catholic school girls, or naughty Girl Scouts," I say with my filthiest smirk.

Cal arches a reproachful brow. He's good at that, the reproachful brow thing. "There's a child present."

"Bravo, naughty babysitter is an excellent idea."

"Boo, maybe you should put him in the basinet."

"He sleeps better in my arms," her pigheaded husband retorts.

"Calvin—" Cam's voice is a lot less saccharine this time.

"You need to put him down."

"I have something I've been meaning to say to you," I interrupt, directing this at the handsome giant who's smiling at the baby sleeping in his arms. The wary expression this elicits almost makes me laugh. "Relax, Cal. It's PG rated. Safe for little and big ears." His expression clears and I take that as my cue to continue. "I know we've had our differences and I've said this to you before but…again, I want to thank you for everything you've done for me. I can't even express how grateful I am. Paying the bail and Ethan and David for their time was—"

"Whoa," the bearded man says, interrupting. I notice the frown on his face and return a frown of my own. Why on Earth would he be frowning?

"I want to pay you back, Cal, I really do, but I don't have that kind of money right now."

Sharing a look I can't decipher, Camilla takes the sleeping baby out of his arms while Calvin stalls the rest of my speech with a raised hand.

"Why do you think I posted bail?"

Is this a trick question? I glance at Cam, and find her wearing a carefully neutral expression. A prickle of unease slides up my neck and over my scalp.

"Because you love your wife and she would've had your nuts if you didn't?" Obviously.

Head shaking, he says, "No. I mean, who told you I posted bail?"

"Ethan did." Calvin's black brows quirk. He glances at Camilla again. "Enough with the googley eyes at each other. What the heck is going on?"

"I called Ethan that night to get a referral, but he insisted on going to get you. He posted bail. I'm not paying him anything, Amber. It was all him. "

The door to Calvin's office swings open and the man in question steps out. One by one, his eyes scan the three faces staring back at him. His smile drops. "What'd I miss?"

CHAPTER TWENTY-SEVEN

I'M INNATELY SUSPICIOUS OF ANYTHING good. A priori it smells like bullshit until I deem otherwise. While I've been having the best sex of my life and happier than a pig in slop, I've also had one ear to the ground waiting for something to inevitably come along and screw it up. A phone ringing in the middle of the night is never a good thing.

The second the fog of sleep clears and I conclude that I'm not dreaming, my stomach clenches. I fumble around the nightstand for a while before my hand lands on the hard square that is my iPhone. My heart rate jumping, I turn away from Ethan so the cold light of the screen doesn't wake him. It reads Sunnyvale Assisted Living and I'm hit with the knowledge that something terrible is about to happen. With my heart thundering under my sternum, I press *accept* while the dread pooling in my gut tells me to prepare for the worst.

"I'm so sorry," the doctor on-call murmurs. One I've never met because before this day my grandmother never had any health issues—aside from the Alzheimer's that had stolen her away from me a small piece at a time.

The doctor is still speaking in what sounds like a foreign language, though rationally I know it isn't. I catch the two most important words—massive stroke. He says a lot more but I've already tuned him out.

Next to me, Ethan stirs awake. His warm hand on my shoulder both grounds me and makes me weak.

"My grandmother's dead."

Moments later he picks me up off the bed and helps me dress. I'm catatonic, my mind incapable of processing anything. He asks me things—where my phone is so he can call my mother, what I want to wear. I can't answer, can't recall anything.

Twenty minutes after that we're in the car headed to the assisted living facility. I have no recollection as to how I even got in the car. The doctor on call greets us at the entrance wearing an appropriately solemn expression. He talks to me and Ethan responds. We're led to a small room where they keep the bodies before the funeral home or morgue comes to retrieve them. I have yet to utter a word.

Ethan's arm has been around my shoulders, securing me to him, since we got out of the car. He holds me tighter as the doctor lifts the sheet off my grandmother. It's not the first dead body I've seen. Not by far. Growing up in a funeral home goes a long way to dispelling any fear of death one may have. It's her—but it isn't. She looks small. Smaller than I remember. How can an entire life be contained by so little? It doesn't seem possible.

I don't cry. I don't scream. I don't really feel much except detachment. I'm a spectator, reading a story in the third person. I nod at the doctor and he lowers the sheet. He says something about arrangements, asks which funeral home the body should be sent to. Ethan responds. I'm not sure what he answered; I find myself not caring.

My grandmother made arrangements to be buried on top

of my grandfather. A double decker I remember her calling it. It's all in the will. The person who bought her business is to handle the funeral—a funeral that will only be attended by myself, Eileen, Audrey and Dan.

Camilla and her parents will want to attend but I don't want them there. I don't want the joy of the birth of their first grandchild tainted by death.

Eileen and Dan rush in. She took the time to put on makeup and real clothes. I'm in my pajama pants and a sweatshirt. It's three am for fuck's sake and she's wearing lipgloss. A spike of anger is the first emotion I register since I got the phone call.

"Did you see her?" Eileen asks, her bright blue eyes shifting quickly between me and Ethan a couple of times until she finally chooses to keep them on Ethan. Typical.

"Yes, I'm sorry. My condolences," Ethan replies.

"Dan Peterson. Thank you so much for bringing Amber," Dan, ever the gentleman, says with an outstretched hand.

"Ethan Vaughn." The men shake hands. "No need to thank me." Ethan tightens his grip on my shoulder again.

"You need to sign off so they can send the body to the funeral home," I tell Eileen in a flat voice I barely recognize.

"I was thinking to send her to Long Island. Easier to make arrangement—"

Her words ignite a fire in my chest. "She left specific instructions. She is NOT going to Long Island because it's easier for you."

"Alright, alright ladies," Dan interrupts. "No need to argue. If she left instructions that she wanted to be sent to her old place then so be it."

"But Dan—" my mother whines.

"Honey—seems only right to follow her wishes."

On Dan's insistence, Eileen pouts and pouts, and eventually acquiesces.

"No use in waiting until Friday. Everyone she knows is dead. Let's do it as soon as possible." With that I start walking away. I hear Ethan giving Dan his number and telling him to call if he needs help with anything.

When he catches up to me, he grabs me by the shoulders and turns me. His face inches from mine, his shrewd eyes dart all over my face—assessing my state of mind no doubt. I stare back with total apathy in my eyes. His mouth tightens and the next thing I know I'm wrapped up in a big hug, his arms steel bands around me, my face buried in his neck and his scent filling my lungs.

"I don't want you to worry about anything," he murmurs. "I'll take care of everything...I'll take care of you."

No. No, I don't want him to take care of anything— especially not me. I'm already so deep in love I'm suffocating under the weight of it.

I pry myself from his firm grip, from his comfort, and look up into his face. "I don't want you to do anything. Everything's been taken care of anyway. My grandmother made all the arrangements."

I don't wait to see what his face tells me. I turn and walk to the parking lot.

* * *

After a long, drawn-out conversation I convince Camilla and her parents not to attend. I want this to be over as quickly as possible and without fanfare. Justin puts up a fuss but I manage him deftly as well. There's only one person that I can't manage to dissuade, and that's Ethan.

"There's no point in you coming. Fredo will drive me to New Jersey. Don't you have a ton of work to do?"

The intense vibes scalding the back of my neck gets my attention. I turn, holding the black dress I retrieved from the closet and find him wearing a disapproving look; I would even go as far as to say that he looks offended. Dressed and ready to go, he shoves his hands into the pockets of his impeccable dark suit.

"Are we friends? We're friends, right?" he says, his expression growing more indignant by the minute.

Looking into determined brown eyes, a melty event happens in the environ of my heart.

"Of course we're friends, you dope." Friends. Right. Sliding the zipper down, I step into the dress and walk over to him for assistance zipping it up.

"So if the situation were reversed, you would do it for me, wouldn't you? Or maybe the definition of friendship needs to be clarified."

There he goes again, lawyering me to death. It's official, I will never win an argument with this man. "Stop out-thinking me. You're being rude."

"You should be used to it by now." Our eyes meet over my shoulder, mine practically stuck in the roll back position. Pleased with himself, he places a kiss on the side of my neck, and zips up the dress. Discussion over.

The day is cloudy. We get there the same time Dan pulls in. Audrey is the first one out of their car. She's wearing a dark shirt, a purple pleated miniskirt and black leggings. Her hair is in princess Leia buns. She runs into me with enough force to almost knock me down, and hugs my waist in a death grip. I smile for the first time in days.

It occurred to me when Ethan was driving us to the cemetery that there is no actual reason for me to speak to, or see my mother ever again. If I want to be, I could be free of her...if I want to be. Because that would mean I would be free of Audrey and Dan as well.

Everyone is quiet as we walk to the gravesite. This cemetery is very large and riddled with hills. I don't fail to note that Eileen is wearing four inch heels. By the looks of the red soles, Louboutins. In contrast, I'm wearing ballerina flats.

Watching her lean on Dan as we traverse hill after hill to get to the plot, her heels sinking into the grass with every step she takes, is the highlight of my week. At one point, she almost drags Dan down with her as she stumbles backwards. In my heart of hearts I know that some time in the future, when I recall this, I will break out it fits of laughter. I glance up at Ethan to see if he's noticed, and watch his lips quiver. I don't know what his eyes are doing because he has his king of studs sunglasses on.

The black comedy portion of the day is over when we reach the plot. The priest is already there. Everything is set to go. Ethan keeps his arm around me on one side while Audrey flanks my other side. Dan has taken Eileen's hand. He rubs her knuckles in comfort.

I used to believe in karma. I used to believe that there's a master plan as to how our lives play out, a heavenly accountant, if you will, keeping track of all the pluses and minuses. I cry foul. I cry foul for the simple fact that Eileen never did a damn thing to deserve a man as good as Dan. How does that equation balance? How does she get to roller-skate through life without a care, without ever once dealing with the consequences of her irresponsibility? How is that fair? Someone explain it to me.

The service starts and concludes with expedience. We thank the priest as the coffin is being lowered, linger for an amount of time that's appropriate, then en masse begin our cross-country trek back to the parking lot. Eileen complains the entire time. I kid you not.

"I don't understand why she had to buy a plot all the way in the back...my shoes are ruined. Dan, my shoes are ruined. Look at the heels, they're ruined."

"I'm sure they're not ruined," St. Dan the doting husband responds.

"Look at how many nice plots there are closer to the road. I would've told her to buy one of these, but did anyone consult me? Of course not. These shoes are seven hundred dollars...Jesus, it's hot. If I knew it was going to get hot I wouldn't have worn this suit...Dan, can't you bring the car around? I can't walk another step in these shoes. This cemetery isn't very well kept..."

"She was trying to save money!" I shout, wheeling around to face her. "For her care! Do you know how much that plot cost? Five thousand! Do you ever think of anyone but yourself?"

Ethan grips my shoulder harder, almost pulling me back, while my mother's eyes narrow on me.

"That's it. We're leaving. I don't need to take this shit from you. God, you're such a bully!"

For a minute, I feel bad...only for a minute.

Dan looks so uncomfortable he looks ready to crawl out his skin. In silence, Audrey follows our mother to the car while Dan is left standing there. "Maybe it's best we all take a time out. Amber, I know you're upset, but she's upset too. She just handles it differently."

With that, Dan turns and leaves. Ethan and I watch the car drive away. It feels like a chapter of my life just ended.

* * *

Two nights later, sleeping restlessly, I wake abruptly in the middle of the night. The cable box reads two am. A loud snore coming from the man next to me says Ethan is soundly asleep. I crawl out of bed and throw on Ethan's hoody over my tank top and underwear. Grabbing my phone just in case, I head out.

I've been on edge the last two days. I never realized it was the weight of my grandmother that was tying me down, anchoring me to this life, until it was gone. Untethered, I feel like I could float away. That I *should* float away...to Los Angeles. Except something keeps whispering in my ear that either way, I won't find any peace.

In the rooftop garden, I sit on the carved wooden bench overlooking the cityscape. It's only June and already warm.

"Hey," I hear coming from the doorway. The voice sounds hoarse, sleep deprived. Ethan stands there in his glasses, a t-shirt and boxer briefs. My heart lurches inside my chest. Not because he's stunning on the outside—because he's even more beautiful on the inside.

"Did I wake you?"

He shakes his head. "Not having you next to me did," he states casually as if he didn't just freaking end me. I wonder if he even realizes the significance of his words. Pain, my heart throbs with it, my throat constricting with all the things I'm too scared to tell him. I have so much love for this man my body can't contain it all.

I watch him rub his eyes with his thumb and index finger,

his eyebrows stretching up. Between juggling work and me, he must be exhausted. I've tried to pretend everything's back to normal—whatever that is—to alleviate some of his concern. It doesn't seem to be working, though.

"I'm going to offer Susan my inheritance. I'm done being patient."

His face stills. "What's the hurry?"

"I'm sick of waiting, Ethan. I'm sick of having this hang over my head. You said this would take three months tops and it's already five."

"I told you David knows what he's doing. He knows what's in your best interest."

In the pause I gather my thoughts, hoping to make him understand this sudden sense of urgency I feel.

"You know, I never considered my grandmother dying. Sounds like a blindspot now that I say it out loud but every doctor we saw told us this disease takes forever to kill a person...so I prepared for forever." Ethan nods, sympathy filling his eyes. "And now that she's gone, I've run out of excuses. I need to go to L.A."

His head tips back, frustration etched in his refined features.

"You need that money," he grinds out. "Moving will be expensive. Just give him a little more time to negotiate. From what Dave's been telling me, I have a feeling she'll come around soon."

"By soon I hope you mean tomorrow because otherwise I'll email Parker. I'll make the offer myself."

Eyes trained on the horizon, he says, "Are you coming to bed?" Ethan grumpy is a rare thing. I chalk it up to lack of sleep.

The gust of chilly wind makes me shiver. I follow him back down without a word. In the bedroom I slip off the hoody and notice an alert on my phone. Audrey has sent me an email.

"What is it?" Ethan asks, his tired expression clearing.

"Audrey." I click on the email and read it out loud.

> I know you're sad and angry at mom but she's sad too. She's been crying a lot since the funeral and I don't think it's about grandma. I think it's because she wants things to be different with you. Don't be mad at her forever. Please.

"There's an attachment," I say and click on the audio file.

"I know you miss Grandma." Her sweet voice drifts through the speaker. "But now you have me...this is Afterlife by Ingrid Michaelson. This is for you."

Ethan's reassuring gaze captures mine.

The first keys of the piano aren't what I'm expecting them to be. They're not as forceful and upbeat as the original. Audrey's rendition is slow and melancholy.

"When the world is breaking down around you, taking everything that you know.

What you didn't know is that we can go forever.

If we want to we can live inside of a moment the one that we own.

You and me
We got this
You and me
We're beautiful
Beautiful"

My sister's lilting voice strips me of the cloak of numbness I've been wearing since that late night call. It gets into my bones and digs in, pushing every emotion I've been hiding for the past week to the surface. A river of tears runs down my face, onto my neck, splashing on my tank top.

"We are
We are
We're going to be alright
We got
We got
We always got the fight in us
We are
We are
We're going to live tonight like there's no tomorrow 'cause we are the afterlife."

Ethan's face is tight, his frustration clear. Three large steps and he's on me, holding me close to his heart like he means to never let go.

My body starts to shake, a catharsis, years of pent up anger and disappointment purging all at once. The urge to get closer turns into a desperate need that reminds me of rats on a sinking ship. My world is sinking and I scratch and claw, holding onto him to stay afloat for one more breath.

Warm hands span my back, holding me securely until the spasms stop. And all the while he whispers sweet reassurances and promises that speak to my soul, to every true fear I harbor but never voice out loud.

That he's here for me.

That I'm not alone.

That he'll never let me go.

"We are
We are
We're going to be alright

We got
We got
We always got the fight in us
We are
We are
We're going to live tonight like there's no tomorrow 'cause we are the afterlife."

CHAPTER TWENTY-EIGHT

THE DOORBELL RINGS AND RINGS and rings. I don't know what I expected when I rip open the door, but it isn't Parker. Standing on the front stoop with his hands shoved into the front pockets of his creased, hipster jeans, everything about him is familiar and foreign at the same time. I used to think him unaffected, above such superficial bullshit. How wrong I was. The messy blond hair and neat beard that I once found so adorably sexy makes me want to barf now.

"What are you doing here?"

He won't hold my burning gaze. His expression is not the same careless one I had the displeasure of seeing five months ago. This time it's sheepish.

"I'm here to invite you to lunch. I need to speak to you and you haven't returned any of my calls." He pushes up a fake smile.

"Last time you invited me someplace I wound up in jail, so you'll excuse me if I invite you to fuck off."

I'm about to shut the door on him when Parker grabs it.

"Amber, I'm begging you. It's the film. The dailies came back and Cheyenne…" His shoulders fall. Head tilted away, I watch his lips press so tight they disappear. "She isn't ready for such a heavy role. We've only shot a week's worth of film.

The only person who knows this character as well as I do is you."

Is this a joke?

"Parker—" Shocked, his name comes out a question. "I...I don't even..." Exhaling harshly, I begin again, "Let's start at the beginning. Does your wife know she's being replaced?"

"We discussed it," he mumbles, the words cautious. "She understands that my career is at stake. I can't fuck this up."

His blue eyes meet mine and in them I see desperation— but not altruism. None. And not one iota of remorse. This is, as usual, about Parker and his career, no regard for other people's needs or feelings. It doesn't matter what he has to do to get what he wants. Begging, lying, dumping fiancées, firing his wife. Whatever it takes, he's willing to do it for the sake of his career. I almost admire his dedication.

"I don't see why you would come all this way for nothing. Thanks to you and your mother I can't leave the state until this case is closed. That is, unless I have to go to jail."

His face twists in confusion. Rubbing his bearded chin, the way he's contemplating me triggers an uneasy flutter in my stomach.

"You don't know?"

The flutter kicks up a notch, a pending sense of dread on its coattails. "Know what, Parker? Spit it out, or I'm shutting this door."

His mouth tilts up in a smug smile. I know that look. This is bad.

"The charges were dropped. The case has been closed for a month. Vaughn paid restitution, for the renovations to my mother's house."

The last few words are a blur, drowned out by the blood

rushing in my ears, my heart pumping hard enough for it to be painful.

A month.

Closed for a month.

Ethan paid for the repairs.

A month. And he never mentioned it. He's been lying to me for a month…and I turned down the part because they were shooting in Canada. Rage descends upon me, my legs shaking from the adrenaline rush.

* * *

"I'm sorry miss, you can't go in…"

Not even bothering to glance at his receptionist, I storm past her. Her objection fades away as I barrel through the door of his office.

Ethan looks up from his computer screen and smiles, his eyes two crescents that take me in from head to toe. When they climb up to my narrow eyed scowl, the joy he's wearing on his too-handsome-for-his-own-good face extinguishes.

Standing to his left, Andi's expression turns owlish. She starts to inch away from him. Her feminine wiles are obviously telling her shit's about to go down and her boss is in all likelihood a marked man. Right before she scurries out of the office, she throws a, "Bye, Amber," over her shoulder.

While Andi closes the door behind her, we stare at each other like we're in a spaghetti western. Meanwhile, his frazzled secretary trots in. "I'm so sorry, Mr. Vaughn—"

"It's fine, June. Miss Jones is always welcome." He smiles at June and the tightness on the secretary's face eases. Then she backs out, closing the door behind her.

Alone at last.

"What's wrong?" he has the nerve to ask, the space

between his eyes puckering.

"What's wrong? *What's wrong?*" My lids are practically pinned to my forehead. "You lying sack of shit."

His shoulders drop, his eyes squeezing shut for a moment. Suspicion confirmed. Parker was telling the truth. And the truth feels exactly like a stake through the heart. When they open again, he aims all the remorse and sorrow in them at me. "Who told you?"

"Parker came by the townhouse. He was overjoyed to discover you're just as bad as he is."

Abruptly, the door opens. "E, what do you want me to do with..." David Pitt's words slide to a stop when he looks up from the paperwork he's holding and sees me standing there. Or, more importantly, sees the expression I'm wearing.

"Perfect. Deceitful sack of shit number two. Come on in, we were just getting started."

Ethan stands and slowly walks around his desk. With every step he takes toward me, I back away from him. When only a few feet separate us, he stops and shoves his hands into the pockets of his slacks.

"How could you? I turned down work because I thought I couldn't leave the state!"

His head drops, his gaze falling on his shoes. He rubs the back of his neck.

"The night I came to the bar—I was going to tell you..."

But we went home and had wild monkey sex. Yeah, I remember.

On the edge of my vision, I see Pitt trying to back out of the office. "Stay right where you are, Pitt," I practically growl. He freezes. My attention whips in his direction. "I want all the paperwork regarding my case emailed to me ASAP."

"Absolutely. The case is closed. I went a step further and expunged all mention of it from your record."

"You're dismissed."

Pitt scurries out of the room without another word. Looking into the flat, sorrowful eyes of the man I love, a pain so caustic burns my lungs that it's impossible to breathe. Rubbing the ache is pointless, nothing can soothe the hole in my chest.

"You know the worst part—I'm not surprised. I should've known you would never do anything to jeopardize your precious career. You would *never risk being disbarred*," I say, repeating the words I'd heard him speak all those months ago.

He takes a step forward. "Amber, listen, I never meant—"

"Don't." I hold out my hands to stop him from coming any closer. "You manipulated me. The one thing you know I can't stomach." He extends a hand, reaching for me, but I step back in time to evade him.

"Damn it! I didn't know you were offered the part. You didn't tell me. I thought we were friends. I thought we were in this together!"

"I did tell you!"

"After the fact—you told me *after*. And by then it was too late. I've been dreading this for *weeks* because..." He exhales sharply, his head shaking, "because I knew once you found out I'd lose you. You're so goddamn hard to get close to. I just...I wanted a little more time with you. I needed a little more time..."

A heavy, suffocating, silence falls.

"For what?"

I glance at his face and watch him swallow, his eyes wide and filled with worry, hold mine. "To show you how much I love you," he murmurs quietly, the edge of his voice as rough as sandpaper.

Shock turns into numbness. I can't feel a thing. Not my tongue, not my limbs. I'm not even sure my heart is still beating. Not in a million years did I expect this. Maybe if I hadn't discovered his lie, maybe someday in the future. But not now, and not under these circumstances. Which is what gives me pause. I don't know what to believe anymore. Is he telling the truth? Is he manipulating my feelings for him? He must know. He must know how I feel about him. And how can I trust him after everything that's transpired. I refuse to let ridiculous romantic notions make an ass out of me again.

"I'm so in love with you I don't know which way is up, or down anymore. I can't see *anything* past it. There's only you and what I feel for you. The rest is an endless, meaningless fucking void."

"So you thought lying to me would work?"

"No." His gaze moves away from me. "No, that's called desperation. I didn't know how to stop you from leaving. I'm sorry."

"Why wouldn't you ask me to stay? Why wouldn't you try honesty?"

"I..." His brow wrinkles, skepticism drawn into the grooves. "Would you have stayed if I asked?"

He really doesn't know. He has no idea how I feel about him. Or if he does, he doesn't believe it. But that sneaking suspicion that he may be manipulating me gets right in my face with a bullhorn before I can spill my guts and tell him everything. I can't keep making the same mistake over and over again. This madness has to stop. Unicorns aren't real. Time to accept that fact.

That's why for the first time in my adult life I don't let my heart rule my intellect. I do the responsible thing, the safe thing. I pull it back and tuck it away.

"I'll forever be grateful for everything you've done for me." My voice cracks. Everything turns blurry, unshed tears gathering at the bottom of my lids make it hard to see.

June walks in after a quick rap on his door. "Sorry, but you weren't answering the intercom. Mr. Tomlinson is here."

"Tell him I'll be a while," Ethan orders, more brusquely than I've ever heard him speak to any of his employees.

"Don't, June. I'm on my way out," I say wiping tears away.

June closes the door quietly.

"Amber..."

For a moment I catch a glimpse of him, the skinny boy with glasses, the one that followed his brother around because he didn't have friends of his own. And my heart breaks for him because manipulation and subterfuge are all he knows, what he's always relied upon. He thinks it's the only way to get what he so desperately wants, which is to be loved and valued for who he is, to be put first. And the crazy thing is that I would have—had he only asked.

"Bye, Ethan."

I turn and walk out, my legs moving of their own accord. I don't take a breath until the elevator doors close, afraid that he'll follow me, afraid that if he tries to stop me from leaving I'll cave.

Outside the sun sears my eyeballs, the sidewalks crowded with people. They flow around me without so much as a stutter in their frenetic pace. I shuffle down Lexington Ave. headed nowhere, without a destination in mind. Just moving.

Because if I stop, I may never start again. My knees will give out from under me and I'll drop like a bag of bones on Lexington between 56th and 55th where I'll remain long enough for the pigeons to mistake me for a stump to take a dump on...sounds about right.

* * *

"Are you okay?"

"Would you stop asking me that. I'm fine," I say into the cellphone cradled between my shoulder and ear as I take the grocery bags from the check out girl.

The streets of Greenwich Village are packed. Up and down the sidewalk, people flow around me, the heat bringing them out in droves.

"You don't sound fine."

I can always tell when Camilla wants to pry. I can also tell when she's trying to not make it sound obvious.

"Well, you sound annoying."

"He was here yesterday. He looks like shit. I've never seen him so...unkempt."

"I don't feel bad. You're not making me feel bad at all. Not even a little bit. I don't care if he goes an entire week without using hair product."

Camilla snorts. "He said you're not returning his calls. Can't you hear him out?"

"Really? It's only been a week. I'm actually more mad today than I was when Parker the prick told me. If I saw Ethan right now, I'd punch his perfect fucking face."

"Wow, salty."

"He LIED to me. Not to mention that I hyperventilate every time I think about how much money he paid that horrible woman."

"I get it."

Half a block from my apartment my steps slow when I spot someone sitting on my stoop. "Speaking of my punching bag," I mutter.

"He's there?"

"Yeah, call you later."

"Wait! Don't hit him in the face. It would be a crime to ruin something so beautiful."

"Goodbye, you traitor." Placing the phone in my handbag, I walk up to the man sitting on the front steps of my building with his elbows on his knees and his head bowed. Camilla was right, he looks exhausted. It hurts to see him this way, it really does. But I'm also equally angry.

He glances up as soon as he spots my feet, eyes sparking as he takes me in. Almost immediately the spark dies and longing and remorse take its place. Standing, he shoves his hands into the pockets of his track pants.

"What do you want, Ethan?"

"Can we talk?"

I walk past him, up the steps, and he follows. We walk into my apartment and his gaze shoots directly to the cardboard boxes stacked against the wall.

"You're moving?" The note of alarm in his voice and his expression shout what he's thinking.

I nod. "In two weeks."

"Amber—" He moves quickly. Grabbing me, he wraps his arms around me. "Amber, listen to me. I'm sorry. I'm sorry for all of it...just don't go yet. Give me a little time."

The mere act of touching him soothes every amped up, raw nerve in my body. And I don't stop him. I don't because as much as I hate what he did I still love him. My heart is clumsy and impulsive. Not only in the way it beats spastically whenever he's near me, but also in whom it chooses to pledge itself to. Ethan was right, he's not perfect, far from it. However, he's still the man I love.

Squeezing me tighter, he places a kiss on the side of my neck and I sigh. His hands slide down over my ass, pressing me against the rock solid erection trapped between us, and I whimper.

One week. Seven days since he touched me and I crave him like it's been ages. The second I raise my chin, his lips meet mine. The kiss turns wild in an instant. All the heightened emotions act as tinder to the fire ever smoldering between us. We fumble with each other's clothing, ripping shit as we go, our lips never once breaking contact. Naked, we sink to the hardwood floor. I'm so lost in him I don't even feel the impact of the wood against my shoulder blades. Though something tells me I will later.

Impatiently, he rubs the head of his shaft against me, while I urge him to hurry. And then he thrusts his hips, burying himself so deep inside of me we're no longer two separate people. Our eyes meet and tears I didn't know I had in me slide down my cheeks. When I try to look away, he cups my face, urging me to stay with him, to see every emotion living openly on his face too.

Pain. Fear. And so much Love.

"This isn't boning, or humping, or fucking. This is me making love to you." His thumbs brush my temples.

All I can do is nod and swallow the words stuck in my throat. His eyes never leave mine once as he begins rocking into me, finding the right pace and angle to drive me wild with pleasure. He gives me his body selflessly. I come twice before he does and as I do, he says, "I love you," over and over again. And as he comes, he grinds out, "I love you," over and over again.

I love you too, my mind screams while the rest of me stays silent.

We manage to crawl to the mattress a short while later, which has been living on the floor since I sold my bed.

"You asked me what I want," he murmurs, his fingers lazily brushing through my hair. Sprawled out on top of him, the vibration of his deep voice tickles my cheek. "I want you to forgive me—but most of all, I want you to think I'm some kind of awesome."

My heart sinks, the groovy feeling I was marinating in after the two epic Os wiped away. Lifting my head off his chest, I look into his soft brown eyes and tell him the truth. Because no matter how painful, it's always valid.

"I thought you were awesome from the very beginning. I thought you were so awesome I didn't think you could be real...but you made me believe in you, and in return you made a fool out of me." Worse yet, he made me doubt myself again.

"That was not my intention and you know that."

Sensing an imminent argument, I sit up. "You've been pulling puppet strings all along, Ethan." I locate my underwear at the foot of the bed, and slip it on. He gets up from the mattress and snatches his boxers off the floor. I can't seem to stop myself from staring at his body. It's so beautiful it hurts to look at him.

"I'm no one's puppet."

"I'm telling you that you mean everything to me." He's mad, his voice forceful. It raises my hackles. What's he got to be mad about? Hands on his lean hips, expression determined—the lawyer is back. He looks into my eyes as if he could will me to believe everything he says.

"Except your career."

It was a cheap shot but it went straight to the heart of the matter. He looks hurt, and for a minute I regret it. I don't want to hurt him. Hurting him would be equivalent to hurting myself.

"Don't get me wrong—I understand. Really, I do. Success requires sacrifice, right? *Art of War* and all that b.s. You were right. I want success as much as you do."

"Tell me what to do—what to say," he murmurs, practically begging. "I'll do it." His eyes move away, lower to the track pants he's putting back on.

"I love you, Ethan." Wide, bewildered eyes slam into mine. I can see more than a small glimmer of hope in them. "And because I love you I would never ask you to give up your dreams for me. I would never ask you to give up anything for me."

As soon as the words hit home, his face falls, hope extinguished in one fell swoop. This isn't a romance novel. This is real life. Shit does not work itself out. It's an uphill climb for most of us. Requiring effort, elbow grease, and sacrifice…success requires sacrifice.

His mouth tightens. Whatever words are on the tip of his tongue, he holds onto them. Silently, he pulls on his t-shirt and walks out the door. And I don't stop him.

CHAPTER TWENTY-NINE

"WHO AM I GONNA TELL all my problems to?"

Justin's been squatting on a mountain of my books since he walked in an hour ago.

"You own a phone," I say while I tape another cardboard box shut. I look up to find sad eyes trained on me. "You're sitting on my books." He was supposed to be helping me pack. What he's actually been doing is slowing the process down by half.

"Dimples, are you sabotaging me?"

"Who me? I would never do that," he says, batting his eyelashes. What a goofball. Also—the worst actor. "But I might be attempting to get in your way just a bit." He raises one ass cheek and motions for me to grab them.

With a smiling smirk, I say, "What's the plan?"

"I'm coming to Cali to train for a few weeks," he replies in a dejected tone.

"See—no need to get mopey."

Twenty minutes later, Justin leaves after a huge hug and a bunch of promises that I'll call at least every other day. Shortly after that my cell phone chimes.

Beauty Queen: Is Audrey with you?

Why would Eileen text me? She usually has to be held at gunpoint to contact me. And why would Eileen be looking for Audrey? Instantly alarmed, I text back.

Me: No. Why?

> **Beauty Queen: Because she ditched school and she's been missing for most of the day.**

Oh, God. A panic, the likes of which I've never experienced, grips me. I press Eileen's number. "I don't know where she is, but I'm on my way to you. I'm catching a train at Penn Station. Tell Dan to pick me up."

"Amber," my mother says, her voice oddly strained. "I'm really worried."

"We'll find her. I'm sure it's teenage drama."

"Okay."

Hanging up, I grab my purse and run out the door barefoot, curse under my breath, and run back in to slip on my Gazelles. Arms flailing, I hail a cab for Penn Station. Sweaty and sucking air into my lungs, I board a train to Long Island fifteen minutes later.

That's when Ethan's text comes in.

> **Fancy: I've got Audrey in case anybody is looking for her.**

All the strength that held my spine upright in the seat a second ago vanishes in a blink. My entire body goes boneless. As exhaustion chases the adrenaline rush burning through my limbs, I hit his number.

"Hi."

I'm incapable of stopping the tears gushing out of my eyes. It's the first time I've heard his voice in two weeks. And like a balm, it soothes every fresh wound, every tender bruise on my heart. One word wipes away two weeks of agonizing pain, of missing him to the point of madness.

"Where are you?" I ask, no preamble necessary.

"Driving to Long Island, to her house…she was too embarrassed to call any of you. Where are you?"

"On a train headed to Long Island—to her house," I answer, biting my bottom lip hard enough to break skin, anything to stop it from trembling.

The middle-aged woman sitting across from me gives me a queer look.

"I'll pick you up at the station after I drop her off."

"Dan's picking me up."

"Text him. Tell him I'll get you and we'll meet at their place."

"Okay." I capitulate because I'm selfish and weak. Because even though my head tells me not to, that it will only make things harder, my heart is willing to put everything on the line to spend one more minute alone with him.

I step onto the platform, still wiping my damp cheeks, and spot him right away. White dress shirt impeccably neat, not a crease to be found on his gray slacks even though it's unusually muggy and hot for the end of June, superstud sunglasses on. So apropos that the end would look like the

321

beginning. With him looking perfect while I'm once again a hot mess.

He removes his glasses and walks toward me, stopping only when he's less than a foot away. I almost sway into him, his gravitational pull turning my knees to jelly. Eyes wide and unblinking, he takes his time drinking me in. As if he hasn't seen me in ages. Then, without warning, he cradles my face and kisses me, kisses the life and love into me, kisses me like he's telling me all the ways he regrets what he did, and I don't stop him. When he finally pulls back, my eyes flutter open.

"I love you," he says, his voice calm and steady while his eyes burn brightly with longing. "And..." He exhales harshly. "And not the flowers and dinner on Valentine's kind of love. It's not soft or sweet. The way I love you is...is—" His face twists in frustration. "It's fucking painful. When you're not near me I feel like Popovitch is sitting on my chest and I can't breathe."

Popovitch, the three hundred and twenty-five pound nose tackle for the Titans. I don't know whether to laugh at the over the top romantic declaration, or cry at the honesty, at the bravery it takes to pour out your most sacred feelings and hope they aren't met with a shrug.

"I know I'm asking a lot. I know I am. But I..." He pauses, breathing roughly, raw emotion breaking through the self-possessions he's famous for. "This—you and me—it doesn't come around often. Don't walk away because I'm selfish when it comes to you. Hate me, stay mad, but don't walk away. I promise I will make it up to you every single day for the rest of our lives if you stay."

I'm being torn in two by my head and my heart. In that moment I live a thousand lives with him, every possible scenario, and come up with the same result.

There is no him and me without me first.

It'll drive a wedge between us eventually. Looking into the pained face of the man I love, I make an attempt at bravery myself. "Ethan—"

"Did I ever tell you how much I love hearing you say my name?" he says interrupting, a noticeable desperation in his voice.

"I can't."

My voice is barely audible, my lungs seizing, unable to draw breath. There's no need for explanations. This has stopped being about who said what or didn't, this is about me making something of myself, not sacrificing my dreams for anyone else—even him.

His eyes briefly flutter closed. Pain. Disappointment. Defeat. None of them linger on his face long because he shuts them down. Slow nodding, his eyes, filled with regret, meet mine again. He won't let go of my face. I wrap my fingers around his wrists and pry them off while I look up, letting him see that it's hurting me as much as it is him. I hold my hand out and he takes it, lacing his fingers through mine. Hugging his arm, I hold on with everything I've got. And that's how we walk to the car. Together, slowly, trying to make the moment last as long as possible.

* * *

"What's your damage? Do you have any idea how scared we all were? This is a big bad world. Kids get kidnapped and sold to people as pets."

Once we got to Eileen's, I said goodbye to Ethan. Few words were spoken. I got out of the car and watched him drive away with my heart. It took everything I had not to run after him screaming like a lunatic. Shortly afterward, I found Audrey in the backyard, rocking back and forth on an old swing set.

"It was my grand gesture," she mumbles, her eyes avoiding me purposely. "I thought...I don't know. I thought if I went to see him he would know that I *like him*, like him."

Oh dear. This is exactly why I should not be allowed near children unsupervised. She looks up with wet green eyes. "And?"

"And he was with his new friends. He acted like he barely knew me."

She might as well have punched a hole in my chest. The pain is that intense. That little fucker. He's lucky he's a minor. Sliding onto the swing next to her, I throw an arm around her bony shoulders. "Happens to the best of us, kid."

"I thought he liked me, too."

"He's a boy. Boys are weird and hard to figure out. The best you can do is be honest with yourself about how you feel, and be honest with them. I wish I could tell you it gets easier but I can't. All I can promise is that if you're honest, one day when you look back on it, you'll smile and hold your head up high because you were brave. And bravery kicks ass."

That gets a wobbly smile out of her. She scrubs her tear stained cheeks with the backs of her hands.

"And Audrey, most importantly, don't ever waste your time and tears on boys that are too stupid to realize that you're awesome."

By the look on her face, I'm not sure she quite gets it. She will eventually, though. I'll be there every step of the way to make sure she does.

"You can't leave," she says with a suddenly determined

expression.

"I have to."

"You can't. We're sisters now, and if you leave, I'll lose you, and I won't have anyone to talk to and—"

"Audrey, Audrey, pump the brakes. First of all, you won't lose me. You'll have an excuse to come to L.A. whenever you have time off from school. And I have to go. I was always going. I have to give it a real chance and part of the reason why is you."

"Me?" She doesn't believe it, her tone rife with doubt.

"Yeah, you." I look down into eyes too big for her delicate features, her expression stoic even though I know she's in despair. "You make me want to be a better grown up. So that my opinion will be worth something to you."

The stoic mask slides off, replaced by a sad acceptance that nothing she says or does will alter the outcome. I almost give in and say I'll stick around a little longer.

"Can I come for the whole summer?"

Teenagers, an endless source of entertainment.

"Nice try. How does two weeks sound?"

When she looks up again, a cheeky smirk lights up her face. "Deal."

* * *

"Thank you."

I look over my shoulder and find the owner of that all too familiar gravelly voice. My mother steps closer to the edge of the patio, and fidgets with the hem of her not-age-appropriate V-neck t-shirt, her breast implants in danger of splitting it in two. She looks contrite, something that has never, not to my knowledge, happened before. Uncork the champagne, this is cause for celebration.

Dan and Audrey insisted I stay for dinner. Dan was barbecuing. I only agreed because he was cooking—knowing Eileen's penchant for cooking with a microwave and only a microwave. She didn't say much during dinner. Instead she chose to watch me from across the patio table with heavy suspicion in her hard eyes. After we ate and cleaned up, I lingered outside a little longer.

"For what?"

"For being a big sister to Audrey...she worships you."

"You don't have to thank me for that. She's my sister. I'd do anything for her." I turn to find my mother watching the horizon. "She's a good kid. A bit dramatic, but good."

Eileen turns to me and smiles. "Wonder who she gets that from." This time we share a smile. Another first. It dawns on me as I watch her. In the process of not becoming my mother, I've shortchanged myself. By letting my fear of becoming anything like her dictate my life, I've given my power away.

"So—did you dump the lawyer?"

Typical. Expecting her to change is about as futile as asking a tiger to become a vegetarian.

Her tone sets me on edge. She's judging me. And her verdict is that I'm an idiot because I'm putting my career before a man. "Let's not pretend we're the Kardashians because we shared a meal."

"Gawd, you're such a bully. I was just asking a question."

"I'm a bully?" I nearly shout, talking over her.

"You're so smart, right? Miss Ivy League," she sneers. "You love to remind me how much smarter than me you are. Well, has it ever occurred to you that I was doing the best I could? That I wasn't equipped to raise a baby at twenty-one because I didn't know how?!"

"Know how? Are you kidding me? You didn't even try. You were always too busy juggling all your boyfriends. You didn't have any time for me."

"Because they were easy to please! I knew what they wanted from me. Sex—and then they went away. But you..." she says head shaking, eyes brimming with unshed tears. "But you wanted things from me that I didn't have to give! I'm not confident like you! I don't know what I'm doing half the time! Who knows where I'd be without Dan!"

Shocked, that's what I am. For the first time I see her through a different lens. One that isn't colored by my memories of her, but rather as an objective bystanders. Mind you, it takes a lot. Images come flooding back. All the times she stumbled into the doorway laughing, hanging onto the latest boyfriend. All the times she ignored me and went about her business with whomever she'd brought back to our apartment over my grandmother's garage. Leaving me at the theater. There are enough memories in my head to fill a The New York City Public Library. However, for the first time I see her as a victim of her immaturity instead of the callous, selfish person she's always been in my eyes.

"I needed you to be there."

"I regret a lot. I regret how I was with you. But you can't blame me for the things that didn't work out for you, and you can't punish me the rest of my life."

"I don't blame you for the things that didn't work out for me. That's on me."

We're quiet for a while, a reflective silence stretching between us.

"I don't expect you to forgive me...I'm asking to start over somehow. I'd like for us to be a family. Dan and Audrey want it. I know I do."

I take in the nervous way she's lacing her fingers together and gripping them closed, the tightness of her full lips, her neck mottled with anxiety.

"I'm not making any promises—but I'll try."

"Ready," Dan says interrupting. I take a last look at Eileen and nod at Dan.

"Have a safe trip," my mother says.

The car ride back to the city is peaceful. Staring out the passenger window, I get lost in the music. Miles Davis, Duke Ellington—a little Charlie Parker. Dan has always been a big jazz aficionado. When we get to my tree lined street in Greenwich Village, he parks. By some act of God we find a wedge of space large enough to fit his Subaru.

"Why'd you marry her, Dan? What was it about her you couldn't live without."

His expression turns wistful, as if he's peering into the past and reliving a memory. A really good one. "It's her enthusiasm for life. She lives every minute like it counts. Back then, when we first met, I had none—" His eyes cut to mine, cloudy with the remnants of an old pain. "You know why." When Eileen crashed into Dan, he was a widower and a single parent of a seven year old boy, having buried his wife, a woman he loved, a year and a half prior. "And she had too much of it. I guess I was hoping a little would rub off on me."

"Did it?"

"Yes," he says, smiling. "Every day. Even after all these years. She fuels me, gives me something to live for."

Tears track down my cheeks. I wipe them away.

"Ya know…" Dan's mouth presses closed, as if he's not sure he should let the words out. "You two are more alike than you think. I hope you take that as the compliment I mean it to be."

"Honestly, I think that's what scares me the most. That I'm so wrapped up in myself that I don't notice all the important stuff going on around me...the important people."

Shaking his head, he stops me from uttering another word. "I mean, you're full of life. You're the kind of woman any man would be lucky to sustain himself on."

"Jesus, Dan, if you don't stop, you're going to turn me into a slobbering mess," I say, wiping more tears away. His low chuckle makes me chuckle, too. I'd liked Dan instantly, which never happened with the men Eileen brought home. And there were plenty. That was another facet to the devastation I felt when she told me I couldn't live with them. I'd never had a father and part of me thought Dan was meant for me.

"How's Billy?"

"Great. He's still at IBM. He married Liz last year."

I nod and smile. Billy is just like his dad, a rock, a solid citizen and a good man.

"There's a question I've been meaning to ask you for a long time." His sage green eyes hold mine for a beat. "Was that you, that left the dog shit when we still lived in Jersey?"

I can't stop the corners of my mouth from creeping up. Holding his amusement filled gaze, I say, "I don't know what you're talking about."

The rumble of laughter starts deep in his chest and explodes out of him. "I knew it. I knew it," he says, head shaking. "Why'd you stop?" The question pops out as if he suddenly realized he needed to know.

"One day, I hid behind the bushes across the street to

revel in my handiwork. I'd made a sling shot that day and chucked it at the white garage doors."

Dan groans. "I remember."

"I was so proud of myself for that one. Until the front door opened and I watched you come out with a bucket and a sponge. It never occurred to me that you were the one paying the price. I should have, though. I should've known she wouldn't be the one cleaning it up." I shrug, stealing a glance at Dan to assess the damage the truth has done and find a smile still gracing his face. "I couldn't do it once I knew it was you bearing the brunt of it."

"Amber." Dan's voice sounds suddenly serious. Glancing in his direction, I find his profile. "I don't have many regrets. But the one at the top of my list is that I didn't fight harder for you when we got married. I was so out of it—in love and dealing with the guilt of moving on without Marie—that you suffered the consequence."

"Dan, you don't have anything to apologize—"

"Let me, please," he says, cutting me off.

"I'm sorry. I hope you'll forgive me."

"There's nothing to forgive, Dan. Really."

Dan smiles. Searching and finding the truth of that statement in my eyes, he nods.

I get out of the car and Dan, ever the gentleman, walks me to my stoop.

"Thanks for the ride."

He hugs me and pats my back and once again, I'm on the verge of another gusher.

"Be safe. Good luck. And come back to us soon."

As soon as I'm back inside my empty apartment I lay down on the bare mattress. The NYU students who live downstairs will be over tomorrow morning to pick it up. The emotional dump makes me sleepy. With any luck, tonight will be the first night that Ethan doesn't invade my dreams. I won't hold my breath, though.

CHAPTER THIRTY

"The guy on table twelve said he wants you to pick the croutons out of his Caesar salad."

Britney holds up the plate for my inspection. Two weeks in California. One of those weeks spent waiting tables night and day at an über trendy restaurant along Sunset Blvd. and I'm already itching to quit.

The guy on table twelve can kiss my skinny ass.

"Welcome to L.A.," she adds with an eye roll.

"I'm surprised they haven't already passed a proposition to ban all carbs from entering the state," I grumble in return.

"Doesn't it makes you want to run back to New York?"

New York. Where all the people I love are. Every cell in my body is screaming to run back and carbs have nothing to do with it. Sleep is an impossible goal almost every night. I bought no less than four new electric boyfriends, and even they proved a total fucking disappointment.

After breaking two of them in my vigor to achieve the unachievable, I finally chucked them all in the trash. Not without some drama; my new seventy year old neighbor was passing me on the way to walk his dog at the same time I was busy smashing one against the sidewalk. According to Mr. Goldman, I need to deal with my anger management issues posthaste.

Missing Ethan is a constant, relentless craving, akin to being hungry twenty-four seven. It dominates my every waking moment, and the few hours of sleep I manage to catch. I so badly want to call him, to see how he is, how he's faring at his new job. But then what? Even if I have forgiven him—which I have—a country separates us. And I owe it to myself to see this through, to not put my own needs on the back burner because I'm afraid of turning into Eileen.

"Nah, I'm livin' the dream." Plastering a fake smile on my face, I head to the bar to pick up a drink order.

"Princess Amber!"

I look around, searching for the faraway voice shouting my name. When nothing else follows, I shake it off and load the tray with drinks.

Outside, on the restaurant patio, sunshine pounds down and reflects off the concrete sidewalk. Squinting, I place the drinks down in front of two hipsters wearing sunglasses that cost as much as the old jalopy I purchased yesterday.

Yay! I have a California driver's license. Woo-hoo. Too bad I broke out in hysterics right as the DMV employee was snapping the picture. Which resulted in the worst driver's license picture ever taken in fifty states. Which, coincidently, looks eerily familiar to my New Year's Eve mug shot. All I could think of was Ethan, and how I wished I could've shared the moment with him.

"Princess Amber Isabelle Jones!"

My feet move of their own accord, following the faraway voice to the edge of the sidewalk. Scanning up and down Sunset Blvd, I watch luxury cars speed by, each more expensive than the next. And then I spot it, the white limo approaching.

There's a man hanging out of the sunroof. A man I recognize all too well because, let's face it, no one would ever forget a face like his. He's holding a bullhorn and waving a bunch of roses back and forth, petals coming loose and hitting the windshield of the car behind him.

"Princess Jones!"

Disbelief and joy explode inside my chest. My heart doesn't skip a beat, it jolts as if I stuck my finger in an electric socket. The concrete beneath me is the only thing keeping me upright.

"*Mama mia*," Britney murmurs. She's hanging over my shoulder, gawking at the same thing I am. "Who is *that*?"

"That's my happily-ever-after," I say in a broken voice while I quickly swipe at my wet cheeks.

As soon as the limo pulls to a stop at the curb, Ethan's eyes find mine. Everything passes between us. Unspoken apologies, joy, relief, love. So much Love. An endless supply of love. Dropping the mangled bouquet of roses and the bullhorn, he jumps out. In his t-shirt and jeans he looks younger than thirty-three. Or maybe it's the less than confident look in his big brown eyes.

Every conversation at the restaurant goes quite as he takes his time walking over to me. I can feel the collective attention of every single customer burning the back of my neck.

"What are you wearing?" the man I love says, his hands stuffed into the front pockets of his jeans, his lips forming into a small shy smile.

"My heart on my sleeve." My voice sounds thin, strangled. My gaze cuts to the white limo. "*Pretty Woman*?"

"Someone once told me every epic love story starts with a

grand gesture."

"So you're not implying I'm a hooker?" My lips twitch, wanting to curve up and failing. Because I'm not only overwhelmed and overjoyed, I'm also scared to death. Seeing him again...I know I'm not brave enough to let him go one more time. I fight to keep what little composure I have left by staring blindly ahead, at the spot in the middle of his chest.

"I believe the moral of the story is that he was prepared to change everything about his life because she was worth it."

"What are you doing here, Ethan?" I ask, cutting to the chase. There is only so much will power I possess when I'm standing before the love of my life, and if I don't touch him soon I am one hundred percent certain that I will die.

"I live here."

In shocked disbelief, my eyes drag back up to meet his steadfast gaze. "Wut..."

"The woman I love is here, and God knows I can't stand to be away from her for a single second." He rubs the spot on his chest where Popovitch likes to sit. "Being without her is not an option."

"But...but what about the job?" My heart is pounding so hard I may be in the midst of an angina attack.

"I turned it down. Nothing's more important than her. Most definitely not a job."

More tears fall. A lot more. The more I wipe, the more keep coming. "Lucky bitch."

"I just hope she takes me back. I did a really shitty thing to her and I'm not sure she's ready to forgive me."

"She's ready," wobbles out. A tidal wave of relief hits me. Being wrong never felt so right. He's not too good to be true. He's the real deal.

Without fanfare or warning, he grabs me and wraps me in a human enchilada. Then he kisses me, kisses me like we've been parted by oceans and wars, like we're standing on the bow of the Titanic. And I kiss him back. I kiss him with everything I've got. For being the man I hoped he was, for not letting me down, for loving me back...for proving that unicorns are real.

The wolf whistles and claps don't stop us from mauling each other. The screams to get a room don't do it, either. On the contrary, I jump him, clasping my legs around his waist and holding on with all my might, holding on as if he's the only fixed point in the universe. And for me, he is.

"No more underhanded moves. No more playing with the truth. I mean it, Ethan. You leave that shit at the office."

"Promise."

"What about your beautiful home?" I say, holding his beloved face, the scruff he almost never has prickly under my fingertips.

"It's a bunch of walls without you."

Ugh. That's gross, and disgusting, and damn near perfect. I'm melting. I'm melting into a puddle of gooey love for this man.

"You wouldn't happen to have a spare bedroom, would you?" I can feel the heavy beat of his heart through our shirts. He's not taking anything for granted.

Stroking his cheek, I force him to look me in the eyes. "Nope. We'll have to share mine."

His grin is immediate and true, beaming joy so brightly sunglasses are required. "I was hoping you'd say that. Also, I'd like to be married before minicamp. I've got a couple of young guys that'll need a lot of—"

"What? That's next month!" I'm screeching. He's got me screeching. "Have you been doing whippets?" I struggle to get out of his grip but he holds on tighter, his big hands squeezing my ass in the process.

"They need a lot of attention so it's got to be next month," he adds without missing a beat. While I huff and glower, he bats those ridiculous eyelashes at me.

"Don't even. That nonsense does not work on me."

"Doesn't it?" the sexy bastard intones, biting his lips to stop the smug smile from spreading across his face.

"Fine, it works. But no kids. Not for a long, looong time."

"I'm thinking five."

"You've definitely been doing whippets. One—at the most. And no crazy names like Echo, or Horizon, or Genesis. That's a hard limit."

"Duly noted. Now tell me how much you love me."

A ghost of something vulnerable passes across his face. It hits me in the gut. How can he not know? How can he not know that he's everything?

And I realize something then, love isn't about grand gestures and romance. It's about forgiveness and acceptance. It's a million tiny moments. Day in and day out, letting the person you love know they're valued, telling them what they mean to you every single day because there are no assurances you'll get another.

"Fancy McButterpants, you're my unicorn. Without you, my story has no happy ending." My bottom lip trembling, I take a fortifying breath and gather the courage to tell him what he should already know. "I love you beyond everything." His mouth curves up, relief smoothing out the baby v between his brows and joy turning his eyes into crescents. Looking into the eyes of my lover, the love of my life, I feel the truth of that statement all the way to the marrow of my bones. "Every piece of me loves every piece of you, Eth…always will."

His lips quirk. "I love you much more than that."

"So competitive," I say, giggling while he wipes the last of my tears away. I drop my face in the curve of his neck, the one place I belong, and breathe him in. "I'll let you win this time."

"Hold my trophy while I kiss you," he murmurs.

"Gladly."

The end…or better yet, the beginning.

EPILOGUE

"Nervous?"

I turn to the owner of the voice, as well as my heart. I mean, can anyone wear a designer tux better that this dude? That's a rhetorical question, the unequivocal answer is no. He squeezes my hand and soothes my nerves with one of his real smiles, the one he reserves only for me. A few silver strands near his ear get my attention. He's even more handsome than when I met him.

"This isn't what makes me nervous, Fancy Pants."

In case you're wondering, Ethan continued representing his clients while Andi made full partner and ran the New York office. I always suspected he was the better one of the two of us and he proved me right. After two years in Los Angeles spent sitting in traffic and logging way too many miles driving from audition to audition, we talked about it and decided to move back to New York. We missed our family and friends. Which turned out to be perfect timing because after five years of missing the playoffs, the NY Gladiators were looking for a new GM and my unicorn got the job.

Audrey and I are closer than ever. Creative streak a mile wide in this family. The love of her life is music. She's attending Juilliard. The kid has an amazing voice. Watching her play the piano and sing gives me goose bumps and brings tears to my eyes.

Ethan's cell vibrates with an incoming text. Lifting it out of the pocket of his tux, he looks at the screen and blinks twice. I watch those yummy chocolate orbs grow wider and wider and a whisper of unease crawls up my spine.

"What is it?"

He hands me his cell phone. One look at the picture on screen and my eyes bug out. This, right here—this is what makes me nervous.

...and the winner for best supporting actress in a Comedy or Musical is...Amber Vaughn, for Lovers and Liars...

I freeze, suddenly ripped out of my thoughts by a roar of applause. My bewildered eyes meet my husband's and everything else melts away. We may as well be the only two people in the galaxy.

"Go," he mouths, the music introducing me making it impossible to say much else. "I'm so proud of you," he adds as I rise out of my seat on unsteady legs. Planting a quick kiss on my lips, he pushes me in the right direction.

For me being in love wasn't about learning how to give love, it was about learning how to accept it, how to allow myself to be loved.

On autopilot I walk up the stairs and take the award from the beautiful Amazon whose job it is to hand them out. Reaching the podium, I take a moment to gather my thoughts. The spotlight heavy and hot on me, I take a deep breath and scan the crowd. I don't have to read this speech. I've been practicing it in the shower my entire life.

"Thank you. Thank you. I'll be as brief as I can be but I've been waiting for this moment for thirty—cough, cough—something years. No way am I coming out of the age closet tonight." A low chuckle permeates the crowd. "I stand before you a misfit, a dreamer, a lover, a fighter, an artist, an actor…I stand before you an actor. It's taken me forever to get here and I won't lie, the ride has been rough." In the crowd, I see a lot of sympathetic expressions, heads nodding in understanding. "In hindsight, however, I can honestly say it made the journey more interesting—this victory sweeter. But if I can impart any knowledge to make the road a little smoother for the next woman, to spare her a little pain, it's this—

"Success isn't glamorous or sexy. It's hard work and perseverance. It's falling down but not staying down. It's never giving up hope. So to all the misfits out there, to all the dreamers, keep fighting, keep working hard. Your chance will come. All it takes is one person to believe in you and that has to start with you."

My eyes connect with the eyes of the man I have the honor to call my husband and best friend. Ethan never slew dragons for me. He didn't have to, because he did even better—he slew the dragon in me and filled the space with love and acceptance.

"Speaking of believing, Marty Glaser, my dear beleaguered agent, this is a farfetched dream without you pushing me every step of the way. And finally, on a personal note, I stand before you a wife, and a mother. To my husband who sustains me every day—this means nothing without you. Thank you for being my one true believer. And to my dear daughter who should be watching at home but isn't—" I stare into the camera, my exasperation as clear as a neon sign.

"Tiger Lily Vaughn, get down from the chandelier. I don't care if Connor Shaw bet you that you couldn't do it."

ABOUT THE AUTHOR

P. Dangelico loves romance in all forms, brick oven pizza, the NY Jets, and to while away the day at the barn. What she's not enamored with is referring to herself in the third person and social media but she'll give you the links anyway.

www.pdangelico.com

Facebook- PDangelicoAuthor

Instagram- PDangelicoAuthor

Goodreads– P. Dangelico Author

Pinterest– P. DangelicoAuthor

Twitter- @PDanAuthor

Made in the USA
Middletown, DE
02 July 2019